AF505655

Le Gothic

Le Gothic

Influences and Appropriations in Europe and America

Edited by

Avril Horner
Professor of English, Kingston University

and

Sue Zlosnik
Professor of English, Manchester Metropolitan University

First published 2008 by
PALGRAVE MACMILLAN
Houndmills, Basingstoke, Hampshire RG21 6XS and
175 Fifth Avenue, New York, N.Y. 10010
Companies and representatives throughout the world

PALGRAVE MACMILLAN is the global academic imprint of the Palgrave
Macmillan division of St. Martin's Press, LLC and of Palgrave Macmillan Ltd.
Macmillan® is a registered trademark in the United States, United Kingdom
and other countries. Palgrave is a registered trademark in the European
Union and other countries.

ISBN 13: 978–0–230–51764–6   hardback
ISBN 10: 0–230–51764–1   hardback

This book is printed on paper suitable for recycling and made from fully
managed and sustained forest sources. Logging, pulping and manufacturing
processes are expected to conform to the environmental regulations of the
country of origin.

A catalogue record for this book is available from the British Library.

A catalogue record for this book is available from the Library of Congress.

10   9   8   7   6   5   4   3   2   1
17   16   15   14   13   12   11   10   09   08

Printed and bound in Great Britain by
CPI Antony Rowe, Chippenham and Eastbourne

*To all the members of the International Gothic Association
in memory of good times and in anticipation of more to come.*

Contents

Acknowledgements

This collection of essays derives from the 'Gothic Voyages' conference we organized in 2004, at the Mona Bismarck Foundation, Paris. The conference attracted scholars from Europe and North America who gathered there to explore the relationship between Anglophone Gothic and European culture. Thanks are due not only to the Foundation, which allowed us to use their magnificent building on the banks of the Seine free of charge, but also to all who took part in three days of stimulating debate.

We should also like to thank our colleagues at Kingston and Manchester for their interest in the project and the members of the International Gothic Association who ensure that Gothic studies continue to challenge established boundaries. Paula Kennedy at Palgrave Macmillan deserves special gratitude for believing that this selection of essays would make a fine book; Christabel Scaife has been most helpful in supporting us through the publication process.

Finally, as ever, a big thank you to our families who always put all of this into a larger context.

List of Figures

Notes on the Contributors

Linnie Blake is Senior Lecturer in the Department of English, Manchester Metropolitan University, where she teaches film. Her core research interest is the philosophy, psychology and politics of horror. She has published widely in film, literary and cultural studies. Her most recent publication is *The Wounds of Nations: Horror Cinema, Historical Trauma and National Identity* (Manchester University Press, 2008).

Carol Margaret Davison is Associate Professor of English Literature at the University of Windsor, Canada. A former Canada-US Fulbright scholar and Fellow at the Institute for Advanced Studies in the Humanities (University of Edinburgh), she is the author of *Anti-Semitism and British Gothic Literature* (Palgrave Macmillan, 2004), the editor of the award-winning collection *Bram Stoker's Dracula: Sucking Through the Century, 1897–1997* (Dundurn Press, 1997), and the co-editor of a special issue on Marie Corelli for the journal *Women's Writing* (2006). She is currently completing *British Gothic Literature, 1764–1824*, an introductory monograph to the Gothic, for the University of Wales Press.

Kathy Justice Gentile is Director of the Institute for Women's and Gender Studies and teaches courses in Gothic fiction at the University of Missouri-St. Louis. She has published a book on the twentieth-century British novelist Ivy Compton-Burnett and is currently completing a book on the American twentieth-century writer Jane Bowles. She has also written essays on the uncanny, female Gothic writers and Henry James's 'Beast in the Jungle'.

Jerrold E. Hogle is Professor of English, University Distinguished Professor and Vice Provost for Instruction at the University of Arizona, as well as a Past President of the International Gothic Association. He has published widely on Gothic texts, as well as Romantic literature and literary theory. Two of his most recent books are *The Cambridge Companion to Gothic Fiction* (Cambridge University Press, 2002) and *The Undergrounds of 'The Phantom of the Opera': Sublimation and the Gothic in Leroux's Novel and Its Progeny* (St. Martin's Press/Palgrave, 2002). He is now at work on a study of the cultural 'baggage' carried by the Gothic into Romantic texts.

Avril Horner is Professor of English at Kingston University, London and co-president of the International Gothic Association (2005–8). Her research interests are mainly focused on women's writing and Gothic fiction. Major publications, co-authored with Sue Zlosnik, include *Daphne du Maurier: Writing, Identity and the Gothic Imagination* (Macmillan, 1998) and *Gothic and the Comic Turn* (Palgrave Macmillan, 2005). They have co-authored numerous articles and chapters on Gothic fiction and are currently working on a scholarly edition of Eaton Stannard Barrett's *The Heroine* (Valancourt Press, 2008). She is also writing, with Janet Beer, a study of Edith Wharton's late fiction, to be published by Palgrave Macmillan.

William Hughes is Professor of Gothic Studies at Bath Spa University. He is the author of *Beyond Dracula* (Palgrave Macmillan, 2000), and, with Andrew Smith, is the co-editor of *Bram Stoker: History, Psychoanalysis and the Gothic* (Palgrave Macmillan, 1998), *Fictions of Unease* (Sulis Press, 2001, edited with Diane Mason and Andrew Smith), and *Empire and the Gothic* (Palgrave Macmillan, 2003). With Richard Dalby he is co-compiler of the definitive *Bram Stoker: A Bibliography* (Desert Island Books, 2004). His current research includes a further edited collection of essays, *Queering the Gothic*, with Andrew Smith, and two volumes on the criticism of *Dracula*. He is the editor of *Gothic Studies*, the refereed journal of the International Gothic Association, published by Manchester University Press.

Raphaël Ingelbien is a Lecturer in Literary Studies at the University of Leuven, Belgium. He is the author of *Misreading England: Poetry and Nationhood since the Second World War* (Rodopi, 2002). His current research focuses on Anglo-Irish writing and cultural nationalism in a European context; recent publications include articles on Yeats, Bram Stoker and Elizabeth Bowen.

Alison Milbank lectures in Literature and Theology at the University of Nottingham. She was formerly teaching at the University of Virginia, where she co-edited a microfilm edition of substantial parts of the Sadleir-Black collection of Gothic novels and chapbooks. Her first book, *Daughters of the House: Modes of the Gothic in Victorian Fiction* (Macmillan, 1992), and later essays – including her contribution to *The Cambridge Companion to Gothic Fiction* (Cambridge University Press, 2002) – explore aspects of the 'female' Gothic. She has edited two Ann Radcliffe novels for Oxford World Classics and is currently working on a theological history of the Gothic and a study of Chesterton and Tolkien.

Rebecca Munford is a Lecturer in English Literature at the University of Cardiff. The editor of *Re-visiting Angela Carter: Texts, Contexts, Inter-texts* (Palgrave Macmillan, 2006) and co-editor of *Third Wave Feminism: A Critical Exploration* (Palgrave Macmillan, 2004), she has published essays on twentieth-century women's writing, the Gothic and contemporary feminist theory and popular culture. Her forthcoming work includes *Decadent Daughters and Monstrous Mothers: Angela Carter and the European Gothic* and, with Stacy Gillis, *Feminism and Popular Culture: Explorations in Post-feminism*.

Barry Murnane graduated with a PhD on Franz Kafka, the Gothic and Modernism from the Universität Göttingen in 2006. His research interests include interactions between German and English fiction, cultural studies, the interfaces between technology, modernization and media in literary texts, representations of the body in Gothic and modernist fiction and the figure of the spectre. Other publications include (with Achim Käflein) *Ireland* (Edition Kaeflein, 2006) and articles on Horace Walpole, Bram Stoker and Franz Kafka.

David Punter is Professor of English and Research Dean of Arts at the University of Bristol. He is the author of many books on Gothic and Romantic literature; modern and contemporary writing; psychoanalysis and critical theory. His most recent publications include *Writing the Passions* (Longman, 2000); *Postcolonial Imaginings: Fictions of a New World Order* (Edinburgh University Press, 2000); *The Gothic* (with Glennis Byron, Blackwell, 2004); and *The Influence of Postmodernism on Contemporary Writing: An Interdisciplinary Study* (Mellen, 2005). His most recent publications are *Modernity*, in the Palgrave Macmillan Transitions series, and *Metaphor*, in the Routledge New Critical Idiom series (both 2007). He is currently working on a book entitled *Rapture: Literature, Secrecy, Addiction*.

Andrew Smith is Professor of English Studies at the University of Glamorgan. He is the author of *The Edinburgh Critical Guide to Gothic Literature* (Edinburgh University Press, 2007); *Victorian Demons: Medicine, Masculinity and the Gothic at the Fin de Siècle* (Manchester University Press, 2004) and *Gothic Radicalism: Literature, Philosophy and Psychoanalysis in the Nineteenth Century* (Palgrave Macmillan, 2000). He has edited eight volumes of essays, mostly on Gothic themes, including *Teaching the*

Gothic (with Anna Powell, Palgrave Macmillan, 2006) and *Empire and the Gothic* (with William Hughes, Palgrave Macmillan, 2003). He is the co-series editor of *Gothic Literary Studies*, and *Gothic Authors: Critical Revisions*, published by the University of Wales Press. He is currently writing a monograph on the Victorian ghost story.

Maria Vara holds an MA in Studies in Fiction (University of East Anglia) and is currently a doctoral candidate in the School of English, Aristotle University, Thessaloniki, Greece, where she teaches courses in writing and fiction. Her research interests and publications focus on the novel and questions of genre and gender. She has recently contributed to a collection of essays entitled *Metafiction and Metahistory in Contemporary Women's Writing*, (eds A. Heilmann and M. Llewellyn, Palgrave Macmillan, 2007), and has contributed a co-authored essay (with K. Kitsi) to *The Reception of British Authors in Europe: Jane Austen* (eds. A. Mandal and B. Southam, Series Ed. E. Shaffer, Continuum, 2007).

Angela Wright lectures in Romantic and Gothic Literature at the University of Sheffield, and is former treasurer of the International Gothic Association. She has published widely on the reception of Gothic fiction during the Romantic era; Scottish Gothic; women's Gothic; and the tensions and connections between French and English Gothic fiction. She is the author of *Gothic Fiction: A Reader's Guide to Essential Criticism* (Palgrave Macmillan, 2007) and is currently completing *The Import of Terror: Britain, France and the Gothic, 1780–1820.*

Sue Zlosnik is Professor of English at Manchester Metropolitan University and co-president of the International Gothic Association (2005–8). Her research interests are mainly focused on women's writing and Gothic fiction. Major publications, co-authored with Avril Horner, include *Daphne du Maurier: Writing, Identity and the Gothic Imagination* (Macmillan, 1998) and *Gothic and the Comic Turn* (Palgrave Macmillan, 2005). They have co-authored numerous articles and chapters on Gothic fiction and are currently working on a scholarly edition of Eaton Stannard Barrett's *The Heroine* (Valancourt Press, 2008). She has published recently on R. L. Stevenson and J. R. R. Tolkien and is currently writing a monograph on the fiction of Patrick McGrath, to be published by the University of Wales Press.

1
Introduction

Avril Horner and Sue Zlosnik

Paris is our starting point. The Franglais of our title indicates not so much insouciance towards our subject as a recognition that in our globalizing world there is a constant need for reassessment of our cultural histories. Paris has loomed large in the British and American imaginations for two centuries, both as the epitome of glamour and culture and as a location where the fabric of political and social stability has been stretched thinly. 1789 and 1968 remain unforgettable dates – the 9/11s of their day. In Paris, political paradigms are shifted. Eighteenth-century Paris was home to the *philosophes' Encyclopédie*, a monumental record of Enlightenment knowledge, yet witnessed in the revolutionary 1790s an irruption of violence and terror that generated cultural reverberations across Europe and beyond. 'The Terror' is widely acknowledged in the history of Gothic fiction, by writers as diverse as the Marquis de Sade and Simon Schama, as a key factor in what Robert Miles calls 'the effulgence of Gothic' in the 1790s.[1] When David Punter challenged the historical boundaries of Gothic writing in 1980, he called his seminal work *The Literature of Terror*, echoing not only Ann Radcliffe's definitions, but also the impact that the terror across the Channel had had upon her work.[2] The vigorous critical debate following Punter – which has given rise to 'Gothic Studies' as we now know it – has, however, been persistently Anglophone in its concerns. Until very recently, critics and theorists of the Gothic, having broadened the definition of 'Gothic' to include film, clothes and popular culture, nevertheless continued to focus on the Anglo-American tradition in literature and confined their attention to writing in English. Although Gothic has now been recognized as a product of the Enlightenment and most scholars would regard it as a key aspect of the project of modernity, the focus on writing in English has, in its critical evaluation, remained. While the distinctiveness of American Gothic has been recognized from Leslie Fiedler onwards, the European dimension of Gothic has received relatively little attention.[3]

This edited collection represents new research into the ways in which cross-fertilization has taken place in Gothic writing from Europe and America over the last two centuries. The relative critical neglect of these dialogues may be due in part to different ways of categorizing literary texts. The French critical tradition, for example, has engaged in a continuing debate about *le roman noir* and *la littérature fantastique*, but has not acknowledged 'Gothic' as a valid literary term, reserving it instead for architecture. British writers and academics, facing one way towards North America (the 'special relationship' marks the academic world too) and one way towards Europe (we are all Europeans since the creation of the European Union), are perhaps particularly well placed to observe and record this intellectual stand-off. It is only comparatively recently that critical exchanges on the Gothic have taken place between scholars working in North America and Europe and only over the last few years that publications have begun to bridge that cultural divide.[4] Interestingly, because of the rise of postcolonial studies, there have been more critical engagements with colonial and postcolonial aspects of Gothic writing than material published on the way in which European and American authors have raided, translated, appropriated and influenced each others' work.[5]

One aim of this collection is to enrich the reader's understanding of the Gothic tradition's international characteristics. As the first chapter argues, the Gothic has always been concerned with the process of 'othering', and particularly with the ascendant 'Other'. Monsters, spectres and uncanny doubles abound in Gothic writing, whatever its original language. This characteristic, as Jerrold E. Hogle argues, is clearly related to historical moment and to anxieties about class, gender, nationality and 'race' within societies facing change. It is not confined to Britain and North America. Anglo-American canonization of Gothic texts has not taken sufficient account of how European authors – themselves 'othered' through differences of language, history and culture – have both created their own uncanny creatures and drawn on transatlantic models to do so. The same is true, of course, of what we claim as our own horrors. The Phantom of the Opera, rising from the dark labyrinths of time and transforming himself into an icon of popular culture during the late twentieth century (thanks to Andrew Lloyd Webber) owes much to Gaston Leroux's novel of 1910 and more than a little to Victor Hugo's *Notre Dame de Paris*, published in 1831.

Thus there needs to be a fuller recognition of the fact that Gothic did not spring fully-formed from the imaginations of British and American authors. Nor was its genesis confined to a dialogue between them or simple mimicry of another country's bestseller. Such dialogue and appropriation are, in any case, immensely complicated by the act of translation, as two recent essays by Terry Hale demonstrate.[6] Again, as much work on the Gothic has shown, it is essential to have an understanding of how historical moment and discourses of theology, medicine and the law (among others) have influenced Gothic writing and its preoccupations. Thus Carol Margaret Davison is able to present Charles Brockden Brown's *Wieland, or the Transformation* and James Hogg's *The Private Memoirs and Confessions of a Justified Sinner* in a new light by tracing how Scottish Calvinist theology helped create the uncanny figure of the double. The Gothic 'Other', who invariably becomes a vehicle of abjection for all that is feared by a particular society at a particular moment, is not only to do with the 'foreign' but also with what Kristeva describes as 'the strange within us'.[7]

An understanding of historical moment and cultural context is, then, vital to a proper understanding of both individual Gothic novels and of how they relate to each other within the stream of Gothic fiction. This is why the intellectual journey that these essays represent begins in Paris. As the seat of the French Revolution and the Terror, and as the first 'modern' city (thanks to Baron Georges-Eugène Haussmann), the city evokes multiple contradictions that suggest the instability of the modern subject. How is it that the march towards democracy – liberty, equality and brotherhood – necessitated such suffering and such body horror? How is it that Haussmann's project to modernize the city in the 1860s resulted not only in elegant architecture and boulevards and the emergence of the supposedly carefree *flâneur*, but also in a new cultural experience of alienation and anomie? *Le Gothic* thus opens with three essays that offer fresh perspectives on the work of several well-known writers, French, Irish and American, who set their works in Paris and who drew on such tensions and contradictions, using the Gothic mode to explore the fractured nature of modern society and the city as an urban Gothic space.

In chapter 2, Jerrold E. Hogle examines Victor Hugo's *Notre Dame de Paris* (1831) and Gaston Leroux's *Le Fantôme de l'Opéra* (1910). While identifying both the novels and their film versions as extensions of the French tradition of the 'Beauty and the Beast' stories (a tradition which is examined in relation to its Hollywood adaptations in chapter 9, by Kathy Justice Gentile) and acknowledging Leroux's obvious debts to

Hugo, Hogle also identifies the adaptation of certain key features of English fiction by these two French authors. He argues that they are expressions of Parisian anxiety concerning class and anti-Semitism in France at particular historical moments. While their concerns appear to be specifically French, Hogle suggests that these two novels, each in their different way, show the process of cultural abjection into 'quasi-antiquated spaces, spectres and characters' of what cannot be accommodated by an emergent Western dominant ideology.

Linnie Blake looks more closely at a French–American connection. Using Edgar Allan Poe's review of Eugène Sue's *Mysteries of Paris* as a starting point for examining Poe's representations of the urban self under capitalism, Blake argues that although Poe's tale, 'The Man of the Crowd', is set in London, it nevertheless reveals an awareness of both the urbanization of American identity and the beginnings of a European theorization (to be developed through writers such as Baudelaire and Benjamin) of the social self within the space of the capitalist metropolis (often exemplified by Paris). Poe's 'disciplining' of his tale's subject matter works as an analogy for the individual's need to order his or her experiences of the city as a dread-inducing place of multiplicity and confusion. This need to 'control' inchoate subject matter is seen not only in Poe's narrative strategies but also in Haussmann's reconstruction of Paris and Baudelaire's conception of the *flâneur*. However, the differences between Poe's old man and Baudelaire's *flâneur* are significant: Poe's old man is seen as a *spiritus loci* of the city, actively breaking free of containing devices, including those of the narrative itself. Unlike Baudelaire's figure, he offers a rejection of 'the instrumental rationality of capitalism'. Implicit in Poe's tale is the need for new modes of being in the city, be it Paris, London or New York.

In chapter 4 on Henry James and Elizabeth Bowen, Raphael Ingelbien draws our attention to the way in which Gothic tropes become assimilated by writers into apparently realist narratives. He compares and contrasts the Gothic representation of Paris in James's *The Ambassadors* (1903) and Bowen's *The House in Paris* (1935), arguing that an awareness of the Gothic vampiric subtext in James's novel helps the reader to understand Bowen's work better and to grasp the ideological function of Gothic echoes in both books. Like James, Bowen often describes human relationships as vampiric. Both authors, setting their plots within old houses, deliberately invite the reader to establish a link between the psychological vampirism of their characters and the bloodshed of the French Revolution. Allegories haunted by the nightmares of history, the psychological intrigues of James and Bowen resonate with memories of the Terror, which – in the case of Bowen – in turn evoke the more recent horrors of the First World War and other 'revolutions'. These, in James's novel, include an aggressive entrepreneurialism that triumphs over the civilized Old World manners of Madame de Vionnet. The author concludes that for Bowen, as for James, the Gothic dimension of Paris, and its association with revolutionary terror(s), offered a way of gesturing towards a tradition in which terror often exceeds the bounds of plot.

Part II, 'Channel Crossings', turns our attention to interchanges between British and French authors in philosophy and literature. These four essays recognize two centuries of cross-fertilizations, ranging from an examination of the impact of Rousseau's work on women writers of the Gothic during the 1790s to new readings of Angela Carter's fiction in the light of European writing. Chapter 5, by Angela Wright, draws attention to the complexity of cross-Channel influences and appropriations in the early phase of Gothic fiction by exploring the links between the work of Jean-Jacques Rousseau, Baculard d'Arnaud (a follower of Rousseau whose work was widely read by English Gothic novelists) and Ann Radcliffe. In spite of the antagonism to his ideas in England during the 1790s, Rousseau was nevertheless highly regarded, Wright argues, by women writers and readers. The influence of *La Nouvelle Hélöise* and *Émile* on Radcliffe's *A Sicilian Romance* and *The Romance of the Forest* is clear; in the case of the latter, the novel seems to dramatize Rousseau's distinction between self-love and self-interest, offering a critique of the French philosopher's argument. Wright also explores the impact of two earlier works by Rousseau (*Discours sur l'Inégalité* [1755] and *Discours sur les Sciences et les Arts* [1775]) on the Gothic mode in England, arguing that their influence on women's Gothic writing in the 1790s has not been fully recognized or understood. Acknowledging that the reception of Rousseau's work in the 1790s in England was greatly polarized, she goes on to examine responses to his famous novel *La Nouvelle Hélöise*, including the anonymous translation of it brought out by the Minerva Press in 1790.

Focusing on horror rather than terror, Alison Milbank, in chapter 6, is concerned with influence and appropriations at the end of the following century and compares the work of Joris-Karl Huysmans with that of the nineteenth-century British writer Arthur Machen. Milbank notes that whereas first-wave English Gothic was respected in France, there was, nonetheless, a divergence of traditions in the nineteenth century.[8] The *fin de siècle*, however, witnessed a new rapprochement in which Huysmans was a key figure, although he has received scant attention to date as a Gothic writer. Considering the 'abhorrent and tormented body' in texts by both writers, Milbank discusses body horror in terms of the literary grotesque, which, as she points out, was linked by Victor Hugo with both modernity and realism. Citing Poe as an influence, she examines Huysmans' *La Bas* in relation to Machen's *The Three Imposters*. The former is characterized as 'a libertine nightmare', which presents in Gothic mode the transcendence of the libertine through the Sadean will to power over instrumentalized bodies. Machen's story, Milbank claims, imitates aspects of Huysmans' novel in its exploration of 'the transcendental purpose of the horrible grotesque'.

In chapter 7, Maria Vara picks up the Sadean theme. Moving beyond accounts of de Sade's own thoughts on the Gothic as they are expressed in his article 'Reflections on the Novel' (1800), it reassesses the link between de Sade's work and Gothic writing. *Justine* (1791) is seen as a hybrid work that emerged at the very moment that the Gothic was establishing itself as a fictional mode in England and France. Of particular importance, Vara argues, is de Sade's representation of the 'persecuted maiden', and she goes on to explore how an appreciation of de Sade's narrative strategies in *Justine* sheds light on the quasi-pornographic tendencies of Ann Radcliffe's *The Mysteries of Udolpho* (1794). Unlike this (and other Gothic fictions of the 1790s) de Sade's text does not conclude by affirming eighteenth-century Enlightenment values. Rather, the exposure of his heroine to all possible dangers and sexual exploitations (which Radcliffe's texts only imply) offers an 'ultra-Gothic' structure that parodies the ideology of the Enlightenment. In fact, the more Justine turns to virtue and to social and legal institutions for aid, the more abused she becomes. Vara then argues that Angela Carter's recognition that de Sade 'contrived to isolate the dilemma of an emergent type of woman' can be seen in her own female protagonists. This accounts, perhaps, for the fact that Carter's heroines do not fit the politically acceptable figure of the strong and active feminist heroine (so popular in the 1970s) and explains why her Gothic fictions enjoyed such a mixed reception from feminist critics.

In the final chapter of Part II, Rebecca Munford also considers Carter's fiction in relation to a European lineage and re-maps the European dimensions of the Gothic tradition in order to destabilize the categories of 'male' and 'female' Gothic traditions. Noting that Carter's work does not sit neatly within the latter category, she argues that the author's engagements with the excesses of a French decadent Gothic lineage – via de Sade and Baudelaire – are vital to her feminist engagement with the Gothic mode. Comparing two novels by Pierrette Fleutiaux (a French author who also draws on the male-authored strand of European Gothic) with Carter's *Nights at the Circus*, Munford argues that the work of both should be recognized as part of a long-established Anglo-French exchange and regarded as attempts to develop a feminist Gothic aesthetic. Munford argues that, in their reworking of the female vampire, Carter and Fleutiaux 're-imagine the position of the unbound Gothic heroine'. However, whereas for Carter this takes place within the confines of traditional male Gothic scripts, Fleutiaux returns to a pre-industrial mythology in order to link vampirism and menstruation in such a way as to free her 'bat girl' from male Gothic sexual and textual boundaries. Neither author's work fits neatly into the category of 'female Gothic' as recently defined in the academy, yet both invest their Gothic revisions with a distinctly feminist agenda – an agenda which evolves from their cross-Channel engagements with established male authors of the Gothic.

Part III, 'Transatlantic Voyages', offers perspectives on the interchange between European and American culture and literature. Whereas Jerrold E. Hogle identifies both *Notre Dame de Paris* and *Le Fantôme de l'Opéra* as derivative of the French Beauty and the Beast tradition, Kathy Justice Gentile focuses on a range of versions of the tale, arguing that depending on the cultural context, the teller and the medium, Beauty is just as likely to be violated and debased as revered and rewarded. Acknowledging that the most pervasive and influential version of the story derives from Mme de Beaumont's 1756 tale in which self-sacrificing Beauty redeems the cursed and enchanted Beast, Gentile considers both Cocteau's 1946 film *La Belle et La Bête* (which presents a gender egalitarianism) and examples of more recent Gothic cinema. Citing Laura Mulvey's argument that Hollywood motion picture codes enshrine the sadistic voyeurism and scopophilia of the male gaze, she finds that the latter has reverted to a dominant sublime/submissive beauty dynamic. In films such as *The Collector*, *Blue Velvet*, the Spanish *Abre los Ojos* and its American remake *Vanilla Sky*, the animal groom tale warns of predatory obsession, lust and inhumanity.

William Hughes takes another look at a key work of the early twentieth century, *The Waste Land* (1922), examining in chapter 10 the intertextual trace of Bram Stoker's *Dracula* and the broader mythological vampire context in T. S. Eliot's poem. Noting that observations on the presence of Stoker's text in Eliot's poem go back as far as 1971 but claiming that scholars of Modernism have overlooked its significance, Hughes offers new insights into this intertextual presence. It is, he argues, more than merely evidence of an ironic playfulness at work. The crowds flowing over London Bridge are a secular form of the undead. Hughes identifies Stetson not as Ezra Pound but as a reference to George R. Stetson, author of 'The Animistic Vampire in New England', which was published in *The American Anthropologist* in January 1896. Noting the desolation of Stetson's representation of New England, Hughes argues that the corpse associated with Stetson in the poem is not a literal or literary vampire ready to rise up to prey upon the West, but a shadow of the dead, buried but still resurgent opinions and attitudes which the anthropologist despairingly encounters even in the 'enlightened' nineteenth century. Eliot's alignment of his poem with a popular novel and anthropological study is purposeful: both are preoccupied with cultural decline. The dead and the undead link all three texts.

The remaining two essays in Part III consider British–American interchanges in the nineteenth century. Carol Margaret Davison examines a sub-genre of Gothic fiction whose predominant characteristics and concerns are marked by a Calvinist sensibility and draws parallels between two studies of troubled subjects on either side of the Atlantic: Charles Brockden Brown's *Wieland* (1798), one of the first American novels, and James Hogg's *The Private Memoirs and Confessions of a Justified Sinner* (1824). Davison claims that there has been a significant critical oversight in the failure to comprehend the theological origins and significance in the uncanny figure of the double, whose provenance may be traced to this sub-genre. Her chapter, therefore, is a contribution to the ongoing project on the historical uncanny first identified and taken up by Terry Castle.[9] She demonstrates how Calvinist Gothic explores the demonic relationship between Calvinism and crimes resulting from theologically sanctioned self-expression or repression. The Calvinist world, dominated by election by faith, is neurosis-inducing and 'an ever-shifting, sign-filled domain of uncertainty, where God the Father is entirely unpredictable and an ineluctably mysterious withholder of truth'. The double is thus seen as the 'spectral conscience' or 'our foremost persecutor and better self'.

In chapter 12 Andrew Smith considers the Gothic dimensions of Charles Dickens's work through an examination of *The American Notes for General Circulation* (1842). Using Dickens's account of his visit to the Massachusetts Asylum for the Blind and the State Hospital for the Insane in Boston as a starting point, he identifies the way in which the text uses the mimicry behaviour he saw there as a metaphor for his inability to account rationally for the perceived peculiarities of America itself. Such mimicry is recorded and identified as a covert national narrative. *The Notes* hints at an element of spectrality that Dickens cannot quite see and the image of ghosting, Smith argues, represents a political drama. Thus Gothic is used by Dickens as a mode of interpretation, which functions as a political critique. The change of tone in *The Notes* follows what Smith identifies as 'a moment of unconscious textual insight' and Dickens's use of the ghost therefore functions as a colonial interjection into the narrative.

Part IV, 'Coda', points to broader horizons. Like Andrew Smith, Barry Murnane is interested in the connection between Dickens and America, but in his chapter this is mediated by Franz Kafka. Murnane notes that although the connection between Dickens and Kafka has been traced in German studies, this has not yet been done in terms of the Gothic novel. Examining both literal Gothic journeys and the metaphorical journey that is translation, Murnane examines the translation of technology into literature through a reading of Dickens's *David Copperfield* and Kafka's German rewriting of it, *Der Verschollene*, which is set in America. Kafka's reading of *David Copperfield*, Murnane demonstrates, condenses and magnifies its Gothic tropes, those of sexual and paternal deviancy and injustice. His modernization of Dickens's novel points to a reading of modernization and technology as it is socially interpreted within the framework of Gothic. Following Walter Benjamin, the argument is based on the premise that each translation contains a trace of foreignness, 'an uncanny returning of that which is to be translated' and that both Dickens's and Kafka's text are each 'haunted by traces of the technology it attempts to incorporate'. The social use of technology is represented as demonic and Kafka's translation and interpretation of Dickens renders this representation in a more extreme form.

The collection ends with a postcolonial reflection on the foreign as macabre. In the final chapter, David Punter examines a truly Gothic curiosity – ghosts of a past Empire in a 'phantom museum': the enormous collection of bizarre artefacts amassed by Henry Solomon Wellcome from across the globe in the early twentieth century and now 'languishing in a huge decaying vault in West London'. Wellcome's intention was to 'trace the history of the human body, in sickness and in health, throughout the whole broad sweep of human history'. The bizarre nature of Wellcome's project is inflected further by the fact that the other partner in his company of 'Burroughs Wellcome' – destined to become a huge corporation – was an ancestor of William Burroughs the novelist. Punter notes that the element of excess, often represented by long lists in Burroughs' prose, anticipates the language of one of the books published to accompany the exhibition of Wellcome's collection. This book, entitled *The Phantom Museum: Henry Wellcome's Collection of Medical Curiosities*, has, argues Punter, a recognizably Gothic dimension. In the second half of his essay, Punter explores the complex relations between the phantom, the relic, the museum, the nature of collecting, archival narratives and what is now known as 'imperial Gothic'. As a finale to this collection, Punter's excursion into this strange collection offers a reminder of the permeability of geographical boundaries in the making of cultural histories.

Notes

1. Robert Miles, '1790s: the Effulgence of Gothic', in *The Cambridge Companion to Gothic Fiction*, ed. Jerrold E. Hogle (Cambridge: Cambridge University Press, 2002), pp. 41–62.
2. David Punter, *The Literature of Terror: A History of Gothic Fiction from 1765 to the Present Day* (London and New York: Longman, 1980).
3. Leslie Fiedler, *Love and Death in the American Novel* (New York: Stein & Day, 1966).
4. Three pioneering conferences that enabled such exchanges were 'The Remains of the Gothic: Persistence and Resistance' (University of Toulouse le Mirail, 2003), 'Gothic Voyages' (Mona Bismarck Foundation, Paris, 2004) and 'Gothic N.E.W.S.' (University of Provence, Aix, 2007). Despite a great deal of recent work on French and German Gothic writing, there is still relatively little published work on how translation and interchange of ideas and plots fed into the rise of the Gothic novel. Publications of note include Jerrold E. Hogle, ed., *The Cambridge Companion to the Gothic* (Cambridge: Cambridge University Press, 2002); Avril Horner, ed., *European Gothic: A Spirited Exchange, 1760–1960* (Manchester: Manchester University Press, 2002); and Daniel Hall, *French and German Gothic Fiction in the Late Eighteenth Century* (New York: Peter Lang, 2005).
5. Work in this area includes William Hughes and Andrew Smith, eds, *Gothic Studies* (Special Issue 'Postcolonial Gothic') Volume 5, No. 2 (November 2003); and Andrew Smith and William Hughes, eds, *Empire and the Gothic: The Politics of Genre* (Basingstoke: Palgrave Macmillan, 2003). Some attention has also been paid to the influence of Caribbean culture in the creation of Gothic. See, for example, 'Zombies and Occultation of Slavery', in Markman Ellis, *The History of Gothic Fiction* (Edinburgh: Edinburgh University Press, 2000); and Lizabeth Parvisini-Gebert, 'Colonial and Postcolonial Gothic: the Caribbean', in Hogle, ed., *The Cambridge Companion to Gothic Fiction*.
6. See Terry Hale, 'French and German Gothic: the Beginnings', in Jerrold E. Hogle, ed., *The Cambridge Companion to Gothic Fiction* (Cambridge: Cambridge University Press, 2002), pp. 63–84; and Terry Hale, 'Translation in Distress; Cultural Misappropriations and the Construction of the Gothic', in Horner, *European Gothic: A Spirited Exchange*, pp. 17–38.
7. Julia Kristeva, *Strangers to Ourselves*, trans. Leon S. Roudiez (New York: Columbia University Press, 1991), p. 191.

8. For example, Maturin's *Melmoth the Wanderer* (1820) became a far more influential text in France than in England during the nineteenth century. See Catherine Lanone, 'Verging on the Gothic: Melmoth's Journey to France', in Horner, *European Gothic: A Spirited Exchange,* pp. 71–83.
9. Terry Castle, *The Female Thermometer: Eighteenth-Century Culture and the Invention of the Uncanny* (Oxford: Oxford University Press, 1995).

Part I
The Paris Nexus

2
Hugo's *Notre Dame de Paris*, Leroux's *Le Fantôme de l'Opéra* and the Changing Functions of the Gothic

Jerrold E. Hogle

The Phantom of the Opera, especially in Gaston Leroux's original French novel (1910), has long been deeply influenced by Victor Hugo's *Notre Dame de Paris* (1831), known in most versions as *The Hunchback of Notre Dame*. After all, there is the basic situation in *Le Fantôme*: the highly musical 'Erik', masking a horrifying visage and living deep within the real Paris Opera of which he knows the most inner workings, falls in love with and eventually captures Christine Daaé, a young singer from the country, whom he tries to keep in his sequestered quarters. This relationship clearly recalls the love of Hugo's grotesque bell-ringer, Quasimodo, for the singing street-gypsy, La Esmeralda, who (like Leroux's Christine) both pities and fears her abductor, especially after he provides her sanctuary in his remote rooms near the bells of the equally real Notre Dame cathedral. On this level, both novels are extensions of the very French tradition of *Beauty and the Beast* stories, which themselves extend the Greco-Roman pattern of *Death and the Maiden* tales (such as the story of Persephone and Pluto), in which a quasi-father figure steals a young woman from a more exogamous marriage to someone closer to her own age, then threatens her with a grotesquely regressive love and a kind of death in a resplendent, but dark underworld of which he is the outcast ruler.[1]

In addition, Leroux's Erik, clearly a scapegoat for many underlying worries in the palace of high culture he occupies (where many of its problems are blamed on the 'Opera ghost'), plays this role – which I see as that of the 'abject' as defined by Julia Kristeva, the locus of inconsistencies in the middle-class 'self' that it 'throws off' or 'throws down' from itself[2] – by compositing the most troubling features in *several* of Hugo's *Notre Dame* characters. First, with his tale set in the 1880s,[3] Leroux's phantom seems a late nineteenth-century repository of the *numerous* 'otherings' of undesirable conditions that late medieval mainstream society throws off onto Quasimodo in Hugo's 1831 rendering of Paris in 1482. Erik is seen by different observers just as the hunchback is by *his* onlookers: as, in Hugo's phrases (pp. 116–17),[4] a 'misshapen ape' (since Erik can 'swing about' on a boat 'with the balance of a monkey' [Leroux, p. 389], suggesting the possibility of human *de*volution in the wake of Charles Darwin's writings) *or* a 'fellow of Oriental architecture' (given that Erik sports costumes, behaviours and weapons from Persia and points further east) *or* 'the offspring of some Jew and a beast', continuing anti-Semitic prejudices of long standing in France – particularly if we note that Erik's skeletal face and figure echo Leroux's own description in 1899 of a now-emaciated Alfred Dreyfus, the French Jewish officer falsely accused of having sold state secrets to Germany and the focal point of the Dreyfus Affair, which brought anti-Semitism out into the open in Western Europe during the years preceding Leroux's *Fantôme de l'Opéra*.[5]

At the same time, Erik also embodies the key qualities of many other *Notre Dame* characters. These include the attributes of a one-time country-carnival performer, vocalist and magician, very 'lowbrow' within the world of 'highbrow' opera, that make him more like Hugo's Esmeralda than his Quasimodo; the mournful longing for sundered family connections, as in the chamber of Erik's subterranean home fashioned like his mother's old bedroom (Leroux, p. 471), equally visible in the 'living skeleton' or 'spectre' of Hugo's recluse 'Gudule', who turns out to be the long-lost mother of Esmeralda herself (Hugo, pp. 177–8 and 373–5); the ironic stance of the struggling poet-playwright, like that of Pierre Gringoire in *Notre Dame,* as when Erik seeks both to subvert and to break into the world of high opera with his own composition, *Don Juan Triumphant* (Leroux, p. 250); and the features of a half-sublime, half-Satanic 'man in black' with 'two live coals' for eyes that recall the gaunt and often cloaked figure of Dom Claude Frollo, the archdeacon of Notre Dame in Hugo's book, who lusts for Esmeralda against his priestly vows (Hugo, pp. 256–62), but in line with his passion for absolute knowledge, his attempts (like Erik's) to penetrate into the darkest secrets of his world (Hugo, pp. 211–14). As a scapegoat for, or 'abjection' of, the multiple and conflicted states of being that the rising middle and the upper classes of Leroux's Paris want to shunt off from themselves, the Phantom of the Opera conflates the major 'othered' figures in *Notre Dame* as if all the conflicted attitudes projected onto Hugo's principal characters have, by the 1880s at least, settled themselves into one 'ghostly' location.

Yet for all of these symbiotic connections between *Notre Dame* and *Le Fantôme,* I want to concentrate here on finally how different from each other these visions turn out to be, especially in the ways they have adapted and transported to France, as some other French writings had done before them, key features of the 'Gothic Story' as it developed in England out of Horace Walpole's *The Castle of Otranto* (1764–5) and its even more popular successors of the 1790s, the decade of Ann Radcliffe's major romances and Matthew Gregory Lewis's *The Monk* (quite well known as *Le Moine* in Paris by the 1820s).[6] As similar as *Notre Dame* and *Le Fantôme* have been and remain, I find that they exemplify the *development* of the Gothic as a mixture of conflicting genres by having it perform a distinct kind of 'cultural work' in each novel.

On the one hand, I would argue, *Notre Dame de Paris*, a signal work of French historical Romanticism written deliberately in the wake of Sir Walter Scott and especially the latter's *Quentin Durward* (1823),[7] plays out with telling power the role of the Gothic as the site of the abjected 'underground' of progressive Romantic aspirations. This is a function the Gothic frequently performs, as I have begun to suggest elsewhere,[8] in texts ranging from those of Scott himself to the works of Chateaubriand, Coleridge, Byron, Mary Shelley and Keats, among others. In this early nineteenth-century variation, a work's Gothic features both drive and undermine the author's progressivist hope for human improvement fuelled, at least in part, by his or her visionary imagination. They do so by harbouring Western culture's most unresolved ideological quandaries at that time, out of which a countering hope attempts to rise by simultaneously acknowledging and 'othering' an abjected multiplicity of conflicting inclinations. These instabilities are left visible, yet also obscured, in the Gothic moments within Romantic works and thereby pull against any desired certainties about human and social betterment.

By the time of *Le Fantôme de l'Opéra* nearly 80 years after *Notre Dame,* on the other hand, the Gothic, in the wake of French *décadence*, imperial conquest, urban decay intermixed with expansion, and the exposure of racism and extreme nationalism in the Dreyfus Affair, among other things, is used less as an abjection of ideological irresolution and more as it is in *Dr Jekyll and Mr Hyde* (1886), *The Picture of Dorian Gray* (1891) or *Dracula* (1897): as a haunting othering of the very process of othering itself. The Gothic, as in Leroux's highly composite phantom, has become a place for throwing off and down, which both conceals and exposes the increasingly anxious fear, in those who believe in Western ideologies of middle-class 'progress', that their gains are mostly illusory and false, based as they are on the classist, racist and Eurocentric impulses, among others, that they claim to rise beyond (all abjected onto the ghost-like denizen in the foundations of the Paris Opera). In crossing from England to France and then from Hugo to Leroux, in other words, the Gothic, I would claim, fulfils its potential as an important enactor of cultural 'haunting' by radically changing what it returns from repression in Parisian and Western culture.

As I turn first to *Notre Dame*, though, I hasten to say that I am not arguing for the most common distinction between this novel and *Le Fantôme de l'Opéra:* that Hugo's book is simply an historical novel *à la* Scott with occasional Gothic elements while Leroux's is more of a truly Gothic pot-boiler influenced by Paris's *Grand Guignol* theatre and several news stories of the day. *Notre Dame* was undoubtedly commissioned by its editor to be fashioned in the style of Scott[9] and is filled with enough re-creations of the physical Paris of 1482 to make the reader sometimes seem to be 'there' by the sheer dint of historical detail. Yet Hugo, as Jeffrey Spires reminds us, had already announced his resistance to sheer historicism in symbolic fiction and his desire, in the tradition of Aristotle, to join historical realism to the mythic, archetypal and dramatic modes, especially as these draw out the *intérieur* of character more than the *extérieur* of history. Consequently, *Notre Dame* tells its story much as Spires says, 'by simultaneously invoking and distancing itself from the model of the historical novel'.[10] One way this book does so is to make crucial characters more reincarnations of established Gothic figures than organic products of the fifteenth century. The most obvious example is the lustful and obsessive Archdeacon Frollo, who is a blatant echo of Lewis's monk, Ambrosio. Particularly when Dom Claude spies on Esmeralda and Captain Phoebus whom she loves by lurking in the guise of a folklorical 'goblin-monk who [supposedly] haunted the streets of Paris at night' (Hugo, p. 229), he recalls Ambrosio, who is just as torn between 'in-born genius' and Catholic 'superstition', going under cover of darkness to the house of the virginal Antonia whom he passionately desires and finally trying to kill (as Frollo does) the person who most stands in his way, all the while (like the archdeacon in Hugo, pp. 301–2) 'conscious of the guilty business on which he was employed'.[11] In addition, Hugo's Esmeralda, with her own brand of virginal innocence, combines the qualities of Antonia with those of the prophetic gypsy-woman Lewis's heroine encounters early in The *Monk* 'whirl[ing] herself repeatedly round and round' and 'danc[ing] in all the eccentric attitudes of folly and delirium' that make her seem a dark sorceress as she foretells Antonia's eventual doom, one quite similar to Esmeralda's at the hands of Dom Claude.[12] *Notre Dame* repeats Gothic archetypes even in harbouring secrets about the lineage of its hero and heroine, as Gothic stories often do from *The Castle of Otranto* to *The Monk* and beyond. Quasimodo turns out to be the child of 'Egyptians' left as a foundling in place of the infant Esmeralda when she was stolen by those same gypsies from the once-beautiful Gudule (Hugo, pp. 173–4 and 383–4).

Notre Dame continues the Walpolean Gothic most, however, at the very point it seems most historical about supposedly authentic Gothic architecture. I refer to the narrator's commentary on the history of Notre Dame itself, especially as that chapter is further glossed later by the section titled 'This Will Kill That' (*Ceci tuera cela*). At first glance, the chapter *called* 'Notre Dame' (Hugo, pp. 89–94) is so specific about the 'injuries' inflicted by 'Time', 'revolutions, political and religious' and changes in 'taste' on the 'façade' of Paris's central cathedral – and about its retaining an unchanging 'basilica' structure like the organic 'trunk of a tree' – that Hugo's writing here seems the antithesis of Walpole's interest in the highly inorganic, fake, domesticated and flagrantly theatrical Gothic, as in his Gothicized house at Strawberry Hill.[13] But Hugo's ultimate emphasis is on Notre Dame as a 'transition edifice' where each 'new art ... encrusts itself upon' a 'structure' that is just as artificial originally and does so in very unnatural acts of power, as when he claims that 'the pointed style, brought back from the Crusades [the supposed era of The *Castle of Otranto*], seated itself like a conqueror upon ... Roman ... circular arches'. This conception is very like the emphasis of *Otranto* on the artful refiguration of older objects already artificial, flagrantly visible in that tale when the figure of a portrait walks out of its frame and the gigantic ghost of the castle's original owner turns out to be the enlarged duplicate of both a statue on an underground tomb and the armoured Ghost of Hamlet's father, which Walpole acknowledged as a primary source for his 'Gothic Story'.[14]

Just as much as Walpole's spectres and semi-medieval props, in other words, Hugo's Notre Dame is what I would call a 'ghost of the counterfeit'. By 'the counterfeit'[15] I mean Baudrillard's notion of the dominant type of signifier which prevailed in European discourse, though not always explicitly, from the Renaissance in the fifteenth century through the beginnings of the industrial revolution in the eighteenth.[16] In this sense of the sign, every symbolic surface looks back to a medieval cultural moment where 'symbol' and 'status' were tightly connected by prescribed distinctions of class and role that seemed divinely ordained.

Yet the sign as 'counterfeit' also intimates the fading control of that standard, while simultaneously admitting its continuing draw, and heralds the new post-medieval capacity of signifiers to be transferred between individuals. People, after all, are shifting more freely and rhetorically between classes and roles during the Renaissance and since, often to the point where someone seems aristocratic by being able to purchase the signs of that status and thereby fake it in the public eye. By Walpole's time in the mid-eighteenth century, this kind of signification is itself beginning to fade into the 'ghost' of itself, just as the Walpolean spectre shows by both looking back to the 'counterfeit' as Hamlet defines it (as the true portrait *and* the false image of his father)[17] and resembling what will become the simulacrum of the industrial era in the portrait that separates from its initial canvas, much as manufactured products will become separate from their original, and already counterfeit, moulds. If Hugo does not make it entirely clear in his 'Notre Dame' chapter that he sees his main setting as such a neo-Gothic figure of a fading set of figures, he does so in 'This Will Kill That' (Hugo, pp. 143–53), where he both celebrates and laments the fact that the power of the printing press and what circulates from it, from about the era of his novel's events, has overpowered the seemingly stationary and rooted symbol that is the cathedral. This process has gone so far, Hugo's narrator adds, 'imprinting will kill architecture' (*l'imprimerie tuera l'architecture*), replacing the latter's social dominance and its supposed repetition of a divine Essence or Order with the repetition of floating signifiers in many different printings and thus, as Constance Schick has written in the vein of Paul de Man, 'troping [medieval] symbolism into' the sheer 'allegorical rhetoricity' of 'ciphers'.[18]

By so fully enacting the Janus-faced tendencies, the extreme looking backwards *and* forwards of the Walpolean Gothic symbol, moreover, Hugo's *Notre Dame* allows the contradiction that results to disguise, yet thereby contain, profound cultural contradictions of the author's own moment, very much as the neo-Gothic has done in many different ways since *The Castle of Otranto*. A symbolic construct that is a ghost of counterfeit signification inherently refers (and defers) in conflicting directions; hence the aptness of the Janus analogy. It at once denies the permanent solidity of the old grounds it still seems to long for, if only spectrally, and offers a near-mechanical reproduction of their symbols instead, as when Walpole invokes old Catholic symbology in his *Castle* while denying the validity of Catholicism and promising the future 'expatiation' of literary 'invention' via modern printing in the Preface to his second edition.[19] This Preface is still famous, after all, for announcing a new mode of free enterprise (the 'Gothic Story') that combines 'ancient' with 'modern' romance and the questionably supernatural with the doubtfully, but marketably, historical. Such a tug-of-war is frighteningly perfect for symbolizing the simultaneous draw of contradictory economies, ideologies and psychologies, such as the unresolved push–pull in *Otranto* between waning aristocratic and rising middle-class attitudes towards property, inheritance, marriage, religion and self-determination in the mid- to late eighteenth century. Here also lies the reason for the Gothic's special usefulness as a site for psychological and/or cultural 'abjection' in Kristeva's sense. For Kristeva, what are most abjected, so that we can seem to have coherent identities by contrast, are our pre-conscious memories of primally contradictory states, such as being half-inside and half-outside the mother at birth and thus originally half-dead and half-alive,[20] or, on the cultural front, starting out immersed in a mix of quite different class, racial and gender attributes and levels. The ghost of the counterfeit that defines the most basic neo-Gothic symbolic position oscillates just like these states, even as it disguises that very oscillation behind theatrically false reproductions of the past. Consequently, the Walpolean Gothic symbol serves both to incarnate abjected contradictions and to provide a site of lurid and ghostly 'otherness' into which such unresolved anomalies of being can be thrown off and down and hidden while remaining hauntingly half-visible.

This unsettled and unsettling process is precisely what appears in Hugo's 'Notre Dame' and 'This Will Kill That' chapters, frequently 'expatiating' from there into the rest of the novel. It is that dynamic, full of struggle as it is, that lets the novel *Notre Dame* abject, and so enunciate with some concealment, Hugo's conflicted sense in 1830–1 of history and culture in France and Western Europe in general. The novel's narrator manifestly longs for and mourns the loss of the cathedral's fifteenth-century state, as though it were a once-authentic condition (now ghosted in 1831). At the same time, he acknowledges it as never more than a series of artificial building stages, 'the colossal product of all the force of the epoch' only in that unstable, ever-changing sense – that of the counterfeit, the signifier of what is really just a signifier of previous signifiers (Hugo, pp. 90–3). In addition, his celebration of the rise of printing, from which he and his book benefit, happily *and* sadly renders Notre Dame as no more than a husk of its former being – 'a skull', as the narrator describes the vast church once the life of its monstrous bell-ringer is absent from it (Hugo, pp. 151–2) – and this consciousness of 'spiritual vacuity', to use the words of Victor

Brombert,[21] recalls Walpole's Enlightenment and anti-Catholic sense of medieval relics in his letters as now so 'empty' that playing with and marketing them in Gothic revivals cannot 'disappoint' anyone in the 1760s.[22] To Hugo's narrator, on the one hand, this emptying of past groundings is tragic indeed, full of loss upon loss, as the fate of nearly all his main characters proves to be by the end of his book. Hugo's figures in the main are ground to death, like his Notre Dame, by large forces of history that he views partly as 'ceaseless destruction'[23] and then left primarily as decaying skeletons, again like his Notre Dame, abjected into buried catacombs that will seem more incomprehensible the more time passes (Hugo, pp. 393–4). On the other hand, the rise of printing and the novel's emphasis on the past-ness of its less enlightened era of despotic public punishment both value an emptying-out of all that as necessary for the progress of civilization, for what Hugo's narrator calls 'emancipated humanity' as it 'beholds the arrival of intelligence overcoming faith, opinion dethroning credulity' (Hugo, p. 145). If only, as *Notre Dame* reminds us in its Gothic take on this ideology of progress, the result were not also a production of disseminated signs from 'the press, this giant machine', in 'spirals without end' which pile up empty ciphers into what Hugo famously sees as an ungrounded and ever-proliferating 'second tower of Babel' that threatens to shatter all hope of cultural unity and continuity (Hugo, p. 153). However different these tangles of unresolved ideologies are from those in Walpole or Matthew Lewis or Gaston Leroux, they are the irreconcilables that underwrite Hugo's *Notre Dame de Paris* and appear most vividly in his recasting of the Gothic ghost of the counterfeit throughout his settings, characters, philosophical statements and plotlines.

To be sure, this novel does, as several scholars have commented, render Victor Hugo's own complex of feelings about how France and the West seemed in 1830–1 and how the features of this time parallel those of 1482 in Paris as he then understood it. *Notre Dame de Paris* was composed in the wake of the July Revolution of 1830 which replaced a royalist absolutism with the seemingly more pro-bourgeois king, Louis-Philippe, partly to the anti-royalist Hugo's satisfaction and partly to his dismay, considering his antipathy to working-class mob violence and his anger at (for him) the desecration of several venerated structures, among them Notre Dame, by minions of Louis-Philippe.[24] The year 1482 for Hugo was a moment of incipient revolution, right at the transition of the Middle Ages to the Renaissance, which set the stage for 'all the foundations of modern-day France'.[25] As such it is an avatar of both 1789, the year of the most famous French Revolution, and 1830, the year of the July revolt, but also the latest instance of what Spires rightly calls 'a recurring ritual of social renewal and rebirth', all of which is prefigured in the novel by the carnivalesque Feast of Fools at its opening and the peasant assault on Notre Dame, followed by its brutal suppression under Louis XI, near the end. Hugo's *Notre Dame*, among other things, figures his ambivalence towards the contraries, the gains and destructions, at each stage of this entire cycle. Yet by half-throwing off and half-manifesting this irresolution in a series of 'grotesque images' (as Spires puts it) – which I see as distinctly neo-Gothic in the tradition of Walpole, Lewis and their French adaptors – Hugo does more than borrow relatively new archetypes to fictionalize his personal views. He develops the cultural baggage of deep insecurity about many unresolved conflicts that the Gothic was already carrying for several 'Romantic' authors before him. When his Gothic images suggest the fear of losing past certainties with the gain of new emancipations, the sense that apparent progress via upheavals is destructive of continuous tradition even as it seems to open avenues for cripples, gypsies and itinerant playwrights, and the frightening prospect that the increasing proliferation of printed texts will produce a groundless Babel without a coherent culture, Hugo is echoing many other voices of early nineteenth-century Europe and their uses of Gothic to abject and half-articulate widespread anxieties among the literate and even *liberal* middle classes and the many writers who emerged from that unstable group.

In England, for example, Samuel Taylor Coleridge had reacted to Lewis's *The Monk* in a 1797 review by claiming that such fiction posed serious problems for Western culture in general, setting up his partner William Wordsworth's sweeping condemnation of such 'frantic novels' and 'extravagant stories' in his Preface to the second edition of *Lyrical Ballads*.[26] For Coleridge the problems included the extreme Gothic's recovery of visible sexuality from repression, its blurring of once distinct ideologies (such as 'superstition' and orthodox Christian doctrine) into 'one common mass', its concomitant mixture of styles from different genres (with 'phrases the most trite and colloquial' placed alongside 'solemnity of diction'), its combination of low with high culture as a consequence, and worst of all, 'the multitude of its manufactures' by the 1790s, in which once solid connections of signifiers to signifieds seemed threatened with obliteration (like Hugo's Notre Dame) by a sheer proliferation of blatantly fictional texts in print.[27] These concerns, once echoed by Wordsworth and others striving to set disciplined standards for a near-explosion of printed writing at the end of the eighteenth century, helped turn the Gothic into a kind of whipping post that writers aspiring to 'high culture' could use to scapegoat their fears about the proliferation of printed works as both attractive and threatening to cultural norms. As Michael Gamer has shown, the Gothic came to be 'blamed' for virtually all the 'changes in literary production and consumption' at this time we now recall as 'Romantic'.[28] It was thus quite clearly the *abject* into which writing in search of a new cohesion could throw off the anomalies it sought both to exploit and to overcome. It therefore may not be surprising that many of the authors who condemned this mixed form nevertheless used it extensively in their best-known works, as Coleridge does powerfully in poems from 'The Rime of the Ancient Mariner' (1798) to 'Christabel' (1800, but published with 'Kubla Khan' in 1816).[29] Such works offer the possibility of future salvation through the enlightened imagination, as Hugo later would, precisely by sequestering in their Gothic images, while thereby confronting – as 'The Rime' and 'Christabel' are now noted for revealing – the intermingled and conflicting ideologies and styles out of which a 'brave new world' attempts to rise. The Romantic work projects the supposed identity of its visionary scheme over against a Gothic 'Other' into which the writer abjects, and through which he (or she) still views, the contradictions that might yet undermine an ultimate unity of vision. That very tension is certainly what we see in what the creature embodies for his creator and author in Mary Shelley's *Frankenstein* (1818) but also, as Gamer has shown, in many of the verses and novels of Sir Walter Scott.[30] There the desired emergence of historical accommodation between opposing social groups is eventually proposed only in the face of Gothic anachronisms that remain hauntingly present with all their unresolved contraries still calling us to them, even as they, like Hugo's 'real' Notre Dame, recede to a past that obscures them as well.

After crossing the English Channel, then, the Gothic in Romantic-historical fiction continues to symbolize unsettled contests among belief systems that still motivate and bedevil the hope of an 'emancipated humanity'. What Coleridge sees and fears in *The Monk* is really what Hugo includes throughout *Notre Dame* in its vision of history's jarring progress through a series of revolutions, here epitomized by a moment in 1482 caught between retrogressive and progressive tendencies. That is why we see flagrant genre blurring and a cross-pollination of literary styles at the most Gothic moments of this book – a mixture that Hugo was by now advocating openly[31] – and a sense of *both* Gothic architecture *and* its death behind the rise of printing which raises the spectre of lost cultural groundings, all standing over against the emergence of 'intelligence' over 'faith'. Even the bursting forth of sexual passion in the figures to whom it is most forbidden socially, Archdeacon Frollo and Quasimodo, shows the different ideological positions between which these characters are pulled just as much as Ambrosio does in Lewis's late eighteenth-century vision of the early sixteenth century. Now Hugo's much-discussed hesitation between the power of free will and the dominance of historical necessity over his characters turns out to be one feature of the Gothic penchant in *Notre Dame* for giving equal force to opposed conceptions of causality as the real undercurrents of a progressive story. To be more precise than we have usually been about the tortured Gothic–Romantic relationship in the early nineteenth century, I conclude that *Notre Dame* shows what that relation really came to be: the crafting of an imaginative prognostication of a better existence to come by the vivid abjection, and thus the shadowy revelation, of the unreconciled quandaries of this and past times against which the imagination struggles. Yes, 'the Gothic', as with other Romantics, was 'associated in Hugo's mind with revolution and the rise of democracy', insofar as the medieval Gothic seemed to rebel against strict Greco-Roman classicism. But it was equally connected, in the wake of Walpolean fiction, with 'permanent dislocation', a fear of emergent changes as a loss of stable meaning.[32] It is this contradiction that most haunts Romantic historicism, and exposing precisely that problem is the principal power of the most Gothic features in Victor Hugo's *Notre Dame de Paris*, as was the case, we now discover, in many other fictions of its time.

In Leroux's *Le Fantôme de l'Opéra* eight decades later, by contrast, we are long past any hope for progress being haunted by the disappearance of past layers of meaning. This time the central skull in the book is the title character's rather than a building's, at least once this Erik is unmasked. Leroux reworks, beyond several of Hugo's characters, the medieval French tradition of the *danse macabre*, the skeletal figure appearing at the fêtes of the wealthy and reminding them of their mortality and the wages of sin.[33] Leroux thus makes his phantom the ultimate betwixt-and-between figure, a version of the 'abject' in being alive and the face of the dead at the same time. Onto this blatantly contradictory ghost of a counterfeit (a spectre of a figure who denies the very death he depicts, as well as being the modern image of a very old icon) Leroux and his supporting characters further abject a host of anomalies that are more basic to rising middle- and upper-class society than any patron of the Opera wants to admit in the 1880s *or* 1910: the connection of the operatic to the carnivalesque (as Erik the former ventriloquist shows by making a diva on stage seem to croak like a frog during Gounod's *Faust*; Leroux, pp. 151–5); the inextricable links of what is mainline French (an Erik born in Rouen) to what is Germanic ('Erik' as the phantom's adopted name), what verges on Jewish (Erik as alluding to both Dreyfus and Svengali), and what seems Oriental (Erik as adopting several Eastern accoutrements with a skull-face thinly covered by *yellow* skin; Leroux, p. 21); the affinity between the high-culture operagoer (Erik in tails in his Box Five) and the artisan or hack musician (two of Erik's ongoing occupations below ground); the pretensions of the self-made man (Erik ascending the social scale from the petit bourgeoisie to the Opera) linked to an underlying potential for degeneracy (a skull-face that betokens devolution to a now-fossilized Darwinian past); and the blurring of apparently standard masculinity (Erik as a tall presence in male evening clothes wooing a young woman towards marriage) with an instability of gender (considering Erik's six-octave voice that at times lets him pose as a female Siren singing across the lake beneath the Opera) and a fluidity of sexual status (given that Erik's vocal range recalls that of the operatic *castrato*). Rather than the Romantic contradiction of history as pulling a narrator longingly backwards just as much as hopefully forwards in the 'skull' that is Hugo's Notre Dame, Leroux presents a phantom of the late nineteenth century who abjects all in one place the many linked contradictions on which the aspirations of the supposedly 'evolved' classes are actually based, despite their above-ground denials of this fact. Erik lives, Leroux keeps reminding us, in the very foundations of a primary cultural institution that he also helped to construct originally in the 1860s and 1870s. Through him, the wealthy are now haunted by the wages of their sins in the sense that they must confront their cultural unconscious in one embodiment of the multiplicities, including interracial, cross-class and cross-gender connections, they have thrown off and thrown down in order to achieve the illusion of a high-class Western identity.

Leroux's time in Western history, quite different from Hugo's, saw enough acceptance of a progressivist ideology that such beliefs at least implicitly endorsed Darwinian evolution as apparently justifying the just ascent of the white European middle and upper classes. This 'structure of feeling', as Raymond Williams would call it,[34] became one rationalization for French, as well as English, imperial conquests around the world in the late nineteenth century, especially in the so-called 'Orient', which ranged from Africa to East Asia to southern Russia and for some to *Eastern* Europe in the Western prejudices of this period, just as Edward Said and others have taught us.[35] Earlier doubts about losing past certainties or standards now faded behind the enterprise of establishing cultural and racial superiority, most prominently in the capitals of capitalistic Europe and their most imposing cultural centres, the Paris Opera among them. One ideological process particularly effective at supporting this projection of white, upper-class, evolved identity was clearly an 'othering' at multiple levels by which certain standards of being and behaviour were consolidated against what is 'othered' as the 'core' of proper existence. All deviations from such standards, especially the mixture of supposedly 'proper' and 'improper' states, were then symbolically and philosophically exiled from the core, to the point where the most outcast states were thought the most 'monstrous' in their combinations of the contradictory. We see this process in the Dreyfus Affair, of course, but also increasingly reflected and critiqued in late Victorian Gothic fiction. There is Stevenson's original *Jekyll and Hyde*, where the multiple class-crossings to which Jekyll is inclined are shunted off onto the 'degenerate' and 'troglodytic' Hyde, who is both distinct from and part of him; Oscar Wilde's *Picture of Dorian Gray,* in which bisexuality and thorough class and gender instability are abjected onto a Walpolean portrait of sinful decay as if it were no longer the mirror of the person it nevertheless reflects; Bram Stoker's *Dracula,* wherein a vestige of the faded warrior-aristocracy vampirically feeds on, and thus comes to embody, racial mixing in Western Europe, the growth of venereal diseases in the blood of the upper classes, and the threat of the more powerful 'New Woman' to established gender hierarchies, among many other crossings of conventional boundaries;[36] and H. G. Wells' *The Island of Dr. Moreau* (1896), less than fifteen years before Leroux's most Gothic effort, where the fear that evolution-based science will open up the potential for human *de*volution, or (even worse) a mixing of the evolved and devolved, is joined to the potential horror of miscegenation between the races as a byproduct of imperial conquest.[37] *Le Fantôme de l'Opéra* builds on these abjections of mixed otherness by throwing off more minglings of contradictory states than any monster-ghost had ever done in Gothic fiction, save possibly Frankenstein's creature, and adds the special emphasis that all these abjected compounds really live together in the very foundations of the edifice in which the dominant classes most want to establish their supremacy as the very essence of 'high culture'.

However similar the Gothic mechanisms are between this highly focused abjection and Hugo's earlier images of his age's anxieties, the cultural agenda has clearly changed, if only by carrying earlier tendencies to extremes that were just potential in them previously. Quasimodo in *Notre Dame* is certainly a convenient 'Other', as Erik would later be, for 'monsterizing' multiple West European prejudices, particularly since his first appearance comes when he is chosen as the King of Fools. There he comically embodies the carnivalesque desire of the lower classes to assume the place of the upper in a seemingly bestial figure whom those underlings can also see as inferior to them. Yet Hugo's hunchback, forced into such roles by others more than seeking them himself, is primarily an unwitting symbolic eddy into which cross-currents of history, from class struggles to differing positions on what defines humanity, pour themselves, much as they do into the encrustations of the 'skull' that is Notre Dame. The otherings of quasi-Jewishness and Orientalness, along with apish bestiality, cast onto him, though he acquires more such associations than any other figure, are just some among the 'low' states that the French of 1482 project onto numerous others, from Esmeralda to Gudule to the cathedral to the many vagabonds in the Court of Miracles, as Hugo spreads out the focal points through which he can manifest the cultural conflicts of 1482 and his own era. The phantom of Leroux, on the other hand, abjects all the 'othered' contradictions of post-1890s 'decadence' in one *danse macabre* symbol of utter betwixt-and-betweenness. In doing so, he emphasizes how interconnected the many kinds of othering are at a time when the imperial expansion so celebrated by the Paris Opera and other structures was encountering the fear, partly caused by that expansion, of newly permeable boundaries between races, classes, genders and even sexual orientations (as in the trials of Oscar Wilde in the mid-1890s).[38] The progression of human enlightenment that once had such doubts about the fading stabilities it was losing has become so insistent as an ideology, luring so many Europeans into poses of exclusive cultural supremacy bound up with a supposed 'normality' of qualities, that all the various 'otherings' that 'true believers' have carried out to this end are indeed as interrelated and as mutually reinforcing as their being scapegoated onto the Phantom of the Opera finally shows them to be. The inclination of progressive change in the early nineteenth century (and in 1482 for Hugo) to link itself still to some older ways of scapegoating social conflict onto 'others' has become, many decades later, the systematic abjection of a host of linked anomalies to create the modern gallery of grotesques (the new 'skull') against which class-climbing 'normalcy' can be constructed, if only over a foundation of abjections that keeps haunting it.

Gaston Leroux, partly in memory of Hugo as both national hero and sometime rebel, after all, saw himself as a combination, he once said, of '*honnête homme*' and 'assassin' in his writing,[39] a portrayer of the norms at which middle-class social convention aimed *and* an exposer of their shocking underbellies in the provocative-but-safe disguise of mystery, adventure and occasionally Gothic stories. At the same time, by imitating existing patterns of popular fiction as openly and fully as he did from 1906 until his death in 1927, Leroux became a medium through which those very conventions manifested their capacities for both upholding social proprieties and symbolizing what was outcast, and hence repressed, by those standards. As he thus carried out the drives already building in the Gothic and other kinds of popular fiction during his lifetime, he took a number of inclinations in Hugo's work besides cultural scapegoating to extremes that his predecessor had only begun to imagine. Leroux's quite Gothic use of the carnivalesque in *Le Fantôme* is a case in point. In *Notre Dame de Paris*, carnival, as in the Feast of Fools and its inseparability from the church- and government-sanctioned Epiphany of 6 January, is an open and self-regulating encounter of potentially conflicting class positions and belief systems. There conservative pulls towards maintaining a hierarchical order and liberationist tugs towards a licence that can blur social types into each other (like a king and a deformed bell-ringer) – tendencies contesting in Hugo's own thinking around 1830–1[40] – can act out their contradictions and deflect them into non-violent mock-symbolism, showing and yet mitigating the ideological conflicts of both the late Middle Ages and the time of the 1830 revolution in Paris. By the time of both the events and the writing of *Le Fantôme de l'Opéra*, as Peter Stallybrass and Allon White have shown,[41] carnival had been banned in Paris for some years, relegated to a low-culture status in the countryside, along with other blurrings of distinction, as the urban elite consolidated its constructed centrality in the redesign of the capital around the Place de l'Opéra. Leroux's Erik, the former country-carnival magician, singer and freak, is therefore reinvading Paris and its Opera with carnival in an aggressive return of the repressed, especially when his disguise as Edgar Allan Poe's 'Red Death' at the Opera's masked ball, where his exposed skull is the only unmasked face to appear (Leroux, pp. 187–8), forces this event to confront its own and the whole Opera's relation to the carnivalesque it has tried to throw off, wrenching the *danse macabre* in a symbolic direction that even Poe did not employ in his 1842 'Masque of the Red Death'. Cast off and down into a Gothicized underground, carnival now, like the phantom himself, has been turned into a cultural unconscious, the site of all its world's abjections, that it was not in 1482 or 1830. This eruption of licence in the space from which it has been banned thus joins the myriad 'others' of France's Third Republic in the late nineteenth century to intimate the costs of high-bourgeois supremacy, and the many challenges to it at home and abroad, in Leroux's new Gothic conflation of once-scattered symbols.

Even more striking in Leroux's transformations of Hugo's Gothic, however, is *Le Fantôme*'s fulfilment of the qualms in *Notre Dame* about the murderous power of the printed signifiers, the ghosts of ghosts of counterfeits, on which these two and all writings depend. Although Hugo simultaneously celebrates and laments the capacity of writings in print to distance, and so kill, what they describe while preserving those objects at least dimly in memory, he offers several moments where signifying surfaces – such as Notre Dame, Esmeralda's prison tower and the 'massive' edifice of sixteen gallows that is Montfoucon in 1482 (Hugo, pp. 89–94, 252–4 and 393–4) – can be penetrated to the point of reaching deeper levels where quite real objects seem very tangible even in words: the chambers of Quasimodo, Dom Claude and the actual cathedral bells; the very physical suffering and defiance of Esmeralda as she faces down Frollo in her cell; and the embracing skeletons of Esmeralda and Quasimodo so palpably 'hideous' that they crumble when touched on the last page of the novel. *Notre Dame de Paris*, it can be argued, works hard in its historical realizations to counter its fear of words eclipsing objects as much as it can. Leroux's novel, in a total reversal, makes its deepest points the repositories of sheer signifiers quite theatrically distanced from their referents to the same extent that signs are divorced from reality in the above-ground world of both opera and the fake *poseurs* of high society. We hear from its narrator quite early in this book that in 'Paris, one is always at a masked ball' (Leroux, p. 55), so much so that the visible features of the wider city and its people are indistinguishable in their basic nature from the costume and scenery at the Opera. *Le Matin*, the newspaper for which Leroux wrote most of his journalism in the 1890s, published a front-page editorial in 1896 lamenting the total 'dissimulation', the perpetual 'carnival' of 'masques', in the 'world of life, politics – everything',[42] and Leroux imported that contemporary cultural problem into *Le Fantôme* along with other headlines of his time. But Leroux also makes this tendency primal at the most basic depths in this story's spaces by locating the counterfeiting of the already counterfeit, a layering of simulations without any real bottom, at every level of his phantom's underground domain, the ultimate depth to which the novel's mysteries finally devolve. The chamber of distorting mirrors at the deepest point of his lair, in which Erik traps Christine's would-be rescuers, repeatedly reflects an already artificial tree at its centre, with every image reflecting a *mise en abyme* of other images, to such an extent that each mirroring of mirrors 'multiplied itself to infinity' (Leroux, pp. 435–6), just as Hugo imagines printed signs will increasingly 'spiral'. The 20,000 francs a month that Leroux's phantom demands as protection money from the Opera management, too, goes to pay primarily for all this fakery, and if Erik returns any of this perpetual debt to the world of sheer surfaces that is Paris above ground, he does so in false bills marked with 'the Bank of St. Farce' (Leroux, p. 303), making the universal counterfeiting in this book quite literal from its deepest point outwards.

Such a thorough realization of Hugo's fears about signs of signs killing off human access to objects stems, Leroux's form of Gothic suggests, from the same pervasive cultural dynamic that has helped produce the 'othering' of the many mixed states with which capitalistic and imperialistic 'high culture' is so involved at the turn of the nineteenth into the twentieth century. As Baudrillard might put it, the passage in Western assumptions about signs from the ghost of the counterfeit in Walpole's era to the standard of the mass-produced 'industrial simulacrum' gaining dominance in Europe by the time of Hugo – one definite reason for his fears about print culture – has given way by 1910 to the simulacrum becoming sheer 'simulation' without an accessible relation to some original mould, however artificial. Since Gothic images start out as ghosts of counterfeits, particularly in deep Walpolean spaces (such as the underground tomb of Alfonso in *Otranto* which is topped with an armoured effigy), they are unusually apt, given that Gothic tales are involved from their beginnings with the proliferation of printed texts, for figuring the cultural transition to the reproducible simulacra (incipient in the ghost of an already painted figure) and then the West's more recent shift to ungrounded simulation (as *Le Fantôme* turns Walpole's subterranean labyrinth of myriad cloisters into a chamber of mirrors of mirrors of mirrors). Leroux's novel is extraordinary in showing how this progression in signification is entirely bound up with social othering and the disguising abjection of it at the time of this story's events and publication. *Le Fantôme* thereby shows us that cultural abjection, in all its variations, depends upon its being hidden by simulations that lead the initial attention of onlookers only to other deceptive images instead of the welter of mixtures and blurring boundaries which is the increasingly problematic Real. Even as he harbours the abjection of both cultural 'otherings' and widespread simulation, Leroux's 'Opera ghost' acts out these very processes himself, becoming an even more comprehensive Gothic symbol. He tries to be a middle-class social climber by masking his more complex blurring of incompatible conditions, yet in that way he makes them more apparent, while also more able to be thrown off and cast down into an underground realm as the inclinations of a villainous freak, however foundational his multiplicity may be to the high culture pursued by him and most of his observers. Slavoj Žižek has helpfully argued that Leroux's phantom incarnates the senseless Real of Jacques Lacan, the confused human tendencies both back to and away from the mother and towards death and life simultaneously, as well as the connection of such 'non-meaning' to the contradictions of 'class struggle'.[43] I would add that the original Erik suggests all this partly because he is also, unlike Hugo's Quasimodo and conflicted sense of Notre Dame, a master of the very simulation of simulations that allows him and others to obscure the cultural otherings he embodies. Such symbolic richness can be achieved because the Gothic itself has moved beyond Hugo's Romantic hesitation between fearing a loss of groundings and embracing middle-class aspirations and instead has half-confronted and half-disguised the Gilded Age's rarely acknowledged roots in both unbounded simulation and the abjection of a great many discriminatory 'otherings'.

This difference in the end, though, does not mean that *Le Fantôme de l'Opéra* is somehow better or more important than, or should be more separated than it has been from, Hugo's *Notre Dame de Paris*. For our purposes here, in fact, both these texts, in their interconnectedness and their historical and symbolic difference from each other, mark the phenomenal cultural power of the Gothic, as it develops across continents and periods, to partly expose and partly obscure the most fundamental social conflicts and the complexes of feelings about them during every historical era since the mid-eighteenth century. At one time in academia, within the standards of the American-born 'New Criticism' that valued the organic integration of already textualized contradictions (all in the name of shoring up definitions of Western high culture in the face of the Cold War), *Notre Dame de Paris*, the original *Phantom of the Opera* and the Gothic in general were regarded as 'lesser' texts, too inorganic, cross-generic, conceptually conflicted and merely popular in their adaptability to be worthy of serious scholarly study. Now, with the advent of cultural studies and the resurgence of the various critical perspectives that have contributed to it from post-structural psychoanalysis and Marxism to New Historicism, we rightly view the writings, theatre and films that make up 'the Gothic' as key indicators of what a culture most values and what it most fears and abjects within those values as it struggles to keep defining itself in many symbolic venues. *Notre Dame de Paris* and *Le Fantôme de l'Opéra*, alongside other Gothic texts, can now come more fully into their own, linked to their adaptations or not, as strongly indicative documents of cultural aspiration and the sublimated contraries it struggles against at different points in time, with each historical moment raising its own set of issues for the Gothic to symbolize and disguise. Granted, we can use the penchant for extreme concealment and layers of simulation in this highly counterfeit mode to keep ourselves from seeing the abjected undercurrents of unresolved ideological debates and blurred distinctions that Gothic settings, characters and descriptions frequently hold out to us, even as they also work to protect us from them in the terror-with-safety that Gothic fictions usually offer. But we can also return to and analyse *Notre Dame* and *Le Fantôme*, as I have tried to do here, and find there how recurrent Gothic symbolic elements move with great cultural power from work to work and yet, in doing so, permit each variation to symbolize and struggle with the most irresolvable cultural quandaries of its own time and place.

Notes

1. See Jerrold E. Hogle, *The Undergrounds of* The Phantom of the Opera: *Sublimation and the Gothic in Leroux's Novel and its Progeny* (New York: Palgrave, 2002), pp. 10–11; and Catherine Clément, *Opera, or The Undoing of Women*, trans. Betsy Wing (Minneapolis: University of Minnesota Press, 1988), pp. 23–4.
2. See Julia Kristeva in *Powers of Horror: An Essay on Abjection,* trans. Leon S. Roudiez (New York: Columbia University Press, 1982), esp. pp. 1–10; and Hogle, *The Undergrounds of* The Phantom of the Opera, pp. 51–2.
3. See Gaston Leroux, *Le Fantôme de l'Opéra* (Paris: Le Livre de Poche, 1959), p. 10 (where 'the events do not date back further than thirty years' from 1910). Henceforth all citations from the original *Fantôme* will be accompanied in my text by 'Leroux' and page numbers from this edition. The translations from Leroux's and Hugo's French are mine.
4. I quote Hugo's *Notre Dame de Paris* from a complete French text (Paris: Les Editions de Paris, 1956), which will be cited throughout with 'Hugo' and page numbers from this edition.
5. See Leroux's report on the opening day of Dreyfus' retrial in the Paris daily *Le Matin*, 2 July 1899, 1–2.
6. See Fernand Baldensperger, '*Le Moine* de Lewis dans la Littérature Française', *Journal of Comparative Literature*, 1 (1903), 201–19.

7. Hugo develops his *Notre Dame* characterization of France's Louis XI (Hugo, pp. 335–58) directly from Scott's rendering of him in *Quentin Durward*, intro. C. L. Bennett (Clinton, MA: Airmont, 1967), esp. pp. 174–86.

8. See Jerrold E. Hogle, 'The Gothic-Romantic Relationship: Underground Histories in "The Eve of St. Agnes"', *European Romantic Review*, 14 (2003), 205–23.

9. Hugo's contract for *Notre Dame* called explicitly for him to write an historical romance 'à la Walter Scott', according to Jacques Seebacher, 'Introduction', *Notre Dame de Paris,* Bibliothèque de la Pléiade edition (Paris: Gallimard, 1975), p. 1052.

10. Jeffrey Spires, 'Victor Hugo's *Notre Dame de Paris:* The Politics and Poetics of Transition', *Dalhousie French Studies*, 61 (2002), 41, n. 4.

11. I quote Matthew Lewis here from *The Monk*, ed. Howard Anderson and Emma McEvoy (Oxford: Oxford University Press, 1995), pp. 238 and 298–304.

12. Lewis, *The Monk*, pp. 34–9.

13. See Dianne S. Ames, 'Strawberry Hill: Architecture of the "As If"', *Studies in 18th-Century Culture,* 8, ed. Rosanne Runte (Madison, WI: University of Wisconsin Press, 1999), 351–63.

14. See Horace Walpole, *The Castle of Otranto: A Gothic Story*, ed. W. S. Lewis and E. J. Clery (Oxford: Oxford University Press, 1996), pp. 26–7, 21 and 10–11.

15. Discussed already in Jerrold E. Hogle, 'The Ghost of the Counterfeit in the Genesis of the Gothic', *Gothick Origins and Innovations*, ed. Allan Lloyd Smith and Victor Sage (Amsterdam: Rodopi, 1994), pp. 23–33.

16. See Jean Baudrillard in *Symbolic Exchange and Death*, trans. Iain Hamilton Grant (London: Sage, 1993), pp. 50–61.

17. See *Hamlet* in the Arden Shakespeare edition, ed. Harold Jenkins (London: Methuen, 1982), pp. 321–4 (III.iv.53–88).

18. Constance Gosselin Schick, 'Death Comes to the Cathedral: Romantic Allegorizations of the Symbol', *French Forum*, 22 (1997), 161.

19. See the 1765 second Preface in Walpole, *The Castle*, pp. 9–14, plus the virulent anti-Catholicism in the 1764 first Preface, pp. 5–8.

20. See Kristeva, *Powers of Horror*, pp. 3–10.

21. Victor Brombert, *Victor Hugo and the Visionary Novel* (Cambridge, MA: Harvard University Press, 1984), p. 64.

22. Here I quote *The Yale Edition of Horace Walpole's Correspondence*, ed. W. S. Lewis et al. (New Haven, CT: Yale University Press, 1937–83), X, p. 192.

23. Joan C. Kessler, 'Babel and Bastille: Architecture as Metaphor in Hugo's *Notre-Dame de Paris*', *French Forum*, 11 (1986), 187.

24. See Kessler, 'Babel and Bastille', 196, n. 7.

25. Spires, 'Victor Hugo's *Notre Dame de Paris*', p. 42. I cite Spires again in what soon follows from p. 43.

26. See 'Preface to *Lyrical Ballads, with Pastoral and Other Poems* (1802)', in William Wordsworth, *The Poems*, ed. John O. Hayden (London: Penguin Books, 1990), I, 873.

27. Samuel Taylor Coleridge, 'Review of *The Monk*', *Critical Review*, 19 (1797), 194–200, rpt. in *Gothic Documents: A Sourcebook*, ed. E. J. Clery and Robert Miles (Manchester: Manchester University Press, 2000), pp. 185–9.

28. Michael Gamer, *Romanticism and the Gothic: Genre, Reception, and Canon Formation* (Cambridge: Cambridge University Press, 2000), p. 67.

29. See Anne Williams, 'An "I" for an Eye: *The Rime of the Ancient Mariner*', *Art of Darkness: A Poetics of the Gothic* (Chicago: University of Chicago Press, 1995), pp. 182–99; and Jerrold E. Hogle, '"Christabel" as Gothic: The Abjection of Instability', *Gothic Studies*, 7 (2005), 18–28.

30. See the studies in *Frankenstein: Contemporary Critical Essays*, New Casebooks, ed. Fred Botting (London: Macmillan, 1995), and Gamer, *Romanticism and the Gothic*, pp. 163–200.

31. See Brombert, *Victor Hugo and the Visionary Novel*, pp. 2–55; and Ilinca M. Zarifopol-Johnston, '*Notre Dame de Paris:* The Cathedral in the Book', *Nineteenth-Century French Studies*, 13 (1985), 22–35.

32. In this and the previous sentence, I quote Suzanne Nash, 'Writing a Building: Hugo's *Notre-Dame de Paris*', *French Forum*, 8 (1983), 122–33.

33. See Hogle, *The Undergrounds*, pp. 5–7.

34. See Raymond Williams, *Marxism and Literature* (Oxford: Oxford University Press, 1977), pp. 128–35.

35. See especially Edward Said's *Orientalism* (New York: Pantheon, 1978).

36. See the essays collected under 'Criticism' in Bram Stoker, *Dracula*, Norton Critical Edition, ed. Nina Auerbach and David J. Skal (New York: Norton, 1997), pp. 411–82.

37. See H. G. Wells, *The Island of Dr. Moreau* (1896), Signet Classics (New York: Penguin Books, 1988), including the 'Afterword' by Brian W. Aldiss, pp. 207–16.

38. See Elaine Showalter, *Sexual Anarchy: Gender and Culture at the* Fin de Siècle (New York: Viking, 1990).

39. This 1904 statement can be found in a collection of Leroux's nonfiction writings, *Du Capitaine Dreyfus / Au pole sud*, ed. Francis Lacassin (Paris: Union Générale Editions, 1985), p. 7.

40. See Brombert, *Victor Hugo and the Visionary Novel*, pp. 52–85; Kessler, 'Babel and Bastille'; Nash, 'Writing a Building'; and especially Spires, 'Victor Hugo's *Notre Dame de Paris*', pp. 42–4.

41. See Peter Stallybrass and Allon White's *The Politics and Poetics of Transgression* (London: Methuen, 1986), esp. pp. 23 and 177.

42. I refer to the columns credited to the pen-name 'Etincelle', in *Le Matin*, 12 February 1896, 1.

43. See Slavoj Žižek, 'Grimaces of the Real, or When the Phallus Appears', *October*, 58 (1991), 44–68.

References

Ames, Dianne S., 'Strawberry Hill: Architecture of the "As If",' *Studies in 18th-Century Culture*, 8, ed. Rosanne Runte (Madison, WI: University of Wisconsin Press, 1999).

Auerbach, Nina and Skal, David J. Bram, eds, *Dracula*, Norton Critical Edition (New York: Norton, 1997).

Baldensperger, Fernand, '*Le Moine* de Lewis dans la littérature française', *Journal of Comparative Literature*, 1 (1903), 201–19.

Baudrillard, Jean, *Symbolic Exchange and Death,* trans. Iain Hamilton Grant (London: Sage, 1993).

Botting, Fred (ed.), *Frankenstein: Contemporary Critical Essays*, New Casebooks (London: Macmillan, 1995).

Brombert, Victor, *Victor Hugo and the Visionary Novel* (Cambridge, MA: Harvard University Press, 1984).

Clément, Catherine, *Opera, or The Undoing of Women*, trans. Betsy Wing (Minneapolis: University of Minnesota Press, 1988).

Coleridge, Samuel Taylor, 'Review of *The Monk*', *Critical Review*, 19 (1797), 194–200, in *Gothic Documents: A Sourcebook,* ed. E. J. Clery and Robert Miles (Manchester: Manchester University Press, 2000).

Gamer, Michael, *Romanticism and the Gothic: Genre, Reception, and Canon Formation* (Cambridge: Cambridge University Press, 2000).

Hogle, Jerrold E., *The Undergrounds of* The Phantom of the Opera: *Sublimation and the Gothic in Leroux's Novel and its Progeny* (New York: Palgrave, 2002).

______ 'The Gothic-Romantic Relationship: Underground Histories in "The Eve of St. Agnes"', *European Romantic Review*, 14 (2003), 205–23.

______ 'The Ghost of the Counterfeit in the Genesis of the Gothic', *Gothick Origins and Innovations*, eds Allan Lloyd Smith and Victor Sage (Amsterdam: Rodopi, 1994).

Hugo, Victor, *Notre Dame de Paris* (Paris: Les Editions de Paris, 1956).

Kessler, Joan C., 'Babel and Bastille: Architecture as Metaphor in Hugo's *Notre-Dame de Paris*', *French Forum*, 11 (1986), 187.

Kristeva, Julia, *Powers of Horror: An Essay on Abjection*, trans. Leon S. Roudiez (New York: Columbia University Press, 1982).

Leroux, Gaston, *Le Fantôme de l'Opéra* (Paris: Livre de Poche, 1959).

______ Report on the opening day of Dreyfus' retrial in the Paris daily *Le Matin,* 2 July 1899, 1–2.

______ *Du Capitaine Dreyfus / Au Pole Sud,* ed. Francis Lacassin (Paris: Union Générale Editions, 1985).

Lewis, Matthew, *The Monk*, ed. Howard Anderson and Emma McEvoy (Oxford: Oxford University Press, 1995).

Lewis, W. S. et al., eds, *The Yale Edition of Horace Walpole's Correspondence* (New Haven, CT: Yale University Press, 1937–83).

Nash, Suzanne, 'Writing a Building: Hugo's *Notre-Dame de Paris*', *French Forum,* 8 (1983), 122–33.

Said, Edward, *Orientalism* (New York: Pantheon, 1978).

Scott, Sir Walter, *Quentin Durward*, intro. C. L. Bennett (Clinton, MA: Airmont, 1967).

Seebacher, Jacques 'Introduction', *Notre Dame de Paris*, Bibliothèque de la Pleïade Edition (Paris: Gallimard, 1975).

Schick, Constance Gosselin, 'Death Comes to the Cathedral: Romantic Allegorizations of the Symbol', *French Forum*, 22 (1997), 161.

Shakespeare, William, *Hamlet*, Arden Shakespeare edition, ed. Harold Jenkins (London: Methuen, 1982).

Showalter, Elaine, *Sexual Anarchy: Gender and Culture at the* Fin de Siècle (New York: Viking, 1990).

Spires, Jeffrey, 'Victor Hugo's *Notre Dame de Paris:* The Politics and Poetics of Transition', *Dalhousie French Studies*, 61 (2002) 41.

Stallybrass, Peter and Allon White, *The Politics and Poetics of Transgression* (London: Methuen, 1986).
Walpole, Horace, *The Castle of Otranto: A Gothic Story*, ed. W. S. Lewis and E. J. Clery (Oxford: Oxford University Press, 1996).
Wells, H. G., *The Island of Dr. Moreau* (1896; New York: Penguin Books, 1988).
Williams, Anne, *Art of Darkness: A Poetics of the Gothic* (Chicago: University of Chicago Press, 1995).
Williams, Raymond, *Marxism and Literature* (Oxford: Oxford University Press, 1977).
Wordsworth, William, 'Preface to *Lyrical Ballads, with Pastoral and Other Poems* (1802)', in *The Poems*, ed. John O. Hayden (London: Penguin Books, 1990).
Zarifopol-Johnston, Ilinca M., '*Notre Dame de Paris:* The Cathedral in the Book', *Nineteenth-Century French Studies*, 13 (1985), 22–35.
Žižek, Slavoj, 'Grimaces of the Real, or When the Phallus Appears', *October*, 58 (1991), 44–68.

3
Edgar Allan Poe in Paris: The *Flâneur*, the *Détournement* and the Gothic Spaces of the Nineteenth-Century City

Linnie Blake

In November 1846[1] Edgar Allan Poe published an excoriating review of a new translation of Eugène Sue's 1842 novel *Mysteries of Paris*.[2] Sue's was a tale of politicized sensation, portraying in lurid detail the opulent depravity of the Parisian upper classes and the miserable, squalid lives of the city's poor. To Poe's horror, the novel's sentimental treatment of the nineteenth century's core conceptual opposition of 'nature' and 'the city', its titillating *exposé* of urban prostitution and its populist political concern with proletarian hardship had already caught the public imagination in the United States where its first cities were coming into being. At the time of the review, moreover, the novel had launched a host of imitations which had transposed the Frenchman's anti-elitist concerns, his populist rhetoric and sexually lurid set-pieces onto the emergent American cityscape. All of modern urban life was here, it seemed, and Poe was horrified at the prospect: dismissing the populists' concern with 'the amelioration of society' as mere 'cant', being nothing less than a 'trick' designed to impart 'a tone of dignity or utilitarianism'[3] to artistically worthless because politically dangerous fictions.

This chapter illustrates how Poe's aesthetic and ideological repudiation of America's French-inspired 'miseries and mysteries genre' informed and influenced both the form and the ideological project of his seminal Gothic tale 'The Man of the Crowd',[4] that ultra-reactionary voyage into the dark heart of the emergent capitalist metropolis. In the course of my argument I will return to the work of subsequent theorists of 'the city', writers such as Charles Baudelaire and Walter Benjamin, who deployed Poe's tale in their own explorations of the relationships between capitalism and the city. For although 'The Man of the Crowd' is purportedly set in London, I believe it is impossible to undertake a contemporary reading of it without an awareness of the ways in which

the 'material insecurity, social instability, historical fluidity and imaginative liquidity'[5] engendered by the birth of the capitalist metropolis
(and embodied in the very structure and subject matter of Poe's tale)
was subsequently theorized by a range of European thinkers who were
not only linked to the city of Paris but who frequently took Poe's tale
as an exemplum of the invidious effects of urban-industrial capitalism
on pre-modern conceptions and representations of the social self. From
Baudelaire to Benjamin to Debord and the Situationist International,
that which is called Paris has thus generated a series of questions of
vital importance to any study of the self under capitalism, and hence
to any study of art objects (such as 'The Man of the Crowd') which
take 'the city' as an overarching metaphor for the modern condition.
In Poe's tale, as in the intrinsically political theorizations of the streets
of Paris promulgated by writers as diverse as Baudelaire, Benjamin and
Debord, we may therefore witness a range of debates concerning the
nature and culture of modernity, the process by which the city and the
urban self are both liberated and enchained by capitalism and hence
the relation of the city, the individual and the monetary economy
to the means available to the artist and activist first to experience
and then to represent the city's whirling multiplicities in time, space,
language, thought and deed.

As is the case with many of Poe's tales, 'The Man of the Crowd' opens
with a little pseudo-philosophical chicanery, designed to confuse the
reader and set an authoritative and learned tone. Here is an observation from La Bruyère (in French of course) on the alienating proximity
of modern urban life: *'ce grand malheure, de ne pouvoir être seul'* (MC,
p. 389) (the great tragedy is that it is impossible to be alone). Here also
is an alleged quotation from an unnamed German book on the modern
text's self-reflexive resistance to interpretation: *'es lasst sich nicht lesen'* – it
will not, Poe says, permit itself to be read (MC, p. 389). From the very
outset, in other words, it is apparent that 'The Man of the Crowd' is a
tale of two characters – three if you count the city itself. First is the
highly unstable narrator who glimpses, at nightfall from a fogged café
window, the figure of an elderly man walking along the crowded street.
This is the second human protagonist, a man whose fiendish counten-
ance inspires the physiognomically informed narrator to speculate on
the highly contradictory qualities the man must possess, qualities:

of vast mental power, of caution, of penuriousness, of avarice, of
coolness, of malice, of blood-thirstiness, of triumph, of merriment,
of excessive terror, of intense – of extreme despair. (MC, p. 389)

So intriguing is the old man, in fact, that the narrator follows him out into the street. And so begins the chase, as our narratological double-act leads us through the crowded and carnal city from square to bazaar to theatre, to slum to gin-palace and back again. This continues all night, for the whole of the next day and into the following evening; from dusk to dawn to dusk again. Finally, exhausted by the multiple sensations and emotions that he has experienced in his wanderings, but unable to draw any firm conclusions from them, the narrator stops before the old man and looks him in the face. There is no hint of recognition or even acknowledgement of the narrator's existence, however, leading him to proclaim: *'es lasst sich nicht lesen'* (MC, p. 389). The old man will not permit himself to be read. The tale then comes to a well-timed, if entirely inconclusive, end.

Rejecting the urban scene that threatened not only to destroy the spirit-infused world of nature that Poe consistently fetishized but also to overturn the divinely sanctioned social hegemonies upon which Poe's very cosmology rested, 'The Man of the Crowd' is, I would argue, a doomed attempt to impose rationality on the chaotic spectacle of the emergent metropolis. In fact, prior to even glimpsing the enigmatic old man, the narrator attempts to define by occupation, and then to stratify by class, the inhabitants of the city that surrounds him. Accordingly, his gaze moves from 'merchants, [to] attorneys, [to] tradesmen, [to] stock-jobbers', and thence to 'the common-placers of society', (MC, p. 389), coming to rest finally on the criminal underworld 'with which', he unequivocally asserts, 'all great cities are infested' (MC, p. 390). The class politics of his gaze closely echoes the author's own, Poe asserting in 'The Colloquy of Monos and Una' and 'Some Words with a Mummy' that the 'evil' of 'omni-prevalent Democracy',[6] that 'most odious and insupportable despotism that ever was heard of upon the face of the Earth'[7] was a cosmological abomination, contravening the 'laws of *gradation* so visibly pervading all things in Earth and Heaven' and hence flying 'in the face ... of God'.[8] The modern urban world's fall from divinely sanctioned social hegemonies had thus, for Poe, robbed people of their humanity, transforming them into 'insolent, rapacious, filthy' urban animals with 'the gall of a bullock ... the heart of a hyena and the brains of a peacock'.[9] Democracy, their chosen means of social administration, was nothing more that a 'very admirable form of government – for dogs'.[10] And it is with such attitudes firmly in place than Poe's narrator embarks on his voyage into the contemporary urban world.

Poe's perspective on the city can be seen, therefore, to embody both the sociologist Georg Simmel's observation that the God of Christianity is the God of the individual and Max Weber's belief that such a faith equated spiritual salvation with material success. In such a world, as Weber observed, the individual may be king, but he was also victim of an unprecedented sense of isolation, cut off from others, from his world, from all that lay beyond himself. On the one hand, then, Poe's tale is pervaded by that sense of Weberian loneliness that is the destiny of the self under capitalism. On the other, it deploys a range of narrative strategies that attempt to rationalize and hence contain and control the terrifying irrationality of the city, that bombards the individual with myriad inchoate sensations and in so doing places any sense of integrated subjectivity and unique individuality under threat. In an era of mass communications coming into being, moreover, Poe recognized that the individual reader and the individual city-dweller had 'more facts ... to think about' than ever before.[11] Accordingly, the generic structure of 'the tale' was a means of marshalling the inchoate experience of modern life into a cogent fictional form that for all its arabesque meandering would enable the reader to rationalize his or her experiences of the city in the world in their consumption of the city on the page. Stressing that 'the tale' was a 'mere construction', Poe claimed that each of his was written with 'the precision and rigid consequence of a mathematical problem', its brevity preventing 'worldly interests intervening' which may 'modify, annul, or counteract, in a greater or lesser degree, the impressions intended' by the author.[12] Thus attempting to construct the tale with all the pragmatic rationality of a grid-plan city, a programme of utter narrative control emerges here – control of the diverse and potentially explosive elements that constitute the city in the world and predetermination of the reader's response to and relationship with those elements, both on the page and in the world.

Inescapable here are the parallels between Poe's narratological project and the rebuilding of the Paris of the Second Empire under which Baudelaire's *flâneur* emerged. For throughout the 1850s and 1860s the Prefect of Paris, Georges Eugène Haussmann, acting under the orders of Napoleon III, refashioned the medieval city in an insistent attempt to destroy those very aspects of the city that the narrator of 'The Man of the Crowd' finds so very distressing. Under Haussmann, for example, those neighbourhoods where the potentially revolutionary working-class communities had lived for centuries were erased, facilitating massive expansion of trade and industry on behalf of the ascendant middle classes whilst enabling the military to move swiftly against any popular uprisings by the city's dispossessed. Thus, despite

Walter Benjamin's claims, neither Poe, nor the old man nor the narrator of this tale can be read convincingly as Baudelairean *flâneurs* wandering through the city and rejoicing in the transitory newness of its elements.[13] For, like Haussmann, author and narrator alike operate as agents of control, working to contain the potentially explosive diversity of the city, struggling to wrestle its contingent ephemerality into a controllable form. Far from being the *flâneur*, then, author and narrator are nothing less than the agents and instruments of the substantive rationality of the capitalist economy; the cyclical narrative moving from dusk to dawn to dusk, echoing capitalism's transparently ideological naturalization of the economic status quo, a means of control that is echoed in the narrator's obsessive mapping of the old man's anti-rational wanderings from the thoroughfare to the square to the bazaar, to the theatre to the slum and back again. But as we shall see, it is a means of control that is ultimately doomed to fail – as the old man, and all that he represents, breaks free of the narrator's attempts to order the chaotic spaces of urban life in a spectacular display of Gothic excess that denies all order, repudiates all containment and promises not only a radical challenge to nineteenth-century capitalism but foreshadows new ways of being in and of the city.

Clearly, what I am arguing here runs counter to a great deal of literary critical thought which, since the nineteenth century, has insisted upon associating characters within the tale with Baudelairean formulations and celebrations of the modern world from which it came. Key to such a critique is Baudelaire's 1860 essay 'The Painter of Modern Life', where the poet famously defined the 'modern' as 'the ephemeral, the fugitive, the contingent, the half of art whose other half is the eternal and the immutable', and had pointed to the peculiarly 'modern' artistic consciousness of the poet's friend Constantine Guys, being one who gazed upon the landscape of the great city, delighting in its variety and noting with an 'eagle eye' the minute-by-minute mutations of urban fashion.[14] Certainly, one may be able to spot certain superficial parallels between Poe's old man and Baudelaire's modern artist – both locating themselves within the midst of the modern crowd 'in the heart of the multitude, amid the ebb and flow of motion, the midst of the fugitive and the infinite'.[15] The old man may even 'enter into the crowd as though it were an immense reservoir of electrical energy', another characteristic of the modern artist.[16] But unlike that artist, he is neither internally energized by his contact with other massed subjectivities nor prompted to externalize his creative genius by the 'luminous explosion in space' that is the city.[17] Clearly, the old man is neither the painter of modern life nor, as Walter Benjamin claimed, the *flâneur* – that *blasé* dandy flourishing in the transitional period between aristocracy and democracy whose sole occupation was the pursuit of happiness and whose struggle against the *ennui* of respectable bourgeois life Baudelaire described as 'the last spark of heroism amid decadence'.[18] In such a formulation, Baudelaire seems to argue that absorption in the crowd is nothing more than a prelude to a reaffirmation of individual identity. And this is most certainly not the case with Poe's old man, for all his 'absolute idiosyncrasy of expression' (MC, p. 392).

But if Poe's narrator attempts to retrench those strategies by which the urban self is controlled and conditioned in his very narrative practice, then what is so fascinating for me, and what has been insufficiently explored by critics hitherto, is the way in which the old man as *genius* or *spiritus loci* of the city actively breaks free of the structural devices by which the tale attempts to order the chaotic spectacle of everyday urban life. In both the aporias that characterize this tale, what Benjamin would term the dialectic at a standstill, and in its Gothic excesses we can see an entirely unintended and entirely radical repudiation of the instrumental rationality of capitalism as it manifests itself in the metropolis and in the realist literary text.

In reworking my own thoughts on Baudelaire, Benjamin and Poe, in rejecting both Poe's narrator and his eponymous protagonist as *flâneurs* and yet remarking on the textual instability of the tale's representation of urban life, I was drawn back to the work of the Situationist International on the *dérive*. Emerging in the late 1950s out of the ruins of the less well-known Lettriste movement (and other European *avant-garde* groups) the Situationists were artists (often in a broadly Surrealist tradition), activists (being key movers in the events of May '68) and theorists. In essence, they worked towards a form of cultural criticism that sought to engage actively with the lived realities of everyday life in the form of political projects that:

> Focus[ed] on the recognition and legitimation of differences which they advocate in the hope of transforming the reactive and generally oppressive structures of power that continue to animate late-capitalism even at its most postmodern extremes.[19]

One of the most celebrated aspects of this attempted transformation is, of course, the *dérive*: an experimental (and essentially group-based) mode of behaviour that is intrinsically linked to the conditions of urban society, being a transient passage through the varied ambiences of the city. It entails a playful yet constructive awareness that the city's many regions, spaces and areas have precise affects on the mood and behaviour of the individual, what the Situationists would term the city's psycho-geographical affects. It was this awareness that for Debord and others distinguished the *dérive* from both the journey and the stroll and the *dériveur or dériveuse* from both the traveller and the *flâneur*. In fact, it could be argued (as Patrick ffrench has done) that for the Situationists, the *dérive* was a conceptual integration of the *flâneur*'s urban meanderings into a politicized critique of urban space, and the effect of that space on the behaviour, emotion and mood of the individual who moves within it. The *dérive* thus functions as an implicit critique of the *flâneur*'s project. To *dérive* is to undertake a *détournement* of the *flâneur*, to use the Situationist term. And the fact that one can be a female *dériveuse* and not a female *flâneuse* adds, of course, a further dimension to that *détournement*.

With the psychogeographical consciousness of the Situationist *détournement* in mind, then, I began to read Poe's text anew. I was drawn in particular to the second issue of the *Situationist International*, published in December 1958, in which Guy Debord outlined how in order to undertake a *dérive*, one should let go of one's usual motives for moving about the city (to work, to shop, to visit, for example) and wander, in the full awareness that cities:

> have a psychogeographical relief, with constant currents, fixed points and vortices which strongly discourage entry into or exit from certain zones.[20]

Such an action, Debord proposed, enables the psychogeographer to trace what he called the precise laws and specific effects of the geographical environment (underscored by spectacular capitalism) on the emotions and behaviour of individuals. In so tracing the control of everyday life by existing influences, Debord believed, one could begin to subvert that control. Unlike the Surrealists, who had taken similar journeys but for Debord had failed to engage with the psychogeography of the city due to their misrecognition of the nature of the human unconscious, the *dériveurs* actively explored the city as a spatial field domesticated by capitalism and affective of human emotion. If the *flâneur* had conceived of the city as a series of binarisms – self and other, individual and crowd, home and street, leisure and labour – then the Situationists sought ludically to deconstruct said categories in the collective intoxication of psychogeographical experience and for the purposes of social revolution.

As I thought more about this, Poe's old man, like Debord's psychogeographical drifters, came to illustrate not only the absurdity of all attempts to map, to chart and to fix in writing the drifting contingency of the city, but also to offer a decidedly Gothic means whereby one may destroy the maps of old and reach for new modes of being in the city, new strategies of artistic representation predicated on new forms of politically grounded action. For as Debord put it: 'Written descriptions can be no more than passwords to the great game'[21] of city life. And that endlessly motile life, as Baudelaire observed, is always changing; as is Poe's old man.

For all the narrator's rationalizing and hegemonizing project, the old man, like urban culture itself, cannot be contained in words. He is continually with the crowd and yet continually alone, continually projecting himself onto the pavement whilst simultaneously retreating into the shelter of his own inscrutable subjectivity. He is self *and* other, self *as* other, and this makes him very dangerous indeed. The narrator may observe that 'a wild history is written in that bosom' (MC, p. 392), but like the Situationist city, the old man resists reduction to a monologic text and struggles against predetermined social hierarchies in his insistent refusal to be (pseudo-) individualized and hence to be read as 'subject'.

All this becomes clear when the narrator observes that through a rent in the old man's jacket, he 'caught a glimpse both of a diamond and of a dagger' (MC, p. 393) – the diamond and the dagger, of course, signifying many things. The former is a precious stone which refracts light and indicates hidden wealth, being thus indicative of the subtext of secrecy which characterizes this quest for urban meaning; an impression that is heightened by the similarly concealed dagger. The diamond is also a geometric shape, reminiscent of Poe's 'scientific' plotting of the tale or Haussmann's refashioning of the streets of Paris. Most importantly, though, it was a contemporary name of a size of printers' type, of which Poe the editor would have been well aware. The 'dagger', too, was a printing term, also known as an obelisk, itself a deathly motif, used to indicate a cross-reference, usually a footnote. As his own feet take him across the page of the city, the man of the crowd is thus revealed as a peculiarly playful eruption of the irrational urban world into the purportedly rational realm of the text, one who challenges all authorial attempts to lend order, stability and structure to the tale and, in so doing, undercuts the ideological certitudes of Poe's representations of modern urban life; our own certainty (perhaps) of what living in the city might be said to comprise, constitute or 'mean'.

Like urban life itself, the old man is unpredictable. Like the narrator he is never a 'character' in the realist sense but a psychogeographical *dérivateur* upon whose experience of urban space the city's 'dark secret' is finally imprinted: the sense that beneath the conditioning and habit of the everyday world there is another 'reality', another mode of experiencing the city and hence existing as 'self'. As the Situationists would put it in one of their better known rallying cries: 'Beneath the paving stones is the beach!' Thus crossing and re-crossing his own trajectory 'by a great variety of devious ways' (MC, p. 395) as if to erase once more the certitude of this narrative's will to order and control; led not by reason by the varied psychogeographical ambiences of the city's many districts, the old man thus leads us from the commercial centre to the broken hinterland that is the slum, enabling us to see, to smell, to feel this literary city *in toto*, and in so doing to witness its newly apparent relations of affluence and poverty, commerce and criminality, excess and deprivation as the travesties of equality, liberty and brotherhood that they are. This is a journey to the 'verge' of the city – the margins of the urban text scrawled with the graffiti of destitution, daubed with 'the worst impress of the most deplorable poverty and the most desperate crime' (MC, p. 395). Here strategies of control lie as broken paving stones beneath the old man's feet as the text's will to hegemony is sucked into his psychogeographic *dérive*. All is left as a whirling vortex of impressions: of injustice and poverty, crime and suffering, disease and addiction, resistance and rage, and dark impenetrable mystery.

The old man, like the 'secret' of the city, is said to be thankfully illegible. He is urban man as polyvocal and self-subverting textual practice most akin, the narrator remarks, to the *Hortulus Animae*, that metaphysical grotesquery that juxtaposed religious writings and pornographic pictures. As the tale reaches its close, then, the motif of circling fictionality returns as the man is aligned to criminality through 'type', becoming for the already modern, already alienated narrator a metaphysical abomination: one who wanders relentlessly through the ages, refusing in each era to be consigned to a class, a subject-position, a region and hence a fixed hegemonized identity. In this, of course, he becomes an archetypal practitioner of the *détournement* – the 'man of the crowd' as printing block who challenges the pseudo-individuation of spectacular capitalism by running off endless copies of himself on the streets of the city, each of which refuses to be rationalized, to be interpreted or to be ordered. Not for him the broad boulevards of Paris that forced the city's inhabitants into calm acceptance of their lot. Not for him the conventions of realist fiction, with its overweening narrative drive to order the fundamental irrationality of the human psyche.

Thus the old man, as urban culture itself, cannot be contained in words and becomes the locus of previous narrative tensions: between the mass and the individual, the sociable and the introspective, the material reality of the city and the self-reflexive narrative evasion of the street. He is continually with the crowd and yet continually alone, continually projecting himself onto the street whilst retreating into the shelter of his own inviolable subjectivity. In so being, he becomes a highly Gothic though avowedly Situationist 'genius' (MC, p. 395) for an age of modernity. For like the Roman spirit of that name, the old man will watch over the city from its inception to its spiralling end, will move through its endlessly shifting ambiences until the city itself ceases to exist.

In the final analysis, then, the old man emerges as the *animus* of the *détournement*. In his anarchic and unlocatable subjectivity we can perceive the Situationist belief that 'urbanism doesn't exist, it is only an "ideology"' in Marx's sense of the word'.[22] Here we can see how 'the development of the urban milieu is the capitalist domestication of space',[23] how 'traffic circulation is the organization of universal isolation'[24] how, in Debord's words:

> the main achievement of contemporary city planning is to have made people blind to the possibility of unitary urbanism, namely a living critique, fuelled by all the tensions of everyday life, of this manipulation of cities and their environment.[25]

In him, we become aware that 'it is necessary to undertake a revolution of everyday life which appropriates the conditioning of everyone by everyone and *détourns* it for the purpose of de-alienation'.[26] Far from being the Baudelairean painter of modern life or even the *flâneur*, the old man of the crowd is in fact a fine textual illustration of what it would be to *dérive* through the city of Poe, to throw off the God-given hierarchies of the author's metaphysical conservativism and the narrator's narrative practice and hence to repudiate the strategies of material and psychological control which underpin the spectacular city under capitalism. A highly Gothic project indeed.

Notes

1. Edgar Allan Poe, 'Marginalia', *Southern Literary Messenger* (July 1849), *Edgar Allan Poe, Essays and Reviews*, ed. G. R. Thompson (New York: Library of America, 1984), pp. 1404–8.
2. Eugène Sue, *Mysteries of Paris* (1842), trans. C. H. Town (New York: Harper and Brothers, 1846).

3. Poe, 'Marginalia', p. 1404.

4. Edgar Allan Poe, 'The Man of the Crowd', *Burton's Gentleman's Magazine* (7 December 1840), in *Edgar Allan Poe, Poetry and Tales*, ed. Patrick F. Quinn (New York: Library of America, 1984), pp. 388–96. Page numbers in the text hereafter, prefaced by MC.

5. Cornell West, *The American Evasion of Philosophy: A Genealogy of Pragmatism* (London: Macmillan, 1989), p. 26.

6. Edgar Allan Poe, 'The Colloquy of Monus and Una', *Graham's Lady's and Gentleman's Magazine* (August 1841), in *Edgar Allan Poe*, ed. Quinn, pp. 449–57, p. 451.

7. Edgar Allan Poe, 'Some Words with a Mummy', *American Review* (April 1945), in *Edgar Allan Poe*, ed. Quinn, pp. 805–21, p. 820.

8. Poe, 'The Colloquy of Monus and Una', p. 451.

9. Poe, 'Some Words With a Mummy', p. 820.

10. Edgar Allan Poe, 'Mellonta Tauta', *Godey's Lady's Book* (February 1849), in *Edgar Allan Poe*, ed. Quinn, pp. 874–84, p. 880.

11. Edgar Allan Poe, 'Marginal Notes', *Godey's Lady's Book* (September 1845), in *Edgar Allan Poe*, ed. Thompson, p. 1377.

12. Edgar Allan Poe, 'Review of *Twice Told Tales* by Nathaniel Hawthorne', *Godey's Lady's Book* (November 1847), in *Edgar Allan Poe*, ed. Thompson, p. 586.

13. Benjamin, in fact, was so keen to deploy the concept of the *flâneur* in his exploration of this tale (or, more accurately, to deploy this tale in service of his thesis on the *flâneur*) that in the 1935 sketch for the Arcades Project: 'Paris – the Capital of the Nineteenth Century', he applied the term to Poe; in 'On Some Motifs in Baudelaire' (1939) he applied it to the narrator and in 'The Paris of the Second Empire in Baudelaire' (1938) to the old man. As I argue here, however, it is apposite to none of them.

14. Charles Baudelaire, 'The Painter of Modern Life', in *The Painter of Modern Life and Other Essays*, trans. and ed. Jonathan Mayne (London: Phaidon Press, 1964), pp. 1–40, p. 14.

15. Baudelaire, 'The Painter of Modern Life', p. 12.

16. Baudelaire, 'The Painter of Modern Life', p. 18.

17. Baudelaire, 'The Painter of Modern Life', p. 18.

18. Baudelaire, 'The Painter of Modern Life', p. 14.

19. David Banash, 'Activist Desire, Cultural Criticism, and the Situationist International. http://www.reconstruction. ws/021/Activist.htm, pp. 1–14, p. 1. Accessed 30 August 2006.

20. Guy Debord, 'Theory of the *Dérive*', *Internationale Situationist # 2*, *Situationist International Anthology*, ed. and trans. Ken Knabb (Berkeley, CA: Bureau of Public Secrets, 1981), pp. 50–4, p. 50.

21. Debord, 'Theory of the *Dérive*', p. 53.

22. Guy Debord, 'Elementary Program of the Bureau of Unitary Urbanism', in Knabb, *Internationale Situationist # 2* pp. 65–76, p. 65.

23. Debord, 'Elementary Program of the Bureau of Unitary Urbanism', p. 65.

24. Debord, 'Elementary Program of the Bureau of Unitary Urbanism', p. 65.

25. Debord, 'Elementary Program of the Bureau of Unitary Urbanism', p. 66.

26. Debord, 'Elementary Program of the Bureau of Unitary Urbanism', p. 65.

References

Banash, David, 'Activist Desire, Cultural Criticism, and the Situationist International'. http://www.reconstruction.ws/021/Activist.htm, pp. 1–14. Accessed 30 August 2006.

Baudelaire, Charles, 'The Painter of Modern Life', in *The Painter of Modern Life and Other Essays,* ed. and trans. J. Mayne (London: Phaidon Press, 1964), pp. 1–40.

Debord, Guy, 'Theory of the *Dérive*', *Internationale Situationist # 2*, in *Situationist International Anthology,* ed. and trans. Ken Knabb (Berkeley, CA: Bureau of Public Secrets, 1981), pp. 50–4.

—— 'Elementary Program of the Bureau of Unitary Urbanism', *Internationale Situationist # 5*, in *Situationist International Anthology,* ed. and trans. by Ken Knabb (Berkeley, CA: Bureau of Public Secrets, 1981), pp. 65–76.

ffrench, Patrick, '*Dérive*: the *détournement* of the *flâneur*', in *The Hacienda Must be Built: On the Legacy of the Situationist Revolt,* eds Andrew Hussey and Gavin Bowd (Manchester: AURA, 1996), pp. 26–41.

Poe, Edgar Allan, 'The Colloquy of Monos and Una', *Graham's Lady's and Gentleman's Magazine* (August 1841), in *Edgar Allan Poe, Poetry and Tales,* ed. Patrick F. Quinn (New York: Library of America, 1984), pp. 449–57.

—— 'Fifty Suggestions', *Graham's Magazine* (May–June 1849), in *Edgar Allan Poe, Essays and Reviews,* ed. G. R. Thompson (New York: Library of America, 1984), pp. 1297–1308.

—— 'Marginal Notes', *Godey's Lady's Book* (September 1845), in *Edgar Allan Poe, Essays and Reviews,* ed. G. R. Thompson (New York: Library of America, 1984), p. 1377.

—— 'Marginalia', *Graham's Magazine* (November 1846), in *Edgar Allan Poe, Essays and Reviews,* ed. G. R. Thompson (New York: Library of America, 1984), pp. 1404–8.

—— 'Marginalia', *Southern Literary Messenger* (July 1849), in *Edgar Allan Poe, Essays and Reviews,* ed. G. R. Thompson (New York: Library of America, 1984), p. 1465.

—— 'The Man of the Crowd', *Burton's Gentleman's Magazine* (7 December 1840), in *Edgar Allan Poe, Poetry and Tales*, ed. Patrick F. Quinn (New York: Library of America, 1984), pp. 388–96.

—— 'Some Words with a Mummy', *American Review* (April 1845), in *Edgar Allan Poe, Poetry and Tales*, ed. by Patrick F. Quinn (New York: Library of America, 1984), pp. 805–21.

Simmel, Georg, *The Philosophy of Money,* trans. T. Bottomore and D. Frisby (London: Routledge, 1978).

Sue, Eugène, *Mysteries of Paris* (1842), trans. by C. H. Town (New York: Harper and Brothers, 1846).

West, Cornel, *The American Evasion of Philosophy: A Genealogy of Pragmatism* (London: Macmillan, 1989).

4
Blood in Paris: Transformations of Revolutionary Gothic in Henry James and Elizabeth Bowen

Raphaël Ingelbien

The work of Henry James and Elizabeth Bowen bears a complex relation to the Gothic. Both writers occasionally use ghostly and supernatural elements in their fiction, but their Gothic quality can be as elusive as their own positions in different literary traditions. The Anglo-American James and the Anglo-Irish Bowen often challenge the categories of literary history, and their works also raise generic questions about the Gothic, confirming that the term should often be put in the plural. The Gothic in James can be analysed in terms of his debt to Nathaniel Hawthorne and other explorers of the dark side of New England's Puritan consciousness, but James could also deliberately engage with the English tradition of female Gothic in tales like *The Turn of the Screw*, or use the Gothic to deal with *fin-de-siècle* decadent motifs.[1] Bowen has often been productively discussed as a modern practitioner of Anglo-Irish Gothic, dissecting the anxieties of the Protestant Ascendancy in its terminal phase,[2] but many of her tales are conscious variations on the English ghost story, while yet other short stories develop a peculiar kind of Gothic to capture the atmosphere of wartime London.[3] Her debt to Henry James further complicates the picture: it shows in her style, her focus on psychology and manners, her interest in the international theme and, last but not least, in the influence of James's own protean Gothic.

The affinities between James and Bowen can be illuminated by looking specifically at the Gothic treatment of Paris in two of their novels. Paris is a location of special significance in English Gothic: it was the centre of the Revolution that provided the haunting subtext of the Gothic rage at the turn of the eighteenth and nineteenth centuries. It is also the setting for both James's *The Ambassadors* (1903) and Bowen's *The House in Paris* (1935).[4] Although neither of the novels can be classified as thoroughly Gothic, the Parisian setting confers Gothic associations on the psychological dramas which are the authors' main concern. That Gothic dimension is precisely what is brought out by Bowen's variation on a Jamesian theme in *The House in Paris*: the Jamesian echoes in Bowen's text, in other words, serve as a confirmation of the Gothic strain that runs through *The Ambassadors*. They further testify to the lasting fascination of Paris's Gothic dimension for Anglo-Saxon writers, regardless of those authors' affiliations with more narrowly defined Gothic traditions. But if James and Bowen perpetuate a long-standing association in English literature between the Gothic and (French) revolutionary violence, they also transform that link. Recent critical work on the Gothic has qualified the 'received piece of wisdom' that 'the Gothic explosion was collateral damage from the French Revolution':[5] the connection between the Terror and the Gothic novels of Ann Radcliffe, Matthew Lewis and their contemporaries was more often than not a product of the political anxieties of English readers and reviewers, instead of a deliberate authorial strategy. Late eighteenth-century Gothic novelists, after all, only exploited a genre that Horace Walpole had pioneered in less suspicious times. James and Bowen, by contrast, will clearly suggest such a connection in their texts, thus turning the latent or imputed revolutionary subtext of earlier Gothic novels into a metaphor that endows their own intrigues with a broader ideological significance. The comparison that follows will also be concerned with the conditions and the possible purposes of that transformation.

James's *donnée* in *The Ambassadors* is not obviously Gothic: his preface makes much of his New England protagonist Strether and of the temptations afforded by Paris to his 'blest imagination' (*The A*, xxxvii). The preface further tends to play down the importance of Paris: the 'surrounding scene' of Strether's drama is 'itself a minor matter, a mere symbol for more things than had been dreamt of in the philosophy of Woollett' (*The A*, p. xxxviii). Strether was sent from Woollett to the French capital in order to rescue his young fellow American Chad Newsome, but he hesitates when it turns out that his mission consists in saving Chad from the mysterious 'virtuous attachment' between the young American and his exquisite mentor in Parisian society, Madame de Vionnet. That attachment turns out to conceal a Gothic, or more specifically a vampiric, subtext. Chad grows physically older under Madame de Vionnet's influence ('The change in [Chad] was perhaps more than anything else, for the eye, a matter of the marked streaks of grey, extraordinary at his age, in his thick black hair' [*The A*, p. 99]), while his older mentor remains mysteriously young. Strether's involvement in their relationship, meanwhile, means that he 'will be used to the last drop of [his] blood' (*The A*, p. 305). After the virtuous attachment is exposed for the intimate affair it really is, a violent reversal occurs in this vampiric relationship. Madame de Vionnet suddenly grows much older in Strether's eyes, while Chad regains some of his youth:

> It was actually moreover … as if he could think of nothing but the passion, mature, abysmal, pitiful, she represented, and the possibilities she betrayed. She was older for him tonight, visibly less exempt from the touch of time. (*The A*, p. 409)

> Strether saw in a moment what it was – it was that [Chad] was younger again than Madame de Vionnet. (*The A*, p. 426)

The mutual, alternate draining of life forces that goes on between Chad and Madame de Vionnet is a perfect illustration of what various critics have called the 'vampire theme' in James's work.[6] Since James developed vampiric imagery in other works like *The Sacred Fount* and *The Golden Bowl*, there may seem to be little or no connection between his vampiric subtext and the Parisian setting of *The Ambassadors* (which, according to the preface, is largely incidental). Yet James's Paris also invites both readers and characters to draw links between vampiric bloodshed and other Gothic associations that inhere in parts of the setting. Indeed, hints of revolutionary Gothic were always likely to lurk behind the façades of Strether's Paris, as James's protagonist himself becomes all too aware at the end of his adventure.

Madame de Vionnet lives in a house that has survived Hausmann's transformation of the old Paris, whose narrow streets were thought to facilitate popular uprisings and mob violence. Strether's first visit to Madame de Vionnet's apartments is framed by a description that dwells on the relative antiquity of the 'old house' where she lives:

> the house, to his restless sense, was in the high homely style of an elder day, and the ancient Paris that he was always looking for – sometimes intensely felt, sometimes more acutely missed – was in the immemorial polish of the wide waxed staircase and in the fine *boiseries*, the medallions, mouldings, mirrors, great clear spaces, of the greyish-white salon into which he had been shown. He seemed at the very outset to see her, in the midst of possessions not vulgarly

numerous, but hereditary cherished, charming ... he found himself making out, as a background of the occupant, some glory, some prosperity of the First Empire ... The place itself went further back – that he guessed, and how old Paris continued in a manner to echo there ... (*The A*, pp. 171–2)

If Strether first enjoys those surroundings as a Baudelairean *flâneur* might, delighting in an antiquarian love of 'le vieux Paris', he later senses the ominous historical connotations that the place conceals. It is during his last visit to Madame de Vionnet's apartment that the Parisian location of Strether's adventure reveals its full, violently Gothic nature:

From beyond this, and as from a great distance – beyond the court, beyond the *corps de logis* forming the front – came, as if excited and exciting, the vague voice of Paris. Strether had all along been subject to sudden gusts of fancy in connexion with such matters as these – odd starts of the historic sense, suppositions and divinations with no warrant but their intensity. Thus and so, on the eve of the great recorded dates, the days and nights of revolution, the sounds had come in, the omens, the beginnings broken out. They were the smell of revolution, the smell of the public temper – or perhaps simply the smell of blood.

It was at present queer beyond words, 'subtle', he would have risked saying, that such suggestions should keep crossing the scene; but it was doubtless the effect of the thunder in the air, which had hung about all day without release. His hostess was dressed as for thunderous times, and it fell in with the kind of imagination we have just attributed to him that she should be in simplest coolest white, of a character so old-fashioned, if he were not mistaken, that Madame Roland must on the scaffold have worn something like it. (*The A*, p. 401)

The Gothic violence of the old, revolutionary Paris is now figuratively revisited on Madame de Vionnet, as she faces the prospect of losing Chad and confesses to Strether that she is 'afraid for [her] life' (*The A*, p. 409). The reversal of her vampiric relation with Chad is indeed a revolution of sorts, and we will return to the significance of Chad's new role at the end of *The Ambassadors*. But the fate of Madame de Vionnet already illustrates the process by which James's exploration of the vampire theme here becomes tinged with revolutionary Gothic. From their incarnations in Romantic writing to Bram Stoker's Dracula, vampires in the nineteenth century had often assumed aristocratic manners.[7] Madame de Vionnet is no exception. When the nature of her relation with Chad becomes clear, the spell of the vampire and of the old order she stands for is broken, and she now awaits her execution while the odour of blood hangs in the air of the capital. The vampire theme in *The Ambassadors* does not contribute to a climate of psychological terror in a traditional Gothic vein; instead, James links his vampiric subtext to the Terror of the French Revolution itself.

Sparse and confused though they may seem at first, the Gothic hints that punctuate *The Ambassadors* nevertheless constitute a coherent subtext. Like the anamorphic death's head that ominously slashes the foreground of Holbein's painting 'The Ambassadors',[8] the Gothic subtext of James's novel can only be discerned through a change of perspective: it requires an interpretive position that takes a step away from a straightforward, realist focus on the glittering (but deceptive) surface of Strether's Paris. Coming to James from her Anglo-Irish perspective, with an almost inbuilt sensitivity to Gothic themes, Elizabeth Bowen was ideally placed to read *The Ambassadors* in precisely that way. She herself proceeded to mix vampirism and revolutionary Gothic in her 1935 novel *The House in Paris*, which is also one of her most Jamesian works. Much can be made of its likeness to *What Maisie Knew*, since it partly adopts the point of view of children immersed in a shady adult world of sexual intrigue.[9] But the Gothic subtext of *The Ambassadors* is another Jamesian intertext that can shed light on *The House in Paris*, and will help us grasp the ideological function of Gothic echoes in both Bowen's and James's novels.

Bowen's novel opens as her first Jamesian centre of consciousness, the appropriately named Henrietta, arrives in Paris. She is a young English girl who is in transit between England and Mentone, and who will spend one day in Paris in the care of Madame Fisher, an acquaintance of her grandmother. She is introduced to a young boy, Leopold, who is also staying there in transit, and to the eerie atmosphere of the *pension Fisher*, whose dark past is revealed to the reader (but *not* to the children) through a series of flashbacks. The secret that haunts the *pension Fisher* is the suicide of Leopold's father, Max. An anxious, lonely Jew working for an investment bank, Max had formed an ambiguous attachment to the older Mme Fisher. Their relationship strongly resembles that between Chad and Madame de Vionnet, and is only more virtuous in that it may not have been sexual. As Max himself explained to Karen, the woman who became Leopold's mother:

I was given a letter to her when I first came to Paris ... Till this year, I have not tried to separate what she made me from what I am. From the first, she acted on me like acid on a plate ... I had never had the excitement of intimacy. Our brains became like senses, touching and drawing back. (*House*, pp. 138–9)

Even though Jamesian adultery is never openly suggested in Bowen's novel, the intensity of the relationship means that it is every bit as vampiric: its dénouement will actually make that vampiric dimension even more explicit than was the case in *The Ambassadors*. Max eventually became engaged to Mme Fisher's demure daughter Naomi – a development that also recalls *The Ambassadors*, where Strether suspects that Chad might end up marrying Madame de Vionnet's daughter Jeanne. But Max's engagement ended when he embarked on a relationship with a former guest of the *pension Fisher*, a bored, adventurous, upper-class English girl named Karen, and made her pregnant. Unable to see a way out of his entanglements, Max slashed his wrists during a dramatic last meeting with Mme Fisher, and fled the house leaving a trail of blood behind him.

Henrietta arrives in Paris as night has already fallen on the French capital, and her first view of the Paris streets sets the tone for the rest of her brief visit:

They swerved right, round the dark railings of a statuey leafless garden – 'Look, Henrietta, the Luxembourg!' – then engaged in a complex of deep streets, fissures in the crazy gloomy height. Windows with strong grilles looked ready for an immediate attack (Henrietta had heard how much blood had been shed in Paris); doors had grim iron patterns across their glass; dust-grey shutters were almost bolted fast ... (*House*, pp. 21–2)

Since she remains unaware of Max's fate, Henrietta's reference to the 'blood that had been shed' is drawn from her knowledge of history, and yet it immediately prepares her – and the reader – for the atmosphere of the house where Max's blood was shed. Henrietta will not see much of Paris in daytime, since she will stay the whole day inside the *pension Fisher*. She will never quite leave the 'complex of deep streets' that eventually lead her to the gloom of 'fissures'/Fishers[10] in a corner of the capital. She is immediately confronted by the darker side of Paris, whose Gothic danger she is made to sense much earlier (and much more vividly) than the endlessly procrastinating Strether in

The Ambassadors. Bowen's is a much shorter and more claustrophobic novel than James's; it zooms in on and brings out the Gothic potential of its Jamesian intertext. As a framing consciousness, Strether may seem quite an unlikely model for Henrietta, although it may be significant that James's naïve New England protagonist is recurrently described as a child left to 'toddle' in Paris (*The A*, pp. 231 and 239). If it takes Strether quite some time to see through Paris's façade to its Gothic heart, Henrietta is possessed with an acute sensitivity to the traces of historical violence that still pervade the French capital. Once she arrives in the *pension Fisher*, she strongly resembles those Gothic heroines lost in gloomy foreign castles, as well as Alice exploring a hostile Wonderland:

> She felt the house was acting, nothing seemed to be natural; objects did not wait to be seen but came crowding in on her, each with what amounted to its aggressive cry. Bumped all over the senses by these impressions, Henrietta thought: If *this* is being abroad ... (*House*, p. 24)

Mme Fisher herself does her best to add to the atmosphere of Gothic menace:

> Mme Fisher was not in herself a pretty old lady. Waxy skin strained over her temples, jaws and cheek-bones; grey hair fell in wisps round an unwomanly forehead; her nostrils were wide and looked in the dusk skullish; her mouth was graven round with ironic lines. (*House*, p. 47)

Mme Fisher's *pension*, it should be noted, is untypical of early twentieth-century Paris. Like the house where Strether visits Madame de Vionnet, it is one of the remnants of an older era, a hereditary possession that dates back to much older and, by implication, more dangerous times. Its antiquity thus deepens the Gothic gloom and menace of the now deserted boarding house where the bed-ridden Mme Fisher rules like a latter-day Miss Havisham. As Mme Fisher herself proudly announces to her guest:

> This house? It does very well. It is uncommon chiefly in being a house at all. It was always in my family, and was left to me by my grandfather, who was a notary; it is such a house as you find only now in the provinces. When I am dead, it will be sold at once. One cannot afford to live in a house, in Paris. But I prefer to die here. (*House*, p. 50)

The *pension Fisher* is also a natural setting for the Anglo-Irish aristocrat Bowen, who often preferred to set her narratives in atmospheric old houses, and who jeered at the cheap, practical impersonality of what she ironically called 'Attractive Modern Homes'.[11] Houses in the narrow sense of the word are exceptional in Paris, where taller buildings dominate most streets, and yet Bowen chooses to set almost all the Parisian scenes of her novel in the *pension Fisher*. The confined, suffocating space of the house has been analysed in terms of its symbolical role in the psychological development of the characters (mostly Henrietta and Leopold),[12] but the Parisian location of the *pension Fisher* opens up other possibilities, namely the exploitation of a revolutionary Gothic vein. As the only 'house in Paris' that Bowen explored in any great detail, the *pension* is (or rather was) an all too appropriate setting for bloodshed – not the historical bloodshed which Henrietta nevertheless senses on her arrival in Paris (p. 22, see above), but the bloody climax of vampiric relationships which memories of revolutionary violence can metaphorically recall or adumbrate. Like James, Bowen often described human relations as vampiric,[13] and nowhere more so than in *The House in Paris*. At various stages, the novel drops hints about the quasi-vampiric nature of the emotional entanglements of Mme Fisher, her protégé Max, her daughter Naomi and their former guest Karen. Max comments on his fiancée Naomi:

> I said something, and she started and pricked her finger. I saw from the pitying way she sucked the bead of blood from her finger how much she pitied me, and saw at the same time that hers was the only pity I did not resent. I wished the blood were on my own finger. (*House*, p. 162)

After Max's suicide and the birth of their son Leopold, Karen turns back to her fiancé Ray, with whom she contracts a melancholy, vampiric marriage:

> Karen had ... drained [Ray] into herself, so that nothing in him resounding or fluid was left, no nerves and no blood, so that when he had had to come here, as he saw he had had to come here, he came as brittle and as dry as dried cuttlefish. (*House*, p. 212)

It is no wonder that the most vampiric relation of all, that between Max and Mme Fisher, leads up to a scene of literal bloodshed in the *pension Fisher*, in a way that echoes and underscores the vampiric relationship that existed between Chad and Madame de Vionnet. This is how Naomi reports what she saw of the scene:

> I saw then that all her life her power had never properly used itself, and that now it had used itself she was like the dead, like someone killed in a victory. Her lips were stiff and she could not speak at first; then she said: 'Go after him,' and when I stood there she said: 'You fool, he is dying.' I thought she meant in the spirit. But she moved herself on the sofa and, with a frown like she has when someone spills wine or ink, made me look at the mantelpiece. The room is not light, and till then I had only looked at her. But then I saw his blood splashed on the marble, on the parquet where he had stood and in a trail to the door, smeared where I had trodden without knowing. I saw his penknife with the long blade open, fallen between where he had stood and where my mother sat. She said: 'He cut his wrist across, through the artery, to hurt me.' (*House*, p. 183)

The ailing Madame Fisher whom Henrietta gets to meet lives out the fate of an abandoned Madame de Vionnet: confined to a state of death-in-life in her bedroom, she too is a defeated vampire. But Bowen's Gothic imagery is not just vampiric. Just before Max slashed his wrists, Mme Fisher already assumed the Gothic shape of a disembodied head, in a description that seems lifted from those Gothic texts that drew explicitly on revolutionary horrors:[14]

> You know our hall is dark and she wears black; I only saw her face, which seemed to be hanging there. When he opened the door she smiled and came in calmly, with the quiet manner she has when there is no more to know. (*House*, p. 181)

In the same way that the prospect of an abandoned Madame de Vionnet had called up images of revolutionary terror for Strether, the scene where Mme Fisher's vampiric spell over Max was dramatically broken also contains hints of revolutionary Gothic.

The old Paris that James and Bowen explore remains replete with the blood that was shed within its walls; as such, it is the ideal setting for the crises which constitute the climaxes of their psychological novels. The connection between the historical violence of the Terror and their Gothic scenes, however, is even less obvious than it was in earlier Gothic novels. The link between the French Revolution and the rise of

Gothic fiction is a highly complex one; indeed, English Gothic novelists were once at pains to dismiss, deny or conceal any link between the horrors of their texts and what took place in Paris under the Terror, for fear of being branded members of the infamous 'terrorist school' of fiction.[15] James and Bowen, on the other hand, deliberately invite readers to establish a link between the psychological vampirism of their characters and the bloodshed of the Revolution. Of course, neither of them needed to fear a charge that had lost all relevance in the early twentieth century, and neither was noted for revolutionary sympathies of any kind. Their fascination with revolutionary bloodshed might even look superficial: the Gothic dimension of their Paris, in such a reading, would be seen as a way of infusing much-needed blood into the otherwise anaemic, desiccated world of their super-subtle psychological games. Bowen's and James's fictions, like the characters who inhabit them, would then resemble vampires tapping into the blood that they lack, lifeless novels battening on the historical energies latent in their setting.

There may be something in this variation on a charge often levelled at both writers,[16] but in both novels the Gothic dimension of Paris also affords more than a sensational, but purely metaphorical thrill. To the extent that the psychological intrigues of James and Bowen are also allegories haunted by the nightmares of history, the Gothic quality of the Parisian setting actually turns out to be more functional. In James's and Bowen's conservative imaginations, memories of the Terror became paradigmatic of subsequent threats (real or imagined) to the forms of order that were central to their fiction. Stephen Spender argued that James's later novels were 'parables of Western civilization', presciently haunted by the horrors of the First World War.[17] As well as being boldly anachronistic, Spender's argument also tried to enlist the conservative James in an essentially Marxist analysis of Europe's decay. Yet Spender may not have been alone in offering a political reading of James in 1935. The Gothic subtext of *The Ambassadors* invites one to discern a historical parable in James's Parisian novel, and that allegorical quality was precisely one of the aspects that Spender's contemporary Bowen exploited in her turn when she drew on James's example.

For Lambert Strether walking the streets of Paris at the turn of the century, and remembering an earlier visit he made to the French capital decades earlier, the *Commune* of 1870 is no distant memory. Paris is the place where revolutions still occur, and what takes place before his eyes at the end of *The Ambassadors* can also be read as the allegory of a revolution that haunted James in those years: the triumph of an aggressive entrepreneurialism, embraced by a renegade Chad Newsome in the last chapters of the novel, over the civilized Old World manners of Madame de Vionnet, who had previously allowed herself to be sustained by the young man's energies. The vision of Madame de Vionnet walking up the scaffold may be purely metaphorical but is nonetheless apposite: as a society hostess who played a central role in Girondin circles, and thus belonged to a moderate upper bourgeoisie with aristocratic connections, Madame Roland was finally executed when the Girondins were swept away by the *Commune*. Revolution, in Madame de Vionnet's case, comes from America with a vengeance. Chad is an improbable *Communard*, but to James's conservative imagination, the capitalism of Woollett represented a more likely and more powerful threat to the civilization embodied in Madame de Vionnet than any popular revolution.

Bowen's variation on revolutionary Gothic in *The House in Paris* is perhaps less easy to grasp, but its complexity does not make it any less functional. Karen, the English girl whose irruption into the lives of Max and the Fishers brings about the fatal crisis, is one of the bored children of upper-middle-class English (or Anglo-Irish) society whom Bowen often chose as her protagonists. In their jaded world-view, historical violence can often look titillating. *The Last September* (1929) provides the best examples: Lois and her cousin Gerald are both fascinated by the violence that rages outside the confines of the big house they inhabit. Laurence declares that he 'should like to be here when this house burns' and 'fire a gun out of a window', while Lois 'hoped that instead of fading to dust in summers of empty sunshine, the carpet would burn with the house in a scarlet night': 'she did not want adventures, but she would like just once to be nearly killed'.[18] The morbid thrill afforded by historical violence is also perceptible in *The House in Paris*. Although she cannot help being profoundly loyal to her class, Karen similarly dreams of revolutions – much to the unease of her aunt Violet, who married an Anglo-Irish landowner whose big house was burned during the Troubles (*House*, 75):

> 'Surely so much has happened,' said Aunt Violet, 'And mightn't a revolution be rather unfair?'
> 'I shall always work against it,' said Karen grandly. 'But I should like it to happen in spite of me.' (*House*, p. 86)

Like other texts that Bowen wrote in those troubled years, *The House in Paris*, despite its claustrophobic atmosphere, remains haunted by the revolutions that took place in Russia and Ireland at the end of the

Great War, and perhaps also by hints of the new war that is looming.[19] *The House in Paris*, it is worth remembering, was published in the same year as the study in which Spender read James's novels as parables of a Western civilization on the edge of the abyss. Politically speaking, the Marxist Spender and the conservative Bowen were poles apart, but both could alternately stress James's powers as a psychologist and (mis)read his *oeuvre* as an allegory of contemporary history.

The charged political context of the 1930s also provides more specific keys for an allegorical reading of the crisis at the heart of Bowen's novel. Although her characters might not be invested with the social aura or representativeness of Chad or Madame de Vionnet, *The House in Paris* is the only novel in which Bowen specifically foregrounds Jewishness. The victimization of Max Ebhardt and the uncertain status of his posthumous child Leopold take on ominous connotations in a novel which, as Jean Radford has pointed out, was published in a period when anti-Semitic legislation was being passed in Germany and when France itself was in the grip of xenophobic agitation. Bowen's treatment of anti-Semitic prejudice further shows up the limitations of the genteel English liberalism of Karen's family, whose response to Max simply rehearses worn-out prejudices.[20] Karen's own attitude may be at odds with those values, but it is also a perfect illustration of the fascination with destruction that Bowen often diagnosed in the upper-middle-class sets who people her fiction. Revolution may be a fantasy to Karen, whom history has often spared. Her family emerged unscathed from the Great War (*House*, p. 126); she had 'grown up in a world of grace and intelligence, in which the Boer War, the War and other fatigues and disasters had been so many opportunities to behave well' (*House*, 70). History, for Karen, is chiefly the safe con-versational medium through which her forbidden courtship with Max is conducted:

> They could remember nothing that they could speak of, and memory is to love what the saucer is to the cup. But for lovers or friends with no past in common the historic past unrolls like a park, like a ridgy landscape full of buildings and people ... His view of the past was political, hers dramatic, but now they were free of themselves they were of one mind ... they surrounded themselves with wars, treaties, persecutions, strategic marriages, campaigns, reforms, successions and violent deaths. History is unpainful, memory does not cloud it; you join the emphatic lives of the long dead. May we give the future something to talk about. (*House*, pp. 143–4)

The authorial 'we' in the last sentence of this passage betrays Bowen's irony towards her still safe, bored protagonist. Although she is not yet aware of it, Karen's role in the Gothic tragedy that will unfold in the house in Paris means that she will not completely escape the violence that fascinates her imagination. Karen too will 'give the future something to talk about' – or, if the secret will not out, something to be uncannily haunted by on visits to Paris. Henrietta's awareness of 'the blood that had been shed in Paris' (*House*, p. 22) retrospectively turns out to be as ambivalent as James's description of a Paris readying itself for Madame de Vionnet's execution. In *Seven Winters*, Bowen wrote of her own early experience of Dublin: 'Perhaps a child smells history without knowing it.'[21] Henrietta, as a young, quasi-Gothic heroine abroad, is a perfect receptacle in which intimations of private tragedy can mix with her author's sense of wider historical forces at work. Henrietta's unconscious confusion between a sordid *fait divers* and revolutionary violence still reveals a strain in Bowen's novel, but the discrepancy that persists between private and political bloodshed is also a comment on Karen's alienation from the history she fantasizes about. Bowen's choice of setting, and the Jamesian echoes that pervade her novel, should at any rate alert us to the manifold uses of Gothic in *The House in Paris*. For Bowen as for James, the Gothic dimension of Paris, and its association with revolutionary terror(s), offered a way of gesturing towards a tradition in which terror often exceeds the bounds of the plot.

Notes

1. See Martha Banta, *Henry James and the Occult* (Bloomington: Indiana University Press, 1972); and T. J. Lustig, *Henry James and the Ghostly* (Cambridge: Cambridge University Press, 1994).
2. See W. J. McCormack, *Dissolute Characters: Irish Literary History through Balzac, Sheridan Le Fanu, Yeats and Bowen* (Manchester: Manchester University Press, 1993); R. F. Foster, 'The Irishness of Elizabeth Bowen', in *Paddy and Mr Punch* (London: Penguin Books, 1995), pp. 102–22; Margot Gayle Backus, *The Gothic Family Romance: Heterosexuality, Child Sacrifice, and the Anglo-Irish Colonial Order* (Durham, NC: Duke University Press, 1999); Raphaël Ingelbien, 'Gothic Genealogies: *Dracula*, *Bowen's Court* and Anglo-Irish Psychology', *ELH* 70.4 (Winter 2003), pp. 1089–105; and the first chapter of Neil Corcoran's *Elizabeth Bowen: The Enforced Return* (Oxford: Oxford University Press, 2004).
3. Elizabeth Bowen, *Collected Stories* (London: Vintage, 1999). For book-length treatments of Bowen's fiction in its various contexts, see Hermione Lee,

Elizabeth Bowen (London: Vintage, 1999); and Maud Ellmann, *Elizabeth Bowen: The Shadow across the Page* (Edinburgh: Edinburgh University Press, 2003); and Corcoran, *The Enforced Return*.

4. Subsequent references to the novels are given parenthetically in the text; they refer to the Oxford World's Classics edition of *The Ambassadors* (Oxford: Oxford University Press, 1985) and the Vintage edition of *The House in Paris* (London: Vintage, 1998).

5. See Robert Miles, 'The 1790s: the Effulgence of Gothic', in *The Cambridge Companion to Gothic Fiction*, ed. Jerrold E. Hogle (Cambridge: Cambridge University Press, 2002), p. 42.

6. See, for instance, Banta, *Henry James and the Occult*, pp. 81–104; and Leon Edel, *Henry James: A Life* (Hammersmith: Flamingo, 1996), pp. 16ff.

7. For an overview of the evolution of the vampire in nineteenth-century literature, see Christopher Frayling, *Vampyres. Lord Byron to Count Dracula* (London: Faber and Faber, 1991), pp. 44–60.

8. On James's use of Holbein's painting, see among others Adeline Tintner's *Henry James and the Lust of the Eyes* (Baton Rouge: Louisiana State University Press, 1993); and Hazel Hutchison's 'James's Spectacles: Distorted Vision in *The Ambassadors*', *Henry James Review* 26.1 (2005) 39–51.

9. See Lee, *Elizabeth Bowen*, p. 96.

10. The pun is noted by Maud Ellmann, *Elizabeth Bowen: the Shadow across the Page*, p. 112.

11. *Collected Stories*, pp. 521–8.

12. See R. B. Kershner, 'Bowen's Oneiric House in Paris', *Texas Studies in Literature and Language*, 28.4 (Winter 1986) 407–23.

13. John Halperin, 'Elizabeth Bowen and Henry James', *Henry James Review*, 7.1 (Fall 1985) 46.

14. See, for instance, Terry Hale, 'French and German Gothic: the Beginnings', in *The Cambridge Companion to Gothic Fiction*, p. 78.

15. See Miles, 'The 1790s: the Effulgence of Gothic', pp. 43–4.

16. The most familiar critique of James remains Maxwell Geismar's *Henry James and his Cult* (London: Chatto and Windus, 1964). For similar critiques of Bowen, see Lee, *Elizabeth Bowen*, pp. 223–5.

17. Stephen Spender, *The Destructive Element* (London: Cape, 1935), pp. 67 and 21.

18. *The Last September* (London: Vintage, 1998), pp. 44, 107, 98 and 99.

19. Bowen's next novel *The Death of the Heart* (1938) is another psychological study of failed relationships, but the deteriorating European context obtrudes symbolically in the jigsaw puzzle that the protagonist Portia receives from her friend Major Brutt: as she puts the pieces together, the puzzle 'soon promised to represent a magnificent air display ... The planes massing against an ultramarine sky began each to take a symbolic form, and as she assembled the spectators she came to look for a threat or promise in each upturned face.' See *The Death of the Heart* (London: Penguin Books, 1962), p. 182.

20. Jean Radford, 'Late Modernism and the Politics of History', in *Women Writers of the 1930s: Gender, Politics and History*, ed. Maroula Joannou (Edinburgh: Edinburgh University Press, 1999), p. 42.

21. *Bowen's Court and Seven Winters* (London: Vintage, 1999), p. 492.

References

Backus, Margot Gayle, *The Gothic Family Romance: Heterosexuality, Child Sacrifice, and the Anglo-Irish Colonial Order* (Durham, NC: Duke University Press, 1999).

Banta, Martha, *Henry James and the Occult* (Bloomington: Indiana University Press, 1972).

Bowen, Elizabeth, *Collected Stories* (London: Vintage, 1999).

—— *The House in Paris* (1935; London: Vintage, 1998).

Corcoran, Neil, *Elizabeth Bowen: The Enforced Return* (Oxford: Oxford University Press, 2004).

Ellmann, Maud, *Elizabeth Bowen: The Shadow across the Page* (Edinburgh: Edinburgh University Press, 2003).

Frayling, Christopher, *Vampyres. Lord Byron to Count Dracula* (London: Faber and Faber, 1991).

Hale, Terry, 'French and German Gothic: the Beginnings', in *The Cambridge Companion to Gothic Fiction*, ed. Jerrold E. Hogle (Cambridge: Cambridge University Press, 2002).

Ingelbien, Raphaël, 'Gothic Genealogies: *Dracula, Bowen's Court* and Anglo-Irish Psychology', *ELH* 70.4 (Winter 2003) 1089–105.

James, Henry, *The Ambassadors* (1903; Oxford: Oxford University Press, 1985).

Lustig T. J., *Henry James and the Ghostly* (Cambridge: Cambridge University Press, 1994).

Miles, Robert, 'The 1790s: the Effulgence of Gothic', in *The Cambridge Companion to Gothic Fiction*, ed. Jerrold E. Hogle (Cambridge: Cambridge University Press, 2002).

Part II
Channel Crossings

5
'How do we ape thee, France!' The Cult of Rousseau in Women's Gothic Writing in the 1790s

Angela Wright

The Gothic's novel's liberal nourishment from a range of foreign, domestic, literary, aesthetic and scientific sources has been acknowledged by both its authors and critics since its first apologetic beginnings in the 1760s. Horace Walpole inaugurated this confessional tradition with his Preface to the second edition of *The Castle of Otranto* (1765). There, in a bid to excuse the literary hoax established in the first Preface, where he had posed as the putative translator of the text, William Marshall, Gent., Walpole adopted a more considered literary approach to his novel. Citing 'diffidence of his own abilities' as the reason for his initial disguise, he proceeded to defend *Otranto* as 'an attempt to blend the two kinds of romance, the ancient and the modern'. He justified his new hybrid creation by acknowledging his indebtedness to Shakespeare:

> The result of all I have said is to shelter my own daring under the cannon of the brightest genius this country, at least, has produced. I might have pleaded, that having created a new species of romance, I was at liberty to lay down what rules I thought fit for the conduct of it: but I should be more proud of having imitated, however faintly, weakly, and at a distance, so masterly a pattern, than to enjoy the entire merit of invention, unless I could have marked my work with genius as well as originality.[1]

Walpole used Shakespeare as a literary defence for his own bold, novelistic innovation. He celebrated his humble imitation of the bard, arguing that he gained more pleasure in imitating Shakespeare than in literary innovation. However, Walpole's disarming humility masked a more serious nationalistic gesture. By taking 'shelter' under England's greatest literary 'genius', he distanced himself from the continental origins of his romance, and participated in defending English literature against the advancing front of French ideas.

Following Walpole's literary example, Ann Radcliffe also took considerable care to highlight the impressive array of literary sources from which she drew inspiration in the poetic and dramatic epigraphs that she used for *The Romance of the Forest* (1791), *The Mysteries of Udolpho* (1794) and *The Italian* (1797). The liberal amounts of Shakespeare, Milton, Gray and Thomson that Radcliffe quoted alongside her own poetry were, arguably, an attempt to secure her a position in a national literary heritage that was specifically English. As a technique this was largely successful. Nathan Drake famously called Radcliffe 'the Shakspeare [*sic*], of Romance writers', thereby associating her recognizably English literary inspiration with her undisputed position as England's most successful author of Romance.[2] The phraseology of Drake's approval suggested that a careful emulation of England's bard was the pinnacle of achievement in the creation of Gothic Romance. He thus seemingly concurred with Walpole's overwriting of the specifically continental origins of the Romance genre, instead reinventing it as an English literary tradition presided over by Ann Radcliffe. Her careful invocation of a specifically English literary tradition thus achieved two important aims: it both secured her reputation as a recognizably English author and exonerated her from the charges of literary sedition that many of her 'Gothic' contemporaries attracted.

The reverent homage that Radcliffe paid to Shakespeare, Milton, Thomson and Gray, however, conveniently glossed over a rather more suspect continental inheritance. This literary legacy was invariably overlooked during Radcliffe's lifetime, but it was a legacy that she shared with other late eighteenth-century Gothic novelists, such as Sophia Lee, Charlotte Smith and Regina Maria Roche. All of these writers drew literary and political inspiration from some of the major French literary figures of the eighteenth century. Lee and Smith adapted (and translated in the latter's case) the works of the Abbé Prévost, with Lee's 1785 Gothic novel *The Recess* deriving considerable inspiration from the French author's *Cleveland*, and Smith's creative translation of *Manon Lescaut* (1785) attempting to render Prévost's ideas more palatable to a British audience. Whilst Roche did not translate eighteenth-century French fiction, her Gothic novels *The Children of the Abbey* and *Clermont* are considerably indebted to the literary and philosophical ideas of Jean-Jacques Rousseau. In both novels, she begins by portraying rural idylls where her heroines are educated by a parent in seclusion from the corrupting influence of the city. Like the initial relationship sketched between Emily St Aubert and her father in Radcliffe's *The Mysteries of Udolpho*, Roche's portrayals of the ideal education was influenced both by Rousseau's *Julie, ou la Nouvelle Héloïse* (1760) and by his later educational work, *Émile* (1762).

Of the aforementioned authors, Charlotte Smith paid the highest price for her continental inspiration in terms of literary reputation. Thomas James Mathias's satirical poem *The Pursuits of Literature*, published in four dialogues between 1794 and 1797, was one of many anti-Jacobin reactions in Britain to the perceived encroachment of ideas from the continent. He was quick to attack female novelists' espousal of 'seditious' ideas from France. In particular, he pinpointed the work of 'Mrs. Charlotte Smith, Mrs. Inchbald, Mrs. Mary Robinson, Mrs. &c. Mrs. &c.', condescendingly complaining, 'Though all of them are very ingenious ladies, yet they are too frequently *whining* or *frisking* in novels, till our girls' heads turn wild with impossible adventures, and now and then are tainted with democracy'.[3] Mathias specifically connected the use of literary sensibility – 'whining or frisking' – with the import of dangerously democratic ideals from France. Linking the invasion of French literary ideals with the threat of political revolution, he pinpointed the source of Britain's literary contamination when he complained that 'Translation to a pest is grown'. Of the three novelists targeted, Smith and Inchbald's translation ventures were well known to the critics. Their multiple talents – both were successful novelists, dramatists and poets as well as translators – created anxiety around the morals and politics that they portrayed in their own creations. Inevitably, Smith and Inchbald's facility with foreign languages, and success in translation, came to be synonymous with the dubious 'democratic' ideals that their works portrayed. Smith's translation of Prévost's *Manon Lescaut* had particularly drawn the venom of the critic George Steevens, who, accusing Smith of both plagiarism and 'licentiousness', forced her publisher Thomas Cadell to withdraw the sale of her translation.[4]

In a gesture that was emblematic of the broader critical consensus, Mathias took especial care, however, to exempt Ann Radcliffe from his list of literary subversives.[5] Her exemption was due both to her invocation of English literary forbears in her epigraphs, and the fact that, unlike many of her contemporaries, she did not supplement her income by translation. Radcliffe's unique exoneration from the charges of literary sedition, however, is misleading. Not only did she exchange ideas with both Charlotte Smith and Sophia Lee through regular correspondence, but she also looked across the Channel for much of her literary and political inspiration. Alongside many of her literary contemporaries, Radcliffe drew qualified inspiration from the work of Rousseau, the citizen of Geneva whose philosophical and literary ideas became strongly associated with the French Revolution in the British psyche. The following section traces the potent combination of literary and political sedition that were laid at Rousseau's door by the conservative British periodical press.

Rousseau the Gothic villain

The reception of Rousseau's writing in 1790s Britain was polarized to such an extent that it undoubtedly scared those writers into silence who were more ambivalent about his influence. As a consequence, is often difficult to discern what writers who did not refer to him directly thought of him. Those who nailed their flag to the mast were largely negative about his influence. In 1791, spearheading the campaign against Rousseau, Edmund Burke described the general morality of Rousseau's work as 'an unfashioned, indelicate, sour, gloomy, ferocious medley of pedantry and lewdness'.[6] Burke's attack was applauded in a letter by Horace Walpole whose *Otranto*, published four years after Rousseau's most famous sentimental novel, *Julie, ou la Nouvelle Héloïse*, caricatures and punishes the sentimentality of the heroine Matilda with death.[7] Walpole's one-dimensional quasi-parodic portrayal of Matilda was undoubtedly a riposte to what he viewed as Rousseau's over-indulgent sentimentalization of his heroine Julie.

As the 1790s progressed, however, so did Rousseau's reputation in Britain decline. Initial objections to his use of sensibility became more overtly hostile, and the political paranoia that characterized the late 1790s in Britain led to his vilification. Over the course of that decade, he was transformed in the conservative press from a relatively benign pedant to a democratically endowed Gothic villain who sought to ensnare an unsuspecting British female readership. In the fourth dialogue of *The Pursuits of Literature*, Mathias bombastically referred to 'chief Equality's vain priest, Rousseau' as 'By persecution train'd and popish zeal'.[8] Conveniently neglecting Rousseau's more moderate Swiss origins, Mathias associated him with a peculiarly hostile, Gothic background. He thus contributed to Rousseau's emergent association with bigotry, terror and Catholicism which the anti-Jacobin faction persisted in linking to France.

Continuing this attack for the periodical the *Anti-Jacobin* in 1798, George Canning ascribed sensibility's invasion of English literature entirely to Rousseau. In his poem 'New Morality', Canning addressed sensibility as the:

> Sweet child of sickly Fancy! – her of yore
> From her loved France ROUSSEAU to exile bore;
> And, while midst lakes and mountains wild he ran,
> Full of himself, and shunn'd the haunts of man,
> Taught her o'er each lone vale and Alpine steep
> To lisp the story of his wrongs, and weep;
> Taught her to cherish still in either eye,
> Of tender tears a plentiful supply,
> And pour them in the brooks that babbled by ...[9]

Canning's portrayal of Sensibility being made to 'lisp the story of [Rousseau's] wrongs' in 'each lone vale and Alpine steep' indirectly referred to how Rousseau's model of sensibility was invoked in particular by Gothic novelists in Britain. The mountainous settings that many such as Radcliffe and Roche chose for parts of their Gothic tales were particularly influenced by Rousseau's alpine settings.

Canning portrayed Rousseau as a self-indulgent Gothic villain who had kidnapped the 'sweet child' Sensibility to England, and exiled 'her' from her native and beloved France. The poem implied the prostitution and corruption of Sensibility by Rousseau. Under Rousseau's direction, Sensibility 'lisp[ed] the story of his wrongs', and cultivated lachrymose narratives to engage the British public's sympathy. Canning's poem suggested that, in itself, 'Sensibility' was a 'sweet, innocent child', but its parent, 'sickly Fancy', had already been infected by French morals.

The point cleverly conveyed by Canning's verse is that Sensibility is not in itself dangerous, but that its rightful location is France. In Canning's vision, Sensibility, an untutored and unprotected child, is unleashed irresponsibly upon Britain. The connections to the worries surrounding the Gothic novel are clear. Sensibility's vulnerable status becomes synonymous with both the young, unprotected heroines depicted in so many Gothic narratives and with the young, unsupervised female readership of Gothic fiction in Britain. On both a literal and figurative level, Rousseau's covert import of Sensibility into Britain became a potential source of continental corruption for Britain's young female readers.

Canning's reactionary remoulding of Rousseau as a Gothic villain was also supported by Hannah More. In her corrective work *Strictures on the Modern System of Female Education* (1799), More commented that 'there never was a net of such exquisite art and inextricable workmanship, spread to entangle innocence and ensnare experience as the writings of Rousseau'.[10] Her observations were equally suggestive of Rousseau's premeditated Gothic villainy. For More, Rousseau's writing set out to capture innocent and experienced readers alike. No British reader was safe from his web.

Despite such deep-rooted suspicion of Rousseau's work, however, Charles Palissot de Montenoy recognized that Rousseau's widespread influence and popularity in England was due to the high regard in which he was held by women.[11] Even one of Rousseau's most outspoken female critics, Mary Wollstonecraft, shamefacedly admitted in a letter to her husband, William Godwin, that she was 'half in love' with Rousseau.[12] The simultaneous repulsion and attraction that he evoked was inevitably reflected in the Gothic novel, and most particularly in the sustained engagement with Rousseau's ideas undertaken by Ann Radcliffe. However, as I shall argue in the next section, the reason that Radcliffe escaped the cultural contempt that her peers suffered was due to her qualified engagement with Rousseau's ideas. These qualifications were crucial to the contemporary reputation that she enjoyed as a promoter of a British literary tradition rather than a French one.

Radcliffe's appraisal of Rousseau

The swift translation of all of Rousseau's works into English bears witness to the urgent demand that his fame commanded. In 1760, *Julie, ou la Nouvelle Héloïse* was translated as quickly as possible into English. The booksellers Becket and De Hondt advertised the translation for a full three months before the first volumes of William Kenrick's translation appeared.[13] Kenrick also translated *Émile* two years later with similar expediency for the same booksellers.[14]

We have no evidence that Radcliffe read Rousseau's writing in the original French, and it is more than likely that she would have read Kenrick's authoritative translations. The influence of *Julie, ou la Nouvelle Héloïse* (1760) and the educational text *Émile* (1762) on Radcliffe's work has been recognized in part.[15] In his critical biography of Ann Radcliffe, *Mistress of Udolpho*, for example, Rictor Norton notes how Radcliffe's second novel, *A Sicilian Romance* (1790), bears a possible tribute to Rousseau through its heroines. The names of Julia and

Emilia, the sisters who embody the different attributes of sensibility, are indebted to the characters of both *Émile* and *Julie, ou la Nouvelle Héloïse*.[16]

Radcliffe's third novel, *The Romance of the Forest* (1791), transforms her Rousseauvian tribute from mere naming to the less certain realm of ideas and thematics. Chloë Chard's excellent edition of *The Romance of the Forest* charts the novel's indebtedness to Rousseau's *Émile* through the father of the hero, Theodore. Theodore's father, La Luc, is clearly modelled on the benevolent 'vicaire savoyard' of Rousseau's *Émile*.[17] For example, at one point in a long conversation with the secondary character M. Verneuil, La Luc argues that: 'Vicious inclinations not only corrupt the heart, but the understanding, and thus lead to false reasoning. Virtue only is on the side of truth.'[18] This debate between the two men adds nothing to the narrative, but it does rehearse some of Rousseau's key thinking in *Émile*.

One of the central arguments of *Émile* centres on self-love (*l'amour de soi*). Rousseau argues that 'the source of our passions, the origin and chief of every other, that which alone is born with man, and never leaves him while he lives, is SELF-LOVE'.[19] However, perhaps contrary to expectations, self-love is not presented as a negative trait. On the contrary, it is described as 'always right', an emotion that 'regards our own personal good only'.[20] As a concept, self-love for Rousseau stands in contrast to self-interest (*l'amour propre*) which itself competes with the good of others. 'Thus', says Rousseau, 'we see how the soft and affectionate passions arise from self-love, and the hateful and irascible ones from self-interest'.[21]

The Romance of the Forest is intimately concerned with the moral construction of the self. In many ways it is a dramatization of this key Rousseauvian distinction between self-love and self-interest. Its plot is driven by villains who act purely from motives of self-interest against a young, embattled, isolated heroine who must acquire the right qualities of self-love. Exceptionally in Radcliffe's *oeuvre*, the romance begins from the perspective of a criminal, Monsieur La Motte. He acts from self-interest when he becomes the unwilling rescuer and guardian of the heroine, Adeline. After his questionable rescue of her, the next threat Adeline confronts occurs when the unwilling guardian trades her to the libertine Marquis de Montalt in exchange for the latter's silence on his whereabouts. During the two villains' commercial exchange, the marquis freely confesses to La Motte: 'I will not pretend that my desire of serving you is unalloyed by any degree of self-interest. I will not affect to be more than man, and trust me those who do are less.'[22]

Montalt believes that self-interest is at the foundation of human nature and that those who profess otherwise are 'less than men'. His positioning is one on which Rousseau had elaborated at length throughout his writing. In his earlier 1755 *Discours sur l'inégalité*, Rousseau argued that the development of civil society had brought with it conditions of economic inequality. These had served to alienate man from his state of mutual respect and equality. Rousseau contended here that as social conditions began to reshape man's self-perception, man's behaviour became oriented towards competing jealousy with his fellow men. Selfishness, or *amour-propre*, began to replace self-respect. This is precisely the posturing adopted by Radcliffe's villains, La Motte and Montalt. The conditions of economic inequality that exist between the two men (La Motte being an exiled gentleman; Montalt a propertied aristocrat) immediately serve to ground their transactions upon self-interest. This in turn replaces any self-respect that the lesser of the two villains, La Motte, may still entertain. *The Romance of the Forest* fleshes out these Rousseauvian arguments. In pitching the benevolent, pastoral environment of La Luc's Switzerland against the shady, entangled forest setting of the marquis's French abode, Radcliffe establishes a dialogue with Rousseau's theories of virtue and vice, or self-love and self-interest.

However, *The Romance of the Forest*'s dramatization of Rousseau's arguments does not necessarily imply its complete endorsement of them. Radcliffe adds one crucial qualification to Rousseau's arguments on self-love in her portrayal of her heroine. Left under the protection of the penniless Monsieur and Madame La Motte, Adeline becomes their surrogate daughter in their makeshift ruined accommodation in the forest. The affectionate familial relationships initially assumed by the three, however, do not withstand the test of a long, enforced seclusion. There comes a point in the story when Madame La Motte, unfairly suspects the surrogate daughter of having an affair with M. la Motte. Instead of challenging Adeline on this misplaced belief, Madame la Motte chooses to neglect her. During this unconvincing narrative interlude, there is a scene where the unfairly suspected Adeline continues with a piece of sewing she is doing for Madame la Motte, not, as the narrative takes pains to explain, to reconcile Madame La Motte to her, but because it is not in her nature to resent:

> For many hours [Adeline] busied herself upon a piece of work, which she had undertaken for Madame La Motte; and this she did, without the least intention of conciliating her favour, but because

she felt there was something in thus repaying unkindness, which was suitable to her own temper, her sentiments, and her pride. Self-love *may* be the center, round which the human affections move, for whatever motive conduces to self-gratification may be resolved into self-love; yet some of these affections are in their nature so refined – that though we cannot deny their origin, they almost deserve the name of virtue. Of this species was that of Adeline.[23]

If we recall, Rousseau's argument in *Émile* posits that self-love 'regards our own personal good only'. Radcliffe's narrative description here modifies this position. Suddenly, there is a dramatic shift in the novel from the use of past tense in retelling the story ('Adeline busied herself'), to a modal verb in the present tense ('Self-love *may*'). The narrative qualifies Rousseau's argument on self-love as if it were carrying on an internal argument with him with the emphasis on the crucial word 'may', and the accompanying shift in tense. This tense transition swiftly transports the reader from the plot of the 'Romance' to a more universal, philosophical statement on self-love. It is so sudden that it can take the reader by surprise, but it presumes knowledge of these philosophical debates in its eighteenth-century readership. Radcliffe's heroine thus functions both as the narrative subject in the past tense and as a philosophical proposition through which Radcliffe rehearses her revisions of Rousseau. In direct contrast to Rousseau's careful distinctions in *Émile*, the narrator cautiously suggests that Adeline does not act from self-love at all, but from 'affections' that '*almost* deserve the name of virtue' (emphasis added). For Adeline, the concept of self-love is intertwined with self-gratification, and does not correspond to her selflessness. Adeline acts purely from altruistic duty, and never considers her self. To her cost, Adeline is probably the most selfless of Radcliffe's heroines. This is precisely because Radcliffe uses Adeline, in E. J. Clery's term, as an 'everyman' in order to disagree with Rousseau's distinctions between self-love and self-interest.[24] Radcliffe instead argues that self-love is all but indistinguishable from self-gratification, a concept more akin to Rousseau's concept of self-interest.

As if to drive home her disagreement, further on in *The Romance of the Forest*, Radcliffe offers another critique of Rousseau's unambiguous championing of self-love, again through the characterization of Adeline. When her suitor Theodore fails to turn up in the forest for a pre-arranged meeting, Adeline examines her own past conduct to discover why. She concludes that she has betrayed her partiality for Theodore – the gravest sin that a heroine can possibly commit – and that as a consequence Theodore is now neglecting her. Adeline's self-accusation, believing that only *she* can be the possible reason for Theodore's absence, is described by the narrative thus: 'When these emotions subsided, and reason resumed its influence, she blushed for what she termed this childish effervescence of self-love.'[25] Here again Radcliffe provides a clear indication of her disagreement with Rousseau's distinctions between self-love and self-interest. Whereas for Rousseau self-love is akin to self-respect, and entirely distinct from self-interest, for Radcliffe self-love is far more self-interested, and blends into the egotistical interests of its Rousseauvian counterpart. The narrator, nonetheless, is careful to provide this critique from Adeline's perspective alone: Adeline 'term[s]' self-love as childish. However, as I have argued above, she acts as the conduit for Radcliffe's disagreements with Rousseau, the hypothesis through which Rousseau's educational theories are tested and found wanting.

In his ground-breaking 1995 study *Ann Radcliffe: The Great Enchantress*, Robert Miles notes Radcliffe's indebtedness to Rousseau throughout her fiction. He argues that *The Romance of the Forest* in particular 'stood four-square behind Rousseau and sensibility'.[26] On the level of language and terminology, however, I think that Radcliffe uses Adeline to distinguish her arguments from Rousseau's, and that this standing-apart would have been noted by her eighteenth-century readership. Whilst Radcliffe does indeed pay homage to Rousseau's thinking throughout *The Romance of the Forest* she does not wholeheartedly endorse his philosophies. Instead, she complements Rousseau's thinking in part by turning to an influential French thinker who challenged Rousseau in another educational text.

The philosophical arguments that permeate *The Romance of the Forest* were equally influenced by the 1782 educational work *Adèle et Théodore ou Lettres sur l'éducation* by Madame de Genlis. Like Rousseau's work, Madame de Genlis's educational fiction was swiftly translated into English, with *Adelaide and Theodore; or, Letters on Education* being published in 1783. The translation of this three-volume educational work was well received in Britain, with the *Critical Review* deeming it 'much superior to the usual novels, in the general strictness and purity of its precepts'.[27] The novel concerns a mother's education of her two children, Adelaide and Theodore. On a superficial level, the names of the children undoubtedly influenced Radcliffe's naming of her couple Adeline and Theodore in *The Romance of the Forest*.[28] Through a series of letters, a mother writes in great detail about the upbringing of her children, an education that she has undertaken far from the corrupting temptations of Paris. Throughout these letters de Genlis, through the mouthpiece of the mother, frequently corrects Rousseau's insights on education as they are expressed in *Émile*.

Of more immediate significance to Radcliffe's *The Romance of the Forest*, however, is de Genlis's writing on self-love. The children's mother, the Baronness d'Almane, writes to her more dissipated Parisian friend:

> The pleasures of self-love, as transient as vain cannot leave deep impressions: they are only produced by the imagination, whose flame is soon extinguished, if the allurement of novelty does not rekindle it. The pleasures of the heart, less tumultuous, but milder and more lasting, can alone ensure our felicity.[29]

Self-love for de Genlis is 'transient' and 'vain', more consonant with the themes of self-interest that Rousseau outlined in *Émile*. As we have seen, Radcliffe similarly does not view self-love as a good characteristic in her heroine, deriding its appearance as a 'childish effervescence'. Radcliffe's nuancing of Rousseau's position on self-love was undoubtedly informed by de Genlis's work. Both female writers view self-love as a transient entity with no lasting, permanent value.

Radcliffe's reproving attitude to her heroines, which is particularly prominent in her third and fourth novels, *The Romance of the Forest* and *The Mysteries of Udolpho* (in the latter Emily St Aubert continually wages war against the excesses of sensibility), is undoubtedly inspired by the educational thinking of Rousseau, but the nuances of her portrayals come from Madame de Genlis. She uses the latter's arguments on education in *Adelaide and Theodore* most particularly to qualify her engagement with Rousseau's *Émile* in *The Romance of the Forest*. Adeline's route towards a lasting model of virtuous happiness takes her through the enticing arguments of Rousseau. Having negotiated these arguments, she achieves a more nuanced appreciation of the transient perils of self-love. It is a route that is also more implicitly pursued by Radcliffe's next heroine, Emily St Aubert, in *The Mysteries of Udolpho*. In order to achieve the idyllic pastoral serenity offered at the conclusion to each novel, both heroines must negotiate a well-trodden, hotly debated path on the relative merits of self-love. The perils that this path offers are potentially just as dangerous to the heroine as any physical threat that she suffers from the villain.

The complex, philosophical arguments that Radcliffe explored and debated in her fiction demonstrate just how widely read in continental thinking she was. Her novels are as embedded within philosophical educational arguments emerging from France as they are in the English literary heritage that she flagged up with so much care through her careful choice of epigraphs. Perhaps her judiciously balanced approach to both literary cultures is best summarized by Adeline's views on literature in *The Romance of the Forest*:

> Adeline found that no species of writing had power so effectually to withdraw her mind from the contemplation of its own misery as the higher kinds of poetry, and in these her taste soon taught her to distinguish the superiority of the English from that of the French. The genius of the language, more perhaps than the genius of the people, if indeed the distinction may be allowed, occasioned this.[30]

Again following Walpole's example, Radcliffe draws attention to the 'genius' of Britain's literary culture. She nonetheless sees fit to qualify this position when she distinguishes between the 'genius of the [English] language' and the 'genius of the [British] people'. Her qualification here offers us a vital clue to her considered literary approach. The *language* of England has produced literature truly endowed with the properties of genius; on the platform of ideas and beliefs, 'the genius of the people', though, the legacy of Britain's inhabitants is less certain. She renders this slight qualification palatable to her British audience through the hesitantly apologetic 'if indeed the distinction may be allowed'.

On the level of ideas and debate, like many of her contemporaries, Radcliffe dared to look across the Channel in a climate that was particularly hostile to Gallic influence. She drew both inspiration and disenchantment from the vilified Rousseau. Radcliffe then chose to critique his thinking independently. She did not effect this critique through the reactionary zealous conservative response from Britain, but through the more intellectually considered work of Madame de Genlis.

George Canning's attack on Rousseau's influence in England in 'New Morality' concluded by referring to Britain's 'colder, servile spirits' with the repeated lament, 'How do we ape thee, France!' Through the model of Radcliffe, I hope to have shown that Britain's Gothic engagement with France was far more complex and infinitely less servile than Canning suggested. Thanks to Radcliffe's uniquely discerning blend of French and English influences, her dual literary heritage truly does qualify her work for inclusion under this essay collection's French/English title 'Le Gothic'.

Acknowledgement

I would like to thank my colleague Dr Joe Bray, of the University of Sheffield, for his careful reading of this chapter and for his excellent suggestions. The editors of this collection, Professors Avril Horner and Sue Zlosnik, also created a conducive climate with the excellent conference 'Gothic Voyages' which they organized in Paris in 2004. For this, as well as for their excellent editorial support, I would like to extend my thanks to them.

Notes

1. Horace Walpole, Second Preface to *The Castle of Otranto*, ed. E. J. Clery (1764/5; Oxford: Oxford World's Classics, 1996), p. 14.
2. Nathan Drake, *Literary Hours or Sketches Critical and Narrative* (London: Cadell and Davies, 1798), p. 249.
3. Thomas James Mathias, *The Pursuits of Literature, A Satirical Poem in Four Dialogues with Notes*, seventh edition (London: T. Becket, 1798), p. 58.
4. Charlotte Smith's translation of *Manon Lescaut* was entitled *Manon L'escaut, or, The Fatal Attachment*. For a fuller account of the literary debacle that followed, see Lorraine Fletcher's *Charlotte Smith: a Critical Biography* (London: Palgrave Macmillan, 1998), pp. 82–3; and Terry Hale, 'Translation in Distress: Cultural Misappropriation and the Construction of the Gothic', in *European Gothic*, ed. Avril Horner (Manchester: Manchester University Press, 2002), pp. 18–20.
5. Mathias added this questionable encomium of Radcliffe's talents: 'Not so the mighty magician of THE MYSTERIES OF UDOLPHO, bred and nourished by the Florentine muses in their sacred, solitary caverns, amid the paler shrines of Gothick superstition, and in all the dreariness of inchantment' (Mathias, 1798, p. 58).
6. Edmund Burke, *Letter to a Member of the National Assembly, in answer to some objections to his book on French affairs* (London: J. Dodsley, 1791), p. 40.
7. Horace Walpole, letter to Mary Berry (1791), in *The Letters of Horace Walpole*, ed. Mrs Paget Toynbee, 16 volumes (Oxford, Clarendon Press, 1903–5), XIV, 439.
8. Mathias, *The Pursuits of Literature, A Satirical poem in Four Dialogues with Notes*, pp. 235–6.
9. George Canning, 'New Morality', *The Anti-Jacobin Review*, 9 July 1798, in *Poetry of the Anti-Jacobin*, ed. Charles Edmonds (London: G. Willis, 1854), p. 229.
10. Hannah More, *Strictures on the Modern System of Female Education* (1799; New York: Garland, 1970), p. 34.
11. Charles Palissot de Montenoy, *Memoires de Rousseau* (c. 1779); cf. the review in the *Monthly Review*, LX (1779), 136–43.
12. Mary Wollstonecraft, letter to William Godwin, 22 September 1798, *Posthumous Works of the Author of 'A Vindication of the Rights of Woman'* (London, 1798), III, 59.
13. For further information on this, see James H. Warner, 'Eighteenth-century Reactions to *La Nouvelle Heloise*', *PMLA*, LII (1937), 803–19.

14. Jean-Jacques Rousseau, *Emile* (1762), trans. William Kenrick, *Emilius and Sophia: or, a new system of education*. Translated from the French of J. J. Rousseau, Citizen of Geneva. (London: Griffiths, Becket and De Hondt, 1762).

15. The publication in 1760 of Jean-Jacques Rousseau's *Julie, ou La Nouvelle Héloïse* was translated as quickly as possible into English. As James H. Warner documents, the booksellers Becket and De Hondt advertised the translation of it for a full three months before the first volumes of the translation by William Kenrick appeared. (Warner, 'Eighteenth-century Reactions to *La Nouvelle Héloïse*', *PMLA*, LII (1937) 803–19). Despite such a speedy dissemination in the 1760s, however, the debate over this, and much of Rousseau's other writing, continued well into the 1790s, with an anonymous sequel to *La Nouvelle Héloise* appearing as late as 1790 from the Minerva Press. (Anon., *Laura; or, original letters. In two volumes. A sequel to the Eloisa of J.J. Rousseau, from the French.* (London: William Lane, 1790).

16. Rictor Norton, *Mistress of Udolpho: The Life of Ann Radcliffe* (London: Leicester University Press, 1999), p. 138.

17. Norton's *Mistress of Udolpho* also notes this, but qualifies it by noting analogies between La Luc and Radcliffe's uncle, Bentley, who had a great influence upon her fiction.

18. Ann Radcliffe, *The Romance of the Forest* ed. Chloë Chard (1791; Oxford: Oxford University Press, 1986), p. 270.

19. Jean-Jacques Rousseau, *Emile* (1762). Here, I have used Kenrick's original eighteenth-century translation, *Emilius and Sophia: or, a new system of education*. (London: Griffiths, Becket and De Hondt, 1762), II, 127.

20. Rousseau, *Emilius and Sophia*, II, 128.

21. Rousseau, *Emilius and Sophia*, II, 140 and 141.

22. Radcliffe, *The Romance of the Forest*, p. 221.

23. Radcliffe, *The Romance of the Forest*, p. 82.

24. E. J. Clery, 'Ann Radcliffe and D.A.F. de Sade: Thoughts on Heroinism', in 'Female Gothic' ed. Robert Miles, *Women's Writing*, 1:2 (1994) 7. In this important essay, Clery also views *The Romance of the Forest* as 'the most philosophical of Radcliffe's novels', and examines the tropes shared by Rousseau and de Sade through the problematic of Rousseau's influence.

25. Radcliffe, *The Romance of the Forest*, p. 107.

26. Robert Miles, *Ann Radcliffe: The Great Enchantress* (Manchester: Manchester University Press, 1995), p. 154.

27. Review of Madame de Genlis, *Adelaide and Theodore; or letters on education* trans. (London: Bathurst and Cadell, 1783), in the *Critical Review*, 56, October 1783, p. 301.

28. I am indebted to Dr Gillian Dow, of the University of Southampton, for initial guidance on de Genlis's work. See her forthcoming edition of de Genlis's work: Gillian Dow, ed., *Adelaide and Theodore*, by Stéphanie-Félicité de Genlis (London: Pickering and Chatto, 2007).

29. Stéphanie-Félicité de Genlis, *Adelaide and Theodore; or letters on education* 3 volumes, trans. (London: T. Cadell, 1783), vol. I, p. 44.

30. Radcliffe, *The Romance of the Forest*, p. 261.

References

Primary sources

Anon., *Laura; or, original letters. In two volumes. A sequel to the Eloisa of J.J. Rousseau, from the French* (London: William Lane, 1790).

Anon., Review of Madame de Genlis, *Adelaide and Theodore; or letters on education* trans. (London: Bathurst and Cadell, 1783), in the *Critical Review*, 56, October 1783.

Burke, Edmund, *Letter to a Member of the National Assembly, in answer to some objections to his book on French affair* (London: J. Dodsley, 1791).

Canning, George, 'New Morality', *The Anti-Jacobin Review*, 9 July 1798, in *Poetry of the Anti-Jacobin*, ed. Charles Edmonds (London: G. Willis, 1854), p. 229.

Drake, Nathan, *Literary Hours or Sketches Critical and Narrative* (London: Cadell and Davies, 1798).

Genlis, Stéphanie-Félicité de, *Adelaide and Theodore; or letters on education.* trans., 3 volumes (London: T. Cadell, 1783).

Mathias, Thomas James, *The Pursuits of Literature, A satirical poem in four dialogues with notes*, seventh edition (London, 1798).

More, Hannah, *Strictures on the Modern System of Female Education* (1799; New York: Garland, 1970).

Radcliffe, Ann, *The Romance of the Forest*, ed. Chloë Chard (1791; Oxford: Oxford University Press, 1986).

Roche, Regina Maria, *The Children of the Abbey, a tale*, 4 volumes (London: William Lane, 1797).

—— *Clermont. A tale.* 4 volumes (London: William Lane, 1798).

Rousseau, Jean-Jacques, *Julie, ou la Nouvelle Héloïse* (1760), trans. William Kenrick, *Eloisa, or a Series of Original Letters* (London: Becket and De Hondt, 1760).

—— *Émile* (1762), trans. William Kenrick, *Emilius and Sophia: or, a new system of education* (London: Griffiths, Becket and De Hondt, 1762).

Smith, Charlotte, *Manon L'escaut, or, The Fatal Attachment*, a translation of Prévost's *Manon Lescaut* (London: T. Cadell, 1785). Withdrawn from publication.

Walpole, Horace, *The Castle of Otranto*, ed. E. J. Clery (1764/5; Oxford: Oxford World's Classics, 1996).

Secondary sources

Clery, E. J., 'Ann Radcliffe and D. A. F. de Sade: Thoughts on Heroinism', in 'Female Gothic', ed. Robert Miles, *Women's Writing*, 1:2, 1994.

Dow, Gillian, ed., *Adelaide and Theodore*, by Stéphanie-Félicité de Genlis (London: Pickering and Chatto, 2007).

Fletcher, Lorraine, *Charlotte Smith: a Critical Biography* (London: Palgrave Macmillan, 1998).

Hale, Terry, 'Translation in Distress: Cultural Misappropriation and the Construction of the Gothic' in *European Gothic*, ed. Avril Horner (Manchester: Manchester University Press, 2002).

Miles, Robert, *Ann Radcliffe: The Great Enchantress* (Manchester: Manchester University Press, 1995).
Norton, Rictor, *Mistress of Udolpho: The Life of Ann Radcliffe* (London: Leicester University Press, 1999).
Warner, James H., 'Eighteenth-century Reactions to *La Nouvelle Héloïse*', *PMLA*, LII (1937) 803–19.

6
Huysmans, Machen and the Gothic Grotesque, Or: The Way Up is the Way Down

Alison Milbank

Despite the early admiration for British Gothic writing in France, illustrated both by celebrated remarks by de Sade and by immediate translations and imitations of Ann Radcliffe and Matthew Lewis by French writers, French exploration of Gothic themes took a very different course.[1] A great Gothic novel like Victor Hugo's *Notre Dame de Paris* is regarded as a work of Romantic historicism, while the prevalence of corpses, ghosts and other horrific material in the *conte fantastique* is accounted for as initially Hoffmannesque[2] and later in the tradition of Poe, who tends to be read in France in terms of a sceptical Romantic epistemology.[3] So although English Gothic is still referred to with respect in France long after its loss of status in Britain or assimilation into the sensation novel, it is hard to find a language and a mode of real congruence between the two national productions.

By the end of the nineteenth century, however, the cultural supremacy of Charles Baudelaire, Baudelaire's Poe and the Symbolists over *fin de siècle* British writing brings about a rapprochment, and, as I shall argue, a common aesthetic of the grotesque that allies French philosophical dualism with British temporal historicism. And the French writer who most clearly illustrates this turn to the grotesque in fictions that chart a spectacular personal dialectical progression is Joris-Karl Huysmans. Yet, despite his employment of horror and his obsessive attention to rotting and confining old houses, Huysmans has received scant attention as a Gothic writer. He makes his way only obliquely into Gothic criticism via the shadowy textual presence of his decadent masterpiece, *A Rebours* (1884), the mysterious novel in yellow papers to which Dorian Gray attributes his fall in Oscar Wilde's study in horror, *The Picture of Dorian Gray*.[4] In this chapter I shall seek to allow Huysmans passage into Gothic terrain by comparing him to the

British *fin-de-siècle* horror writer Arthur Machen. I shall then offer a new reading of the two novelists' engagement with the abhorrent and tormented body in terms of the grotesque which, I shall argue, is the means by which they endeavour to find that philosopher's stone of the nineteenth century: namely, the real.

In instalments appearing in the *Echo de Paris* during the early spring of 1891, *Là-Bas* ('Down There'; or 'The Damned' in English translations) was a literary and popular success. It charts the intellectual, erotic and gastronomic adventures of Durtal, a solitary Parisian writer based on Huysmans himself, engaged in preparing a biography of Gilles de Rais, Joan of Arc's Marshall, whose later horrendous crimes against young children and his sorcery led to his arrest and execution in 1440.[5] *Là-Bas* also describes Durtal's affair with the ambiguously sacrilegious Hyacinthe de Chantelouve, who takes him to a black mass, and his encounters through his friend Des Hermies, with a range of modern-day occultists. It thus provides both a synchronic and a diachronic dialectical structure: medieval and modern society, contemporary Satanism versus Catholicism. In *The Three Imposters*, published in 1895, Arthur Machen similarly describes the adventures of two friends and urban *flâneurs*, Dyson and Phillips, and their encounters with occultism through the discovery of an ancient gold coin lost as a young man in spectacles flees from a murderous secret society. It contains a number of tall stories narrated by the 'imposters' of the novel's title, each of which reaches a horrendously violent conclusion, only outdone by the discovery of an actual corpse by the two Londoners in the last chapter.

While it is not known whether Machen read *Là-Bas*, he refers to *A Rebours* in his own writing, and was a translator of Margaret of Navarre and other early French writers, so that he certainly had the ability to read Huysmans' novel before its translation into English in 1927.[6] Although direct influence cannot be proved, there are a number of similarities between the two works that serve to illuminate their respective projects and effects. In each case the contemporary urban frame allows a pair of male protagonists to glimpse a mysterious and awesomely different past, which both critiques the banality of the present by its critical distance and simultaneously exerts an influence on the seemingly discrete present day in the manner of a Gothic narrative. So Durtal lovingly narrates the trial of de Rais, which is more real to him than Boulanger's Paris, while Phillips and Dyson are presented by tales such as 'The Novel of the Black Seal' in which 'Miss Lally' describes the quest of Professor Gregg into primeval survivals in the Welsh Marches, which become manifest in the metamorphosis of a local boy into a creature with tentacles, and in the professor's own disappearance as the past literally swallows him up. In both novels the past reveals itself as a potent source of evil as well as fascination, capable of reaching out and enfolding the present in its murderous embrace.

A second feature the two novels share is an emphasis on the disgusting and the horrible. The late nineteenth century has been studied in this regard by a number of critics who interpret the enervations of the vampiric bite, the evolutionary reversals of Rider Haggard's Ayesha in the flames from goddess to monkey, and Dorian Gray's sudden fall from immortality to unrecognizable corpse as responses first, to *fin-de-siècle* anxieties about degeneration and the possibility of evolutionary reversal, and secondly, to the perceived instability of human identity in a post-Darwinian worldview.[7] Indeed, Machen's description of Miss Leicester's brother's reduction to 'a dark and putrid mass, seething with corruption and hideous rottenness, neither liquid nor solid, but melting and changing before our eyes'[8] is a perfect example of what Kelly Hurley terms the 'abhuman' ablative in its repeated gesture of departure from the norm and threatening in its unmaking of any recognizable human form.[9] Machen here and in the horrendous experiments of *The Great God Pan* (1890) is something of a specialist in offering set-pieces of the rendering and liquefaction of the human form. Huysman's *Là-Bas* similarly details De Rais's dismemberments. He slashes a boy's chest to drink from his lungs, 'macerat[ing] himself in excrement' and gouging out eyes 'rubbing between his fingers the bloody, milky discharge'.[10] The disgusting also finds a place in the language of Durtal, whose estrangement from and dislike of modern society and its corruptions finds expression in an extremity of abuse. Famously, the last sentence of the novel excoriates those who 'will stuff their guts with food and evacuate their souls through their bowels' (*LB*, p. 265).

Yet while these two texts stage and display examples of abjection, disgust and the horrid, there is more to them than the prophylactic catharsis usually advanced by Gothic critics, although I do not deny that there is evidence of Kristeva's 'powers of horror' at work in these texts. But while psychologically influenced criticism explores the fluidity and swooning ambivalence of the gesture of abjection and compares it to the early attempts towards individuation of the child, I wish to draw attention to a more settled, indeed excessively violent digestive evacuation by discussing the disgust and horror of these two novels in terms of the literary grotesque. There may, indeed, be a psychological basis to our fearful reaction to grotesque images, but there is also no doubt that writers such as Huysmans and Machen are employing it for specific strategic aims.

In using this category of aesthetic discourse I am employing a term overtly invoked in both works. Early in *The Three Imposters*, for example, Dyson observes the 'gangrenous decay' of the ruined house and announces:

> I yield to fantasy; I cannot withstand the influence of the grotesque. Here, where all is falling into dimness and dissolution ... I cannot remain commonplace. I look at that deep glow on the panes, and the house lies all enchanted; that very room, I tell you, is within all blood and fire. (*TTI*, p. 104)

In using the grotesque, Huysmans and Machen are not only imitating Poe, who entitled his collected stories 'Tales of the Grotesque and Arabesque' (1839 for 1840), but engaging a term central to aesthetics ever since the archeological discovery of Roman wall paintings in the fifteenth century – hence the word 'grotesque', from grotto or cave. These murals showed half-human, half-animal figures and topped vegetable arabesque decorations with human heads.[11] The term was developed in art criticism to describe the playful fantastic and the monstrous and bizarre admixture of disparate forms. Hence in origin it is a visual category, although from the seventeenth century onwards the term was applied to visual effects in literary works such as Dante's *Commedia* and Rabelais's *Pantagruel and Gargantua*.[12] In German Romanticism it was used (sometimes interchangeably) with the arabesque to delineate a kind of Romantic irony and express the creative freedom of the artistic imagination, until in August Schlegel's formulation it came to express a thoroughgoing epistemological uncertainty.[13] The Romantic grotesque finds its fullest fictional expression in Hoffmann's 'Night Pieces', where it takes on a more threatening aspect, for example in the famous 'Sandman' tale in which Nathaniel falls in love, unwittingly, with a mechanical doll, and spectacles seem to take on a life of their own.[14]

In the nineteenth century it is France and Britain that develop further the theory of the grotesque. First, Hugo in his 'Preface to *Cromwell*' of 1827 realigned the fantastic Romantic grotesque with realism and with modernity.[15] The monstrous yoking of the grotesque image paralleled the democratic and hybrid nature of modern literature and politics, in contrast to classical stylistic and generic decorum.

Its monstrosity, like that of Hugo's own grotesque creation, the hunchback Quasimodo, has a revolutionary energy. It exists, moreover, in tension with the sublime: 'while the sublime represents the soul as it is, purified by Christian morality, the grotesque plays the part of the human beast'.[16] The democracy of the grotesque allies humanity with the rest of creation, something that *Notre Dame de Paris* carries out by extensive animal similitude for its protagonists,[17] and by Esmeralda's quasi-human little goat, which is rescued in preference to the girl herself. The duality of human nature as half-ape, half-angel is central to Hugo's conception.

Influenced by Hugo, the British cultural theorist John Ruskin turns this comic theory in a theological direction, so that the grotesque enacts and bears witness to the gulf between human and divine as the result of sin, or that between humanity and death caused by fear. It is still, however, a source of energy and creativity. While having a playful element, Ruskin's 'noble' or Gothic grotesque is a response to 'the dreadfulness of the universe'.[18] Hence for him Dante's sportive satirical demons in *Inferno* 21 and 22 are admired for their mingling of horror and the ludicrous. As grotesque they are religious conceptions because, as the human imagination is a distorted mirror of the divine it is still a mirror and 'the vaster the truths into which it obtains an insight, the more fantastic their distortion is likely to be'.[19] Indeed, the more terrible and extreme the grotesque effect, the more it witnesses to the power and infinitude of the Divine.

While Ruskin's writing (and that of Walter Bagehot) led to the valorization of medieval sculpture and the poetry of Robert Browning in Britain, it had an effect in France also through the Ruskin devotee Marcel Proust and his translation of *The Bible of Amiens* with its references to the grotesque in its introduction.[20] Much earlier however, in Gautier's anthology of grotesque poetry of 1853, it had become a quasi-national form, which may go some way to explaining the immense influence of Edgar Poe on the French imagination. The French fantastic tale, following both Poe and Hoffmann, tends in an increasingly grotesque direction. Furthermore, in both British aestheticism and French symbolism of the latter part of the nineteenth century, the grotesque was a mode of renewing an increasingly jaded apprehension of beauty and of renewing the perceived decadence of language, which seemed to have become increasingly abstract and disconnected with the materiality of experience.[21]

Hence, when Dyson declares his yielding to the grotesque in Machen's story he invokes a whole history of interpretation. He alerts his reader to the novel's monstrous Hugoesque hybridity, its Hoffmannesque yoking of realism and fantasy, humour and horror, and he invokes the Schlegelian grotesquely creative imagination for a work about style itself. Moreover, he prepares the reader for the 'terrible grotesque' of Ruskin, for we shall later discover that the sun's enchantment will break upon literal 'blood and fire'. What is particularly grotesque about the literalization of the blood and fire is the way in which the signifier and referent come too close: they become one in a monstrous hybrid because the dying body of the young man in spectacles visibly bleeds and burns. It is a kind of reverse of the usual theoretical attention to the instability of the relation between signifier and signified in the sign.

Similarly in *Là-Bas* Durtal uses the word 'grotesque' quite frequently, but the concept is central also to the novel's structure and method. By his use of deliberately unstable pronouns and adverbs for the titles of his novels – *En Ménage* (1881), *En Route* (1895), *En Rade* (1887), *A Vau-L'Eau* (1882), *A Rebours* (1884) and *Là-Bas* (1891) – Huysmans seems to open a space of deliberate liminality and fluidity in his novels. Yet he fills these spaces of epistemological quest with physical grotesque items and images, like Des Hermies in *A Rebours* filling his house with excessive quantities of artworks and embroideries. An example can be seen in Durtal's excessive use of the language of excrement: 'What whirlpools of ordure lie in wait for us on the horizon,' he declares in words that seem bizarrely inappropriate to describe an abstract movement of thought: namely, the onset of modern agnosticism about God's existence. Durtal is indirectly alluding to the tortures of the devil endured by the long-suffering saintly nun, Lydwina of Schiedam, whose biography Huysmans was later to write in 1901, and who was regularly assailed in this way. The grotesque arises in the case of Durtal and the nun from a mismatch of categories: spiritual and supernatural warfare described in terms of natural faeces, all-too physical words to describe a mental attitude. The 'stuff their guts' and excretion of the novel's last sentence quoted above is grotesque not just because of the alimentary language so much as the fact that it is the immaterial *soul* that is excreted. Durtal here imitates Dante's devil in *Inferno* (*LB*, p. 149), who signals to his demonic troops by making a trumpet of his arse. In both cases the grotesque element is the perversion of communication involved in the action and the mismatch of categories.

Grotesque in the sense of a monstrous union of contraries also characterizes the narrative structure of *Là-Bas* in which revelations of Gilles de Rais's appalling and extreme acts of cruelty are juxtaposed with the banalities of modern-day Satanism, which lack his sublime excess. In the present the most violent act is the spiritual persecution an astrologer claims to be undergoing by long-distance spells from a rival supernaturalist, which cause nothing worse than the occasional head-ache. All this Satanic practice in Huysmans' novel is, again grotesquely, narrated in conversation around the dinner table of the pious bell-ringer of St Sulpice, Carhaix. Grotesque above all in its satirical presen-tation is the eagerly awaited black mass, at which wrinkled and painted homosexuals hobble about as acolytes, while the celebrant, the rogue priest Canon Docre, shows his sock-suspenders along with his tumes-cent penis as he desecrates the host with a variety of transgressive fluids. For much of the time Huysmans' text employs the grotesque method as a mode of satire by means of monstrous juxtaposition in the style of his friend Villiers de l'Isle Adam, who in one celebrated fantastic tale describes the Paris Bourse systematically in terms of the Morgue, to such effect that the reader is unsure right to the end as to which institution is the primary reference and which the metaphor.[22]

The Gothic critic who has done most to attend to the disgustingly grotesque elements of fiction at the turn of the twentieth century is Kelly Hurley in her 1996 study, *Gothic Body: Sexuality, Materialism and Degeneration at the Fin de Siècle*. She reads effects such as I describe above as due to a terrified but also ecstatic attention to the ruin of the unified subject, while the ability of ungraspable matter to take on a life of its own is evidence of the victory of an appalling and all-conquering materialism. This latter putrid 'thingness' she accords the term 'Gothicity of matter'. But while she herself occasionally uses the term 'grotesque' adjectivally or adverbially, she does not analyse the excess of form as well as matter that characterizes literature from this period. Similarly, Geoffrey Harpham's study of the grotesque talks of 'grotesqueries' as standing at 'a margin of our consciousness between the known and the unknown, the perceived and the unperceived', but fails to note that though our mind is in a state of fluidity as to the categories in which to fit the image, our eyes most assuredly see it.[23] Were the image purely material and without form there would be a different philosophical question: is there anything at all? But in the horrible grotesque there is form or rather forms, but no one category in which to unify or settle what one sees. The world of phenomena available to sight thus becomes truly mysterious. So, for example, in Huysmans the intangibility of the whirlwind is held in tension with the specificity of ordure and the spiritual actually invades the category of the natural. Indeed, faeces are viscous, but they famously have form – even art as the earliest mode of infant creativity. The problem is how this form could relate to the form of abstract speculation. Similarly, a story like that of de l'Isle Adam is one of *too much* form, an overdetermination of signs. Coppola's cascade of spectacles in 'The Sandman' is grotesque precisely because it is both a cascade (liquid and formless) and one of spectacles (objects with definite shapes).

For the grotesque works by opening two divergent ideas or pictures in the brain, neither of which fits with the other. In this way it makes the perceiver imitate the hesitation that Tzvetan Todorov accords to the reader or protagonist of the fantastic tale.[24] For Todorov a specifically post-Enlightenment genre, the fantastic allows a seemingly supernatural fact or experience to disturb a believable realist narrative, so that the protagonist or reader hesitates, unable to hold together the two realities. In the German Romantic tale such a procedure leads to ambiguous and ironic conclusions and even madness for the protagonist, as in the conclusion to 'The Sandman', in which Nathaniel cannot bear a reality in which Clara's rationalism and Coppola's seeming supernaturalism coexist, and grotesquely throws the real woman off the tower as a puppet. The reader too is left in doubt as to whether it was really Coppelius below in the square or not. In the Gothic grotesque of Machen and Huysmans however, it is not so much the supernatural that disturbs the real as the material cosmos itself that behaves 'supernaturally', refusing to keep to its material limits and its 'natural' character. Hence here the grotesque is far from a materialist trope, but rather renders the material realm – the thingness of the phenomenal world – itself problematic.

A good example can be found in the scene in *Là-Bas* in which Durtal imagines de Rais wandering in the woods near his stronghold at Tiffauges. Seeking respite from his overwhelming desires he finds those same desires embodied in nightmarish form in what is described as 'the immutable lubricity of trees', whose roots and branches couple in 'stationary fornication' (*LB*, p. 146). The various barks become the translucent skin of his child victims, with incisions like enormous lips, while in the sky clouds 'swell into breasts, divide into buttocks, bulge with fecundity' (*LB*, p. 147). The landscape alters only to reveal 'exostosis and ulcers' and becomes an 'arboreal venereal clinic' (*LB*, p. 147). Overwhelmed by lust of a vegetable kind de Rais sleeps, only to dream of the corpses of his victims reviving in the larval state and attacking his lower organs. Is this not a perfect example of a confluence between entropic terrors and their converse: the chaotic domination of pure matter now with a life of its own? And yet what is terrifying about this transformation is not that it lacks form and meaning, but that it has all too much: matter has been transmuted into form and intentionality of a quasi-human nature. There are indeed holes, but they prove to be the 'puckered anuses' of animals. Indeed, the landscape of 'abomination' is 'in a state of flux', but it orchestrates 'frightful tumours and goitres' in the trees, 'exostosis and ulcers, pustulent sores the size of rocks' and 'tubercular chancres' (*LB*, p. 147). And it is not the vegetation that is objectified but de Rais who falls on his bed 'like an inert object'.

This unpleasant scene presents a libertine nightmare, in which the Sadean will-to-power expressed by the instrumentalization of bodies as pleasure machines that will allow the transcendence of the libertine, is universalized and Gothicized. The gnostic denial of the material and physical is revealed in the same moment as its failure. For de Rais is *confined* by the bodily nature of his desires. In this section Huysmans employs and even coins reflexive verbs – *se Satanise, se pervertisse* (*LB*, pp. 169 and 170) – as if to emphasize the desire for self-transcendence that turns backwards to confirm the ego's self-imprisonment.

Indeed, not just this scene but the whole of *Là-Bas* can be interpreted as an investigation into the various ways to deal with, and escape from, matter. If de Rais sought the transcendent by freeing himself from matter, Durtal himself used his sexual relations with the succubus Madame de Chantelouve as a 'trampoline' to 'pass far beyond the physical cravings of the flesh', only to be reduced 'grotesque[ly]' to a new awareness of his dependence on the body (*LB*, 160). Satanists like Canon Docre 'force' Christ into their black mass or feed hosts to white mice to deify themselves. And de Rais's murderous career is an exercise in substitutionary sacrifice in which the broken bodies allow him diabolical passage from the natural to the supernatural in a manner soon to be adumbrated by Hubert and Mauss in their 1898 revision of sacrificial theory as an act that, through a victim, enables the sanctification of the sacrificer, in contrast to earlier theories like that of Robertson Smith which stressed the participatory communion of the sacrificial meal. In each of these examples of a drive to transcend matter, the novel employs grotesque effects to illustrate the fruitless nature of the enterprise.

There is, however, a mode of transcendence of matter offered in *Là-Bas*, but paradoxically it involves an embrace of the real and the material. After the descriptions of de Rais's sadism and its rebounding nightmare, the most horrific scene of the novel is Durtal's ekphrasis of the crucifixion of Christ then at Cassel by the fifteenth-century Flemish painter Mathais Grünewald. With its exaggerated, almost mannerist gestures, it is already an exercise in the grotesque mode, but Huysmans goes even further in rendering it a monstrosity:

> Dislocated, almost ripped from their sockets, the arms of the Christ seemed bound their entire length in bulging cords of muscles; the tortured tendons of the armpits looked ready to snap; the hands, wide open, brandishing fingers contorted in a confused gesture of benediction and reproach … Purulence was setting in; the seeping wound in the side dripped thickly, inundating the thigh with blood that was like congealed blackberry juice; a milky puss tinged with a pinkish hue, similar to those Moselle wines, oozed down the chest and over the abdomen with its rumpled loin-cloth.[25]

In every way grotesque, this is a tortured and tensile body that is a more effective trampoline to the transcendent than his mistress for Durtal because it represents an acceptance of the realm of matter to such an extent that Christ becomes a thing, an 'erupting cadaver' (*LB*, p. 8), not by seeking to transcend the physical but by making it speak through his deliberate giving himself up to it. Hence the importance of the painting for Durtal is that it is both utterly realist in its content and utterly idealist: 'a masterpiece of the impossible was revealed, an art ordered to render the invisible and the tangible' (*LB*, p. 10). But it is still grotesque because humanity – even Divine humanity – remains dual: 'two beings, one perishable, the other immortal, one carnal the other ethereal' as Hugo puts it, and argues for the grotesque mode in art as being true to our divided nature.[26] It is particularly true to French thought which, from Descartes onwards, has found mediation from dualist conceptual models hard to achieve except through heroic use of paradox by a Pascal, a Péguy or a Derrida. So here Huysmans' way out is to imitate Christ: to embrace it and to render it dynamically productive through the grotesque, so that while his divine Christ is also a putrid mass of pus, his de Rais is shown as equally grotesquely dual in his move from diabolical violence to spectacular repentance and redemptive death. This is morally grotesque: how can a mere confession weigh against the torture and eating of scores of children? But for *Là-Bas*, the enormity of the abyss below, 'down there', only dramatizes the unbelievable depth of *Là-Haut* (up there), and the way up is the way down, as it was also for Charles Baudelaire according to T. S. Eliot, who wrote in his introduction to Baudelaire's journal that his

'Satanism was in itself an attempt to get into Christianity by the back door ... It is a way of affirming belief'.[27] In a similar way modern artists employ blasphemously religious imagery and artefacts to provoke meaning in a world from which it seems to have drained.

So if, as I postulate, Machen imitates aspects of Huysmans' novel in *The Three Imposters*, what does this reveal about Machen's own presentation of dissolving and tortured bodies? Are we not here more comfortably within identity breakdown? Indeed we are, but the subtitle of *The Three Imposters*: *'Or: the Transmutations'* reveals another attempt to move beyond materialism. Transmutation is a term used in alchemy for the changes undergone by the substances used in its attempts to make gold; and for Machen style was the philosopher's stone that could transmute his horrors into art. The novel goes further in replicating alchemical procedure than many *fin de siècle* fictions however, since it also replicates the various stages of the process, such as 'nigredo' in the 'novel of the black seal', in which the substance is destroyed and gives off a smell of putrefaction, and the 'albedo' stage in 'the novel of the white powder' in which Leicester is reduced to a liquid mass like the alembic bath, ending with the 'rubedo' stage, which involves both heat (fire) and blood in the production of the philosopher's stone or the fifth essence.[28] In Machen, the blood and fire Dyson intuits in the ruined house being endured by the young man in spectacles completes the rite.

What I would argue is at stake in this alchemical figuration is not just the alchemy of style that Machen describes in his critical apologia *Hieroglyphics* (1902), but the embrace of matter as a means to transcendence typical of the theurgic Platonism that would later be so important to literary modernism in the work of W. B. Yeats and Ezra Pound. Machen, like Yeats and Bram Stoker (who is, in my view, equally theurgic) belonged to the Order of the Golden Dawn,[29] which taught this mode of occultism and sought like Huysmans to align Eleusis with Christianity in a participatory and sacramental neo-Platonism: 'man is a sacrament, soul manifested under the form of body', as Machen put it in *Hieroglyphics*.[30] Theurgic Platonism delineates a spiritual journey that does not flee the material but descends to its depths in order to ascend.[31] Alchemy forms a symbolic language for this embrace of matter, and for that reason is discussed also at length in *Là-Bas*, both in relation to de Rais's experiments and in terms of its practical possibilities in the present. Hugo too gives us an alchemist, Claude Frollo, in his *Notre Dame de Paris*, who tries at various points to hold both the arabesque Esmeralda and the grotesque Quasimodo under his control, but cracks under the tension to become another de Rais in his cruelty and will-to-power.

The disturbing ending of *The Three Imposters* then does not just leave the reader horrified at the breakdown of the human as we view the 'shameful ruin' of the young man in torment. Unlike Dorian Gray's transmutation into an unidentifiable mass of decrepitude, this form is still recognizable:

> The body was torn and mutilated in the most hideous fashion, scarred with the marks of red-hot irons, a shameful ruin of the human shape. But upon the middle of the body a fire of coals was smouldering; the flesh had been burnt through. The man was dead, but the smoke of his torment mounted still, a black vapour.
> 'The young man with spectacles,' said Mr. Dyson. (*TTI*, p. 234)

That he is a 'ruin' gestures towards his original form, making the reader hold both images in tension, just as his former identity as 'the young man with spectacles' still obtains. So the horror of what has happened lies in the act itself but also in the effort of accommodating both tortured and spectacled body in mental connection – as a sort of interior alchemical wedding in the mind of the reader. This is a deliberate use of the grotesque that forces the reader to acknowledge the duality of human nature as a mystery. Indeed it was this very insight that Machen valued in Robert Louis Stevenson's *Jekyll and Hyde*:

> I think that I see here that Mr. Stevenson had received a vision of the mystery of human nature, compounded of dust and of the stars, of a dim vast city, splendid and ruinous as a drowned Atlantis deep beneath the waves, of a haunted quire where a flickering light burns before the veil.[32]

In asserting the transcendental purposes of the horrible grotesque I am, of course, taking a different trajectory from that of Mikhail Bakhtin's secularizing *Rabelais and His World*, in which he reads the monstrosity of the grotesque body as an opening up to a social cosmos that involves a deliberate 'uncrowning' of the spiritual in favour of a cosmic bodily cycle of becoming and dissolution.[33] Indeed, in my opinion, the arboreal lubriciousness of de Rais's nightmares is an imitation of Panurge's city architecture of female genitalia which Bakhtin presents as evidence of the porous, fecund sociality of the carnivalesque inversion of the 'closed' canonical body.[34] A Bakhtinian reading of *Là-Bas* would interpret the erotic inversions of the black mass and its raping of the crucifix as liberatory uncrownings of the sacred/profane divide, which are now reconnected by the porous double nature of the grotesque body.

However, by being so anxious to assert the joyous carnivalesque release of the grotesque, Bakhtin paradoxically removes much of its transgressive and dialectical character. If life is death and sacred and profane are one, the grotesque is no longer grotesque: calling a church tower a phallus only works comically if the taboo nature of the sacred is invoked to render a frisson of profanity. Without Lent, carnival becomes a consumerist spectacle and loses its participatory character. Pantagruel's hat with assorted body parts is only comic because we have a clear conception of the 'normal' body. For Machen, Rabelais was a not a secular but a religious writer: 'he brings before you the highest by positing that which is lower than the lowest, and if you have the prepared, initiated mind, a Rabelaisian "list" is the best preface to the angelic song'.[35] These words appear in *Hieroglyphics* and are part, therefore, of Machen's elucidation of his own literary practice. Matter is not an inert objectified reality but itself participatory in the Divine, and by a theurgic descent, Rabelais, according to Machen, presupposes an ascent.

The paradox of *The Three Imposters* and *Là-Bas*'s Satanic initiates is that the search for the gold Tiberius or the mystery of human suffering eludes them precisely because they resist the Rabelaisian grotesque: instead they instrumentalize the human body by torture and death. In this sense they are truly the 'imposters' of Machen's title, which is a reference to an anonymous atheist tract denouncing Christ, Moses and Mahomet as requiring sacrifice and doing evil.[36] In contrast to the tract, however, it is not the world religions that are held up for blame for a murderous monotheism in Machen but the libertine occultists: both Miss Lally and her co-conspirators, like Gilles de Rais, use the deaths of others as a means to avoid the duality of their own human-ity. They employ substitutionary sacrifice in a ritualistic mode to allow them access to power and sacrality. And yet such murderous uni-tariness rebounds to bring de Rais to his knees, while the unrepentant Lally and her friends are bound like Joyce's similarly circuitous *Finnegans Wake* to 'a commodious vicus of recirculation'[37] in the repeti-tive arabesques of Machen's circular tale. They keep telling stories which end in the grotesque but, like de Rais in the forest of body parts, they cannot escape from matter or from their own physicality. It is for the reader that the alchemy of style becomes productive as she holds in the imagination like an alchemical retort the conflicting energies of the Gothic grotesque, and proves for herself that the way down is indeed also the way up.

In the grotesque, therefore, French philosophical dualism could find a Gothicized version of itself rendered as a monstrosity, and move beyond its instrumentalization of matter into a new and more energized duality. British simultaneous loss of and fear of its own history could find expression in Gothically grotesque effects, as it had done from its eighteenth-century origins in Walpole's *The Castle of Otranto* (1764), in which stylistic anachronism and oversized supernatural helmets had energized a text in the playful Gothic mode. In both French and British horror fiction, Huysmans and Machen, horror deliberately provokes the conceptual *aporias* (blockages to thought) of the grotesque, but in so doing, it allows the world of matter to reveal its mystery and transcendence and humanity itself, in all its bestiality, the duality of the Divine.

Notes

1. See Marquis de Sade, in 'Idée sur les romans' (extract), in Victor Sage (ed.), *The Gothick Novel: A Casebook* (Basingstoke: Macmillan, 1990), pp. 48–9; and Terry Hale, 'Translation in Distress: Cultural Misappropriation and the Construction of the Gothic', in A. Horner (ed.), *European Gothic: A Spirited Exchange 1760–1960* (Manchester: Manchester University Press, 2002), pp. 23–4.
2. J-H. Retinger, *Le Conte fantastique dans le romanticisme français* (Paris: B. Grasset, 1909); and R. Journand-Bautry and J-F. Perrin, *Le Conte Merveilleux au XVIIIe Siècle: une Poétique Expérimental* (Paris: Kimé, 2002).
3. P. Quinn, *The French Face of Edgar Poe* (Carbondale, IL: South Illinois University Press, 1957).
4. O. Wilde, *The Picture of Dorian Gray*, ed. D. Lawyer (New York: Norton, 1998), pp. 98–9.
5. G. Bataille, *The Trial of Gilles de Rais*, trans. R. Robinson (Paris: Pauvert, 1965).
6. M. Valentine, *Arthur Machen* (Bridgend: Poetry Wales Press, 1995), p. 18.
7. S. Arata, *Fictions of Loss in the Victorian Fin de Siècle* (Cambridge: Cambridge University Press, 1996); W. Greenslade, *Degeneration, Culture and the Novel, 1880–1940* (Cambridge, Cambridge University Press, 1994); K. Hurley, *The Gothic Body: Sexuality, Materialism and Degeneration at the Fin de Siècle* (Cambridge: Cambridge University Press, 1996); and M. Nordau, *Degeneration*, second edition (London: Heinemann, 1898).
8. A Machen, *The Three Imposters and Other Stories*, ed. S. T. Joshi (Oakland, CA: Chaosium, 2000), p. 203. Page number prefaced by *TTI* hereafter in the text.

9. Hurley, *The Gothic Body,* p. 144.
10. J-K. Huysmans, *The Damned [Là-Bas],* trans. Terry Hale (Harmondsworth: Penguin Books, 2001), pp. 143 and 146. Page numbers hereafter in the text prefaced by *LB*.
11. W. Kayser, *The Grotesque in Art and Literature* (New York: Columbia University Press 1957), pp. 19–22; and G. Harpham, *On the Grotesque: Strategies of Contradiction in Art and Literature* (Princeton, NJ: Princeton University Press, 1982), pp. 48–76.
12. Kayser, *The Grotesque in Art and Literature,* pp. 26–7.
13. Kayser, *The Grotesque in Art and Literature,* pp. 48–81.
14. G. Hoffmann, *Tales of Hoffmann,* trans. S. Humphries, V. Humphries and R. J. Hollindale (Harmondsworth: Penguin Books, 1982), pp. 85–125.
15. V. Hugo, *Cromwell,* ed. A. Ubersfeld (Paris: Garnier Flammarion, 1986), pp. 61–109.
16. Hugo, *Cromwell,* pp. 78–9, my translation.
17. V. Hugo, *Notre Dame de Paris,* ed. A. Krailsheimer (Oxford: Oxford University Press, 1993), pp. 275, 262, 249 et passim.
18. J. Ruskin, *Complete Works of John Ruskin,* Library Edition, ed. E. T. Cook and A. Wedderburn, 35 volumes (1905–12), 11, p. 158.
19. Ruskin, *Complete Works,* 11, p. 181.
20. M. Proust, *Against Sainte-Beuve and Other Essays,* trans. J. Sturrock (Harmondsworth: Penguin Books, 1988), p. 109.
21. L. Dowling, *Language and Decadence in the Victorian Fin de Siècle* (Princeton, NJ: Princeton University Press, 1982), pp. 56ff.
22. I. Calvino, *Fantastic Tales: Visionary and Everyday* (New York: Vintage, 1997), pp. 389–93.
23. Harpham, *On the Grotesque: Strategies of Contradiction in Art and Literature,* p. 3.
24. T. Todorov, *Poétique* (Paris: Éditions du Sueil, 1973), p. 21.
25. J-K. Huysmans, *The Damned (Là-Bas),* trans. Terry Hale (Harmondsworth: Penguin Books, 2001), p. 18.
26. Hugo, *Cromwell,* p. 78.
27. T. S. Eliot, *Selected Essays* (London: Faber, 1991), p. 421.
28. See L. Braun, *De l'alchiemie/Paracelse* (Strasbourg: Presses Universitaires de Strasbourg, 2000); and A. Roob, *Alchemy and Mysticism: The Hermetic Museum* (London: Taschen, 2001).
29. Valentine, *Arthur Machen,* pp. 77–8.
30. A. Machen, *Hieroglyphics* (London: Grant Richards, 1902), p. 126.
31. G. Shaw, *Theurgy and the Soul: The Neoplatonism of Iamblichus* (University Park, PA: Pennsylvania University Press, 1995), pp. 21–58.
32. Machen, *Hieroglyphics,* p. 125.
33. M. Bakhtin, *Rabelais and His World,* trans. H. Iswolsky (Bloomington, IN: Indiana University Press, 1984), p. 312.
34. Bakhtin, *Rabelais and His World,* p. 313.
35. Machen, *Hieroglyphics,* p. 127.
36. A. Nasier (1904) *The Three Imposters,* http://www.infidels.org/library/historical/unknown/three_imposters.html. Accessed 2 September 2006.
37. J. Joyce, *Finnegans Wake,* intro. S. Deane (Harmondsworth: Penguin Books, 1992), p. 3.

References

Arata, S., *Fictions of Loss in the Victorian Fin de Siècle* (Cambridge: Cambridge University Press, 1996).

Bataille, G., *The Trial of Gilles de Rais*, trans. R. Robinson (Paris: Pauvert, 1965).

Dowling, L., *Language and Decadence in the Victorian Fin de Siècle* (Princeton, NJ: Princeton University Press, 1982).

Greenslade, W., *Degeneration, Culture and the Novel, 1880–1940* (Cambridge: Cambridge University Press, 1994).

Hale, Terry, 'Translation in Distress: Cultural Misappropriation and the Construction of the Gothic', in A. Horner (ed.), *European Gothic: A Spirited Exchange 1760–1960* (Manchester: Manchester University Press, 2002), pp. 17–38.

Harpham, G., *On the Grotesque: Strategies of Contradiction in Art and Literature* (Princeton, NJ: Princeton University Press, 1982).

Hugo, V., *Notre Dame de Paris*, ed. A. Krailsheimer (Oxford: Oxford University Press, 1993).

—— *Cromwell*, ed. A. Ubersfeld (Paris: Garnier Flammarion, 1986).

Hurley, K., *The Gothic Body: Sexuality, Materialism and Degeneration at the Fin de Siècle* (Cambridge: Cambridge University Press, 1996).

Huysmans, J-K., *The Damned (Là-Bas)*, trans. Terry Hale (Harmondsworth: Penguin Books, 2001).

—— *Là-Bas* (Paris: Plon et Nourrit, c. 1939).

—— *Against Nature (A Rebours)*, trans. R. Baldick, intro. P. McGuinness (Harmondsworth: Penguin Books, 2003).

D'Isle-Adam, A. V., 'The Very Image', in I. Calvino (ed.), *Fantastic Tales: Visionary and Everyday* (New York: Vintage, 1997).

Journand-Bautry, R. and Perrin, J-F., *Le Conte Merveilleux au XVIIIe Siècle: une poétique expérimentale* (Paris: Kimé, 2002).

Joyce, J., *Finnegans Wake*, intro. S. Deane (Harmondsworth: Penguin Books, 1992).

Kayser, W., *The Grotesque in Art and Literature* (New York: Columbia University Press, 1957).

Machen, A., *The Three Imposters and Other Stories*, ed. S. T. Joshi (Oakland, CA: Chaosium, 2000).

—— *Hieroglyphics* (London: Grant Richards, 1902).

Mauss, M and Hubert, H., *Sacrifice: Its Nature and Functions*, trans. W. Hall (1964; Chicago: Chicago University Press, 1981).

Nasier, A. *The Three Imposters* (1904), http://www.infidels.org/library/historical/ unknown/three_imposters.html. Accessed 2 September 2006.

Nordau, M., *Degeneration*, second edition (London: Heinemann, 1898).

Proust, M., *Against Sainte-Beuve and Other Essays*, trans. J. Sturrock (Harmondsworth: Penguin Books, 1988).

Quinn, P., *The French Face of Edgar Poe* (Carbondale, IL: South Illinois University Press, 1957).

Retinger, J-H. *Le Conte fantastique dans le romanticisme français* (Paris: B. Grasset, 1909).

Ruskin, J., *Complete Works of John Ruskin*, Library Edition, ed. E. T. Cook and A. Wedderburn, 35 volumes (1905–12).

de Sade, D. A. Marquis, 'Idée sur les romans' (extract), in V. Sage (ed.), *The Gothick Novel: A Casebook* (Basingstoke: Macmillan, 1990), pp. 48–9.

Shaw, G., *Theurgy and the Soul: The Neoplatonism of Iamblichus* (University Park, PA: Pennsylvania University Press, 1995).

Valentine, M., *Arthur Machen* (Bridgend: Poetry Wales Press, 1995).

Wilde, O., *The Picture of Dorian Gray*, ed. D. Lawyer (New York: Norton, 1988).

7
Gothic Permutations from the 1790s to the 1970s: Rethinking the Marquis de Sade's Legacy

Maria Vara

It is now received wisdom that the machinery of the Gothic novels written in the 1790s by authors such as Ann Radcliffe and Matthew Lewis gradually evolved into a recyclable set of images, motifs and narrative devices that surpass temporal, spatial and generic categories. Recent literary criticism has reconfigured the Gothic spectrum both synchronically – by acknowledging its influence on numerous postmodern fictions – and diachronically – by rescripting, in hindsight, the history of the Gothic canon to allow space for ambiguous presences such as that of the Marquis de Sade.

De Sade's association with the Gothic has, however, been treated in a rather perfunctory manner, critical commentary on the issue usually limited to citing epigrammatically de Sade's own thoughts on the Gothic. This chapter focuses instead on the narrative strategies in *Justine, or Good Conduct Well Chastised* (1791) in order to explore more fully the link between de Sade and Gothic fiction. It will also touch on the narrative methods employed in *Justine*'s various rewrites – especially those produced by British and American women writers in the 1970s.

Justine, de Sade's notorious protagonist, might exhibit some crucial differences from those prototypical 'virtuous' heroines of Radcliffe, but she does share their passivity – as do many female characters who appear in 1970s Gothic texts written by women. While fusing detective and fairy tale elements, a number of these novels and short stories utilize the Gothic narrative potential of Justine to chart issues of gender politics. I shall examine French, American and British texts from two historical moments when notions about gender in the Western world were drastically changing.[1] In so doing, I hope to show how the Gothic novel's topography forms and reforms itself by sly exchanges and interactions across time and space.

'The shadow of the divine marquis'

From being an unmentioned outcast during the nineteenth century, de Sade came to literary prominence during the twentieth century. Scholars from diverse disciplines, such as Beauvoir, Queneau, Camus, Bataille, Klossowsky, Adorno, Horkheimer, Blancot, Sollers, Lacan, Barthes, Foucault, Deleuze, Carter and many others, positioned de Sade solidly within the literary canon, thereby initiating an ongoing discussion concerning the narratological, socio-political, ideological and aesthetic aspects of his *oeuvre*. In spite of this, however, as the authors of a recent introduction to de Sade's narrative put it, 'his intellectual legacy has hardly been resolved'.[2] Both transgressive and hybrid in form and content,[3] the Sadean *oeuvre* emerged at a moment in history when the Gothic – as defined by the works of Radcliffe and Lewis – was beginning to acquire momentum. Yet until recently the two have been kept separate in the realm of literary criticism; from the late twentieth century, however, the Gothic has been accepted as a malleable genre, flexible enough to contain, in Borgesian fashion, some problematic precursors. Furthermore, de Sade's novels – which have resisted categorization within movements (such as surrealism) or discourses (such as psychoanalysis) now need re-reading in the light of postmodernity's theories of subjectivity. Thus, claims for the notorious marquis's ambivalent affiliation with the Gothic novel have been made only comparatively recently. With the exception of two articles, such claims have, however, connected de Sade and the Gothic adventitiously, not intrinsically.[4] For example, when C. Anderson cites de Sade as one of the 'father-figures' of the Gothic,[5] she does not elaborate but instead, with a footnote, directs the reader to an article by B. Neumeier,[6] which supposedly gives more information. There, too, the reference to de Sade is equally short and vague: he is cited together with E. T. A. Hoffmann and E. A. Poe as a father-figure of Gothicism, the term explained in relation to Angela Carter's work as 'a blend of fairy-tale and pornography' that 'most obviously shows the replacement of the ontological by the iconographic'.[7] This rather cursory treatment of de Sade is surprising, given Mario Praz's argument in *The Romantic Agony* as early as 1933 that Lewis, Radcliffe and de Sade belong to 'the same mental climate, that climate which ... produced so many incarnations of the theme of the persecuted maiden'.[8]

Praz describes his book, *The Romantic Agony*, as 'a study of Romantic literature ... under one of its most characteristic aspects, that of erotic sensibility' and his reason for dealing with de Sade is the fact that he was 'a sinister force in the Romantic Movement'.[9] Sinister forces are, in fact, dominant in most of Praz's chapters, including 'The Beauty of the Medusa', 'Metamorphoses of Satan', 'La Belle Dame Sans Merci', 'Byzantium', 'Swinburne and "Le Vice Anglais"'. But my interest is in the chapter called 'The Shadow of the Divine Marquis', the ramifications of which reach far beyond Romantic literature. In attempting to investigate the (medieval) origins of the romantic trope of the persecuted maiden, Praz, somewhat unintentionally, placed de Sade within the realm of the Gothic. Richardson, in creating Clarissa Harlow, is perceived by Praz to have first 'refurbished' the theme in the eighteenth century with an innocent girl, 'a pitiful little lamb among greedy wolves', who faces a cruel fate in a novel that uses pietism as a veneer to cover its 'sensual, turbid background'.[10] Richardson's use of a shallow moralism, an aspect of the dominant materialist philosophy of the times, had its imitators in France, Praz postulates, 'who sought in the subject of the persecuted woman chiefly an excuse for situations of heightened sensuality'. Diderot's *La Religieuse* is seen by Praz as an 'anticipation of *Justine*' because the heroine's virtue is highlighted only to 'add a sharper spice to the cruelty of her persecution'.[11] For Praz, de Sade (like Diderot) is also an exponent of materialism, in the sense that he 'moves in an opaque atmosphere of mere matter,in which his characters are degraded to the status of instruments for provoking the so-called divine ecstasy of destruction'.[12] Praz concludes these observations by claiming that 'the butcheries of Sade are hardly different from experiments in a chemical laboratory'.[13]

Obviously, Praz is resisting here the contemporary favourable reaction by the Surrealists to de Sade's writing.[14] However, Praz goes on to recognize de Sade's 'influence on a whole century of literature' in the sense that 'the success of the persecuted beauty as a subject in the novel of the eighteenth century owes more to the motives which dictated the work of the Divine Marquis than to those which caused Richardson to write *Clarissa*'.[15] So, de Sade's novels become for Praz an indispensable tool for tracing the origins of and the reasons for the success of the maiden-in-flight as romantic figure, which is also a key motif in the Gothic. The word Gothic is never mentioned, but the references to 'tales of terror' or to 'horror' and 'horrifying stories' clearly demarcate the Gothic topography.

Recent critical commentary on the issue, as I have noted, usually limits itself to referring to de Sade's thoughts on the Gothic novel – called by de Sade the novel of 'sorcery and phantasmagoria' – that are expressed in his preface to *Les Crimes de l'amour*, entitled 'Idée sur les romans' ('Reflections on the Novel'),[16] written in 1800:

> Let us concur that this kind of fiction, whatever one may think of it, is assuredly not without merit: twas the inevitable result of the revolutionary shocks which all of Europe has suffered. For anyone familiar with the full range of misfortunes wherewith evildoers can beset mankind, the novel became as difficult to write as monotonous to read. There was not a man alive who had not experienced in the short span of four or five years more misfortunes than the most celebrated novelist could portray in a century. Thus, to compose works of interest, one had to call upon the aid of hell itself, and to find in the world of make-believe things wherewith one was fully familiar merely by delving into man's daily life in this age of iron.[17]

The epigrammatic power of this work's most renowned phrase – that the rise of the Gothic 'was the inevitable result of the revolutionary shocks which all of Europe has suffered' – has, as Victor Sage postulates, 'proved highly influential in later critical debate, marking a tradition of linking the Gothic novel with the French Revolution'.[18] In other words, it has become a critical commonplace that the political events of the eighteenth century gave the Gothic a new importance. De Sade's expression, because of its very power and insight, may have worked as a barrier and obscured any further reflection on the relation between his novels and the Gothic.

Here it is worth remembering that although *Justine* is often spoken of as a single text, there are several editions of the story. The novel was first composed in 1787 as *Justine ou les Infortunes de la vertu* (*Justine or the Misfortunes of Virtue*), a 200-page 'philosophical tale', as the author describes it, a first version of the novel that was eventually published as late as 1930, with Maurice Heine as editor. In de Sade's time two other version appeared: in 1791 the novel-length *Justine ou les Malheurs de la vertu* (*Justine, or Good Conduct Well Chastised*) was published, followed in 1797 by *La nouvelle Justine ou les Malheurs de la vertu* (*The New Justine*) which, with further additions, became a huge, ten-volume edition. The first two versions are first-person narratives. The second of these is much longer than the first, and 'more violent and sexually explicit';[19] in it Justine retrospectively narrates her own story, albeit entrapped within the narrative frame of a voyeuristic narrator. Unlike the third version which, according to Angela Wright, 'is not a Gothic novel' as it portrays a third-person narrator who 'makes us entirely complicit in his mockery of Justine',[20] the second version – upon which my own analysis is based – upholds both the genre's stock features (dark, enclosed spaces, a maiden fleeing her predators) and an invisible, but intense, preoccupation with power, all of which allow the reader to locate it firmly within the genre of the Gothic.

Justine,[21] or narrating against the aesthetics of the Enlightenment

Foucault, in his seminal essay 'Language to Infinity', has maintained that de Sade's attempt to 'tell all is not simply that of breaking prohibitions, but of seeking the limits of the possible'.[22] As Donald F. Bouchard explains, de Sade, together with Flaubert and Nietzsche, figured 'that it is no longer the sleep of reason which breeds monsters ... but the attentiveness of scholarship, an insomniac knowledge, and the gray patience of genealogy'.[23] In other words, the so-called Age of Reason (when 'abstraction' became a leading doctrine, 'the number became the canon' and 'mathematical procedure became, so to speak, the ritual of thinking'),[24] with its totalizing systematization of thought, is taken by de Sade to its extreme limit, and is shown to be self-destructive. De Sade draws on the materialist philosophers of the Enlightenment, but at the same time extends this very philosophy, Phillips contends, 'to its logical extreme'.[25] This is evident in his notorious novel *Les 120 Journées de Sodome* (*120 Days of Sodom*), where the manic preoccupation with symmetry and numbers leads to an unprecedented cataloguing of all known sexual perversions. It also results in de Sade's impatience with the limitations of neoclassical taste and in the creation of Justine, who evolves into a counter-Enlightenment Gothic trope which proliferates down the centuries.

The eighteenth-century passion with encyclopaedias, the attempt to 'tell all', is pushed in *Justine* to its limits and finally exploded by the employment of narrative techniques that flout the rules laid out by the classical Gothic fiction of the time. For example, by the time *Justine* was published in France, Ann Radcliffe, in her novel *A Sicilian Romance*, published a year earlier in England (1791), had already introduced and established the 'explained supernatural' as a highly recognizable narrative device whereby all supernatural events are eventually given a rational explanation. The notorious marquis displayed familiarity with the evolution of Gothic fiction in England by claiming that Matthew

Lewis's *The Monk* 'is superior in all respects to the strange flights of Mrs. Radcliffe's brilliant imagination'.[26] Despite de Sade's preference for Lewis's labyrinthine, chaotic and self-reflexive plot games over Radcliffe's more subdued narratives, it is with her novels that his *oeuvre* shares rather similar plot motifs.[27] The simplicity of the narrative and the portrayal of a passive central heroine whose 'virtue' is in 'distress' make *The Mysteries of Udolpho* (1794) an exemplary paradigm for the reader to grasp how de Sade's delineation of the virtuous heroine departs from the classical line and initiates a new type of heroine-centred Gothic text.

The plot in *The Mysteries of Udolpho* follows the simple narrative line of the misfortunes of Emily, whose goodness finally triumphs over evil, drawing the novel to a straightforward moral close. Radcliffe's dexterity in using suspense is evident when the novel's dark figures who loom so large are finally revealed as projections of Emily's state of mind and excess of sensibility. Emily's happy union with Valancourt (the lover necessary to propel the story forward) needs to be forestalled for narrative convenience until the very end as a reward for all her hardships and misfortunes; alongside this main narrative there exists a coherent alternative subtext reinforcing enlightenment values. According to Clery:

> the course of narration echoes the history of enlightenment itself. The reader progressively moves from the sense of mystery that encourages fearful, false ideas to the full knowledge of the facts, intelligibility of causes, means and ends, and confirmation of the truth of reason: in other words, reliving the passage from gothic to modern times, a process here invested with a pleasurable blend of relaxation and control, licence and restraint.[28]

Unlike the 1790s Radcliffean Gothic, Sadean transgression does not end by offering a solid sense of identity or by restoring morality and a social order that confirms the power of reason and sustains eighteenth-century enlightenment values. Holland and Sherman, who refer to rationality as the 'counter-Gothic', have argued that de Sade's texts belong to the realm of the 'ultra-Gothic'. Unlike Poe's use of rational explanations to 'balance off and limit the horror of his various burnings alive', de Sade 'goes beyond the suspense and mystery to carry out those terrible mysterious urges in full view of the literent [*sic*]'.[29] I would argue that the same relationship exists between the Radcliffean and the Sadean text. *Justine or Good Conduct Well Chastised* features

Justine's stubborn and meaningless adherence to virtue, contrary to what takes place in the classical Gothic, which presents a heroine who is finally compensated in the narrative for her good conduct. The manic attempt of de Sade to expose his heroine to all the possible dangers and sexual acts that Radcliffe's texts frequently suggest but never actually portray[30] can be read as an 'ultra-Gothic' structure that parodies the whole ideology of the enlightenment.

Justine begins in a relatively common eighteenth-century manner whereby an authoritative narrative voice ponders the objective of philosophy. The reader is soon presented with two orphans whose juxtaposition is immediately posited: Juliette's 'artifice, artifice, wiles' prepare the reader for a vicious character and throw Justine's perfection – 'large blue eyes very soulful and appealing, a dazzling fair skin, a supple and resilient body, a touching voice, teeth of ivory and the loveliest blond hair' – into sharp contrast (*Justine*, p. 459). The novel opens at the point when Justine, on her way to her execution for crimes she has not committed, retrospectively recounts the story of her life to a rich lady, who miraculously proves to be her sister Juliette:

> 'To recount you the story of my life Madame' this lovely one in distress said to the Countess, 'is to offer you the most striking example of innocence oppressed, is to accuse the hand of Heaven, is to bear complaint against the Supreme Being's will, is, in a sense, to rebel against His sacred designs...I dare not...' tears gathered in this interesting girl's eyes and, after having given vent to them for a moment, she began her recitation in these terms ... (*Justine*, p. 468)

Here Justine – an 'ambiguous victim, endowed with narrative speech' according to Roland Barthes[31] – evidently complies, through her posture, with a voyeuristic (pornographic) code that places emphasis on her 'loveliness' and 'innocence'. However, her suggestion that the 'hand of Heaven' would have opposed her complaint against her abuse invalidates any comforting Enlightenment narrative: here de Sade takes his mocking conflation of God and the oppressive sadist patriarch to its limit. Moreover, when the narrator calls Justine 'lovely one in distress' – an idea indebted to Edmund Burke's 'beauty in distress' proposition in *A Philosophical Enquiry into the Origin of Our Ideas of the Sublime and the Beautiful* (1757) – an echo of the classical Gothic version of 'virtue in distress' is introduced. According to *The Handbook of Gothic Literature*, in his depiction of 'virtue in distress' the marquis, 'a marginal figure in the Gothic tradition', seems 'to subscribe to the conventions of Gothic writing'.[32] In the classic Gothic, however, the presentation of a 'distressed' heroine aims at arousing sympathy on the part of the other characters and the reader. Conversely, in *Justine* this idea is carried to its logical (pornographic) limits when it actually arouses not pity but the villain's erotic desire, as Justine confesses later on in the novel:

> The violence of my movements had disturbed what veiled my breast, it was naked, my dishevelled hair fell in cascades upon it, it was wetted thoroughly by my tears; I quickened desires in the dishonest man. (*Justine*, p. 720)

Similar episodes appear several times, but this is not to claim that de Sade's text defiantly ignores, without blanching, the codes of virtue; the codes are there, through Justine's unflinching expectations that her condition will ultimately procure her the sympathy of others. This somewhat excessive depiction of 'virtue in distress' signifies a relentless refusal on the part of the text to allow sentimental pampering of both the heroine and the reader. As the narration proceeds, the reader discovers that the common eighteenth-century tradition of instability and incongruities in narrative technique (such as abrupt interchanges between present and past tense) are compounded by the fact that there is no reward, no moral triumph to Justine's misfortune.

Justine's obstinate devotion to virtue, her inability to suspect the abuse that awaits her, her persistence in looking for the good in people despite her numerous hardships, has been interpreted as exposing the innocent and virtuous Gothic heroine's hypocrisy.[33] When Justine takes innocence to such an extreme she also exasperates the reader, who becomes impatient with an excess of purity and goodness that seems to verge on folly.[34] The experience of reading is one of struggling with readerly resistance and the atmosphere of horror is constantly renounced and replaced by a feeling of excessive claustrophobia; this prefigures postmodern reappropriations of the genre to be found in work by authors such as Muriel Spark and Patricia Highsmith in which all sense of mystery is deviously drained away.

Thus de Sade disrupts the passive reading experience of Gothic, whereby we succumb to the enchantment of the image of the 'maiden in flight'. By blatantly refusing the reading pleasures classic Gothic depends on, *Justine* can be seen as a *writerly* text of *bliss* (to borrow

Barthes' terminology in *S/Z*),[35] one which discomforts and demands an active labour of reading. The exhausting (for the reader) recurrence of similar episodes that mirror each other *ad infinitum* as *mises en abyme* of the whole novel is brought to an end by the lightning that strikes Justine so that, finally, contingency triumphs over any stock happy resolution. The novel does not offer a climactic point that would have confined Justine within an ethical frame, within an economy of crime and retribution. Because the plot line of the novel resembles that of an ancient Greek tragedy (in the sense that, as readers, we know more than Justine, who mistakenly perceives herself as a free adventurer), we cannot indulge in borrowing her stubbornly innocent eyes or in seeing her as a tragic heroine. Catharsis is precluded by this abrupt ending.[36]

Justine becomes 'a gratuitous victim' as Angela Carter has explained in *The Sadeian Woman*,[37] because she exhibits a pose of defencelessness that is not compensated for 'by a convention of respect which is largely false'.[38] Thus, in reading de Sade's *Justine*, we are in the realm of the dismantling of myths, Carter asserts. The 'illusory metaphysic' of the 'perfect woman'[39] that commands Justine's 'expectation of reverence' is deflated by de Sade, when Justine's obstinate adherence to virtue is mercilessly 'well chastised', despite her hope that it 'will procure her some reward, some respite from the bleak and intransigent reality which surrounds her and to which she cannot accommodate herself'.[40] All 'mythic versions of women' are suspect for Carter, even those of the blameless and morally superior victim, a cultural construction that, she believes, the notorious marquis exposes as yet another 'consolatory nonsense' for women's 'lack of access to the modes of intellectual debate'.[41]

The legacy of the 1970s

The slippery narrative pattern de Sade adopts in *Justine* deprives the reader of both sublimity and escapism. But this reading experience of excess is arguably what renders the text so novel. Foucault included Radcliffe among the 'initiators of discursive practices' because her novels 'put into circulation a certain number of resemblances and analogies patterned on her work – various characteristic signs, figures, relationships and structures that could be integrated into other books'.[42] This is the point where de Sade's and Radcliffe's contributions to the literary realm converge. Angela Carter was the first to discern that the influence of the Sadean text reaches far beyond the literary realm that Praz had demarcated and that it extends into 1970s novels of paranoia and Gothic intensity, such as Judith Rossner's *Looking for Mr Goodbar*:

> There is presumably no direct literary influence from the eighteenth-century philosophical pornographer to these contemporary women novelists; but in the character of Justine, Sade contrived to isolate the dilemma of an emergent type of woman. Justine, daughter of a banker, becomes the prototype of two centuries of women who find the world was not, as they had been promised, made for them and who do not have, because they had not been given, the existential tools to remake the world for themselves. These self-conscious blameless ones suffer and suffer until it becomes second nature.[43]

Taking up Carter's argument as a cue, one can traverse from a different angle a number of controversial novels from the 1970s which portrayed heretical Gothic heroines and which adopted an amoral, anti-essentialist stance in relation to the clearly demarcated feminist imperatives of the time. In a period when cultural feminism demanded texts that presented women as privileged subjects, the titles of Joyce Carol Oates' *Do with me What you will* (1973), or Patricia Highsmith's collection of short stories entitled *Little Tales of Misogyny* (1977) suggested heresy; they seemed to shrug off feminist expectations, while their protagonists formed an array of contemporary monstrous Justines who pushed to extremes the roles allotted to them.

For example, N. Hexam, the scared protagonist in Diane Johnson's *The Shadow Knows* (1974),[44] is another avatar of Justine. Almost thirty, divorced and abandoned by her lover, N. complies externally with the Sadean stereotype of fair, vulnerable beauty – 'Outside I am a round faced little woman with golden curls and round blue eyes, with round breasts and toes' (*The Shadow*, 8) – and writes in daily instalments about her fear of being murdered. Like the Gothic heroine, she flees her persecutor. However, she is finally raped, an experience which leaves her disturbingly satisfied. We meet N. at the point when she is in the process of losing herself through fear, which allows her a new vantage point on her own marginality, a point of view behind the scenes of the legal and social fictions that have positioned her among the powerless and the morally degenerate N.'s narrative is constantly undercut by a sub-plot of imaginary encounters with a Famous

Inspector, whom she visualizes summoning her after her death when, as a consenting corpse, she will be stretched out under his dissecting gaze:

> I can hear the mellifluous tones of some Famous Inspector instructing his flock – here my children here in this corpse you see the embodied, or rather, the disembodied perils of erotic self-indulgence and wilfulness. A person cannot do just what he wants. (*The Shadow*, p. 93)

N. here envisages her imminent future in a way that encapsulates the mechanics of the social and legal discourses inscribed on her body that mark her as a wayward woman. These make her wonder 'if someone is trying to kill you, do you maybe deserve it?'(*The Shadow*, 160), a question that disturbingly articulates the idea that the victim might be *asking for it* when a criminal act occurs. She is finally attacked and raped by somebody she cannot see and therefore cannot recognize. After the rape, N postulates:

> But I couldn't see him; he could have been anybody. ... I was shaking with terror and amazement, and also with a strange elation. ... I don't know. I felt happy. ... Most likely it was some madman neighbor who has been lustfully watching us all along, unknown to us. It could even have been the Famous Inspector.... Perhaps it doesn't matter at all. (*The Shadow*, p. 276)

This extract suggests why *The Shadow Knows* is not usually regarded as a progressive novel in terms of gender politics (and why it invited attacks by feminists). But it is the economy of punishment that N. subtly upsets here. Once again we are in the sphere of Justine's legacy, the dismantling of myths, and N. is *in the know* in this respect. Although N. has no choice but to experience her existence as a marginal occurrence, what differentiates her from Justine is *knowing* what this bleak situation entails. Unlike Justine, though, who, as Carter has suggested, is blind to the fact that 'her poverty, her weakness, her femaleness, her goodness put her on the wrong side of the law' (*The Sadeian Woman*, p. 41), N. knows the story in advance, knows the disciplinary logic concerning wanton women who supposedly deserve such a fate. If all is seen in advance, then being aware of the scheme written *for* her and *on* her body, gives her a kind of *amoral* advantage. To struggle against the feeling of elation at finally becoming what she already knew she would become, a victim, would have been absurd, would have endowed her with a false sense of hope, a sham roundness of character. After the rape N. takes on 'the thinness and the lightness of a shadow' (*The Shadow*, p. 277), turning into a non-character, with the reader's expectations for closure also renounced and replaced by a reading exuberance when the roles of victim and criminal end up as interchangeable (as in Borges, Pynchon, Eco, Spark). Lise, in Muriel Spark's *The Driver's Seat*,[45] is another character through whom contingency prevails at the expense of a linear, cause-and-effect plot. Lise seeks death, not a lover, in a chilling Gothic twist of the holiday romance plot. She is literally *asking for it*, asking for death, in a grotesque inversion of the terrified woman, a trope that is here reprocessed and emptied of its tragic dignity.

More aware of their precarious and culturally defined status as victims, these heroines can see their strings being pulled by others, and can recognize the intentions of their adversaries. The main difference between de Sade's Justine and these rewritings resides in a shift of narrative dynamic that results in the heroines' knowledge of their victim status. Most female characters in these novels know that they represent the idealization of femininity. Unlike Justine, they *know* that '[t]o exist in the passive case is to die in the passive case – that is to be killed. This is the moral of the fairy tale about the perfect woman' (*The Sadeian Woman*, p. 77). This amoral advantage deprives them of their traditional heroine status, but also asserts the importance of dismantling myths, making us see more clearly Justine's legacy as encapsulated in Carter's claim that de Sade 'treats the facts of female sexuality not as a moral dilemma but as a political reality' (*The Sadeian Woman*, p. 27).

The Gothic, then, in its postmodern reconfiguration, has acquired a permeability of tropes and images that can be found scattered as a driving force behind much contemporary work. The exchanges and interactions between the 1790s Sadean tropes and 1970s Gothic texts by women might thus help us rethink the tensions inherent within the genre and grant it the elasticity it always entailed.

Acknowledgements

I am grateful to Professor Ruth Parkin-Gounelas for help in compiling the bibliography and for obtaining certain articles for me. I am also grateful to the editors of this collection for providing help beyond the common call of editorial duty.

Notes

1. For changes in 1790s notions on gender, see Clery's insightful account of the correlations between gender issues and the circularization of books in libraries (E. J. Clery, *The Rise of Supernatural Fiction, 1762–1800* [Cambridge: Cambridge University Press, 1995] and Hoeveler, who informs us that 'notions about gender in Western Europe radically altered sometime during the middle to late eighteenth century'. D. L. Hoeveler, *Gothic Feminism: The Professionalization of Gender from Charlotte Smith to the Brontës* [Pennsylvania: Pennsylvania State University Press, 1998], p. 245). The fact that the emergence of Second Wave feminism in the1970s also resulted in challenges to traditional concepts of gender is clearly beyond dispute.

2. D. Allison, M. Roberts and A. Weiss, 'Introduction', in *Sade and the Narrative of Transgression*, ed. D. Allison, M. Roberts and A. Weiss (Cambridge: Cambridge University Press, 1995), p. 6.

3. According to Allison, Roberts and Weiss, de Sade's texts are 'located between the various traditions of eighteenth-century thought (libertine tracts, materialist philosophy, anti-clerical pamphlets, political writing, the nascent roman noir, as well as the more traditional French theatrical works)'. *Sade and the Narrative of Transgression*, p. 11.

4. See E. J. Clery, 'Ann Radcliffe and D. A. F. de Sade: Thoughts on Heroinism', *Women's Writing* 1:2 (1994), 203–14; and A. Wright, 'European Disruptions of the Idealized Woman: Matthew Lewis's *The Monk* and the Marquis de Sade's *La Nouvelle Justine*', in A. Horner, ed., *European Gothic*, pp. 39–54. (Wright also reminds us of French criticism on the connection between de Sade and the Gothic by citing two articles, M. Heine, 'Le Marquis de Sade et le roman noir' and B. Didier, 'Sade: Une écriture du désir', both written in the 1970s but not translated into English.)

5. C. Anderson, 'Emma Tennant, Elspeth Barker, Alice Thompson: Gothic Revisited', in A. Christianson and A. Lumsden, eds,*Contemporary Scottish Women Writers* (Edinburgh: Edinburgh University Press, 2000) pp. 117–30.

6. B. Neumeier, 'Postmodern Gothic: Desire and Reality in Angela Carter's Writing', in V. Sage and A. L. Smith, eds, *Modern Gothic: A Reader* (Manchester: Manchester University Press, 1996), pp. 141–51.

7. Neumeier, 'Postmodern Gothic', p. 149.

8. M. Praz, *The Romantic Agony* (1933; Oxford: Oxford University Press, 1970), p. 174.

9. Praz, *The Romantic Agony*, pp. xiv and xviii.

10. Praz, *The Romantic Agony*, p. 98.

11. Praz, *The Romantic Agony*, p. 99.

12. Praz, *The Romantic Agony*, p.106.

13. Praz, *The Romantic Agony*, p. 107. In drawing a parallel between a chemical laboratory and the Sadean narrative, Praz acknowledges the existence of 'system' in de Sade – a notion that obsessed the Enlightenment – but also suggests repetition, regularity and detachment, concepts that foreshadow later critical observations which characterize de Sade's *oeuvre* as 'de-eroticized' in the sense that it 'moves the focus away from sexual desire to writing and discourse' because it seeks to convince rather than to seduce (J. Phillips, *Sade: The Libertine Novels* [London: Pluto Press, 2001], p. 56).

14. At the time when Praz published his study, as Allison, Robert and Weiss inform us, de Sade was being rediscovered by the Surrealists, having received hardly any acclaim in Europe during the previous century, when his name was 'stigmatized with a psychological reference to violence' (*Sade and the Narrative of Transgression*, p. 1) by medical scientists. The attitude towards de Sade changed when, at the dawn of the twentieth century, the publication by Maurice Heine of de Sade's works ignited the interest of Breton, Aragon, Eluard, Char and Peret who mythologized de Sade in an effort to upset bourgeois mentality and to acquire a forefather.

15. Praz, *The Romantic Agony*, p. 109.

16. My citations are from an English translation: D.A.F. de Sade, 'Reflections on the Novel', *The 120 Days of Sodom and Other Writings*, trans. Richard Seaver and Austryn Wainhouse (London: Arrow Books, 1991), pp. 97–116.

17. De Sade, 'Reflections on the Novel', pp. 108–9.

18. M. Mulvey-Roberts, ed., *The Handbook of Gothic Literature*, (Basingstoke: Macmillan, 1998), p. 83.

19. J. Phillips, *Sade: The Libertine Novels*. (London: Pluto Press, 2001), p. 87 (subsequent references appear in the text). On the issue of Justine's multiple editions, I have consulted the work of both J. Phillips and A. Wright.

20. Wright, 'European Disruptions of the Idealized Woman: Matthew Lewis's *The Monk* and the Marquis de Sade's *La Nouvelle Justine*', p. 50.

21. All subsequent quotations from *Justine* are from the anthology: D. A. F. de Sade, *Three Complete Novels: Justine, Philosophy in the Bedroom and Other Writings*, trans. R. Seaver and A. Wainhouse (London: Arrow Books, 1991). This book contains the second version of Justine: *Justine, or Good Conduct Well Chastised*. References will appear hereafter in parentheses in the text.

22. M. Foucault, 'Language to Infinity', in *Language, Counter-Memory, Practice: Selected Essays and Interviews*, ed. D. Bouchard, trans. D. Bouchard and S. Simon (Ithaca, NY: Cornell University Press, 1977), pp. 53–67, p. 61.

23. Bouchard, 'Introduction', *Language, Counter-Memory, Practice: Selected Essays and Interviews*, p. 18.

24. T. W. Adorno and M. Horkheimer, *Dialectic of Enlightenment* (New York: Continuum, 1989), pp. 13, 7 and 25.

25. J.Phillips, *Sade: The Libertine Novels* (London: Pluto Press, 2001), p. 23.

26. de Sade, 'Reflections on the Novel', p. 109.

27. E. J. Clery, in her essay 'Ann Radcliffe and D.A.F. de Sade: Thoughts on Heroinism', offers an illuminating account of how Radcliffe's *The Romance of the Forest* and de Sade's *Justine ou les Malheurs de la Vertu* (*Justine, or Good Conduct Well Chastised*) engage in a 'philosophical conversation' (p. 204). Radcliffe's staging of the triumph of sentimentalism is juxtaposed to de Sade's materialism, with the passive heroine being the ideal vehicle for the illustration of both enquiries.

28. Clery, *The Rise of Supernatural Fiction*, pp. 107–8.

29. N. Holland and L. F. Sherman, 'Gothic Possibilities', *New Literary History: A Journal of Theory and Interpretation*, 8:2 (1977), 279–94, p. 287.

30. In the classical Gothic there is always an imminent fear of rape of the heroine, but the word is never actually mentioned, nor is the heroine described as being explicitly aware of the nature of the looming threat.

31. R. Barthes, *Sade/Fourier/Loyola*, trans. R. Miller (London: Jonathan Cape, 1977), p. 31.
32. Mulvey-Roberts, ed., *The Handbook of Gothic Literature*, pp. 204–5.
33. According to D. L. Hoeveler, the Radcliffean heroine is a cultural construct (good, obedient, loving and passive) who plays the victim; this device allows the author to reveal at the end of the novel how or whether such behaviour has been rewarded. In *Gothic Feminism* Hoeveler briefly juxtaposes de Sade's texts with those of Radcliffe, claiming that 'at times *The Mysteries of Udolpho* reads as barely disguised pornography which the Marquis de Sade would later make explicit in his own tedious attempts to unmask the sexual hypocrisy of the Gothic heroine in *Justine* and *Juliette*' (p. 58).
34. There are numerous instances of such behaviour in *Justine*. Having, for example, just escaped from the savage surgeon Rodin, Justine naively seeks refuge in the Benedictine monastery, Saint Mary-in-the Wood, where, once more, as the reader suspects, she will be severely abused. When she first catches a glimpse of the monastery, her hope and goodwill are retained unscathed despite her former ill luck: '… ah! There must all virtues dwell, of that I am certain, and when mankind's crimes exile them out of the world, 'tis thither they go in that isolated place to commune with the souls of those fortunate ones who cherish them and cultivate them every day' (*Justine*, p. 559).
35. R. Barthes, *S/Z* (New York: Hill and Wang, 1974).
36. For further details on the Aristotelian concept of catharsis, see Dalia Judovitz, 'Sex, or the Misfortunes of Literature', in Allison, Roberts and Weiss, eds, *Sade and the Narrative of Transgression*, p. 173.
37. A. Carter, *The Sadeian Woman: An Exercise in Cultural History* (London: Virago, 1979), p. 39.
38. Carter, *The Sadeian Woman*, p. 73.
39. As Carter wryly observes: 'The virtuous, the interesting Justine with her incompetence, her gullibility, her whining, her frigidity, her reluctance to take control of her own life, is a perfect woman' (p. 55).
40. Carter, *The Sadeian Woman*, pp. 141, 72 and 54–5.
41. Carter, *The Sadeian Woman*, p. 5.
42. M. Foucault, 'What is an Author?', in *Language, Counter-Memory, Practice: Selected Essays and Interview*, pp. 114–38, pp. 131–2.
43. Carter, *The Sadeian Woman*, p. 57.
44. D. Johnson, *The Shadow Knows* (New York: Alfred Knopf, 1974). References appear hereafter in parentheses in the text.
45. M. Spark, *The Driver's Seat* (1970; Harmondsworth: Penguin Books, 1974).

References

Adorno, T. W. and M, Horkheimer, *Dialectic of Enlightenment* (New York: Continuum, 1989).
Allison, D., Roberts, M. and A. Weiss, eds, *Sade and the Narrative of Transgression* (Cambridge: Cambridge University Press, 1995).
Anderson, C., 'Emma Tennant, Elspeth Barker, Alice Thompson: Gothic Revisited', *Contemporary Scottish Women Writers*, ed. A. Christianson and A. Lumsden (Edinburgh: Edinburgh University Press, 2000), pp. 117–30.

Bathes, R., *Sade/Fourier/Loyola,* trans. R. Miller (London: Jonathan Cape, 1977).

Carter, A., *The Sadeian Woman: An Exercise in Cultural History* (London: Virago, 1979).

Clery, E. J., 'Ann Radcliffe and D. A. F. de Sade: Thoughts on Heroinism', *Women's Writing* 1:2 (1994) 203–14.

—— *The Rise of Supernatural Fiction, 1762–1800* (Cambridge: Cambridge University Press, 1995).

Foucault, M., 'Language to Infinity', *Language, Counter-Memory, Practice: Selected Essays and Interview.* ed. D. Bouchar, trans. D. Bouchard and S. Simon (Ithaca, Y: Cornell University Press, 1977), pp. 53–67.

—— 'What is an Author?', *Language, Counter-Memory, Practice: Selected Essays and Interviews*, ed. D. Bouchar, trans. D. Bouchard and S. Simon (Ithaca, NY: Cornell University Press, 1977), pp. 114–38.

Hoeveler, D. L., *Gothic Feminism: The Professionalization of Gender from Charlotte Smith to the Brontës* (Pennsylvania: Pennsylvania State University Press, 1998).

Holland N. and Sherman, L. F., 'Gothic Possibilities', *New Literary History: A Journal of Theory and Interpretation*, 8:2 (1977) 279–94.

Johnson, D., *The Shadow Knows* (New York: Alfred Knopf, 1974).

Mulvey-Roberts, M., ed., *The Handbook of Gothic Literature*, (Basingstoke: Macmillan, 1998).

Neumeier, B., 'Postmodern Gothic: Desire and Reality in Angela Carter's Writing', *Modern Gothic: A Reader*, ed. V. Sage and A. L. Smith (Manchester: Manchester University Press, 1996), pp. 141–51.

Phillips, J., *Sade: The Libertine Novels* (London: Pluto Press, 2001)

Praz, M., *The Romantic Agony* (1933; Oxford: Oxford University Press, 1970).

de Sade, D. A. F., 'Reflections on the Novel', *The 120 Days of Sodom and Other Writings*, trans. R. Seaver and A. Wainhouse (London: Arrow Books, 1991), pp. 97–116.

—— *Three Complete Novels: Justine, Philosophy in the Bedroom and Other Writings*, trans. R. Seaver and A. Wainhouse (London: Arrow Books, 1991).

Spark, M., *The Driver's Seat* (1970; Harmondsworth: Penguin Books, 1974).

Wright, A., 'European Disruptions of the Idealized Woman: Matthew Lewis's *The Monk* and the Marquis de Sade's *La Nouvelle Justine*', in A. Horner, ed., *European Gothic: A Spirited Exchange 1760–1960* (Manchester: Manchester University Press, 2002), pp. 39–54.

8
Dracula's Daughters: Angela Carter and Pierrette Fleutiaux's Vampiric Exchanges

Rebecca Munford

Vampiric voyages

The literary vampire is the Gothic voyager *par excellence*. From Lord Byron's *The Giaour* (1813) and Dr John William Polidori's *The Vampyre* (1819) to Charles Nodier's melodrama *Le Vampire* (1820), and from the Baudelairean *flâneur* feeding off the sights and sounds of the modern cityscape to Count Dracula's sea voyages to Victorian England, this liminal figure haunts the nineteenth-century Anglo-French literary imagination. Not only a subject of Gothic narrative, the vampire is also emblematic of its textual practices and processes. In the introduction to *European Gothic: A Spirited Exchange 1760–1960* (2002), Avril Horner foregrounds the voracious character of the Gothic novel as 'a vampire-like phenomenon that thrives on the blood of others'.[1] Focusing on the vital role of translation and the complex rhythms of cross-Channel exchange in its parasitical progression, the essays in Horner's collection overthrow the 'tyranny of Anglo-American narratives of the Gothic'[2] by unveiling both fictional and critical excesses and exclusions, and effecting an exploration of the genre in its neglected European lineage. If the genre's lineages and histories have been mapped largely along an Anglo-American axis, so too have they been delineated by the distinction drawn between 'male' and 'female' Gothic forms – a demarcation, albeit a contested one, that continues to cast its own tyrannical shadow over the history of Gothic endeavours. Redeploying the figure of the vampire as embody-ing the disruption and disempowerment of 'polarized systems of thought' and 'western logical tendencies to con-struct divisive, hierarchical, oppositional structures',[3] this chapter will explore the contributions of two women writers whose Gothic engagements traverse dominant boundaries of both nationality and gender: the British writer Angela Carter (1940–92) and the French writer Pierrette Fleutiaux (1941–).

Angela Carter's fiction sits uneasily in relation to both dominant Gothic conventions and feminist discourse, especially as they converge through the category of the 'female Gothic'. Owing to her interest in pornography and her engagement with the sexual and textual violence of specifically 'male Gothic' scripts – in particular the Gothic scenarios of the Marquis de Sade, Edgar Allan Poe, E. T. A. Hoffmann, Charles Baudelaire and Bram Stoker – Carter's representations have disquieted some feminist critics. In particular, the representations of self-sacrificing femininity and sexual violence in her early novels *Shadow Dance* (1966) and *Love* (1971) suggest a closer alignment with the theatricality of the Sadeian Gothic than with a Radcliffean lineage of women's Gothic writing. In an Afterword published in 1987 she famously described the latter novel as an 'almost sinister feat of male impersonation' in 'its icy treatment of the mad girl' Annabel, with her protruding veins and 'curiously pointed teeth'.[4] Describing the text as 'Annabel's coffin', she identifies 'the ornate formalism' of its style with her desire to write a 'modern-day' version of Benjamin Constant's *Adolphe* (1816). Carter's broader fascination with a male-centred French literary tradition has been documented in biographical accounts of her reading and writing career. In response to a question about 'Gothic' prose styles posed by Lorna Sage, she attributes the 'polish' of her own writing to her acquaintance with the French language.[5] In the same interview she describes the formative influence of French literature: 'we had this very good French teacher, and we did *Les Fleurs du Mal* and *Phèdre*, and the minute I read Racine, I knew that it moved me much more savagely than Shakespeare'.[6] In particular, an enthralment with the exuberant aesthetic of Baudelaire can be traced in her work – from the representation of the dandified Honeybuzzard in *Shadow Dance* and Joseph in *Several Perceptions* (1968) to the vampish prostitutes and performers in her later works, most notably in *The Passion of New Eve* (1977), *Nights at the Circus* (1984) and 'Black Venus' (1985), a fictional autobiography of Jeanne Duval, Baudelaire's mistress and muse. It is precisely Carter's inclination to take 'decadence rather shockingly for granted'[7] that has been situated in tension with her feminist politics – or, as Christina Britzolakis puts it, her 'oft-expressed belief in her fiction as an instrument of social change and intervention'.[8] Nevertheless, re-imagining her particular and perverse engagements with the sexual and textual violence of male literary frameworks through a reconceptualized

European Gothic heritage provides a space in which to re-examine the vexed issue of Carter's gender/genre politics.

If the shape and politics of Carter's Gothic engagements continue to perplex her critics, Pierrette Fleutiaux's feminist and Gothic credentials remain largely unexplored.[9] Although her collection of fairy tale horror, *Métamorphoses de la reine* (1984), and *Nous sommes éternels* (1990), a Gothic novel set in France and New York, were awarded le Prix Goncourt de la nouvelle and le prix Femina respectively, Fleutiaux remains a little known writer outside France. In addition to these two works, several other texts deal with Gothic themes and topoi – from the reworking of female vampirism in her first novel, *Histoire de la chauve-souris* (1975), to the motif of the haunted/haunting painting in *Histoire du tableau* (1977). Nevertheless, while Bettina Knapp locates *Histoire de la chauve-souris* within 'la famille des auteurs de romans noirs, ou romans gothiques, tels Anne [*sic*] Radcliffe, William Beckford, Monk Lewis et d'autres écrivains attirés par ce genre comme Mary Shelley, Byron, Poe, Maupassant, Huysmans, Villiers de l'Isle-Adam ou Kafka', this generic alignment is not extended to her other works, despite their indubitably Gothic gestures and preoccupations.[10] That Fleutiaux's work has thus far been neglected in Gothic scholarship is arguably a symptom of the Anglo-American bias of even European approaches and the absence of a readily mapped French tradition of women's Gothic writing.[11] Yet, a broader conceptualization of the Gothic as a tradition that, to quote Carter, 'grandly ignores the value systems of our institutions ... operate[s] against the perennial desire to believe the word as fact ... [and] retains a singular moral function – that of provoking unease'[12] enables us to situate Fleutiaux firmly within the genre. Indeed, like Carter, Fleutiaux works very much with a male-authored strand of the European Gothic, in particular its nineteenth-century formations, albeit from the 'other' side of the Channel.

Focusing on Carter's and Fleutiaux's feminist reworkings of the female vampire, this chapter foregrounds the gender politics of their cross-Channel Gothic voyages. While the male literary vampire is distinguished by his mobility, nineteenth-century representations of the female vampire are often tied to anxieties about women's 'movements'. As Gina Wisker suggests: 'Female vampires lurk seductively and dangerously in romantic poetry and nineteenth-century fictions, where they chiefly act as a warning against being taken in by appearances and becoming victim to the evils of women's active sexuality, equated with the demonic.'[13] Foregrounding the exchange of bodily fluids and the transgression of corporeal boundaries, the female vampire incorporates the drives of Eros and Thanatos and thus exemplifies the simultaneous desire for and dread of female sexuality that is at the heart of nineteenth-century cultural discourse on both sides of the Channel. Highlighting the vulnerability of the borders of subjectivity and the integrity of the individual, the vampire is an abject body, a body which, as Julia Kristeva proposes in *Powers of Horror* (1982), 'disturbs identity, system, order. What does not respect borders, positions, rules. The in-between, the ambiguous, the composite.'[14] The female vampire in particular embodies those elements of 'defilement' – urine, blood, excrement, etc. – which place the subject 'in perpetual danger'.[15] In the nineteenth-century Gothic imagination, this abject body most often manifests as an unstable and pathologized body and, as the prevalence of the vampire metaphor in nineteenth-century medical discourse indicates, a body that must be the subject of and subjected to classification and normalization; a body that must be 'fixed'.

A woman with wings, Carter's Fevvers in *Nights at the Circus* is a 'physiological anomaly',[16] a body to be scrutinized and surveyed. Her enigmatic physicality is sardonically linked to the very emergence of psychoanalytic discourse: 'In Vienna, she deformed the dreams of that entire generation who would immediately commit themselves wholeheartedly to psychoanalysis.'[17] Likewise, Fleutiaux's nameless narrator in *Histoire de la chauve-souris*, with a furry, membranous bat entangled in her hair, is subject to the enquiry of the various incarnations of the male scientist she meets as she travels through the Gothic spaces of the narrative. Blurring the boundaries between human and animal, the characterization of the protagonists of both of these novels is thus congruent with Kelly Hurley's delineation of the 'abhuman subject' as

> a not-quite-human subject, characterized by its morphic variability, continually in danger of becoming not-itself, becoming other. The prefix 'ab-' signals a movement away from a site or condition, and thus a loss. But a movement away from is also a movement towards – towards a site or condition as yet unspecified – and thus entails both a threat and a promise.[18]

This chapter will explore the ways in which Carter and Fleutiaux rework the highly codified figure of the female vampire inherited from their nineteenth-century literary predecessors and imbue it with morphic possibilities. With particular reference to Carter's engagement with the Baudelairean vamp in *Nights at the Circus* and Fleutiaux's rewriting of Bram Stoker's female vampires in *Histoire de la chauve-souris*, it will interrogate what is at stake in their cross-Channel literary voyages.

Angela Carter and the Gothic vamp

Published in 1984, Carter's *Nights at the Circus* has frequently been identified as a 'postmodern' or, most often, 'carnivalesque' novel. Nevertheless, the prevalence of Sadeian and decadent Gothic topographies – inhabited by vampiric Rosicrucians, sterile dukes and phallic surrogate mothers – situates the novel firmly within a European Gothic tradition. The significance of the novel's French inheritance is highlighted from its very opening and our initial encounter with Fevvers who, although billed the 'Cockney Venus', is immediately identified as a literary voyager: 'Fevvers, the most famous *aerialiste* of her day; her slogan, "Is she fact or is she fiction?" … this query, in the French language, in foot-high letters, blazed forth from a wall-size poster, souvenir of her Parisian triumphs, dominating her London dressing-room.'[19] Moreover, and in keeping with the *fin-de-siècle* setting of *Nights*, the bird-woman Fevvers crafts herself as a pastiche of nineteenth-century male Gothic inscriptions of femininity. In particular, her self-characterization playfully reworks decadent representations of the predatory vamp and the figure of the female vampire – for example, her blonde hair and physical bulk link her to Miss Urania, the acrobat of J. K. Huysmans' *A Rebours* (1884) and, most strikingly, to Emile Zola's Nana, 'la blonde Vénus', whose sexual and financial vampirism is linked to the political and moral destructiveness of the Second Empire.

It is, however, Baudelaire as a literary heir of de Sade, who provides the most striking point of reference for Carter's representation of the vampiric performer in *Nights at the Circus*. In her discussion of the influence of Charles Maturin's *Melmoth the Wanderer* (1820) on the development of nineteenth-century French Gothic forms, Catherine Lanone pertinently identifies Baudelaire as a central figure in the redemption of the Gothic 'in a new era of doubt and darkening political prospects'. Baudelaire, she proposes, was 'that advocate of modernity enamoured with satanic rebellion, who chose as poetical objects skeletons, prostitutes and the depth of the abyss' in his claim for the essentially infernal tendency in modern art'.[20] In *Les Fleurs du mal* (1857 and 1861), a collection notable for its macabre treatment of dark desires, excesses and decay, the figure of the female vamp(ire) as prostitute recurs as 'the perfect image of the savagery that lurks in the midst of civilization'.[21] For it is 'Baudelaire, not de Sade', Jennifer Birkett proposes, 'who places the origins of evil in Nature rather than man, and, most of all, in the women who for him are Nature's chief representatives. Juliette is an exception in the Sadeian world, while Baudelaire's poetry is dominated by the *femme fatale* and her innocent victims.'[22] For example, 'Les Métamorphoses du vampire', collected in *Les Fleurs du mal*, portrays a predatory vamp who, having sucked the 'marrow' from the poet's bones, undergoes an abject, putrescent metamorphosis before dematerializing into a pile of wizened bones. However, like the diseased muse of 'La Muse malade', the subject/object of one of the opening poems of *Les Fleurs du mal*, the grotesque, excessive body of this vampiric *femme fatale* is fixed through the meticulous crafting of the poetic composition. If the materiality of the abject vampire body represents the 'generative power' of the female and especially maternal body, it is this 'dreaded' power that, according to Kristeva, 'patrilineal filiation has the burden of subduing'.[23] As Birkett suggests:

> To reproduce and fix, in art, the process of decomposition, reconciling the desire for chaos and the desire for order, is the purpose of both Baudelaire and de Sade. The wild orgies of tangled bodies in de Sade are careful theatrical productions ... They have their analogy in Baudelaire's poetry, where decayed and rotting flesh and disintegrating mind and spirit are gradually refined and fixed into the abstractions of art.[24]

In Baudelaire's poetry, the figure of the female vamp(ire) represents a fetishistic metaphorization of femininity so that the horror of *decomposition* aligned with the material and protean female body is contained in – or 'subdued' by – the artistic *composition*. If the vampiric *femme fatale* represents an anxiety about female sexual identity – a threat which lays bare the sterile power of the male Gothicist – then the poet takes up the position of the male vampire, feeding off the abject female body as the site over which he negotiates his 'declared aesthetic intention of extracting beauty from evil'.[25]

In her essay on Edgar Allan Poe's 'The Fall of the House of Usher', Carter simultaneously recapitulates and debunks the notion that the female vampire epitomizes:

> the fear of and longing for sexuality, symbolizing sex and femininity as compulsion and disease. She is the woman who takes by force the blood and life and potency of a man. A metaphor. A part of the

décor, in fact – no lonely castle in these abandoned parts is complete without one. The vampire is a tacky theatrical device, too, just like the collapsing house itself.[26]

Female vampires abound in Carter's fiction. However, one of the most poignant explorations of the contingency of female sexual identity on the structural paraphernalia of the male Gothic is realized in *Nights at the Circus*, through the characterization of Fevvers as decadent vamp(ire). Ma Nelson's Academy, where Fevvers begins her journey, is a London brothel explicitly linked to the 'influence of Baudelaire ... a poor fellow who loved whores not for the pleasure of it but, as he perceived it, the horror of it'.[27] Here, the material female body is symbolically evoked by the 'wine-red, figured damask' inner wall of the brothel. This house architecturally represents the 'glittering sterility'[28] of an anti-womb space; this is a very much a male decadent appropriation of a maternal Gothic space within which sex is everywhere but (biological) motherhood is nowhere. The textual inscription of blood here is that of penetration, decapitation and sacrifice: heads of satyrs ornament the banister, and a 'brace of buxom, smiling goddesses' support the mantelpiece, which 'might have served the Romans for an altar, or a tomb'.[29] Ma Nelson's academy thus establishes a Gothic architecture of enclosure and a dynamic of male voyeurism that are reduplicated throughout the narrative. Indeed, it is here, under the guidance of Ma Nelson, that Fevvers learns her trade as a 'living statue' – a *tableau vivant* – and is educated in the art of female performance as the fetishized object of a male gaze.

With its Sadeian architecture and sinister *mise en scène* of female sexuality, Madame Schreck's Museum of Woman Monsters represents the visual and pornographic centrepiece of the novel. Catering for those men who are not merely troubled in their bodies, but 'troubled in their ... souls', it unequivocally invokes the dark horror of the Gothic and, in particular, a decadent Gothic view of female sexuality: 'this place was known as "Down Below", or else, "The Abyss"'. The 'damask' walls of Ma Nelson's brothel are replaced here by the living grotesque bodies of Fevvers and the other 'Woman Monsters', who become *tableaux vivants* 'made to stand in stone niches cut out of the slimy walls'.[30] The topographical contexts of the Museum of Woman Monsters take those of Ma Nelson's Academy to their Gothic conclusion by foregrounding the configuration of the Gothic castle as asylum. Reminiscent of Charcot's Museum of Living Pathology, this is the space of the male vampire who, as Luce Irigaray suggests, 'needs to stay in disguise and do his work at night. Otherwise he is reminded that he is dependent on death. And on birth. On the material, uterine foundations of his mastery. Only if these be repressed can he enjoy sole ownership.'[31] It is this anxiety about the 'generative power' of the female body that similarly informs Fevvers' encounter with Christian Rosencreutz. For Rosencreutz the horror of the female body and its permeable borders signals the unspeakable and unrepresentable domain of birth and thus death: 'the female part, or absence, or atrocious hole, or dreadful chasm, the Abyss, Down Below, the vortex that sucks everything dreadfully down, down, down where Terror rules'.[32] Nevertheless, while Carter parodies Rosencreutz's insecurities about male virility – 'his other weapon, poor thing, that bobbed about uncharged, unprimed, unsharpened'[33] – she warns of the dangers of Fevvers' complicity with it. Fevvers' vampish self-representation reinforces rather than destabilizes Rosencreutz's epistemology: his desire to sacrifice Fevvers to achieve his own immortality is the logical conclusion of her staging of 'Death the Protectress' in Madame Schreck's Museum. It is only by reaffirming the horror of the Freudian feminine, and brandishing the (castratory) sword she has inherited from Ma Nelson, that Fevvers manages, temporarily, to take flight from Rosencreutz's Gothic castle into the open landscape. Even when she enters the carnivalesque space of St. Petersburg, Fevvers' pursuit of economic autonomy – a refiguration of Nana's financial vampirism – leads her to the Russian Grand Duke's Gothic mansion, which 'represents sterile power ... a gothic horror threat of potential disempowerment and reification'.[34]

On one hand, the parodic representation of Fevvers' predatory sexuality suggests that, like de Sade's Juliette in Carter's *The Sadeian Woman* (1979), she is cast in the 'mode of irony' – a sexual (and textual) terrorist who takes on the position of the vamp(ire) to ensure her own survival within the male Gothic fantasy spaces of the narrative.[35] To use Sally Keenan's words, she breaks out of the 'victim/victimizer frame by controlling the narration of her own story through a mixture of flagrant self-display and subterfuge'.[36] Yet, while Fevvers' vampish performance of the *femme fatale* exposes the theatricality of the male Gothic composition, when she finds herself in the wilderness space of Siberia – when her wings are broken and she has no Gothic castles around her – she suffers a crisis of identity: 'Am I fact? Or am I fiction?'[37] In spite of her wings she is unable to take flight from Gothic scripts and, reaffirming the conservative closure associated with the female Gothic, ends her narrative locked in the gaze of her male lover back in a reconfigured bedroom space. At the end of *Nights at the Circus*, Fevvers even yearns to return to the very space from which she has travelled: 'Home! Yes! she would see Trafalgar Square, again; and Nelson on his plinth ... and St Paul's, the single Amazon breast of her beloved native city'.[38] Thus Fevvers continues to subscribe to male Gothic structures and a masculinized codification of the female body (represented here by the evocation of the breast at St. Paul's and the reinstatement of Nelson as Master of her destiny). Her willingness to play the 'vamp' means that she remains caught up in an automated masquerade of femininity that contains her identity at the surface level of her body – which becomes a 'tacky theatrical device, just like the collapsing house itself'.

Pierrette Fleutiaux and the menstrual monster

If Carter's *Nights at the Circus* offers a refiguration and disruption of the predatory vamp/ire, then Fleutiaux's *Histoire de la chauve-souris* [*Story of the Bat*] can be read as offering a counter-model to the pathologized version of femininity underlying Bram Stoker's *Dracula* (1897).[39] While Stoker's novel makes extensive reference to contemporaneous ideas about hysteria and its treatments – most notably the theories of hypnosis developed by 'the great Charcot'[40] – the female vampire is most powerfully codified in relation to menstrual discourse. Proposing that 'the interaction between the vampire and the victim ... is a trope for the relationship between the Victorian male doctor and the female hysteric', and highlighting the novel's reiteration of the iconographies of vampirism haunting the discursive history of menstruation, Marie Mulvey-Roberts has persuasively argued that:

> *Dracula* is, of course, far more than a novel about pathologies .... Its gendering of male blood as good and female blood as bad signals that it is menstrual blood and its pathologies that provoke a sense of horror. ... Stoker's attention to the relationship between women and blood is a surrogate for menstrual taboo.[41]

Indeed, Stoker's Gothic heroines, Lucy Westenra and Mina Harker, are primarily located as menstrual subjects in relation to the bloody bite of Count Dracula, as a personification of menstruation.[42] It is the 'disorder' of menstruation that is regulated and censored by the 'Crew of Light', led by Van Helsing and Dr Seward as representatives of late nineteenth-century institutional medicine and science.[43] Centrally,

Lucy's positioning as menstrual monster is constructed through her identification with the Medusa, an alignment that is foregrounded by Dr Seward's description of her vampiric state: 'The beautiful colour became livid, the eyes seemed to throw out sparks of hell-fire, the brows were wrinkled as though the folds of the flesh were coils of Medusa's snakes ... If ever a face meant death – if looks could kill – we saw it at that moment.'[44] As Mulvey-Roberts highlights, the figure of the Medusa has frequently been associated with the menstrual female subject, the sight of whom was considered to be as deadly (or, rather, as *castrating*) as the gaze of the Gorgon.[45] Ultimately, then, Lucy's dangerous, disordered body must be destroyed; she is penetrated with a stake and then decapitated in an act of explicitly gendered violence that recalls Perseus' slaying of the Medusa. The metaphor of the vampire thus functions to codify, contain – and ultimately eliminate – the threat of female sexual voracity.

Presented as a fictional case study of female pathology, centred on the nameless heroine's narration of the (non-)presence of a bat entangled in her hair, Fleutiaux's *Histoire de la chauve-souris* is similarly concerned with what Hurley describes as the 'gothicity' of medical discourse.[46] However, although, like Stoker's Lucy, the protagonist of Fleutiaux's novel is positioned as representing a 'curious psychological study' for the various incarnations of the scientist/doctors she encounters, *Histoire* is distinguished by its first-person narration. While the infestation of the bat in the hair of the adolescent protagonist recalls pre-industrial mythologies linking menarche to the bite of a vampire bat,[47] the novel's episodic structure, combined with the patterns of ingestion/expulsion governing the bat's feedings, evokes a narrative pulse aligned with the rhythms of the menstrual cycle.[48] The white, pristine and cold asylum-like configuration of the Gothic castle in which the narrator initially finds herself symbolically inscribes the security and stability of the heroine's 'clean and proper' prepubescent body. However, by unfastening the window she has been forbidden from opening, Fleutiaux's Gothic heroine transgresses the law and initiates the arrival of the bat which becomes entangled in her hair (an actualization of Lucy's hallucinatory vision of a 'big bat ... buffeting its wings against the window' in *Dracula*):[49] 'Against the nape of my neck I feel this other flesh ... I feel this great beating of imprisoned wings and a horror without name penetrates me'.[50] The arrival of the bat and the breaking of menstrual taboo literally shake the foundations of this Gothic castle as a codification of paternal law. As such, the menstrual heroine is thrust towards the threshold, 'the gaping hole of the window'[51] – a figuration of the grotesque 'gaping wound' upon which sexual difference is predicated.

While in *Dracula* the figure of the vampire serves as a metaphor for menstruation and its 'morbidification', the location of the bat in Fleutiaux's text marks a shift from a metaphoric to a metonymic inscription of menstrual identity. By positioning the bat by her heroine's head, Fleutiaux's reconfiguration of menstrual subjectivity explodes the mind/body dualism over which nineteenth-century discourses of hysteria are navigated. This shift from a metaphorical to a metonymical configuration of menstrual identity is played out most powerfully in two key scenes in the early part of *Histoire de la chauve-souris*. The first of these is the bat girl's coming out at the annual village festival, for which she is provided with a Gothic ball gown. With its 'repulsive' fabric and 'widely open-necked collar, light and membranous,' the Medusa-like dress exteriorizes her menstrual body.[52] A metaphorical iteration of the bat, this Gothic costume renders the heroine's body a *readable* and, therefore, *containable* spectacle. The dynamics of containment are further foregrounded by the brutal crucifixion/'staking' of the 'real' bat that descends upon the carnival festivities. Thus, in spite of the associations of the village festival with Bakhtinian notions of carnival as the topos of regenerative fiction, this is not a moment where objects are turned 'inside out' to expose the fragility of the social and corporeal body, but a moment that functions to regulate and 'exorcize' difference by fixing bodies and identities.

If the bat girl's encounter at the festival reconfigures the vampiric/vampirized Lucy's confrontation with and obliteration by the Crew of Light in *Dracula*, then her next encounter is with the male vampire, incarnated here as 'the naked man'. Feeding off the discarded waste of a rubbish heap built on an abyss, the naked man embodies an animalistic, 'dirty' and predatory sexuality, signified by the creature living in his groin: 'In the hairs of his genitals, a strange, black creature moves, *similar to mine, and yet different*' (emphasis added).[53] Echoing Count Dracula's vampirization of Mina with its inferences of enforced fellatio, he pushes the bat girl's head to the creature in his groin: 'suddenly, as I am still kneeling down, he grabs hold of my neck and pins my head against his legs and holds me firmly against him ... Then, from the depths of this horror, I feel something moving softly against my head.'[54] Nevertheless, in Fleutiaux's metonymic reconfiguration of menstrual identity, the positioning of the bat by the protagonist's head suggests a different kind of Gothic maidenhead by foregrounding a psychic, rather than a solely bodily, Gothic initiation into womanhood.

Just as the Crew of Light in *Dracula* seek to circumscribe Lucy through medical discourse, in *Histoire de la chauve-souris*, the Gothic heroine is similarly subjected to the attempts of the male scientist/ doctor – in particular, a speleologist, a psychoanalyst and a cineaste – to produce and categorize her 'abhuman' body through the medical gaze. Riveted between 'the Medusa and the abyss',[55] the bat girl seeks out a space of refuge in the dark, underground space of a bat cave. Although this is a place that offers the consolation of sameness amongst the warm, furry bats, the comfort of the bat cave is swiftly interrupted with the invasion of the speleologist and his 'little light'. Metaphorically assuming the position of a gynaecologist, and aligned with the Crew of Light in *Dracula*, he 'illuminates', categorizes and catalogues the bats. Not only does the speleologist attempt to contain and control the bat girl in his exploration of this 'dark continent' space but, after pulling her out of the cave and turning her up 'the right way', he returns her to another Gothic castle reminiscent of the first tower.

However and wherever she tries to travel in search of a place in which to tell her own story about her bat, she is always returned to the Gothic castle as a codification of the structures/strictures of paternal law. This move is exemplified by her confrontation with 'le docteur introspecteur', who attempts to 'fix' her unstable narrative/body within the composition of the psychoanalytic case study:

> 'Did you love your mother? ... And your father, a violent man no doubt? ... try hard to remember, has there not been an event in your childhood that marked you, an event that terrified you, leaving you with an enduring guilt complex?'... He keeps talking, and other elements come and take their place *one by one in the structure.* (emphasis added)[56]

In other words, the doctor attempts to (en)close her story within a hermeneutic derived from the very 'structures' of the initial Gothic castle.[57] Reminding us of the multiple significations of 'the case' – as rule, individual, linguistic notion and container – David Punter argues that '[w]hat Gothic shows is that this case always falls open (and, as it were, things fall out)'.[58] It is such a falling out, then, that underlies the bat girl's request that the analyst touch her bat – not only proving its 'reality' but, at the very moment it vomits mucous onto his skin, disrupting the fragile borders of the psychoanalytic scene.

It is, however, in her final encounter with the cineaste, who wants to make a film of her various journeys, encounters and experiences with the bat, that the bat girl ultimately returns and deflects the (medical) gaze. Seeking to sanitize her menstrual narrative, the cineaste wants to exchange the furry, membranous feminized bat for 'a beautiful white gull'.[59] Nevertheless, once again, the stability of the narrative scene is disrupted by the bat's secretions – the abject once again threatening the boundaries of patriarchal structures and representations. This time, however, the bat's mucus-like emission is supplemented by the abject discharge of the heroine's laughter: 'I hear myself laugh ... the inner emptiness on the verge of which I was standing frozen in a painful cramp *crumbles into dust* ... I laugh again, spewing out with each hiccup sweat, fear, jealousy, frenzy, I laugh, I laugh' (emphasis added).[60] The image of dust echoes the Count's fate – and the metaphorical effacement of the menstrual subject – in *Dracula*. However, here the Gothic heroine's vampiric/menstrual identity is reappropriated as the source of her narrative agency and her metamorphosis from girlhood to womanhood. Finally unravelling the hairs encasing the bat, she emerges as a laughing Medusa.

*　*　*

'The play of fear and laughter', proposes Fred Botting, 'has been inscribed in Gothic texts since their inception'.[61] It is significant, then, that both *Nights at the Circus* and *Histoire de la chauve-souris* end with the bursting forth of their heroines' laughter. Much has been made of the transformative potential of Fevvers' laughter at the end of *Nights at the Circus*. In many respects, Fevvers' bellowing laughter at the prospect of having duped Walser (about her virginity, if not the authenticity of her wings) might be read as a reversal of Baudelaire's 'comique absolu': 'Fabulous creations, beings whose authority and raison d'être cannot be drawn from the code of common sense, often provoke in us an insane and excessive mirth which expresses itself in interminable paroxysms and swoons'.[62] If the 'comique absolu' is the excessive and violent laughter of the grotesque, of fallen humanity, then in Carter's recapitulation it becomes the laughter of redemption. However, while Fevvers' laughter might '[seep] through the gaps in the window-frames and cracks in the door-frames', it is a laughter that nonetheless leaves the structures of the Gothic house of fiction, and her vampish position therein, intact.[63] In contrast, the laughter of Fleutiaux's bat girl is more closely aligned with Kristeva's identification of Célinian laughter as that which 'bursts out, facing abjection, and always originating at the same source ... the gushing forth of the unconscious, the repressed, suppressed pleasure, be it sex or death'.[64] The vampiric identity of her bat girl thus corresponds to Gina Wisker's articulation of the radical potential of feminist re-workings of the female vampire, where the 'transgression of gender boundaries, life/death, day/night behaviour ... is no longer abject, rejected with disgust to ensure identity', but 'enables us to recognize that the *Other is part of ourselves*'.[65] In this respect, it is Fleutiaux who more forcibly unsettles the somatic and textual forms of the vampire narratives inherited from her European Gothic predecessors.

Notes

1. Avril Horner, 'Introduction', in *European Gothic: A Spirited Exchange 1760–1960*, ed. Avril Horner (Manchester: Manchester University Press, 2002), pp. 1–16, p. 1.
2. Horner, 'Introduction', p. 1.
3. Gina Wisker, 'Love Bites: Contemporary Women's Vampire Fictions', in *A Companion to the Gothic*, ed. by David Punter (Oxford: Blackwell, 2000), pp. 167–79, p. 168.
4. Angela Carter, *Love* (London: Virago, 1997), pp. 113, 16.
5. Lorna Sage, 'The Savage Sideshow: A Profile of Angela Carter', *New Review* 4 (1977), 51–7, 55.
6. Sage, 'The Savage Sideshow', p. 54.
7. Sage, 'The Savage Sideshow', p. 51.
8. Christina Britzolakis, 'Angela Carter's Fetishism', *Textual Practice* 9 (1995), 459–75, 465.
9. Aside from one monograph, Bettina L. Knapp's introductory *Pierrette Fleutiaux* (1997), and a handful of articles and book reviews, Fleutiaux's writing has thus far harnessed little critical attention.
10. Bettina L. Knapp, *Pierrette Fleutiaux* (Amsterdam: Rodopi, 1997), p. 9.
11. Horner, for example, laments the lack of 'comprehensive histories of French or Italian Gothic', while Joan Hinde Stewart refers to late eighteenth-century women's writing in French as a 'largely forgotten body of literature'. Horner, *European Gothic*, p. 1; Joan Hinde Stewart, *Gynographes: French Novels by Women of the Late Eighteenth Century* (Lincoln, NB: University of Nebraska Press, 1993), p. ix.
12. Angela Carter, *Fireworks: Nine Profane Pieces* (New York: Penguin, 1987), p. 133.
13. Wisker, 'Love Bites', p. 169.
14. Julia Kristeva, *Powers of Horror: An Essay on Abjection* (1980), trans. Leon S. Roudiez (New York: Columbia University Press, 1982), p. 4.
15. Kristeva, *Powers of Horror*, p. 9.
16. Angela Carter, *Nights at the Circus* (London: Vintage, 1994), p. 15.
17. Carter, *Nights at the Circus*, p. 11.

18. Kelly Hurley, *The Gothic Body: Sexuality, Materialism and Degeneration at the Fin de Siècle* (Cambridge: Cambridge University Press, 1996), pp. 3–4.
19. Carter, *Nights at the Circus*, p. 7.
20. Catherine Lanone, 'Verging on the Gothic: Melmoth's Journey to France', in *European Gothic: A Spirited Exchange 1760–1960*, ed. Avril Horner (Manchester: Manchester University Press, 2002), pp. 71–83, p. 74.
21. Charles Baudelaire, 'The Painter of Modern Life' [1863], in *The Painter of Modern Life and Other Essays*, trans. and ed. Jonathan Mayne, second edition (London: Phaidon Press, 1995), pp. 1–41, p. 36.
22. Jennifer Birkett, *The Sins of the Fathers: Decadence in France 1870–1914* (London: Quartet, 1986), p. 22.
23. Kristeva, *Powers of Horror*, p. 77.
24. Birkett, *Sins of the Fathers*, p. 22.
25. Nicole Ward Jouve, *Baudelaire: A Fire to Conquer Darkness* (London: Macmillan, 1980), p. 157.
26. Angela Carter, 'Through a Text Backwards: The Resurrection of the House of Usher' [1988], in *Shaking a Leg: Collected Journalism and Writings* (London: Chatto and Windus, 1997), pp. 482–90, 489–90.
27. Carter, *Nights*, p. 38.
28. Carter, *Nights*, p. 39.
29. Carter, *Nights*, p. 26.
30. Carter, *Nights*, p. 61.
31. Luce Irigaray, *Speculum of the Other Woman* [1974], trans. Gillian C. Gill (Ithaca, NY: Cornell University Press, 1985), pp. 126–27.
32. Carter, *Nights*, p. 77.
33. Carter, *Nights*, p. 83
34. Wisker, 'Love Bites', p. 240.
35. Angela Carter, *The Sadeian Woman: An Exercise in Cultural History* (London: Virago, 2000), p. 79.
36. Sally Keenan, 'Angela Carter's *The Sadeian Woman*: Feminism as Treason', in *The Infernal Desires of Angela Carter: Fiction, Femininity, Feminism*, ed. Joseph Bristow and Trev Lynn Broughton (Harlow: Addison Wesley Longman, 1997), pp. 132–48, p. 143.
37. Carter, *Nights*, p. 290.
38. Carter, *Nights*, pp. 290–1.
39. For an extended reading of the relationship between these two texts see Rebecca Munford, 'Blood, Laughter and the Medusa: The Gothic Heroine as Menstrual Monster', *Menstruation: A Cultural History*, ed. Andrew Shail and Gillian Howie (Basingstoke: Palgrave Macmillan, 2005), pp. 259–72.
40. Bram Stoker, *Dracula*, ed. Maurice Hindle (London: Penguin Books, 1993), p. 247.
41. Marie Mulvey-Roberts, 'Dracula and the Doctors: Bad Blood, Menstrual Taboo and the New Woman', in *Bram Stoker: History, Psychoanalysis, and the Gothic*, ed. William Hughes and Andrew Smith (New York: Macmillan, 1998), pp. 78–95, pp. 80, 78. See, for example, the nineteenth-century physician Oliver Wendell Holmes' proposition that 'a hysterical girl is a vampire who sucks the blood of the healthy people about her'; quoted in Carroll Smith-Rosenberg, *Disorderly Conduct: Visions of Gender in Victorian America* (New York: Oxford University Press, 1986), p. 207.

42. 'Dracula is represented as a feminized man whose strange fragrance hints at the scent of menstrual blood.' Mulvey-Roberts, 'Dracula and the Doctors', p. 79.

43. As Janet Beizer notes, '[p]aradoxically, it is from the very moment a woman begins to menstruate, becomes *réglée*, regulated, fixed in her (female) role, that her entire being is open to *dérangement* ... It then seems that the specific preoccupation with menstrual disorders hides a more fundamental anxiety about menstruation *as* order, or the essential disorder of the female condition'. Janet Beizer, *Ventriloquized Bodies: Narratives of Hysteria in Nineteenth-Century France* (Ithaca, NY: Cornell University Press, 1993), p. 40.

44. Stoker, *Dracula*, p. 272.

45. Mulvey-Roberts, 'Dracula and the Doctors', p. 87.

46. Hurley, *The Gothic Body*, p. 5.

47. See Claude Lévi-Strauss, *From Honey to Ashes: Introduction to a Science of Mythology, II* [1967], trans. John and Doreen Weightman (London: Jonathan Cape, 1977), p. 382.

48. The heroine's compulsive preoccupation with feeding the bat also suggests that she is re-pathologized via an association with bulimia.

49. Stoker, *Dracula*, p. 185. As Simone de Beauvoir proposes, 'the little girl, not yet in puberty, carries no menace, she is under no taboo and has no sacred character ... But on the day she can reproduce, woman becomes impure; and rigorous taboos surround the menstruating female.' Simone de Beauvoir, *The Second Sex* [1949], trans. and ed. H. M. Parshley (London: Pan-Picador, 1988), p. 180.

50. Pierrette Fleutiaux, *Histoire de la chauve-souris* (Paris: Julliard, 1975), p. 27. All translations are my own.

51. Fleutiaux, *Histoire de la chauve-souris*, p. 26.

52. Fleutiaux, *Histoire de la chauve-souris*, p. 39.

53. Fleutiaux, *Histoire de la chauve-souris*, p. 59.

54. Fleutiaux, *Histoire de la chauve-souris*, p. 60. See also the graphic scene in *Dracula* where the Crew of Light find Mina kneeling before Dracula, sucking the blood from the 'thin open wound' on his chest: 'Kneeling on the near edge of the bed facing outwards was the white-clad figure of [Mina]. By her side stood a tall, thin man, clad in black ... his right hand gripped her by the back of the neck, forcing her face down on his bosom. Her white night-dress was smeared with blood ... Her face was ghastly, with a pallor which was accentuated by the blood which smeared her lips and cheeks and chin; from her throat trickled a stream of blood.' Stoker, *Dracula*, pp. 363–4.

55. Hélène Cixous, 'The Laugh of the Medusa', trans. Keith Cohen and Paula Cohen, in *Feminisms: An Anthology of Literary Theory and Criticism*, ed. Robyn R. Warhol and Diane Price Herndl (New Brunswick: Rutgers University Press, 1993), pp. 334–49, p. 341.

56. Fleutiaux, *Histoire de la chauve-souris*, pp. 163–4.

57. This metaphorical equation between topographical and discursive structures is more striking in the original French: 'Il parle encore, et d'autres éléments viennent prendre leur place *tour à tour dans l'édifice*' (emphasis added).

58. David Punter, *Gothic Pathologies: The Text, The Body and the Law* (Basingstoke: Macmillan, 1998), p. 6.

59. Fleutiaux, *Histoire de la chauve-souris*, p. 169.

60. Fleutiaux, *Histoire de la chauve-souris*, p. 171.
61. Fred Botting, *Gothic* (London: Routledge, 1996), p. 168.
62. Charles Baudelaire, 'On the Essence of Laughter' [1855], in *The Mirror of Art*, trans. and ed. Jonathan Mayne (London, Phaidon Press, 1955), p. 144.
63. Carter, *Nights*, pp. 294–5.
64. Kristeva, *Powers of Horror*, pp. 205–6.
65. Wisker, 'Love Bites', p. 168.

References

Baudelaire, Charles, 'On the Essence of Laughter' [1855], in *The Mirror of Art*, trans. and ed. Jonathan Mayne (London, Phaidon Press, 1955).

—— 'The Painter of Modern Life' [1863], in *The Painter of Modern Life and Other Essays*, trans. and ed. Jonathan Mayne, second edition (London: Phaidon Press, 1995), pp. 1–41.

de Beauvoir, Simone, *The Second Sex* [1949], trans. and ed. H. M. Parshley (London: Pan-Picador, 1988).

Beizer, Janet, *Ventriloquized Bodies: Narratives of Hysteria in Nineteenth-Century France* (Ithaca, NY: Cornell University Press, 1993).

Birkett, Jennifer, *The Sins of the Fathers: Decadence in France 1870–1914* (London: Quartet, 1986).

Botting, Fred, *Gothic* (London: Routledge, 1996).

Britzolakis, Christina, 'Angela Carter's Fetishism', *Textual Practice* 9.3 (1995) 459–75.

Carter, Angela, *Fireworks: Nine Profane Pieces* (1974; London: Penguin Books, 1987).

—— *Love* (1971; London: Virago, 1997).

—— *Nights at the Circus* (1984; London: Vintage, 1994).

—— *The Sadeian Woman: An Exercise in Cultural History* (1979; London: Virago, 2000).

—— 'Through a Text Backwards: The Resurrection of the House of Usher' [1988], *Shaking a Leg: Collected Journalism and Writings* (London: Chatto and Windus, 1997), pp. 482–90.

Cixous, Hélène, 'The Laugh of the Medusa', trans. Keith Cohen and Paula Cohen, in *Feminisms: An Anthology of Literary Theory and Criticism*, ed. Robyn R. Warhol and Diane Price Herndl (New Brunswick: Rutgers University Press, 1993), pp. 334–49.

Fleutiaux, Pierrette, *Histoire de la chauve-souris* (Paris: Julliard, 1975).

Horner, Avril, 'Introduction', in *European Gothic: A Spirited Exchange 1760–1960*, ed. Avril Horner (Manchester: Manchester University Press, 2002), pp. 1–16.

Hurley, Kelly, *The Gothic Body: Sexuality, Materialism and Degeneration at the Fin de Siècle* (Cambridge: Cambridge University Press, 1996).

Irigaray, Luce, *Speculum of the Other Woman* [1974], trans. Gillian C. Gill (Ithaca, NY: Cornell University Press, 1985).

Keenan, Sally, 'Angela Carter's *The Sadeian Woman*: Feminism as Treason', in *The Infernal Desires of Angela Carter: Fiction, Femininity, Feminism*, ed. Joseph Bristow and Trev Lynn Broughton (Harlow: Addison Wesley Longman, 1997), pp. 132–48.

Knapp, Bettina L., *Pierrette Fleutiaux* (Amsterdam: Rodopi, 1997).

Kristeva, Julia, *Powers of Horror: An Essay on Abjection* (1980), trans. Leon S. Roudiez (New York: Columbia University Press, 1982).

Lanone, Catherine, 'Verging on the Gothic: Melmoth's Journey to France', in *European Gothic: A Spirited Exchange 1760–1960*, ed. Avril Horner (Manchester: Manchester University Press, 2002), pp. 71–83.

Lévi-Strauss, Claude, *From Honey to Ashes: Introduction to a Science of Mythology*, 2, trans. John and Doreen Weightman (London: Jonathan Cape, 1977).

Mulvey-Roberts, Marie, 'Dracula and the Doctors: Bad Blood, Menstrual Taboo and the New Woman', in *Bram Stoker: History, Psychoanalysis, and the Gothic*, ed. William Hughes and Andrew Smith (New York: Macmillan, 1998), pp. 78–95.

Munford, Rebecca, 'Blood, Laughter and the Medusa: The Gothic Heroine as Menstrual Monster', *Menstruation: A Cultural History*, ed. Andrew Shail and Gillian Howie (Basingstoke: Palgrave Macmillan, 2005), pp. 259–72.

Punter, David, *Gothic Pathologies: The Text, The Body and the Law* (Basingstoke: Macmillan, 1998).

Sage, Lorna, 'The Savage Sideshow: A Profile of Angela Carter', *New Review* 4 (1977), 51–7.

Smith-Rosenberg, Carroll, *Disorderly Conduct: Visions of Gender in Victorian America* (New York: Oxford University Press, 1986).

Stewart, Joan Hinde, *Gynographes: French Novels by Women of the Late Eighteenth Century* (Lincoln, NB: University of Nebraska Press, 1993).

Stoker, Bram *Dracula* (1897; London: Penguin Books, 1993).

Ward Jouve, Nicole, *Baudelaire: A Fire to Conquer Darkness* (London: Macmillan, 1980).

Wisker, Gina, 'Love Bites: Contemporary Women's Vampire Fictions', in *A Companion to the Gothic*, ed. David Punter (Oxford: Blackwell, 2000), pp. 167–79.

Part III

Transatlantic Voyages

9
Beast's Triumph over Beauty in Gothic Film

Kathy Justice Gentile

Throughout Western cultural history, beautiful women have been courted, pursued and menaced by beasts, ranging from gods and humans in animal form to sociopathic Gothic villains. Some of the early oral versions of the animal groom or animal lover tale were eventually written down as fragmented myths and bowdlerized fairy tales. More recently, Beauty and the Beast tales have been reanimated in lavish and/or lurid cinematic spectacles. A review of historical variations on the Beauty and Beast tale suggests that although the conflict between the 'two antithetical allegorical figures' is often resolved in sexual, romantic and/or marital union,[1] Beauty is just as likely to be violated and debased as revered and rewarded, depending on the teller, the medium and the cultural/historical context.

However, as Jack Zipes has noted, the most pervasive and influential Beauty and the Beast story in Western culture derives from Madame de Beaumont's 1756 version,[2] in which a self-sacrificing Belle redeems the cursed, enchanted Beast. Beaumont's association of female beauty with Christian virtue finds philosophical grounding in Kant's *The Critique of Judgement* (1790), where he associates the concept of beauty with the morally good and 'the furtherance of life' because the contemplation of beauty elicits feelings of delight and positive pleasure from the subject.[3] However, for Kant, beauty is apprehended and estimated against a Platonic concept of perfection, whereas a subject's confrontation with a sublime spectacle evokes both repulsion and attraction, negative pleasure or awe in the face of the immeasurably great.[4] Before Kant in 1757, the English philosopher Edmund Burke attested to the power of the sublime over mere beauty, which he describes as 'comparatively small', 'smooth', 'polished', 'light and delicate',[5] in contrast to the 'terrible' sublime which provokes 'the strongest emotion which the mind is capable of feeling'.[6] Burke suggests that the pleasure in contemplating beauty is a less powerful emotion than the deeper emotions of terror and awe aroused by a sublime spectacle. Theoretically, then, in any contest where a beautiful object may be pitted against the sublime, vulnerable beauty, in its visibility and specific delineation, would be unable to withstand the overwhelming prospect of the terrible, dark, obscure and boundary-less sublime.

In line with the aesthetics of Kant and Burke, Gothic cinema works against Beaumont's Belle as a representation of feminized Christianity and topples Beauty from her pedestal by exalting a beastly sublime in displaying beautiful heroines who seem to have lost all power to soothe or redeem the savage breasts of beast/men. In a disturbing reversal of one of our culture's most cherished myths of romantic love, film codes, directorial visions and the cultivated tastes of the audience for sadistic satisfaction have dictated Beast's triumph over Beauty in a number of Gothic films which restructure and reframe one of our most enduring tales.

In Greek mythology and its transformative retellings, such as Ovid's *Metamorphoses*, beauty has no clear association with moral goodness or inviolate virtue. Beautiful women are pursued, raped and sometimes transformed into beasts themselves by jealous goddesses, whereas predatory, shape-changing gods such as Zeus and Apollo rarely suffer punishment for their crimes against female beauty. Supernaturally powerful gods assert their divine right to satisfy beastly lusts though deceit, tyranny and force.[7] 'Cupid and Psyche' is the Greco-Roman tale most often cited as the predecessor to Beaumont's tale and other Beauty and the Beast fairy tales that proliferated in seventeenth- and eighteenth-century France.[8] Strictly speaking, however, there is no beastly suitor or husband in Apuleius' second-century tale. Psyche's jealous sisters deliberately misinterpret the oracle's proclamation that Psyche's husband will be a 'winged pest', whose power is so potent that even the gods fear him.[9] Instead, they insist that Apollo's oracle foretold that Psyche's unseen husband and nighttime lover would be a 'savage wild beast' whom she must slay.[10] However, instead of a monster, Psyche's husband is revealed to her as the beauteous god of love, Cupid. After proving her worth through a series of trials prescribed by Venus, her jealous mother-in-law, Psyche, the beautiful mind, is reunited with Eros in the realm of immortality. The illuminating metamorphosis of the 'beastly' husband unites the two beautiful lovers in a divinely happy ending.

In contrast to the relatively powerless mortal beauties of classical myth, in the oral annals of the fairy tale, the beautiful woman was reputed to exercise great power over her beastly suitor. Citing the German folklorist Heide Gottner-Abendroth, Zipes argues that animal groom tales have evolved from a matriarchal oral tradition, in which 'the male figure is a wild, roving beast ... and this condition represents his homelessness and undomesticity . ... It is up to the woman to bring him salvation by making human clothes for him and accepting him into her house as a domesticated inhabitant.'[11] When the educated class began to transcribe and revise oral tales into written tales, a number of variant versions of the animal groom tale were published in late seventeenth- and eighteenth-century France,[12] although Jeanne Marie LePrince de Beaumont's 'La Belle et la Bête', published in *Magasin des Enfants* in 1757, has endured as our cultural paradigm of the beautiful female–beastly male encounter. Intended as a tale of instruction for her students when she was living in England, Beaumont's parable of exemplary Christian female conduct portrays a Beast whose physical characteristics and habits are unspecified and a Beauty whose selfless love redeems him into a courtly lover and handsome prince, worthy of Belle's hand in marriage.[13]

According to the psychoanalyst Bruno Bettelheim, the tale is an Oedipal drama of sexual maturation for Beauty, who must learn to overcome her disgust at male sexuality, transfer her affections from her father, and accept herself as a woman and the beast/man as a lover.[14] In a more empowering feminist interpretation, Phyllis Ralph argues that Belle makes choices, such as offering herself for slaughter as a substitute for her father and returning to save the Beast, unlike the more passive Cinderella and Snow White, and thus offers a more desirable model of female development.[15] Betsy Hearne sees the tale as a vision quest for Belle who must learn to see beneath appearances to the Beast's essential goodness.[16] And in a recent cinematic version of Beaumont's tale, Disney's book-smart Belle redeems a prince turned into a Beast by a powerful fairy because he is spoiled, selfish and loves no one but himself. Belle teaches him not only how to love, but also good manners and a smattering of literary knowledge.[17]

In the 1946 film version, Jean Cocteau's *La Belle et la Bête* cites Beaumont's fairy tale as its source while transforming the children's story into Gothic cinema. A filmmaker and poet, Cocteau declared that 'every man harbours a night in himself, that the work of the artist is to bring out this night into broad daylight'.[18] He also admitted in his film diary that he identified very closely with his monster.[19] Using innovative technical effects Cocteau creates an eerie Gothic atmosphere and a conflict between a tormented Beast/lover and a defiant, yet compassionate Belle, played by Josette Day. Upon initially beholding Jean Marais's upright wolfish, leonine, bear-like creature, Belle is horrified at the spectacle of alien, animalistic masculinity, as she faints away in the style of a true Gothic heroine. In Cocteau's revision, however, Beauty is active and daring in her virtue. She takes charge of her destiny by stealing away on the white horse to substitute herself for her father in the enchanted realm of the Beast. Upon arrival, she literally runs into a crumbling Gothic castle of dark chambers and long corridors lit by disembodied arms holding candelabra, then floats to angelic music past wind-blown white drapes. When she later explores the castle at night, her every move is followed by the eyes of living statue heads. Mists and fogs veil the grounds, the glove and the claws of the beast exude smoke, and the bedroom door and magic mirror speak to Belle. The Beast walks stiffly and awkwardly, as if he is struggling to control and rectify his animal nature, as if his upright human stance is agonizingly painful. The Beast's passion and shame at his animal drives are also powerfully conveyed in a scene where through the gaze of Beauty we see his royal clothing torn, his fur dishevelled and his body steaming after a wild run through the woods where he stalks and kills animal prey as an outlet for his jealousy of Belle's human suitor, Avenant.

Cocteau's Gothic darkening of the fairy tale culminates in a vertiginous series of magical transformations that many viewers have found confusing, rather than satisfying. Yet these magical reversals constitute the thematic heart of Cocteau's vision which is the revolutionary transformative power of reciprocal love. Earlier in their relationship, Beauty and the Beast debated the subject of who was master, Beauty acknowledging that Beast had power over her, while Beast insisted that all he had was at her command. Just before he dies, the Beast tells her, 'Love can make a man a beast. Love can beautify ugliness'. To further demonstrate these contradictory maxims, he promptly expires and is transformed into a handsome prince who is the image of Avenant, Beauty's suitor, who at the same instant is shot with an arrow by an animated statue of Diana as he smashes the glass of the skylight and drops into her sacred pavilion as the slain Beast.

The paradoxical equation that love can degrade a man into a beast because of ungovernable passion or transform the ugliest beast into a beauty is further illustrated by Belle's frantic, impassioned search for '*Ma bête!*' when she is overcome by her love and concern for the Beast, who has grown deathly ill in his frustrated longing for the absent Beauty. Beauty's search is prompted by seeing her own image in the magic mirror change into an image of the dying Beast. When she finds him stretched out by the pool, she renames herself to her suffering Beast by declaring, 'I am the monster'. The Beast within her is roused and she embraces her passionate nature and establishes an egalitarian, non-hierarchal relationship with her beast turned princely husband-to-be. After these magical reversals have established the perfect compatibility of the two lovers, Belle then teases the disenchanted prince with a series of feminine contradictions as he questions her about her feelings for Avenant and the Beast. She first says she did not love Avenant, then says she did and that she also loved the Beast. When the manly prince tells her that he will fly away with her to his kingdom and asks if she will be afraid, Belle has a coy reply, 'I'd like to be afraid – with you', again affirming the unsettling pleasures of romantic attraction, as the two lovers fly above the Gothic darkness and into a transcendent realm of happily ever after.[20]

Cocteau constructs a model of oscillating reciprocity in *La Belle et la Bête* by shifting positionality back and forth between Beauty and the Beast. A few years after Cocteau's film, Simone de Beauvoir sketched an existential theory of reciprocal love and sexual satisfaction in *The Second Sex* (1949). She suggests that an individual woman can break the shackles of centuries of culturally imposed passivity and 'Otherness' by establishing a relation of reciprocity with her partner through 'mutual recognition of the ego and of the other in the keenest awareness of the other and of the ego'.[21]

Instead of extending the radical precedent of Cocteau's gender egalitarianism and moving towards de Beauvoir's ideal of sexual reciprocity, notable films in recent Gothic cinema suggest a reversion to a dominant sublime/submissive beauty dynamic. Beauty loses her redemptive power and virtuous activism and instead is subjected to degradation, abuse, and even murder by the power of the beast in modern Gothic man. The animal groom tale becomes a warning tale of predatory obsession, lust and inhumanity in films such as *The Collector*, based on John Fowles' novel, David Lynch's *Blue Velvet* and his television series *Twin Peaks*, and the Spanish film *Abre los Ojos*, and its American remake *Vanilla Sky*. Mary Ann Doane notes that 'woman's beauty, her desirability, becomes a function of certain practices of imagery – framing, lighting, camera movement, angle';[22] that is, how a director chooses to deploy the apparatus of filmmaking deftly manipulates meaning construction and viewers' perceptions of cinematic narrative.

According to Laura Mulvey's influential formulation, Hollywood motion picture codes have enshrined the sadistic voyeurism and fetishistic scopophilia of the male gaze, thus structurally determining the inter-actions and Gothic conflicts between the beastly male villain or pro-tagonist and the female object of his and the camera's gaze.[23] Passive Beauty is acted upon by a beastly antagonist who is threatened by Beauty's difference (the threat of castration). Sadistic acts perpetrated against Beauty are valorized by the camera eye, and the spectator becomes complicit in Beast's predatory perspective and active degrada-tion, dismemberment, and/or silencing of the threat Beauty poses to masculinized beastliness.

In *The Collector* (1965), the director, William Wyler, demystifies the Beauty and the Beast encounter by dramatizing the Gothic banality of evil. The socially inept, amoral, predatory collector, Freddie Clegg (played by Terence Stamp), kidnaps and confines a beautiful young art student, Miranda (Samantha Eggar) in the cellar of an isolated Tudor farmhouse, partly because he wants to keep her as a possession like the butterflies in his collection, but also because he hopes that she will fall in love with him. However, the kidnapper resists transformation and is not redeemed by Miranda's love, because she cannot bring herself to love or esteem someone so emotionally stunted and sexually dys-functional and perverse. She tells him, 'I know you and I hate you'. Eventually, her confinement and her thwarted attempts to escape extinguish her spirit, and she develops pneumonia and dies in the killing 'care' of her admirer.[24]

In scenes from John Fowles' novel which were deleted from the film because of the Hollywood sex codes of the 1960s, Freddy undresses Miranda and takes photos of her when she is unconscious and later when she is sick and unable to resist, thus degrading Beauty into pornography for his impotent, life-denying obsession. While Fowles' novel gives equal time to Freddy's and Miranda's points of view,[25] Wyler privileges Freddy's predatory perspective by giving him voice-overs and more often following his gazing at his captured prey. Yet the camera also gives us Miranda's view of her captor, an ordinary, phy-sically unassuming, former bank clerk, who has captured Beauty and is slowly and systematically stifling the life out of her by denying her the fresh air, spatial freedom, art, intelligent conversation and human contact that she needs to thrive. At one point she tells him her own version of 'Beauty and the Beast', a story with a happy ending, where a monster loves his female prisoner so much that he grants her the freedom to leave him, but Caliban/Freddy does not grant Miranda her wish and she has no Prospero/father to save her. Her captor matter-of-factly tells her, 'There would be more of this [kind of thing] if people had the time and money', suggesting that more men would kidnap, imprison and sexually violate girls and women if they felt they could escape punishment. After Miranda's death, Freddy continues to pursue his obsession by planning to stalk and kidnap another young woman, less beautiful and educated than Miranda, and therefore more malleable and suitable for his purposes.

In a climactic scene which takes place in darkness and rain, Freddy is taking Miranda back to the cellar after allowing her a bath in the main house when she realizes that he is never going to let her go and although her hands are tied, she manages to grab a large stick and strike him. When he falls she is unable to channel the beast within and raise the weapon again to finish him off, enabling him to grab her leg and drag her kicking and screaming back into the cellar-cave. Virtuous, civilized Beauty is unable to muster the killer instinct necessary to escape from her caveman Beast and is subdued by brute force.

A number of critics have remarked on the Gothicism of David Lynch's film *Blue Velvet*, his television series *Twin Peaks* and its motion picture prequel *Fire Walk with Me*.[26] These films slip in and out of surrealistic dream and nightmare states, which exist alongside the more realistic narratives. Within his Gothic vision, Lynch incorporates a pathologically sinister version of the Beauty and Beast story. His beast-men, BOB in *Twin Peaks* and *Fire Walk With Me* and Frank in *Blue Velvet*, are wild and demoniac, and perpetrate rape, physical and psychological abuse and murder against their beautiful female victims. In *Blue Velvet* (1986), the small town gangster figure Frank (played by Dennis Hopper) kidnaps the child of the lounge singer Dorothy (Isabella Rossellini), so he will have power over her and can terrorize her sexually. Frank's demonic claim 'I'll fuck any-thing that moves!' is a sublimely grotesque boast of sexual prowess that terrifies with its chilling hollowness when we witness his per-formative impotence with Dorothy. The young hero Jeffrey (played by Kyle McLachlan) covertly watches Frank's abuse of Dorothy and sees that Frank achieves his demented climax by donning a gas mask, inhaling helium, acting out as Dorothy's baby and calling her 'Mommy' in a high, squeaky voice. Viewers are complicit in Jeffrey's voyeuristic peeping at the disturbing spectacle of Dorothy, the beauty Frank has abused and degraded to the point that she sees herself as worthless and deserving of the abuse Frank inflicts on her.

With Frank's example imprinted on his imagination, Jeffrey too succumbs to the sadistic desire to abuse Beauty and imitate Frank's beastly
behaviour as he feeds Dorothy's masochism by striking her in the act
of love. In a later scene, when Jeffrey and his girlfriend, Sandy (the
innocent virgin in Lynch's virgin/whore Manichean Gothic vision),
find a naked, battered and dazed Dorothy wandering outside Jeffrey's
house, Dorothy's beast-like abjection and degradation are offered up to
the viewer as well. She has been so traumatized by Frank's perverse
appropriation of her child, her life and her body that she regresses to
child-like status, no longer capable of resistance or moral choice.
Although Jeffrey later kills Frank, and Dorothy is reunited with her
child, the slick, glossy ending is ironized by its obvious contrivance.
The Gothic underworld is lurking, as close as the next nightmare. The
blue velvet curtains that open and close the film are sleazy symbols of
the Gothic veil that conceals the secret, shameful nature of human
desire and propensity for violence.[27]

BOB, the demonic serial rapist and killer who freely roams as a
lawless drifter in the Twin Peaks community and also manifests as an
evil double in the hearts and bodies of men, is a supernatural exten-
sion of Frank. His role as the devil or embodiment of evil in the television series and film further confirms the pessimistic Christian
eschatology of Lynch's Gothic vision. The question that begins
the series 'Who killed Laura Palmer?' also establishes the premise
that Beauty is already dead – raped, battered, murdered, bound and
drowned – an overdetermined killing that immediately draws the viewer
into sadistic complicity with this horrific crime against the female body.
With each episode, and especially in the prequel, *Fire Walk with Me*,
the viewer learns that the 'wholesome', homecoming queen, Laura,
was actually a very bad girl, engaging in prostitution, drugs and other
bodily degradations, despite her compensatory attempts to perform
social service and help others. Her boyfriend, Bobby, tells the psychologist, Dr Jacoby:

> She said people tried to be good, but they are really sick and rotten –
> her most of all. And every time she tried to make the world a better
> place something terrible came up inside her and pulled her back
> into hell and took her deeper and deeper into the blackest night-
> mare. Every time it got harder to go back up to the light.[28]

Laura has internalized the masculine view of herself as an evil tempt-
ress and debased sexual object. Towards the end of the series and at the

conclusion of *Fire Walk with Me*, the viewer is horrified to discover that Laura's rapist and killer was her own father, Leland Palmer, who, possessed by the spirit of BOB, began a cycle of incest by sexually abusing his daughter at home in her bedroom and finally, in a frenzy of sadistic rage and jealousy, brutally murders her. In a bizarre echo of the ending of Cocteau's film when the two lovers rise into the starlit sky, Laura's fleshless embodiment sprouts wings and her transfigured, angelic form ascends into the light and the heaven above.[29]

Unlike Cocteau's *La Belle et la Bête*, Lynch's films do not envisage redemption in the form of reciprocal love. In sum, Lynch's 'Beauty and the Beast' narrative seems to redefine original sin as the father's crime against the daughter, a sin that can never be washed clean as long as we inhabit our physical bodies. The father's forbidden desire for his innocent child is the root of evil, and the shame and self-loathing he feels because of his desire lead him to degrade and violate the loved and detested female object of his lust. The ending of the television series evokes the illimitable sublime, when the good Agent Cooper (Kyle McLachlan again) looks into the mirror the morning after his descent into the underworld in a quest to save another young Beauty and sees the image of BOB. This blood-chilling transfiguration heralds the triumph of the beastly sublime, a force that cannot be suppressed by civilized models of Christian manhood. In Lynch's Gothic world, Beauty's demise is predetermined by man's original sin. Laura Palmer never stands a chance in this world; only, perhaps, in the final scene/dream of a celestial afterlife in *Fire Walk with Me*. However, as with the dissonant saccharine conclusion of *Blue Velvet*, the culminating scenes of *Fire* evoke not sublimity, but sentimental stereotypes of feminine goodness, either angelic innocence or the image of maternal love that closes *Blue Velvet*. The viewer is left wondering whether Lynch is sincere in his visions of feminized redemption or whether he is pulling our collective leg.

Finally, I would like to consider a recent Gothic/sci-fi Beauty and the Beast film, *Vanilla Sky* (2001), a faithful remake of the Spanish film *Abre los Ojos* (1997), written and directed by Alejandro Amenabar. To summarize the complex plot, young, handsome, wealthy David Ames (Tom Cruise) is a self-centred, self-indulgent entrepreneur, who lost his parents at an early age and has never known love. He has had and discarded many women. One of his conquests, Julie (Carmen Diaz), resents his cavalier treatment and when he is drawn to another woman, Sophia (played by Penelope Cruz in both the Spanish and American films), Julie entices him into her car and attempts to kill herself and David by crashing the car. Julie dies and David survives, but in an altered state. His arm and face are destroyed and a series of reconstructive surgeries cannot restore his masculine strength and appearance. When he looks in the mirror he sees a monster.

Broken and battered in body and spirit, he realizes that Sophia, whom he now longs for and loves, can never love him in his monstrous form and so he overdoses. His suicide, however, is the beginning of his lucid dream, which he has purchased from an Internet outfit called Life Extensions, which freezes bodies at the moment of death and supplies the frozen consciousness with an alternative dream-life. In David's dream, Sophia returns to him, his face is restored, and he and Sophia are happily in love – until she morphs into the dead Julie before his eyes, a haunting image from his repressed past. Out of guilt, revulsion and paranoia, he smothers Julie/Sophie with a pillow while in the act of sexual intercourse. The violent ugliness that rises up within him, his unleashed beast, snuffs out Beauty. Having obtained love and his feminine ideal in his lucid dream, his unconscious sabotages this utopian fantasy and sends him on a tormented voyage of discovery. At the end of the film, David has learned the truth from a man who serves as Technical Support, and he chooses to wake up – open his eyes – to the uncertain, ugly, but real world of the future.[30] This ending suggests that perfect beauty or a life without pain or nightmare is itself monstrous because the attainment of this ideal thwarts rather than satisfies the beast within us, our unconscious fears and desires, our imperfect humanity.

Laura Mulvey and other Lacanian feminist film theorists might suggest that the Beast reigns over Beauty in Gothic films because the camera eye fetishizes, imprisons and punishes women as the objects of the male gaze, whereas monstrous masculinity attains brutalizing subjectivity by creating a sublimely aweful spectacle of active animality and resistance to objectification. Transfixed in passive loveliness, Beauty incites a physical reaction and unleashes a savage spring in her beastly admirer. According to the terms of the sadistic male fantasy that seems to dominate Gothic cinema, Beauty is culpable of inciting a desire that can only be satisfied by her degradation, and therefore is deservedly and justly diminished.

Gender critiques of masculinity take this analysis beyond Freudian/ Lacanian terminology by acknowledging that in most Western cultures which promulgate stereotypical gender distinctions, men often feel powerless and frustrated because of unfulfilled sexual longing, and these feelings may progress into active anger at the women who arouse these feelings, whether involuntarily or intentionally. Timothy Beneke and Michael Kimmel have argued that many men fear and resent the helplessness and humiliation they sometimes feel in response to public and private displays of female sexuality. Gothic film would seem to provide a fantasy enactment of satisfying those poisonous feelings of lust, fear, anger and desire to dominate.[31]

However, as a counter to the view that the camera is lasciviously and obsessively fixated, that Beauty is immutably passive and helpless to resist her attacker, and that the beast within man must find release in active sadism, we have only to return to Cocteau's revolutionary revision of the fairy tale, wherein Beauty acts according to a virtuous, self-sacrificing, ultimately self-regarding code and Beast conquers his animal urges to unite with his opposite number in a magical, oscillating, egalitarian relationship of love, respect, acceptance and understanding.

Notes

1. Maria Tatar, 'Introduction: *Beauty and the Beast*', in *The Classic Fairy Tales*, ed. Maria Tatar (New York: Norton, 1999), p. 25.
2. Jack Zipes, 'The Dark Side of "Beauty and the Beast": The Origins of the Literary Fairy Tale for Children', *Proceedings of the 8ᵗʰ Annual Conference of the Children's Literature Association* (Minneapolis: University of Minnesota Press, 1981), p. 123.
3. Immanuel Kant, *The Critique of Judgement*, trans. James Creed Meredith (Oxford: Clarendon Press, 1964), p. 91.
4. Kant, 'Analytic of the Beautiful', pp. 50–89, and 'Analytic of the Sublime', pp. 90–165, in *The Critique of Judgement*.
5. Edmund Burke, *A Philosophical Enquiry into the Origin of Our Ideas of the Sublime and Beautiful*, ed. James T. Boulton (South Bend: Notre Dame University Press, 1958), p. 124.
6. Burke, *A Philosophical Enquiry*, p. 58.
7. Apparently, one of Zeus's favourite seduction techniques was to transform himself into tame, pleasing animal shapes in order to gain access to mortal female loveliness, as when he appears as a friendly bull to Europa and a swan to Leda. From the evidence of the fragmented tales, Zeus took on animal forms not so much to make himself more desirable or less threatening, but to escape the detection of his jealous wife, Hera, who, instead of punishing her husband, degraded the objects of his lust into animals, transforming Io into a heifer and Callisto into a bear, although Zeus later cast her into the heavens as a constellation. See Ovid, *Metamorphoses*, trans. Arthur Golding, 1567 (New York: Macmillan, 1965).
8. Because Psyche is ignorant about sex and fearful that the intimate acts she enjoys each night with her invisible husband are unnatural and beastly, she is persuaded by her malicious sisters to slay her husband before her lamp reveals him as the young god Cupid, whereupon he flies off because she has broken his injunction not to look at him. See Apuleius, 'Cupid and Psyche',

The Transformations of Lucius Otherwise Known as the Golden Ass, trans. Robert Graves (New York: Farrar, Straus and Giroux, 1979), pp. 96–143.

9. Apuleius, 'Cupid and Psyche', p. 100.

10. Apuleius, 'Cupid and Psyche', p. 114.

11. Jack Zipes, *Breaking the Magic Spell: Radical Theories of Folk & Fairy Tales* (Lexington, KY: University Press of Kentucky, 2002), pp. 33–4.

12. Beaumont's immediate predecessors published contending versions of the Beauty and Beast conflict which have proven less enduring, including Perrault's 'Ricky of the Tuft' (*Riquet à la Houppe*, 1696), Madama D'Aulnoy's *The Ram (Le Mouton*, 1697), and Madame de Villeneuve's novel, *Beauty and the Beast* (1740), which supplied many of the elements for Beaumont's much shorter version. Perrault's Ricky is not a literally a beast, but rather a hideously ugly man, whose superior male intelligence subdues the unruly, fickle princess to his will. In *The Ram*, the princess comes to love a prince who is condemned to the body of a ram for five years, but forgets about him and her promise to return after she goes home to her father and sisters. Because of her heartless neglect, the ram/prince pines away and dies. The divergent and sometimes unfavourable treatments of Beauty in earlier tales contend with Beaumont's portrayal of a virtuous Beauty with the power to restore bestial man to humanity through love and acceptance, the romantic utopian ending which has been imprinted on our collective Western consciousness.

13. See Jeanne-Marie Leprince de Beaumont, 'Beauty and the Beast', in *The Classic Fairy Tales*, pp. 32–42.

14. See Bruno Bettleheim, *The Uses of Enchantment: The Meaning and Importance of Fairy Tales* (New York: Knopf, 1976), pp. 303–10.

15. Phyllis Ralph, '"Beauty and the Beast": Growing Up with Jane Eyre', in Diane Long Hoeveler and Beth Lau, eds, *Approaches to Teaching Jane Eyre* (New York: MLA, 1993), pp. 56–61.

16. Betsy Hearne, *Beauty and the Beast: Visions and Revisions of an Old Tale* (Chicago: University of Chicago Press, 1989).

17. See *Beauty and the Beast*, dir. Gary Trousdale and Kirk Wise, animated, Walt Disney Pictures Productions (1991).

18. Rebecca M. Pauly, '*Beauty and the Beast*: From Fable to Film', *Literature and Film Quarterly* 17:2 (1989), p. 88, trans. from Jean Cocteau, *Journal d'un inconnu* (Paris: Grasset, 1953).

19. Michael Popkin, 'Cocteau's "Beauty and the Beast": The Poet as Monster', *Literature and Film Quarterly* 10:2 (1982), pp. 100–9.

20. See *La Belle et la Bête*, dir. Jean Cocteau, screenplay Jean Cocteau (1946), based on 'Beauty and the Beast' by Jeanne-Marie Leprince de Beaumont.

21. Simone de Beauvoir, *The Second Sex*, trans. H. M. Parshley (New York: Random House, 1989), p. 401.

22. Mary Ann Doane, 'Film and the Masquerade: Theorising the Female Spectator', ed. Sue Thornham, *Feminist Film Theory: A Reader* (New York: New York University Press, 1999), p. 133.

23. See Laura Mulvey, 'Visual Pleasure and Narrative Cinema' and 'Afterthoughts on "Visual Pleasure and Narrative Cinema", inspired by King Vidor's *Duel in the Sun* (1946)', in *Feminist Film Theory*, pp. 58–9 and 122–30.

24. *The Collector*, dir. William Wyler (1965), based on the novel by John Fowles.
25. See John Fowles, *The Collector* (New York: Dell, 1963). The first section of the novel is told from Freddy's point of view, and then Miranda's journal entries recount her kidnapping and imprisonment up to the point of her death. She comes to refer to Freddy as Caliban, indicating that she views him as an unevolved beast/man. The final, brief section of the novel gives us Freddy's reflections on Miranda's death, so that Miranda's more literate, upper-class narrative is contained by Freddy's less articulate, obsessive desire for the unobtainable feminine and class privilege that Miranda represents.
26. See David Lavery, ed., *Full of Secrets: Critical Approaches to Twin Peaks* (Detroit: Wayne State University Press, 1995).
27. See *Blue Velvet*, dir. David Lynch, written by David Lynch (1986).
28. Quoted in Christy Desmet, 'The Canonization of Laura Palmer', in Lavery (ed.) *Full of Secrets*, p. 96.
29. See *Twin Peaks*, dir. David Lynch, Mark Frost et al., written by David Lynch, Mark Frost et al., 30 episodes (8 April 1990–23 May 1990 and 30 September 1990–10 June 1991), ABC Network, and *Twin Peaks: Fire Walk with Me*, dir. David Lynch, written by David Lynch and Mark Frost (1992).
30. *Vanilla Sky*, dir. Cameron Crowe, screenplay Cameron Crowe (2001), based on the film *Abre los Ojos*, written by Alejandro Amenabar and Mateo Gil (1997).
31. See Timothy Beneke, *Proving Manhood: Reflections on Men and Sexism* (Berkeley, CA: University of California Press, 1997); and Michael Kimmel, *The Gender of Desire: Essays on Male Sexuality* (Albany, NY: State University of New York Press, 2005).

References

Apuleius, 'Cupid and Psyche', *The Transformations of Lucius Otherwise Known as The Golden Ass*, trans. Robert Graves (New York: Farrar, Straus and Giroux, 1979), pp. 96–143.
de Beaumont, Jeanne-Marie Leprince, 'Beauty and the Beast', in *The Classic Fairy Tales* ed. Maria Tatar (New York: Norton, 1999).
La Belle et la Bête dir. Jean Cocteau, screenplay Jean Cocteau (1946). Based on 'Beauty and the Beast' by Jeanne-Marie Leprince de Beaumont.
Bettelheim, Bruno, *The Uses of Enchantment: The Meaning and Importance of Fairy Tales* (New York: Knopf, 1976).
Blue Velvet, dir. David Lynch, written by David Lynch (1986).
Burke, Edmund, *A Philosophical Enquiry into the Origin of Our Ideas of the Sublime and Beautiful* (1757; South Bend: Notre Dame University Press, 1958).
The Collector, dir. William Wyler (1965). Based on the novel by John Fowles.
Fowles, John, *The Collector* (New York: Dell, 1963).
Hearne, Betsy, *Beauty and the Beast: Visions and Revisions of an Old Tale* (Chicago: University of Chicago Press, 1989).
Kant, Immanuel, *The Critique of Judgement*, trans. and ed. James Creed Meredith (Oxford: Clarendon Press, 1964).

Lavery, David, ed., *Full of Secrets: Critical Approaches to Twin Peaks* (Detroit: Wayne State University Press, 1995).

Ovid *Metamorphoses*, trans. Arthur Golding (1567; New York: Macmillan, 1965).

Popkin, Michael, 'Cocteau's "Beauty and the Beast": The Poet as Monster', *Literature and Film Quarterly*, 10:2 (1982), 100–9.

Ralph, Phyllis, '"Beauty and the Beast": Growing up with Jane Eyre', Diane Long Hoeveler and Beth Lau, eds, *Approaches to Teaching Jane Eyre* (New York: MLA, 1993), pp. 56–61.

Thornham, Sue, ed., *Feminist Film Theory: A Reader* (New York: New York University Press, 1999).

Twin Peaks, dir. David Lynch, Mark Frost et al., written by David Lynch, Mark Frost et al. 30 episodes (8 April 1990–23 May 1990 and 30 September 1990–10 June 1991, ABC Network).

Twin Peaks: Fire Walk with Me, dir. David Lynch, written by David Lynch and Mark Frost (1992).

Vanilla Sky, dir. Cameron Crowe, screenplay Cameron Crowe (2001). Based on the film *Abre los Ojos,* written by Alejandro Amenabar and Mateo Gil.

Zipes, Jack, *Breaking the Magic Spell: Radical Theories of Folk & Fairy Tales* (Lexington, KY: University Press of Kentucky, 2002).

—— 'The Dark Side of "Beauty and the Beast": The Origins of the Literary Fairy Tale for Children', *Proceedings of the 8th Annual Conference of the Children's Literature Association* (Minneapolis, MN: University of Minnesota Press, 1981), pp. 119–25.

10
'Who is the third who walks always beside you?' Eliot, Stoker and Stetson in *The Waste Land*

William Hughes

Academic criticism has long speculated regarding the influence of Bram Stoker's *Dracula* (1897) on T. S. Eliot's *The Waste Land* (1922), though the novel itself is named neither in the poem nor in its at times ironic endnotes. The interface of the two works is inevitably problematic. Stoker's 'prurient, highly coloured sensationalist prose', according to A. N. Wilson's introduction to the 1983 Oxford World's Classics edition of *Dracula*, ensures that 'It is not a great work of literature'.[1] Conversely, *The Waste Land*, according to Calvin Bedient, is 'the quintessential poem of Anglo-American modernism' – a text, in other words, unequivocally worthy of serious study and a suitable recipient, therefore, of a more favourable critical hyperbole.[2] It is this gap between the serious and the sensationalist, between the unanimously accepted and the merely tolerated – in genre as much as in choice of texts – that has coloured the way in which academic criticism has reacted to the apparent presence of *Dracula* in *The Waste Land*. The intertextual trace of Stoker's novel has been noted, but never explored at length. Unlike the allusions to Dante, Spenser or Shakespeare in *The Waste Land*, *Dracula*, a text neither historically canonical nor venerably antique, is conventionally mentioned merely in passing during analysis. If not an embarrassment, then it is an inconvenience for criticism – a private joke on Eliot's part, never adequately explained, never worthy, indeed, of the effort of explanation, at least in the rarefied field of Modernist criticism. *Dracula*, after all, lies within the field of the Gothicist rather than the Modernist – and seemingly *The Waste Land* is to be found outside of that critically fertile field. A subtle and unacknowledged pressure, as it were, restricts the debate. Yet, there is more to be said about *Dracula* in *The Waste Land*, as indeed there are further matters to be considered in the poem's relationship to the broader meaning of the mythological vampire, at first sight an odd figure in Modernism's mechanical landscape of the urban and rational.

Conventionally, the perceived intertextuality between the two works is centred solely on an episode in 'What the Thunder Said', the final section of the poem. This phase of *The Waste Land*, which depicts an arid and desolate landscape of 'cracked earth' peopled by 'hooded hordes', first recounts how, to the sound of a 'Murmur of maternal lamentation', an unnamed 'city over the mountains' spectacularly 'cracks and reforms and bursts in the violet air'. The poem then ponderously intones a litany of civilizations either already despoiled or seemingly poised on the brink of cultural collapse – 'Jerusalem Athens Alexandria Vienna London'. These cities are the locations, one assumes, of the 'Falling towers', literal or figurative, which precede their funereal tabulation here; the places in which one has witnessed, may presently witness or may come to witness, the life in death of a culture.

From such apocalyptic generalizations, the poem turns to a more intimate scenario:

> A woman drew her long black hair out tight
> And fiddled whisper music on those strings
> And bats with baby faces in the violet light
> Whistled, and beat their wings
> And crawled head downward down a blackened wall[3]

This appears an obvious enough allusion. In Stoker's novel, Jonathan Harker's madness is in part triggered by such a scene as this, where the imprisoned solicitor sees not a bat but his host, Count Dracula, 'slowly emerge from the window and begin to crawl down the castle wall over that dreadful abyss, *face down*, with his cloak spreading out around him like great wings' (*Dracula*, p. 34; author's emphasis).[4] Eliot's adaptation of this striking scene from *Dracula* was noted as early as 1971 in a short article in *The Explicator* by Lee J. Richmond. It becomes the starting point for a speculation which really fails to develop the intertextual implications to their full potential. Eliot's Waste Land, in common with the Count's desolate demesne, embodies a despoiled chapel, and this particular edifice is considered by Richmond first in connection with the journey to the Perilous Chapel of the Grail Legend – acknowledged by Eliot in his notes (*The Waste Land*, p. 79) – and subsequently with a 'perilous cemetery haunted by the Un-Dead', ambiguously the place in the West to which the Count has brought 'the curse of the living dead', his infectious and debilitative vampirism.[5] Curiously, for Richmond, Eliot's meditative but seemingly harmless Tiresias, one who has suffered rather than brought suffering, is obliquely related to Stoker's malign count merely because he is 'neither living nor dead'.[6] Maxine Rance, writing sixteen years later and seemingly unaware of Richmond's article, makes essentially the same points, though in less detail, in a contribution to *Notes and Queries*. The downward crawl is again regarded as being less an allusion to *Dracula* and more a suitable device to portray the no doubt surreal 'hallucinations of the Knight in search of the Chapel Perilous'.[7] *Dracula*, seemingly, is a less worthy text than *Parzifal*.[8]

Richmond's speculation is taken up by Donald Beagle in the most recent consideration of this question, again in *The Explicator*. As Beagle asserts, 'the allusion [to *Dracula*] was more explicit' in an earlier draft of *The Waste Land*, not available to his two predecessors in criticism. In this draft the equivalent passage from 'What the Thunder Said' reads:

> A woman drew her long black hair out tight
> And fiddled whisper-music on those strings
> The shrill bats quivered through the violet air
> ~~Sobbing~~ Whining, and beating wings
>   distorted
> A man, ~~one withered~~ by some mental blight
>   contorted
> Yet of abnormal powers
>   Such a one crept
>   I saw him creep head downward down a wall.[9]

Two other undated manuscript revisions, not mentioned by Beagle, also recall the scene in *Dracula*. In the first, written in Eliot's own hand, 'A ~~man~~/form crawled downward down a blackened wall'. The second, a revision of a typescript which dates from as late as January 1922, excises 'a form', effectively merging the singular Count into the bats that descend the wall of the published poem.[10] What was an obvious allusion is thus made more subtle in the transition between manuscript and publication. The case for Eliot's allusion to *Dracula*, if one reads Beagle's article and, indeed, supplements his evidence with the further manuscript revisions to this scene from *The Waste Land*, appears convincing, if not closed.

Like Richmond, Beagle is keen to stress the connections between the empty chapel of the poem and the ecclesiastical edifice of the Grail legends, which he argues is replicated in *Dracula*. All are associated, he suggests, with a quest, the shedding and sharing of blood, and (via the poem's opening epigraph from the *Satyricon*) an eventual release into death and peace, 'shantih', for the Sybil or the vampire who 'longs for death' and 'is unable to die'.[11] Again, there would seem to be a determination in the work of the commentator on Modernism, when acknowledging the presence of Stoker's novel within *The Waste Land*, to stress only the alleged high-cultural or scholarly authorized mythological content of the former. The novel itself is again apparently incapable of being a referent in its own right, becoming little more than an allusion which itself teasingly alludes to a more appropriately elitist source.

There is a little more to say, however, with regard to the presence of *Dracula* in 'What the Thunder Said'. Further allusions to the novel, *as* a novel rather than as a *bricolage* of references to more worthy works, are apparent, and these have been singularly overlooked by Modernist scholars. The setting for the closing stages of the novel in particular strikingly prefigures the landscape of Eliot's poem. Mina Harker and her defenders end their quest in the count's exhausted and culturally backward Carpathian homeland, where 'The country gets wilder' as they travel, becoming, at the threshold of the castle, 'a more wild and desert land' still (*Dracula*, pp. 362 and 365). Historically, the troops of Attila, the count's own ancestor, have roamed these desolate plains (*Dracula*, p. 29), rather in the manner of Eliot's chronologically vague 'hooded hordes'. It is in this wilderness that absolute darkness succumbs to 'a light of some kind, as there ever is over snow' (*Dracula*, p. 366), a chromatic correspondent, arguably, of the violet light that suffuses the decline of cultural and personal life on two occasions in Eliot's poem.[12]

It also seems odd that no consideration has been given as to the identity of the woman with the 'long black hair' and, indeed, the significance of her curious pose. Mina Harker, the count's second victim, might appear a likely candidate for this role, for though the colour of her hair is never explicitly mentioned in the novel, it is clear that she wears it both long and loose (*Dracula*, p. 296).[13] Being bitten by the vampire, she draws it round her as a covering for her shame, 'as the leper of old his mantle', emitting not 'whisper music' but a mournful keening of hopelessness and self-abasement (*Dracula*, p. 296). In this inhospitable region there are faces that express fear of the vampire's victim from house doorways (*Dracula*, p. 361), even if they should not go so far as to 'sneer and snarl' in the manner of those depicted by

Eliot (*The Waste Land*, p. 72). Finally, if, as Calvin Bedient suggests, the bats of *The Waste Land* are ambiguously born of Eliot's dark-haired woman – 'driven out of sheltering dark female enclosures ... in a parody of birth' – their status as 'horrid little infantile Count Draculas' links them utterly to Mina, the count's victim, child, bride and, after the ritual disposal of Lucy Westenra, the matrix of his prospective English heirs and descendants (*Dracula*, pp. 288 and 306).[14]

Reference to the cancelled drafts of *The Waste Land* may further suggest that *Dracula* was originally envisaged as a considerably more central text than it eventually became in the poem. One can discern the count not merely through his habit of descending his castle walls 'head downward', as Beagle observes, but also through his depiction as:

distorted
A man, ~~one withered~~ by some mental blight
contorted
Yet of abnormal powers ...[15]

The count is twice analysed in the novel through the scientific criminology of the *fin de siècle*, a popular as well as clinical discourse which systematically relates both physical deformity and mental deviance to a predisposition to violence and crime. On meeting the count for the first time, Harker dwells on his host's physicality – his domed forehead, sharp teeth, pointed ears and hairy palms all being signifiers in a common currency of moral and physical degeneration.[16] It is Harker's wife, Mina, who is most explicit with regards to the count's mental state, however, when she states, 'The Count is a criminal and of criminal type. Nordau and Lombroso would so classify him, and *qua* criminal he is of imperfectly formed mind' (*Dracula*, p. 342). Van Helsing similarly considers the count to 'be of child-brain in much', given that the criminal 'has not full man-brain. He is clever and cunning and resourceful; but he be not of man-stature as to brain' (*Dracula*, p. 341). The 'abnormal powers' here are thus not merely the count's supernatural ones. Because of the contextual use of late Victorian scientific criminology they include, ostensibly, his 'mental blight' and deviant practices, the very things with which this atavistic Eastern invader whom Harker is 'helping to transfer to London' will exercise in order to 'create a new and ever widening circle of semi-demons to batten on the helpless' (*Dracula*, p. 51). The count's curse, in certain respects, is the imposition of mere replication and repetition upon creativity, the subsuming of individuality under monotonous, all-consuming appetite.

The count's destructive force, as critics of the Gothic have frequently argued, is intimately bound up with this infection of the West by the East, and with its tendency to 'Eastern' practices or standards inimical to Western standards.[17] With all due respect to Richmond's reading of *The Waste Land*, Eliot's destructive, Dracula-style entity ought not to be not the flaccid, tired Tiresias but the more sinister Mr Eugenides, the unshaven 'Smyrna merchant' of 'The Fire Sermon' who, one assumes, has travelled to London from Turkey, the heartland of Richard Burton's Sodatic Zone, and who inducts Western heterosexuals into deviant 'Eastern' practices in Brighton hotel rooms.[18]

The allusions to *Dracula* in *The Waste Land* arguably extend beyond their accepted inclusion in 'What the Thunder Said'. In the published version of Eliot's poem, the fourth section, 'Death by Water', the three-stanza elegy of Phlebas the Phoenician is considerably shorter than the voyage originally projected in the manuscript. This latter is a fishing voyage in Eastern seas, rounding an unnamed cape in uncertain weather. As is the case in Stoker's *Dracula*, where a sailing vessel passes Cape Matapan in Greece *en route* to England (*Dracula*, p. 82), the crew is anxious and disgruntled, one man in particular expressing unease at the vessel's inability to sail to any course dictated by the mortal Master.[19] This phase of the unpublished poem appears to be narrated by the ship's captain, as is the case with the log of the *Demeter*, the Russian vessel in which Stoker's vampire is carried from the Black Sea port of Varna.[20] As with the *Demeter*, Eliot's ship sails at the mercy of the winds and the sea, 'leaping beneath invisible stars' as the *Demeter* too had voyaged without hope or purposeful direction within the obscurity of fog and high seas (*Dracula*, p. 83).[21] Both ships are deprived of navigational landmarks, their only guide to position being sounds heard through the gloom or brief glimpses of distant terrain (*Dracula*, p. 84).[22] Sunrise is sensed, rather than actually seen, by the two captains (*Dracula*, p. 85).[23] Both vessels finally encounter a port whose visible boundary is 'A wall, a barrier, towards which we drove'.[24]

On watch, Stoker's captain eventually encounters the vampire that has decimated his ship's crew and blighted his voyage (*Dracula*, p. 85). Eliot's master mariner, though, sees not this singular figure but rather a tableau of apparitions reminiscent of an earlier episode in *Dracula*. The grouping recalls both the sirens of classical mythology and the trio of female vampires who entrance first Harker and later Van Helsing in *Dracula* (*Dracula*, pp. 37 and 367).[25] The narrator recalls how:

>   … One night
> On watch, I thought I saw in the fore cross-trees
> Three women … leaning forward, with white hair
> Streaming behind, who sang above the wind
> A song that charmed my senses, while I was
> Frightened beyond fear, horrified past horror, calm,
> (Nothing was real) for, I thought, now, when
> I like, I can wake up and end the dream.[26]

Stoker's erotic women lack the white hair, though their laughter is hypnotically 'musical' (p. 37). The recognition in Harker's account of a 'voluptuousness … both thrilling and repulsive (*Dracula*, p. 38) generates a sense of anticipation both fearful and delightful, and mobilizes an intensity of experience beyond anything previously encountered. Harker recalls how, passive and 'in a languorous ecstasy', he 'waited – waited with beating heart' (*Dracula*, p. 38). Reactions such as these proclaim what Victor Sage terms 'the abnegation of the will' of the perceiver, the sense of powerlessness of one who might otherwise be the master of his own destiny, at sea or in the castle.[27] One observes, but is powerless to act. The two perceivers may attempt to disarm the horrors of this collapse of volition by vainly claiming the whole thing to have been a dream (*Dracula*, p. 40), though the fear vested in the possibility of the apparitions' reality cannot be dismissed, whether one assertively wakes the self or passively awakes.

It is too easy, though, to reduce any reading of *Dracula* in *The Waste Land* to a mere acknowledgement of quotations or apparent paraphrases, fragments which the critic may recognize, though not always apply successfully in order to impose a semblance of order or meaning upon Eliot's commodious ruins. Even the attempt to allocate meaning to appropriation might be specious itself, an act of 'bogus scholarship' as blatant as Eliot's attributions by way of his falsely authoritative footnotes.[28] In evading such closure – or speculation – the critic must consequently confront not the allusion but the source of the allusion, the author and novel which sit so uneasily, perhaps, within a poem populated by canonical luminaries as diverse as Dante, Spenser, Shakespeare, Baudelaire, Ovid and Virgil. Given that, as Pound asserted in a letter to Eliot, *The Waste Land* is 'for the elect or the remnant or the select few or the superior guys', a popular text such as *Dracula* seems a strange bedfellow for such illustrious company as the *Aeneid*, the *Metamorphoses* or *The Divine Comedy*.[29] On one level, this might all be another act of ironic playfulness: Eliot defying, as it were, the elite,

1920s reader not so much to recognize as to admit a personal knowledge of the mass-culture referent. On another level, though, it might
as easily be argued that the poet's apparent attitude to Stoker's novel
has more in common with the criticism of the 1980s than that of the
1920s. Sometimes a vampire novel may be read as being much more
than simply a popular, formulaic horror story.

If the elitist, thoroughly twentieth-century critic of Eliot's own time
might be forgiven for overlooking – or preferring not to recognize – the
presence of an author from late Victorian popular culture in this
most aristocratic of works, then he or she might well have recognized
a much earlier reference to the Un-dead in *The Waste Land*. This context, though obscure to the twenty-first-century reader, has both an
American origin and an intellectual resonance of accredited scholarship quite in keeping with the tastes of Pound's 'elect' or 'select few'.
The matter in question is to be found near the end of the first section
of *The Waste Land*, 'The Burial of the Dead', and is intimate to its
hellish Dantean vision of a London seen 'Under the brown fog of a
winter dawn'.[30] Within this landscape flows a tide of humanity, mobile
yet seemingly dead, the drones – as Calvin Bedient suggests – of an
urban, anonymous and hopeless capitalist system.[31] These are another type of the Un-dead, a secular rather than occult version of
hopeless damnation, consumption and replication driven by appetite
alone.

Within this seemingly undifferentiated mass, one figure only catches
the eye of the poem's narrator:

> There I saw one I knew, and stopped him, crying: 'Stetson!
> 'You who were with me in the ships at Mylae!
> 'That corpse you planted last year in your garden,
> 'Has it begun to sprout? Will it bloom this year?
> 'Or has the sudden frost disturbed its bed?
> 'O keep the Dog far hence that's friend to men,
> 'Or with its nails he'll dig it up again!
> 'You, hypocrite lecteur! – mon semblable, – mon frère![32]

Bedient reads the sprouting corpse as a Gothicized version of the
Hyacinth Girl encountered earlier in 'The Burial of the Dead', one who,
when emotionally overwhelmed, envisaged herself as 'neither living
nor dead'.[33] Bedient rapidly retreats, though, from such Gothic possibilities in order to configure Stetson and the narrator as brothers in
a Freudian primal crime, with the blooming corpse as the murdered

father or mother.[34] The syntax of the piece, Bedient asserts, 'pins Stetson to a bloody history'.[35]

There is a great deal of unintended irony vested in this remark, as Stetson does indeed have 'a bloody history' of sorts, even though for most critics he has no history at all. Eliot's choice of name here – a curious appellation for an apparent participant in the first Punic War of 261–240 BC – has never been satisfactorily explained.[36] Reputedly, Valerie Eliot is supposed to have assumed Stetson to be Pound. Subsequent critics, though, are either vaguer or less certain. In more recent times, Hugh Kenner (1959) has called Stetson, somewhat blandly, 'the speaker's acquaintance', Steve Ellis (1994) has delineated the Punic sailor as nothing more than 'a colleague', and – extraordinarily, given Eliot's taste for references and word games – the magisterial Cleanth Brooks (1939) has presumed the name to have 'no ulterior significance', being 'merely an ordinary name such as might be borne by the friend one might see in a crowd in a great city'.[37]

Stetson is not Pound in a big hat.[38] Nor is he Count Dracula, or Tiresias. He is, though, a brother-in-letters to Bram Stoker, albeit on the level of textual preoccupation rather than actual or direct quotation. Charles Powell, reviewing *The Waste Land* for the *Manchester Guardian* in 1923, asserts the poem to be 'not for the ordinary reader' and effectively inexplicable other than to 'anthropologists and *literati*'.[39] If Stoker's novel was allegedly all but invisible to the elitist *literati*, then the name of Stetson – in full, George R. Stetson – ought to have stimulated a response among those familiar with Anglo-American anthropology at the turn of the century. Stetson's article, 'The Animistic Vampire in New England', published in *The American Anthropologist* in January 1896, some twelve months before *Dracula*, is neither quoted nor paraphrased in *The Waste Land*, though its depressive tone and appreciation of contemporary culture arguably informs the poem's own lament on the decline of quality of life.

The corpse associated with the Stetson of the poem is, in this respect, not a literal or literary vampire ready to rise up to predate on the West, but a shadow of the dead, buried but still resurgent opinions and attitudes which the anthropologist despairingly encounters in America, even in 'the enlightened nineteenth century'.[40] Stetson's vampire is not so much animistic as atavistic. The anthropologist argues that the present cultural state of New England represents 'an extraordinary instance of a barbaric superstition outcropping in and coexisting with a high general culture'.[41] Superstition itself appears to be but one symptom of a culture rendered so stagnant that it has become also 'the tramping ground of the book agent, the chromo peddler, the patent-medicine man and the home of the erotic and neurotic modern novel'.[42] Folk superstition, in other words, sits easily alongside the modern mythologies of quasi-science and paranoiac fiction. In consequence, Stetson's anthropological New England has become as much a waste land as Eliot's poetic terrain. The anthropologist notes how 'Farm-houses deserted and ruinous are frequent, and the once productive lands, [are] neglected and overgrown with scrubby oak'.[43] Youth has migrated from the countryside to the drone-occupations of the city and neither environment seems to offer hope or any indication of cultural progress. There is no wounded Fisher King in Rhode Island, no grail to seek and crave succour from. The problem is that 'the superstitions of a much lower culture have maintained their place and are likely to keep it and perpetuate it, despite the church, the public school, and the weekly newspaper'.[44] For Eliot, arguably, superstition is not the issue: rather, it is the debilitative influence of the 'lower cultural order'. Eliot's poetic dog in 'The Burial of the Dead' may equally not be there simply to dig up the corpse of such beliefs. He may have a biblical antecedent in the Book of Proverbs: 'As a dog returneth to his vomit, so a fool returneth to his folly.'[45] In the context of Eliot's poem, 'a fool' may as easily be a culture as an individual, this return to folly being a collective and atavistic retreat from progress. The hooded hordes of the East have their parallel in the bowed heads and downcast eyes of the West: barbarianism need not be promulgated solely by the sword. This sprouting corpse is not likely to bring forth a cornucopia in the manner of those ritually efficacious beings recorded by Frazer.[46]

It is this 'lower cultural order', not socially proletarian but culturally barbaric, not localized but general, which Eliot mobilizes both in his Dantean, densely peopled streets and in the bleak intimacies of the typist's bedsit, the homosexual's hotel room and the working-class public house. Eliot has taken the cultural corpse from the country to the city, from generalization to synecdoche. Regional isolation, proclaimed as the source of decline in Stetson's article, is replaced by a more personal application of exclusion, a loneliness or temporariness in everyday lives, within Eliot's poem. Viewing the broader picture, as Stetson says, 'it is fortunate' that such isolation 'has produced nothing worse'.[47] In *The Waste Land* it does not *produce* anything, but participates in and perpetuates a general and depressing sense of immobile meaninglessness. This is the 'indifference' or the boredom of 'the violet hour', the locking of 'each in his prison', the consequence of a mechanical and repetitive world without metaphorical 'controlling hands', the guides, as it were, of living rather than stagnant culture.[48]

Cause and effect thus become cause and protracted decline. Eliot may have suggested that *The Waste Land* was less 'criticism of the contemporary world' and more 'the relief of a personal ... grouse against life', though taken broadly, that 'grouse' may well have been connected with the isolated life emblematized in the persons of any one of the living dead peopling Eliot's streets or buildings.[49] These are small lives, lives not truly lived. In this light, *The Waste Land* evokes a cultural despair as emphatic as that in Matthew Arnold's *Culture and Anarchy*, for all the facetiousness and mock grandeur which punctuates the poem.

One cannot argue that either Stoker or Stetson provides an essential or singular key to the mysteries of *The Waste Land*, the vampire being but one signifier among many. Eliot's alignment, though, of a popular novel and an anthropological study is undeniably significant. Both works are preoccupied with cultural decline, though *Dracula* only became acceptable as a serious commentary on the *fin de siècle* some six decades after the publication of *The Waste Land*. It is not to be suggested that Eliot has made this connection years in advance of modern literary criticism. His achievement, rather, is to layer fictional allusion with intellectual commentary, to create an alignment which might be productive of such interfaces. Eliot is writing in England about a West which seems to be exclusively European – no American cities are mentioned, after all, in his litany of social or urban decadence.[50] Yet it is a text treating of cultural decline, rather than advance, in the United States that is the vehicle for part of the poem's rhetoric. If Eliot's declining 'Eastern Europe' juxtaposes, and in this way threatens, his contemporary West in London, then so surely may Europe be seen as the Eastern Other to America's own Western location.[51] Bleakly, if Stetson is to be believed, superstition and ignorance are practised in the New World almost as diligently as they are celebrated in Stoker's *Dracula*.[52] By the end of *The Waste Land*, notably, 'London bridge is falling down falling down falling down', and in its train are falling culture and stability also.[53] With Stetson's authority acknowledged, there is no forward-looking West to anticipate on the other side of the Atlantic.

The dead and the un-dead thus link all three texts – *The Waste Land*, *Dracula* and 'The Animistic Vampire in New England'. The two referential texts, though, have until now been largely forgotten. To borrow a line from 'The Dry Salvages' (1941), 'We had the experience but missed the meaning' – or possibly we had the meaning, but lost the context.[54]

Notes

1. Bram Stoker, *Dracula*, ed. A. N. Wilson (Oxford: Oxford University Press, 1983), p. xiv. Subsequent quotations are taken from this edition, and page references will be given in parentheses in the body of the text.
2. Calvin Bedient, *He Do the Police in Different Voices: The Waste Land and its Protagonist* (Chicago: University of Chicago Press, 1986), p. ix.
3. T. S. Eliot, *The Waste Land* in *The Complete Poems and Plays of T. S. Eliot* (London: Faber and Faber, 1970), pp. 59–80, p. 73. Subsequent references are to this published edition of the poem unless specified.
4. For a medical reading of this scene see: William Hughes, '"Terrors that I dare not think of": Masculinity, Hysteria and Empiricism in Bram Stoker's *Dracula*', in Elizabeth Miller, ed., *Dracula: The Shade and the Shadow* (Westcliff-on-Sea: Desert Island Books, 1998), pp. 93–103, pp. 96–7.
5. Lee J. Richmond, 'Eliot's *The Waste Land* 380–395', *The Explicator*, 30 (1971), 11–13. Cf. Stoker, *Dracula*, p. 23; Eliot, *The Waste Land*, pp. 68, 73. The annotated manuscript of *The Waste Land* became available in facsimile form in 1971, and it appears that Richmond did not have access to this reprinted work whilst researching his article. The location of the manuscript, which left Eliot's possession in 1922, became public knowledge in 1968, following a formal announcement by the New York Public Library.
6. Richmond, 'Eliot's *The Waste Land* 380–395', p. 12.
7. Maxine Rance, 'Dracula in *The Waste Land*', *Notes and Queries*, 34 (1987), 508–9.
8. Clive Leatherdale considers the Grail context of *Dracula* in conjunction with the Tarot, which Eliot makes extensive use of in *The Waste Land*, in *Dracula: The Novel and the Legend* (Wellingborough: Aquarian Press, 1985), pp. 192–205, passim.
9. Donald Beagle, 'Eliot's *The Waste Land*', *The Explicator*, 47 (1989), 40–1, p. 40; T. S. Eliot, *The Waste Land: A Facsimile and Transcript of the Original Drafts including the Annotations of Ezra Pound*, ed. Valerie Eliot (London: Faber and Faber, 1971), p. 113.
10. Eliot, *The Waste Land: A Facsimile*, pp. 75, 87. Vivien Eliot notes that the annotations to the typescript reproduced on p. 87 of the Facsimile edition of the poem postdate Eliot's visit to Pound in Paris in 1922, where the earlier version of the work was annotated by the latter: ibid., pp. xxii, 83.
11. Beagle, 'Eliot's *The Waste Land*', p. 41.
12. Eliot, *The Waste Land*, pp. 68, 73.
13. Lucy Westenra, the count's first victim, is usually regarded as being fair-haired, though changes made between the first and second editions make this ambiguous in later reprints. See Leatherdale, *Dracula: The Novel and the Legend*, p. 236, n. 10.
14. Bedient, *He Do the Police in Different Voices*, p. 186.
15. Eliot, *The Waste Land: A Facsimile*, p. 113.
16. For a detailed critical reading of these signifiers see Daniel Pick, '"Terrors of the Night": *Dracula* and "Degeneration" in the Late Nineteenth Century', *Critical Quarterly*, 30/4 (1988), 71–87.

17. See, for example, Stephen D. Arata, 'The Occidental Tourist: *Dracula* and the Anxiety of Reverse Colonization', *Victorian Studies*, 33 (1990), 621–45, pp. 630–2.
18. Eliot, *The Waste Land*, p. 68. Eliot suggests in his notes that all the males of the text are but one male, and Tiresias, with his 'wrinkled female breasts' (p. 68) unites the two sexes: see p. 78.
19. Eliot, *The Waste Land: A Facsimile*, p. 57. Appreciation of the situation faced by the ships in both texts is probably dependent also upon familiarity with Coleridge's 'The Rime of the Ancient Mariner'. The latter is quoted in the newspaper report of the loss of the *Demeter*: Stoker, *Dracula*, p. 76.
20. Demeter, as both Eliot and the university-educated Stoker would have known, is a significant Greek corn deity. She is mentioned extensively in Frazer's *The Golden Bough* (1922), which Eliot acknowledges in his notes to *The Waste Land*, particularly in association with the juxtaposition of 'the melancholy gloom and decay of autumn ... to the freshness, the brightness, and the verdure of spring'. See Eliot, *The Waste Land*, p. 76; J. G. Frazer, *The Golden Bough: A Study in Magic and Religion*, abridged edition, 2 volumes (London: Macmillan, 1960), Vol. 2, p. 525.
21. Eliot, *The Waste Land: A Facsimile*, p. 59.
22. Eliot, *The Waste Land: A Facsimile*, p. 59.
23. Eliot, *The Waste Land: A Facsimile*, p. 61.
24. Eliot, *The Waste Land*, p. 61, cf. Stoker, *Dracula*, p. 78.
25. Though 'two [of the three] are dark', the other is 'as fair as can be, with great, wavy masses of golden hair and eyes like pale sapphires': Stoker, *Dracula*, p. 37.
26. Eliot, *The Waste Land: A Facsimile*, p. 59.
27. Victor Sage, *Horror Fiction in the Protestant Tradition* (Basingstoke: Macmillan, 1988), p. 186.
28. Steve Ellis, '*The Waste Land* and the Reader's Response', in Terry Davies and Nigel Wood, eds, *The Waste Land* (Buckingham: Open University Press, 1994), pp. 83–104, p. 103.
29. Quoted in Eliot, *The Waste Land: A Facsimile*, p. xxiii.
30. Unlike the subsequent matter surrounding the bats and the falling towers, this section of the poem was not substantially modified or annotated in the draft seen by Pound. See Eliot, *The Waste Land: A Facsimile*, p. 9.
31. Bedient, *He Do the Police in Different Voices*, p. 63.
32. Eliot, *The Waste Land*, pp. 62–3, cf. Eliot, *The Waste Land: A Facsimile*, p. 9.
33. Bedient, *He Do the Police in Different Voices*, p. 66; Eliot, *The Waste Land*, p. 62.
34. Bedient, *He Do the Police in Different Voices*, p. 66.
35. Bedient, *He Do the Police in Different Voices*, pp. 72, 67, 72.
36. The naval Battle of Mylae was fought in 260 BC, the Romans defeating the Carthaginians. See F. L. Lucas's review of *The Waste Land* in *New Statesman*, 3 November 1923, reproduced in Cox and Hinchcliffe, eds, *T. S. Eliot: The Waste Land* (London: Macmillan, 1968), p. 37.
37. Hugh Kenner, 'The Invisible Poet' [1959], in Cox and Hinchcliffe, eds, *T. S. Eliot: The Waste Land*, pp. 168–99, p. 183; Ellis, '*The Waste Land* and the Reader's Response', p. 91; Cleanth Brooks, '*The Waste Land*: Critique of the Myth' [1939], in Cox and Hinchcliffe, eds, *T. S. Eliot: The Waste Land*, pp. 129–61, p. 136.

38. The headgear which is today almost exclusively associated with the name Stetson is so named from a 1902 trademark registered by the American manufacturer John B. Stetson (1830–1906), who founded his hat company in Philadelphia in 1865.
39. *Manchester Guardian*, 31 October 1923, quoted in Cox and Hinchcliffe, eds, *T. S. Eliot: The Waste Land*, pp. 29–30, p. 30.
40. George R. Stetson, 'The Animistic Vampire in New England', *The American Anthropologist*, 9/1 (1896), 1–13, p. 7.
41. Stetson, 'The Animistic Vampire in New England', p. 7.
42. Stetson, 'The Animistic Vampire in New England', p. 7.
43. Stetson, 'The Animistic Vampire in New England', p. 8.
44. Stetson, 'The Animistic Vampire in New England', p. 8.
45. Proverbs, 26:11.
46. See, for example, Frazer, *The Golden Bough*, Vol. 1, pp. 418–20, 441–7.
47. Stetson, 'The Animistic Vampire in New England', p. 10.
48. Eliot, *The Waste Land*, pp. 68, 74.
49. Eliot, *The Waste Land: A Facsimile*, p. 1.
50. Eliot, *The Waste Land*, p. 73. Jerusalem, the only exception, is a city formerly occupied, and thus architecturally affected, by European crusaders. The city was in 1922, moreover, subject to a British mandate.
51. Eliot, *The Waste Land*, p. 79.
52. However confident Stoker's rhetoric might have sounded when voiced through Van Helsing, he was notably defensive when mentioning the supernatural content of *Dracula* to the British statesman and evangelical Christian William Ewart Gladstone. In a covering letter enclosing a first edition of the novel, Stoker confides, 'there is nothing base in the book and though superstition is fought in it with the weakness of superstition I hope it is not irreverent': see Bram Stoker to W. E. Gladstone, 24 May 1897, British Library ADD MSS 44525 f. 221.
53. Eliot, *The Waste Land*, p. 74.
54. 'The Dry Salvages', from *Four Quartets*, in *The Complete Poems and Plays of T. S. Eliot* (London: Faber and Faber, 1969), pp. 184–90, p. 186.

References

Arata, Stephen D., 'The Occidental Tourist: *Dracula* and the Anxiety of Reverse Colonization', *Victorian Studies*, 33 (1990), 621–45.
Beagle, Donald, 'Eliot's *The Waste Land*', *The Explicator*, 47 (1989), 40–1.
Bedient, Calvin, *He Do the Police in Different Voices: The Waste Land and its Protagonist* (Chicago: University of Chicago Press, 1986).
Brooks, Cleanth, '*The Waste Land*: Critique of the Myth' [1939], in C. B. Cox and Arnold P. Hinchcliffe, eds, *T. S. Eliot: The Waste Land* (London: Macmillan, 1968), pp. 129–61.
Cox, C. B. and Arnold P. Hinchcliffe, eds, *T. S. Eliot: The Waste Land* (London: Macmillan, 1968).
Eliot, T. S., *The Complete Poems and Plays of T. S. Eliot* (London: Faber and Faber, 1970).

—— *The Waste Land: A Facsimile and Transcript of the Original Drafts including the Annotations of Ezra Pound*, ed. Valerie Eliot (London: Faber and Faber, 1971).

Ellis, Steve, '*The Waste Land* and the Reader's Response', in Terry Davies and Nigel Wood, eds, *The Waste Land* (Buckingham: Open University Press, 1994), pp. 83–104.

Frazer, J. G., *The Golden Bough: A Study in Magic and Religion*, abridged edition, 2 volumes (London: Macmillan, 1960).

Hughes, William, '"Terrors that I dare not think of": Masculinity, Hysteria and Empiricism in Bram Stoker's *Dracula*', in Elizabeth Miller, ed., *Dracula: The Shade and the Shadow* (Westcliff-on-Sea: Desert Island Books, 1998), pp. 93–103.

Kenner, Hugh, 'The Invisible Poet' [1959], in C. B. Cox and Arnold P. Hinchcliffe, eds, *T. S. Eliot: The Waste Land* (London: Macmillan, 1968), pp. 168–99.

Leatherdale, Clive, *Dracula: The Novel and the Legend* (Wellingborough: Aquarian Press, 1985).

Pick, Daniel, '"Terrors of the Night": *Dracula* and "Degeneration" in the Late Nineteenth Century', *Critical Quarterly*, 30/4 (1988), 71–87.

Rance, Maxine, 'Dracula in *The Waste Land*', *Notes and Queries*, 34 (1987), 508–9.

Richmond, Lee J., 'Eliot's *The Waste Land* 380–395', *The Explicator*, 30 (1971), 11–13.

Sage, Victor, *Horror Fiction in the Protestant Tradition* (Basingstoke: Macmillan, 1988).

Stetson, George R., 'The Animistic Vampire in New England', *The American Anthropologist*, 9/1 (1896), 1–13.

Stoker, Bram, *Dracula*, ed. A. N. Wilson (Oxford: Oxford University Press, 1983).

11
Calvinist Gothic: The Case of Charles Brockden Brown's *Wieland, or the Transformation* and James Hogg's *The Private Memoirs and Confessions of a Justified Sinner*

Carol Margaret Davison

> Horror and doubt distract
> His troubl'd thoughts, and from the bottom stir
> The Hell within him, for within him Hell
> He brings, and round about him, nor from Hell
> One step no more than from himself can fly
> By change of place: Now conscience wakes despair
> That slumber'd, wakes the bitter memory
> Of what he was, what is, and what must be
> Worse; of worse deeds worse sufferings must ensue.[1]

'What say of it? What say of CONSCIENCE grim, that spectre in my path?'[2]

The late eighteenth and early nineteenth centuries witnessed a significant development in Gothic literature which may be called Calvinist Gothic. This classification refers not only to Gothic fiction that took Calvinism as its subject but to a sub-genre whose predominant characteristics and concerns are marked by a Calvinist sensibility. To date, several scholars have noted the former aspect of Calvinist Gothic, while the latter has yet to be recognized and assessed in terms of its ramifications for the Gothic genre as a whole. Joel Porte has illustrated, for example, how 'much Anglo-American *genre noir* fiction from Godwin to Poe owes its "Gothic" *ambiance* to a brooding sense of religious terror which is notably Protestant in its origins and bearing', and observed that William Godwin's *Caleb Williams* exhibits 'an internalized Calvinism'.[3] Victor Sage echoes Porte in his theory that the 'rhetoric of the horror novel is demonstrably theological in character', but goes a step further in his argument that the eighteenth-century mortuary tradition was a 'product of the "bourgeoisification" of dissenting Calvinism, rather than of established Protestant tradition', which was subsequently blended 'through the vehicle of growing antiquarianism, with the eighteenth-century interest in the religion of the past and the materials of the "Gothic" romance'.[4] My brief examination of Charles Brockden Brown's *Wieland, or the Transformation* (1798) and James Hogg's *The Private Memoirs and Confessions of a Justified Sinner* (1824), seeks, among other things, to consider the theological origins and significance of the uncanny figure of the double, whose provenance in the Gothic tradition can be traced to the sub-genre of Calvinist Gothic and whose creation had dramatic consequences for literature more broadly.[5] In its consideration of the nature of the double as it is manifested in two particular national contexts and, more specifically, as it is marked by Calvinism, this chapter participates in the ongoing project, first identified and taken up by Terry Castle, of historicizing the uncanny. Special attention will be paid to the unique relationship that exists between Scotland and the uncanny, given that this concept is ushered into the Gothic tradition via Hogg's novel.

In his seminal essay 'In the Hands of an Angry God: Religious Terror in Gothic Fiction', Joel Porte perceptively claims that the terror of classic Gothic fiction 'is usually at bottom theological' and involves 'the dark rites of sin, guilt, and damnation'. The question arises: what happens when the Gothic novel, which began by displacing what Porte describes as 'strikingly Calvinistic' concerns onto Roman Catholic settings,[6] shifts focus to Calvinism? Such a move was predictable given Protestantism's tradition of 'unremitting self scrutiny'[7] and the fact that, especially thanks to the influence of John Milton's *Paradise Lost*, the Gothic was already marked to some degree by the Protestant worldview and its preoccupations. A few things need to be noted, however, regarding the nature of this shift before proceeding to a more specific textual examination. Perhaps the most noteworthy innovation in Calvinist Gothic is its act of mining, in novel ways, the psychological depths of the Gothic hero-villain who sits at the crossroads of saint and sinner, policeman and criminal. Confronted with his story, the reader is mesmerisingly terrified, in turn fascinated by and (here lies the difference) *sympathetic* to his monstrosity and its tragic consequences, which are usually revealed to be the result of both nature *and* nurture.[8] It is not so much that the love plot is absent, as David Punter claims with regard to William Godwin's *Caleb Williams*, the grandfather text of Calvinist Gothic,[9] but that it assumes a new and sinister twist in the form of a seductive demon lover, an *homme fatal*, whose 'immortal passion for what he defines as freedom ... can only be consummated in the grave'.[10] This powerful figure plays a pivotal role in the hero's downfall and demise, and while some may cry 'entrapment', there is no denying the existence of the protagonist's role as a *willing* victim.

In terms of the life-blood it draws from the French Revolution and its aftermath, the Calvinist Gothic has much in common with the classic Gothic tradition from which it springs. These points of contact also extend to the preoccupations of both traditions – they are equally obsessed with origins and the sins of the fathers (although the classic Gothic emphasizes the Rousseauesque ideal of Original Innocence as opposed to the Calvinist Gothic's focus on Original Sin), they aim to police excess and fanaticism in its various manifestations,[11] and to establish parameters of identity. The subject under scrutiny in the Calvinist Gothic, however, is the Protestant self represented at home in a Protestant environment. The inhospitable, labyrinthine castles that once mediated consciousness are abandoned in favour of the direct penetration and representation of consciousness. In the place of encounters with the usually Roman Catholic Other who is key to Protestant self-definition are encounters with an uncanny foreign-yet-familiar Calvinist Other that reveals, time and again, that the self *is* Other or – horror of horrors – may be unwittingly converted into that Other. The seductive *homme fatal* – frequently figured as the devil – may lie within. The ostensibly impermeable boundaries of identity are often blurred, and self-estrangement, usually combined with self-persecution, is the order of the day.

At the risk of reducing literary history to a type of paint-by-numbers set, I would maintain that this shift to the more self-reflexive and nationally critical Calvinist Gothic mode is signalled in *Caleb Williams* at the moment that Caleb declares that Britain is a tyrannical prison akin to France's Bastille.[12] A personalized version of this episode is again presented at the novel's end when the purportedly victimized Caleb has the revolutionary revelation that he has much in common with his alleged persecutor, Falkland. In the decidedly Gothic 'Heart of Darkness' psychomachia that follows in the wake of Godwin's compelling novel, Nathaniel Hawthorne's 'Young Goodman Brown' (1835), Edgar Allan Poe's 'William Wilson' (1840) and Robert Louis Stevenson's *The Strange Case of Dr. Jekyll and Mr. Hyde* (1886),[13] the Calvinist Gothic explores the demonic relationship between Calvinism and crimes resulting from theologically sanctioned/promoted self-expression and repression. This sub-genre exposes how our foremost persecutor *and* better self may exist in the form of a spectral conscience that, in Calvin's own words, acts as a '"kind of sentinel" set over man "to observe and spy out all his secrets, that nothing may remain buried in darkness"'.[14]

The undeniable offspring of Godwin's *Caleb Williams*, Brockden Brown's *Wieland* and Hogg's *The Private Memoirs and Confessions of a Justified Sinner* are fascinating socio-political indictments that fix their lenses on religious fanaticism as it is manifested in various forms of Antinomian Calvinism, an extreme, heretical branch of Calvinism that maintains that no action on the part of an elected ('justified') individual – even murder – will affect their election. Both novels draw on the Gothic to relate the spine-tingling details surrounding a series of purportedly divinely ordained murders undertaken by Antinomians. The subsequent recognition of the true nature of their deeds (the extent of this recognition varies radically in each case) engenders a pronounced horror in these criminals and both ultimately commit suicide. In that they cast a critical glance backwards at their respective nations' political and theological founding fathers and the social order they believe they have established, these cautionary tales are effectively 'veiled sermons', as Fred Lewis Pattee calls *Wieland*,[15] which strategically deploy the uncanny and the double in order to comment on dangerous national weaknesses and propensities. While Hogg advances a predominantly theological and economic critique of the vexed idea of a Calvinist Covenant, Brockden Brown's tale is more socio-political in its concern with establishing a healthy relationship between church and state within the New Republic. Central to both texts, however, is serious concern about the possible negative effects that extreme Calvinism has on its adherents and the nation at large. Intriguingly, both works not only suggest that this theology is ideologically and structurally akin to a demonic secret society, but that it promotes schizophrenia as it produces a treacherous psychological bifurcation in its followers. In the hands of Brockden Brown and Hogg, this split is allegorically emblematic of social, and ultimately national, fragmentation and chaos. Notably, both works are set against a socio-political backdrop characterized by national identity crises: *Wieland* is set in the mid- to late eighteenth century when Puritanism was losing political ground and doubts proliferated regarding the great American socio-political experiment (especially in the wake of the French Revolution); and *The Confessions* is set in the late seventeenth and early eighteenth centuries when, 'in the immediate aftermath of bloody conflict' and the Act of Union, Scotland was experiencing 'profound upheaval affecting the constitutions of Church and State'.[16]

Before elucidating to what ends the Gothic is brought to bear on Calvinism in these novels, I will begin by mapping the Calvinist Gothic make-up of each, and draw on Susan Manning's stellar scholarship on Calvinism in *The Puritan-Provincial Vision: Scottish and American Literature in the Nineteenth Century*. The portrait that emerges in Manning's introduction has undeniable and uncanny resonances for the well-versed Gothic reader: the Calvinist world, dominated by election by faith, induces neurosis. It is fundamentally marked by a sense of division that engenders acute anxiety, paranoia and persecution. Due to the Fall, '[d]istance and disinheritance define the self' and '[d]ivision becomes the structuring principle of life'.[17] The Calvinist pilgrim's progress, from Effectual Calling to Justification and finally Sanctification, is decisively characterized by repeated falls away from an idealized union: man is divided first from God, next from nature, then from and within himself and finally from other people.[18] Two polarized groups inhabit the Calvinist terrain: the elect and the reprobate. In Alice Cooper's words, 'welcome to my nightmare',[19] for this *is* one and just when we think things may get better, they actually get worse for the Calvinist world is an ever-shifting, sign-filled domain of uncertainty where God the Father is unpredictable and an ineluctably mysterious withholder of truth. Confronted by such insecurity regarding one's spiritual status as the question of one's election is 'largely a matter of self-assessment', the Calvinist becomes, as Manning says, 'both an obsessive observer and an obsessive rationalist'.[20] Thanks to a conscience that Calvin describes as assuming the tripartite function of accuser, judge and executioner, the obsessively self-doubting Calvinist essentially splits off, in Manning's words, into 'two selves – an observer and an actor, a saint and a sinner, regenerate and reprobate – two selves utterly opposed and yet (to the external view and the corrupted conscience) perhaps indistinguishable'.[21] Suspicion and paranoia even spill over into society at large. As the notorious witch hunts in Scotland and New England attest, fears of demonic conspiracies arise and a 'grand paradox' wherein neighbours are regarded 'with brotherly love *and* suspicion'.[22]

The Antinomian Calvinist scenarios portrayed by Brockden Brown and Hogg are in keeping with the Gothic genre's fixation on excess.[23] Antinomian adherents, according to the Moderate Calvinist preacher Blanchard, in *The Confessions*, carry their 'points to a dangerous extreme' (*JS*, p. 131). Moderates like Blanchard were 'products of the eighteenth-century Enlightenment, and were characterized by their concern for reason and tolerance'.[24] Doubtless, they regarded Anti-nomianism as 'in its axioms, devilish'.[25] The Antinomian God, as the Gothic suggests, is fashioned in the Antinomians' image,[26] with much in common with such traditional Gothic tyrants as Walpole's Manfred, Lewis's Ambrosio and even Godwin's Falkland. Indeed, this arbitrary sadist is not unlike Percy Shelley's bloodthirsty Jehovah, featured in such works as *The Wandering Jew* and *Queen Mab*,[27] who, it is intriguing to note, is the deity of an earlier Chosen People after whom Calvinists in general modelled themselves. The characters' acts of confounding the ethical nature of their bloody crimes, which both misperceive as sacred missions propagating God's word, blur two boundaries upheld by traditional Calvinists – that between moral and immoral actions, and the two aspects of the Calvinist self as identified by Manning.[28] Thus do the Antinomians become self-loathing and insane megalo-maniacs, demon and deity in one.[29] Their monstrous transgressions are denounced in each instance by way of a cunning and apt stra-tegy of semiotic slippage involving divine covenants and demonic compacts. In these texts obsessed with founding fathers, transgression, misinterpretation and various forms of inheritance, it is intimated that extreme Calvinists in Scotland and the new American republic are misguided pilgrims with fallen senses who have unwittingly struck Faustian compacts with likeminded secret society-style Mephistophelean figures.

In the case of Brockden Brown's *Wieland*, which promotes a balance between rationalism and spirituality, the extreme situation of radical sectarians is taken to task alongside that of Enlightened rationalists. In order to advance Brockden Brown's two-pronged critique, a fair bit of energy is expended at the novel's beginning relating the nature of the sins of Theodore Wieland's forefathers. While his Camissard father shuns social worship[30] and ultimately experiences a monstrous and fatal form of inner light by way of spontaneous combustion, Theodore's enlightened, classical education in his family's Ciceronian-style temple disregards his spiritual self and entirely ignores religion. According to Shirley Samuels, *Wieland* plays out the various anxieties produced by a change in jurisdiction, namely 'the separation of church and state represented by the ratification of the Constitution and the dispersal of the authority of the church into the related institutions of education, law, and the family'.[31] Theodore's plaguing quest for spiritual meaning leads him back, ironically, to his father's extreme Camissard Calvinism and renders him susceptible to the experimental wiles of the foreign biloquist, Carwin, who urges Wieland – in a voice Wieland confuses with God's – to murder his family. A broad spectrum of anxieties about radical French ideas and archaic secret societies current in 1790s America when the Federalists adopted repressive measures regarding resident aliens and prospective sedition[32] are distilled into Carwin's portrait. As David Brion Davis explains, '[a]fter the Revolution, many Americans were haunted by the fear that their fathers' sacrifice had been betrayed and that some dangerous conspiracy threatened to destroy the glorious promise of democracy'.[33] An enlightened Wandering Jew-like rhetorician, the chameleonic Carwin converted to Roman Catholicism in Spain and trained in the arts of secrecy by the feared Jesuits. Theodore's sister Clara, who effectively stands in for the Republic in this national allegory, especially promotes this 'Carwin-conspiracy' association (*W*, 214). Carwin's ultimate revelation, however, that he is native to America (*W*, p. 224), underscores Brockden Brown's most startling suggestion – that the formidable problems facing America may be home-grown rather than imported. While foreign ideas may influence American politics, they are often revealed to be too radical and incompatible with the American context.

Especially in his novel's opening segment minutely detailing the various educational histories of the three generations of Wielands, Brockden Brown suggests that America must look within and cultivate a balance between rationalism and religion if it is to achieve social unity and heal its deep divisions. The apparently ideal rational republic in which Theodore and his sister Clara are raised is ultimately revealed to be damningly incestuous and intolerant, physically and intellectually isolated as it is from society at large. Clara claims that her brother loves her 'with a passion more than fraternal' (*W*, p. 208) and the feeling appears to be mutual, although repressed in Clara's shorthand journal. These intimated incestuous desires are symbolic of solipsism and thus 'antithetical to that kind of voluntary cooperation among citizens demanded by emergent democracies'.[34] Clara's comments in the novel's concluding paragraph underline Brockden Brown's views regarding the perverse theological tenets underpinning Antinomianism and its place in the republic. In her words, 'If Wieland had framed juster notions of moral duty, and of the divine attributes ... the double-tongued deceiver would have been baffled and repelled' (*W*, 273). As the first line of defence, Theodore Wieland is weak. As his devastating life-trajectory illustrates, the Wielands' lack of religious education, combined with Theodore's mode of conceptualizing God as a 'supreme passion' (*W*, p. 185), runs counter to the rational, enlightened conception of the deity espoused by Brockden Brown and promoted in such works as Thomas Paine's *The Age of Reason* (1795) as fundamental to a nation's socio-political stability. Theodore's Calvinist conception of a punishing, selective and merciless God leaves the nation vulnerable to treacherous influences and possible attack. As a result, Theodore slaughters his wife, their three children and an adopted child, attempts to kill his sister and ultimately commits suicide. Thus does Brockden Brown illustrate the incredible susceptibility of even the most apparently ideal republic to both internal and external acts of terrorism.

Turning to a slightly more detailed examination of Hogg, the reader is also confronted in *The Confessions* with a megalomaniacal failed reader[35] who consistently confounds God and the devil. No episode better conveys this than the one that follows Robert Wringhim's apparent election to the 'society of *the just made perfect*' (*JS*, p. 115) when he first meets Gil-Martin, another slippery rhetorician who is either the physical incarnation of Wringhim's dark side or the devil in disguise. While his mother is convinced that Wringhim (who is described as one of the devil's spiritually proud 'hand-fasted children'; *JS*, p. 90) has been demonically converted, or 'translated' as she refers to it (*JS*, p. 121), Robert Wringhim senior assures her, in a scathingly ironic scene, that Gil-Martin is indeed a 'brother' who agrees with every Antinomian precept. The subsequent ritualistic 'baptism' of Wringhim into the 'society of *the just made perfect*' (*JS*, p. 115) as a 'two-edged weapon' that may 'lay waste … [God's] enemies' (*JS*, p. 122) further advances Hogg's crafty and critical depiction of Antinomianism as a loveless, vengeful and demonic secret society. John Bligh astutely observes that a 'natural kinship' exists between the devil and the Antinomian as 'both believe that their eternal destiny is already fixed and cannot be altered by conduct good or bad' (*JS*, p. 155). Bligh also insightfully remarks that 'the devil knows that Antinomianism is false, but he is glad to propogate [*sic*] it because it makes its adherents amenable to his solicitations' (*JS*, p. 155). In forging this devil–Antinomian equation, Hogg undermines the devil–woman association fundamental to both the Scottish witch-hunts and Wringhim's misogynist worldview.[36] Although his misogyny eventually translates into matricide and murder (*JS*, p. 190), Hogg consistently represents women as perceptive creatures of integrity.[37] Indeed, he suggests that if a 'coven' exists in the novel, it is to be found in the unholy alliance of Wringhim and Gil-Martin.

The tacit semiotic slippage between 'covens' and 'covenants' carries over to the term 'Confessions' in Hogg's title and provides another key to his strategy of critique. Wringhim's 'Confession' sits at the crossroads of the Roman Catholic practice of confession and the Presbyterian Negative Confession of 1581, which laid out the basic beliefs of that faith.[38] Time and again, Hogg figures Wringhim's tragedy, among other things, as a regression and fall *into* the damned faith of Roman Catholicism. This equation is most conspicuously suggested when Gil-Martin appears wearing a bishop's mitre (*JS*, p. 208). Perhaps the most damning instance, however, involves Wringhim's vexed compact with Gil-Martin, which confuses the fundamental Calvinist tenet of election by grace with the idea of election as 'earned' by way of good works. Gil-Martin's act of slyly sealing 'a bond of blood' ensuring Wringhim's full physical protection (*JS*, p. 165) and of convincing him that his Crusade-like 'Reformation by blood' is a 'great ... work' (*JS*, p. 141) that will guarantee Wringhim's sainthood betrays both Gil-Martin's true tendencies and his role as a Mephistophelean arch-usurer who, while claiming only to have Wringhim's 'unspeakable profit' at heart (*JS*, p. 44), exacts an exorbitant price in exchange.[39] Such a role positions Gil-Martin as engaging in what is described in *A Cloud of Witnesses* – a volume that Wringhim claims to have read that recounts the final testimonies of executed Covenanters – as Satan's act of Secret Fraud.[40] Albeit on an unconscious level, secular accounts hold tremendous significance for the self-described 'unaccountable' Wringhim (*JS*, pp. 25 and 36).[41] Thanks to his demonic accountant, Gil-Martin, who spews a constant barrage of commercial rhetoric and enacts what Iain Crichton Smith describes as 'the ultimate capitalist transaction' with his young pledge,[42] Wringhim gains control of his elder, half-brother's estates (*JS*, p. 55). In exchange for the creation of what he suggests is a second self who transacts business in his likeness (*JS*, p. 182) and engages in pleasures of the flesh, Wringhim first pays the price of his sanity and then of his soul. The former loss is particularly ironic and significant given Calvin's claim in his *Sermons upon the Fifth Book of Moses* (London, 1583) that fallen men are often 'anxious, depressed, unable to work, given to fantasies of demons, morbid introspection of fearful daydreams'.[43] To varying degrees, Wringhim may be said to exhibit all of these characteristics.

With the rare exception,[44] *The Confessions* has been read as a satire on *extreme* Calvinism.[45] However, I will propose that the anxieties pervading Hogg's novel extend to Calvinism generally. More specifically, *The Confessions* is haunted by repressed uncertainties about Calvinism's moral foundations. Despite Calvin's belief that the elect would *naturally* act morally and perform good deeds, his theory of the elect lends itself, as one scholar has cogently argued, 'to an interpretation which is subversive of morality and social order' in its proclamation of freedom from law.[46] Beyond his concern with such doctrinal propensities, Hogg seems also to be criticizing the Calvinist preachers and writers of his day, in contradistinction to Federalist theologians, who popularly represented the Covenant as a type of commercial contract between God and the Scottish nation.[47]

Notably, the pathologically obsessive relationship between Gil-Martin and Robert Wringhim has a significant historical parallel – overlooked by critics – that provides a key to Hogg's anxieties about Calvinism in general, and its origins in Scotland. John Knox, widely and popularly regarded as the Founding Father of Scottish Presbyterianism, was the constant companion and armed bodyguard of George Wishart, who preached Reformation-driven ideas and was martyred as a heretic for it in 1546. A notorious misogynist like Wringhim, whose early youth may have been similarly notoriously sinful, Knox responded to his moment of election in a manner comparable to Wringhim's with 'a confused ecstasy of awe, terror, relief and self-gratulation'.[48] Knox also condoned the use of violence for the sake of defending and promoting his faith. He ultimately fulfilled that mission through armed organization.[49] While seventeenth-century Episcopalian anti-Presbyterian propaganda deemed all Presbyterians to be 'gun-disciples of Christ' and Knox a possibly insane, self-righteous, bloodthirsty fanatic,[50] pro-Covenanters championed Knox's views and methods. Hogg appears to weigh in, in this debate, by way of the rapier-carrying Robert Wringhim junior whose role as a 'double-edged weapon in … [God's] hand' (*JS*, p. 122) is strikingly reminiscent of Knox's own early role as Wishart's protector when he carried a two-handed sword, the traditional weapon of the Scots.[51] Hogg's promotion of the purgation of Gil-Martin's extreme ideas from the Scottish body politic – ideas that are deemed by the moderate preacher Blanchard too sanguine for the laws of Scotland (*JS*, p. 137) – is enacted in Wringhim's expulsion from Scotland, an expulsion that significantly transpires in the domain of Hogg's home region of the Borders. It has been said that Hogg's novel 'raises more questions … than [it] is capable of answering'.[52] Given the double-edged Knoxian interpretation of Calvinist tenets, *The Confessions* seems to raise more spectres than it is ultimately capable of exorcising.

As a final note, if one takes the longer view of *The Confessions* in terms of the history of the uncanny, it seems to register a vital transition in the

Gothic tradition, particularly in relation to its location and representation of terror. It is now accepted that a significant shift occurred in the early nineteenth-century Gothic whereby internal '[u]ncanny effects rather than [external] sublime terrors' came to predominate.[53] Hogg's novel effectively registers that transition in the figure of Gil-Martin who, in keeping with his final literal location in the novel at the English–Scottish border, is strategically figuratively located for the duration of the novel at the border of the sublime and the uncanny. Like Brockden Brown in *Wieland*, Hogg resists any association between divinity and sublime terror while figuring the supernatural Gil-Martin as sublimely terrifying, particularly in his ideas and logic (*JS*, p. 129). Hogg significantly allows Blanchard to articulate this crucial distinction. Religion, Blanchard says, is 'a sublime and glorious thing, the bond of society on earth, and the connector of humanity with the Divine nature', but, he continues, '[t]here is a sublimity in ... [Gil-Martin's] ideas, with which there is ... *a mixture of terror*; and when he talks of religion, he does it as one that rather dreads its truths than reverences them' (*JS*, p. 131; emphasis added).

Hogg notably does not eradicate the idea of sublime terror in order to introduce the idea of the uncanny, a rich, multivalent concept popular in Scottish society and culture.[54] While, as Ian Duncan explains, the idea of the uncanny appeared 'as a central (if not definitive) topic in the Scottish literature of romance revival, between about 1760 and 1835',[55] 'uncanny' is referenced for the first time in the Gothic tradition in *The Confessions* when Wringhim's companion Gil-Martin is described by the Cameronian Samuel Scrape as a 'strange mysterious person ... that the maist part of folks countit uncanny' (*JS*, p. 186). Although Scrape later informs Wringhim that people think Gil-Martin is the devil (*JS*, p. 195), Gil-Martin's identification as either the devil or an aspect of Wringhim's aberrant psychology opens up what Rebecca A. Pope refers to as 'the double-devil debate' in the novel.[56] As such, Gil-Martin assumes another borderline position in that he is located between a pre-Enlightenment folkloric/theological notion of the uncanny as something supernatural and an Enlightenment conception of the uncanny as defined in relation to human psychology. On the former count, Gil-Martin has much in common with the *coimhmeadh* (co-walker), the famous *doppelgänger* of Scots-Irish mythology who functions in 'every way like the man, as a twin-brother and companion, haunting him as a shadow ... whit[h]er to guard him from the secret assaults of some of its own folks, or only as a sportful ape to counterfeit all his actions'.[57] On the latter count, Gil-Martin is transformed into a figure of the uncanny, an encounter with something, as Freud describes it, 'secretly familiar and old-established in the mind ... which has become alienated from it only through the process of repression' (*JS*, p. 247). By way of this innovative 'double' representation, Hogg earned the praise of André Gide, who helped promote the novel's reputation,[58] and of Walter Allen, who famously said of *The Confessions*, 'it is doubtful whether a more convincing representation of the power of evil exists in our literature'.[59] Hogg also profoundly revitalized and modernized the Gothic and left a profound mark on literary history, paving the way for such later literary masterpieces as Edgar Allan Poe's short stories and Henry James's *Turn of the Screw*.

Notes

1. John Milton, *Paradise Lost* IV, ed. Merritt Y. Hughes (1674; Indianapolis: The Odyssey Press, 1981), ll. 18–26.
2. Chamberlayne's *Pharonnida*, quoted in Edgar Allan Poe, 'William Wilson', in *Selected Tales* (1839; Oxford: Oxford University Press, 1980), p. 79.
3. Joel Porte, 'In the Hands of an Angry God: Religious Terror in Gothic Fiction', in *The Gothic Imagination: Essays in Dark Romanticism*, ed. G. R. Thompson (Washington: Washington State University Press, 1974), pp. 42–64, pp. 45 and 54. The facts that Godwin's father John was a Sandemanian Calvinist minister and that Godwin functioned in his early years in a similar capacity at Ware, Stowmarket and Beaconsfield, are unsurprising in that this theology informs *Caleb Williams*.
4. Victor Sage, *Horror Fiction in the Protestant Tradition* (London: Macmillan, 1988), pp. xvi and 4.
5. Although it does not constitute my focus here, I would maintain that the advent of the double in the persecutor/persecuted dialectic established between the servant Caleb and his master Falkland in William Godwin's *Caleb Williams* had dramatic consequences for literary history more broadly as the double was subsequently imported into a variety of genres.
6. Porte, 'In the Hands of an Angry God', pp. 45 and 50.
7. Susan Manning, *The Puritan-Provincial Vision: Scottish and American Literature in the Nineteenth Century* (Cambridge: Cambridge University Press, 1990), p. 3.
8. In the two primary texts under examination, Theodore Wieland's sister Clara, the narrator of Brockden Brown's novel, repeatedly evokes sympathy for her brother's fall from grace, while the reader responds in a similar manner to the sheer terror experienced by Robert Wringhim while under the tormenting control of Gil-Martin.
9. David Punter, *The Literature of Terror: A History of Gothic Fictions from 1765 to the Present Day* (London and New York: Longman, 1980), p. 134.
10. Robin Morgan, *The Demon Lover: On the Sexuality of Terrorism* (New York and London: Norton, 1989), p. 112. This is especially the case in Hogg's

novel where Robert Wringhim's relationship to Gil-Martin is figured as a marital union. Gil-Martin informs Wringhim, 'I am wedded to you so closely, that I feel as if I were the same person. Our essences are one, our bodies and spirits being united, so, that I am drawn towards you as by magnetism, and wherever you are, there must my presence be with you' (James Hogg, *The Private Memoirs and Confessions of a Justified Sinner* [1824; Oxford: Oxford University Press, 1991], p. 229. Page numbers prefaced by *JS* hereafter in the text.) A similar relationship obtains between Robert Louis Stevenson's Jekyll and Hyde. In a chillingly graphic depiction of their union in the novella's closing segment entitled 'Henry Jekyll's Full Statement of the Case', the reader is told that 'that insurgent horror [Edward Hyde] was knit to him [Henry Jekyll] closer than a wife, closer than an eye; lay caged in his flesh, where he heard it mutter and felt it struggle to be born; and at every hour of weakness, and in the confidence of slumber, prevailed against him, and deposed him out of life' (Robert Louis Stevenson, *The Strange Case of Dr. Jekyll and Mr. Hyde* [1886; Oxford: Oxford University Press, 1987], pp. 74–5).

11. According to Gary Kelly, Hogg had created in Robert Wringhim a figure analogous to a fanatical Jacobin (Gary Kelly, *English Fiction of the Romantic Period 1789–1830* [London and New York: Longman, 1989], p. 265).

12. William Godwin, *Caleb Williams* (1794; Oxford: Oxford University Press, 1988), pp. 181–2.

13. In keeping with the national origins of the works in my list, Susan Manning claims that *Caleb Williams* 'had immediate and lasting effects on Scottish and American fiction, far disproportionate to its influence on English literature but commensurate with its puritan-provincial rationale' (*The Puritan-Provincial Vision*, p. 72). In terms of the Calvinist–Gothic tradition as I identify it, Ian Campbell notes a parallel between how the devil-figure of 'Young Goodman Brown' is curiously pre-echoed in Hogg's Gil-Martin (Ian Campbell, 'Hogg's *Confessions* and the *Heart of Darkness*', *Studies in Scottish Literature* 15 [1980], 187–201, 192).

14. Quoted in Manning, *The Puritan-Provincial Vision*, p. 11.

15. Fred Lewis Pattee, 'Introduction', *Wieland, or the Transformation* (1798; San Diego: Harcourt, Brace, Jovanovich, 1926), p. xxviii. In support of this designation, Pattee cites Brockden Brown's prefacing advertisement for *Wieland* where he claims that 'His purpose is neither selfish nor temporary, but aims at the illustration of some important branches of the moral constitution of man' (p. 3).

16. Adrian Hunter, 'Introduction', *The Private Memoirs and Confessions of a Justified Sinner* (Peterborough, Ontario: Broadview Press, 2001), pp. 8–9.

17. Manning, *The Puritan-Provincial Vision*, pp. 8 and 7.

18. Manning, *The Puritan-Provincial Vision*, p. 13.

19. Notably, David Punter describes Hogg's novel as a 'nightmare book' like William Godwin's *Caleb Williams* 'in the particular sense that moral purpose – often initially present – is in each case eroded by the pressures of psychological obsession' (Punter, *The Literature of Terror*, p. 134).

20. Hunter, 'Introduction', *The Private Memoirs*, p. 15; and Manning, *The Puritan-Provincial Vision*, p. 9.

21. Manning, *The Puritan-Provincial Vision*, p. 21.
22. Michael Walzer, 'The Puritans as Revolutionaries', *Intellectual History in America: Contemporary Essays on Puritanism, the Enlightenment, & Romanticism*, ed. Cushing Strout (New York: Harper & Row, 1968), p. 9, emphasis added.
23. Fred Botting, *Gothic* (London and New York: Routledge, 1996), p. 1.
24. Douglas S. Mack, 'Hogg's Religion and *The Confessions of a Justified Sinner*', *Studies in Scottish Literature*, 7 (1970), 272–5, 273.
25. This is how Crichton Smith refers to Calvinism in his article on *The Confessions* (Iain Crichton Smith, 'A Work of Genius: James Hogg's *Justified Sinner*', *Studies in Scottish Literature*, 28 [1993], 1–11, 4). His view is that Calvinism in general is demonic in its axioms because it maintains that only a certain few will be saved.
26. This terrible truth regarding God's origins and make-up are found in Wieland's father's motto, 'Seek and ye shall find' (*W*, p. 9). His incredible death by spontaneous combustion (*W*, pp. 18–20) brings Jonathan Edwards's graphic images of both notorious hellfire and God's burning wrath (*W*, p. 106) dramatically alive. As such, the exact nature of his demise and his moral nature are ambiguous.
27. Examinations of the insane tyranny and sadism of the construct known as the 'Calvinist God' are carried over into nineteenth-century poetry as well. See, for example, Robert Burns's 'Holy Willie's Prayer' (1785) and Robert Browning's provocative poem from the 1860s, 'Caliban upon Setebos; Or Natural Theology in the Island'.
28. Manning, *The Puritan-Provincial Vision*, p. 21.
29. As regards Hogg's novel, Adrian Hunter argues that it takes as its target all forms of religious fanaticism and 'megalomania as it occurs in people of all dispositions' (Hunter, 'Introduction', *The Private Memoirs*, p. 13).
30. Charles Brockden Brown, *Wieland, or the Transformation* (1798; San Diego: Harcourt, Brace, Jovanovich, 1926), p. 12. Page numbers prefaced by *W* hereafter in the text.
31. Shirley Samuels, *Romances of the Republic: Women, the Family, and Violence in the Literature of the Early American Nation* (New York and Oxford: Oxford University Press, 1996), p. 51.
32. Vernon Stauffer, 'New England and the Bavarian Illuminati'. Dissertation. Columbia University, 1918, p. 132.
33. David Brion Davis, *Homicide in American Fiction, 1798–1860: A Study in Social Values* (Ithaca, NY: Cornell University Press, 1957), p. xv.
34. James D. Wilson, 'Incest and American Romantic Fiction', *Studies in the Literary Imagination*, 7 (1994), 31–50, 50.
35. Hunter, 'Introduction', *Memoirs*, p. 12. Hunter perceptively comments that Wringhim 'is in every sense a failed reader: of himself, of scripture, of history'. Indeed, this seems to be a key element in the construction of Gothic hero-villains from Horace Walpole's Manfred and Matthew Lewis's Ambrosio to Mary Shelley's Victor Frankenstein and Robert Louis Stevenson's Dr Jekyll. While they often fail to convince, these solipsistic megalomaniacs are especially prone to justifying their selfish destructive actions.
36. According to Robert Wringhim, women function as the most dangerous worldly snare, one that he makes concerted efforts to abhor and despise

(*JS*, 113). In a typical yet disturbing instance of blaming the victim, Robert confesses to never having had respect for his mother and he justifies this as a judgment on her from heaven for former sin (*JS*, p. 114). Ultimately, Wringhim's self-loathing is expressed by way of his mother, his site of origins. When he begins to loathe life, he also begins to loathe the woman who bore him and yearn for death (*JS*, p. 184).

37. Robert Wringhim's mother immediately recognizes a major alteration in her son after his first encounter with Gil-Martin. It is she who notes that her son has been 'translated' (*JS*, pp. 120–1). Likewise, towards novel's end, it is the wife of the weaver who has granted Robert shelter who perceives that the devil is besieging their house (*JS*, p. 231).

38. David Stevenson, *The Covenanters: The National Covenant and Scotland* (Edinburgh: The Saltire Society, 1988), p. 29.

39. L. L. Lee correctly notes that 'there is no crude Devil, no magic spells, no familiars, no pact, not even a temptation, at least not a clear temptation' (L. L. Lee, 'The Devil's Figure: James Hogg's *Justified Sinner*', *Studies in Scottish Literature*, 3 [1966], 230–9, 236). Gil-Martin, however, craftily secures a pact with Robert Wringhim after George's wrongful imprisonment on charges of assault and battery. After ascertaining that Robert feels assured of his election and 'the perfect safety of [his] ... soul' for all eternity, Gil-Martin offers the following loaded yet unsolicited promise: 'I give you my solemn assurance, and bond of blood, that no human hand shall ever henceforth be able to injure your life, or shed one drop of your precious blood, but it is on the condition that you walk always by my directions.' Robert's response is that he 'will do so with cheerfulness' (*JS*, p. 165).

40. In his commentaries on Genesis, Calvin defines the concept of Satan's Secret Fraud more broadly as involving his attempt to 'induce wicked and ungodly men openly to oppose our faith ... [and] sometimes, privately and by stealth ... [to assail] us through the medium of good and simple men, that he may overcome us unawares'.

41. According to Ian Duncan, 'unaccountable' is 'one of Hogg's favourite words'. It appears in many of his tales (Ian Duncan, 'Walter Scott, James Hogg, and Scottish Gothic', *A Companion to the Gothic* ed. David Punter [Oxford: Blackwell, 2000], pp. 70–80, p. 77).

42. Crichton Smith, 'A Work of Genius: James Hogg's *Justified Sinner*', p. 4.

43. Quoted in Walzer, 'The Puritans as Revolutionaries', p. 15.

44. John Carey suggests, for example, that because Hogg is a devout Presbyterian, his novel could not be satirizing Calvinism (John Carey, 'Introduction', *The Private Memoirs and Confessions of a Justified Sinner* [1824; Oxford: Oxford University Press, 1991], pp. xi–xxiii, p. xviii). Douglas S. Mack adeptly counters the claim and illustrates how *The Confessions* indicts *extreme* Calvinism. Iain Crichton Smith has argued, contrary to Carey, that Hogg's critique extends beyond the parameters of *extreme* Calvinism to include Calvinism as a whole. Divine Election, Crichton Smith maintains, is 'a damnable thing because the theory is in its axioms devilish, for it states that a certain number are elected to be saved' (Crichton Smith, 'A Work of Genius: James Hogg's *Justified Sinner*', p. 4). This chapter extrapolates, to some degree, on Crichton Smith's by suggesting that deep-seated anxieties regarding Calvinism in general are barely repressed in the novel.

45. See, for example, Walter Allen, *The English Novel: A Short Critical History* (1954; Harmondsworth: Penguin Books, 1965), pp. 130–1; André Gide, 'Introduction', *The Private Memoirs and Confessions of a Justified Sinner* (London: the Cresset Press, 1947), pp. ix–xvi; John Bligh, 'The Doctrinal Premises of Hogg's *Confessions of a Justified Sinner*', SSL, 19 (1984), 148–64, 148; Punter, *The Literature of Terror*, p. 151; Thomas Crawford, 'James Hogg: The Play of Region and Nation', *The History of Scottish Literature*, ed. Douglas Gifford (Aberdeen: Aberdeen University Press, 1988), 3, pp. 89–105, p. 101; Mack 'Hogg's Religion', p. 274.
46. Bligh, 'The Doctrinal Premises', p. 149.
47. Federal theology emerged in the late sixteenth century and granted the idea of the covenant a central place. Notably, federalists borrowed their name from the Latin word *foedus*, meaning covenant. See Stevenson, *The Covenanters*, pp. 31–2.
48. Edwin Muir, *John Knox: Portrait of a Calvinist* (London: Jonathan Cape, 1929), pp. 12 and 14.
49. Jasper Ridley, *John Knox* (Oxford: Clarendon Press, 1968), p. 40.
50. Colin Kidd, *Subverting Scotland's Past: Scottish Whig Historians and the Creation of an Anglo-British Identity, 1689–c. 1830* (Cambridge: Cambridge University Press, 1993), p. 55. In his two-volume *History of Scotland* (London 1759), William Robertson provides what Kidd (p. 191) describes as the standard Moderate interpretation of Scotland's ecclesiastic history, as he concedes 'that such founding fathers of the Reformation as Buchanan and Knox had been rather bloodthirsty' (p. 115).
51. Ridley, *John Knox*, p. 39.
52. Hunter, 'Introduction', *Memoirs,* p. 18.
53. Botting, *Gothic*, p. 11.
54. As the *Oxford English Dictionary* makes clear, the word 'uncanny' appeared in Robert Fergusson's 1789 collection of poems and was later used by Sir Walter Scott in *Guy Mannering; or The Astrologer* (1815).
55. Ian Duncan, 'The Upright Corpse: Hogg, National Literature and the Uncanny', *Studies in Hogg and his World*, 5 (1994), 29–54, 34.
56. Rebecca A. Pope, 'Hogg, Wordsworth, and Gothic Autobiography', *Studies in Scottish Literature*, 27 (1992), 218–40, 232. Intriguingly, the apparent division between the double and the devil is bridged by Ernest Jones, Freud's English disciple, who claimed that the devil is God's dreadful double.
57. Manning, *The Puritan-Provincial Vision*, p. 23.
58. Barbara Royle Bloedé, 'James Hogg's *Private Memoirs and Confessions of a Justified Sinner*: The Genesis of the Double', *Études Anglaises*, 26 (1973), 174–86, 174–5.
59. Allen, *The English Novel*, p. 130.

References

Allen, Walter, *The English Novel: A Short Critical History* (1954; Harmondsworth: Penguin Books, 1965).
Bligh, John, 'The Doctrinal Premises of Hogg's *Confessions of a Justified Sinner*', *Studies in Scottish Literature*, 19 (1984), 148–64.

182 *Carol Margaret Davison*

Bloedé, Barbara Royle, 'James Hogg's *Private Memoirs and Confessions of a Justified Sinner*: The Genesis of the Double', *Études Anglaises*, 26 (1973), 174–86.

Botting, Fred, *Gothic* (London and New York: Routledge, 1996).

Brion Davis, David, *Homicide in American Fiction, 1798–1860: A Study in Social Values* (Ithaca, NY: Cornell University Press, 1957).

Brown, Charles Brockden, *Wieland, or the Transformation* (1798; San Diego: Harcourt, Brace, Jovanovich, 1926).

Browning, Robert, 'Caliban upon Setebos; Or Natural Theology in the Island' (1864), M. H. Abrams, ed., *The Norton Anthology of English Literature*, Vol. 2, sixth edition (New York: Norton, 1993), ll. 1243–50.

Burns, Robert, 'Holy Willie's Prayer' (1789; 1799), M. H. Abrams, ed., *The Norton Anthology of English Literature*, Vol. 2, sixth edition (New York: Norton, 1993), ll. 85–8.

Campbell, Ian, 'Hogg's *Confessions* and the *Heart of Darkness*', *Studies in Scottish Literature*, 15 (1980), 187–201.

Carey, John, 'Introduction', *The Private Memoirs and Confessions of a Justified Sinner* (1824; Oxford: Oxford University Press, 1991), pp. xi–xxiii.

Clark, David Lee, *Charles Brockden Brown, Pioneer Voice of America* (Durham, NC: Duke University Press, 1952).

Coates, Paul, *The Gorgon's Gaze: German Cinema, Expressionism, and the Image of Horror* (Cambridge: Cambridge University Press, 1991).

The Compact Edition of the Oxford English Dictionary, 2 volumes (1971; Oxford: Oxford University Press, 1989).

Crawford, Thomas, 'James Hogg: The Play of Region and Nation', Douglas Gifford, ed., *The History of Scottish Literature* (Aberdeen: Aberdeen University Press, 1988), 3, pp. 89–105.

Crichton Smith, Iain, 'A Work of Genius: James Hogg's *Justified Sinner*', *Studies in Scottish Literature*, 28 (1993), 1–11.

Duncan, Ian, 'The Upright Corpse: Hogg, National Literature and the Uncanny', *Studies in Hogg and his World*, 5 (1994), 29–54.

—— 'Walter Scott, James Hogg, and Scottish Gothic', in David Punter, ed., *A Companion to the Gothic* (Oxford: Blackwell, 2000), pp. 70–80.

Edwards, Jonathan, 'Sinners in the Hands of an Angry God' (1741), in Sculley Bradley, ed., *The American Tradition in Literature* (New York: Grosset & Dunlap, 1974), 1, pp. 98–113.

Freud, Sigmund, 'The Uncanny' (1919), James Strachey, ed., *An Infantile Neurosis and Other Works*. The Standard Edition of the Complete Psychological Works of Sigmund Freud, 24 volumes (London: The Hogarth Press, 1962), 17, pp. 217–56.

Garside, Peter D., ed., 'Introduction', James Hogg, *The Private Memoirs and Confessions of a Justified Sinner* (Edinburgh: Edinburgh University Press, 2002), pp. xi–xcix.

Gide, André, ed., 'Introduction', James Hogg, *The Private Memoirs and Confessions of a Justified Sinner* (London: the Cresset Press, 1947), pp. ix–xvi.

Godwin, William, *Caleb Williams* (1794; Oxford: Oxford University Press, 1988).

Hawthorne, Nathaniel, 'Young Goodman Brown' (1835), R. V. Cassill, ed., *The Norton Anthology of Short Fiction* (New York: Norton, 1995), pp. 730–41.

Hogg, James, *The Private Memoirs and Confessions of a Justified Sinner* (1824; Oxford: Oxford University Press, 1991).

Hunter, Adrian, ed., 'Introduction', James Hogg, *The Private Memoirs and Confessions of a Justified Sinner* (1824; Peterborough, Ontario: Broadview Press, 2001), pp. 7–39.

Jones, Ernest, *On the Nightmare* (London: Hogarth Press, 1931).

Kelly, Gary, *English Fiction of the Romantic Period 1789–1830* (London and New York: Longman, 1989).

Kidd, Colin, *Subverting Scotland's Past: Scottish Whig Historians and the Creation of an Anglo-British Identity, 1689–c. 1830* (Cambridge: Cambridge University Press, 1993).

Knox, John, *The First Blast of the Trumpet Against the Monstrous Regiment of Women* (1558; New York: Da Copa Press, 1972).

Lang, Andrew, *John Knox and the Reformation* (1905; Port Washington, New York: Kennikat Press, 1967).

Lee, L. L., 'The Devil's Figure: James Hogg's *Justified Sinner*', *Studies in Scottish Literature*, 3 (1966), 230–9.

Mack, Douglas S., 'The Devil's Pilgrim: A Note on Wringhim's Private Memoirs in James Hogg's *Confessions of a Justified Sinner*', *Scottish Literary Journal*, 2–3 (1975–6), 36–40.

—— 'Hogg's Religion and *The Confessions of a Justified Sinner*', *Studies in Scottish Literature*, 7 (1970), 272–5.

Manning, Susan, *The Puritan-Provincial Vision: Scottish and American Literature in the Nineteenth Century* (Cambridge: Cambridge University Press, 1990).

Milton, John, *Paradise Lost*, ed. Merritt Y. Hughes (1674; Indianapolis: The Odyssey Press, 1981).

Morgan, Robin, *The Demon Lover: On the Sexuality of Terrorism* (New York and London: Norton, 1989).

Muir, Edwin, *John Knox: Portrait of a Calvinist* (London: Jonathan Cape, 1929).

Oakleaf, David, '"Not the Truth": The Doubleness of Hogg's *Confessions* and the Eighteenth-Century Tradition', *Studies in Scottish Literature*, 18 (1983), 59–74.

Paine, Thomas, *The Age of Reason* (1795; Harmondsworth: Penguin Books, 1984).

Pattee, Fred Lewis, 'Introduction', *Wieland, or the Transformation* (1798; San Diego: Harcourt, Brace, Jovanovich, 1926), pp. ix–xlvi.

Poe, Edgar Allan, 'William Wilson' (1839) *Selected Tales* (Oxford: Oxford University Press, 1980), pp. 79–96.

Pope, Rebecca A., 'Hogg, Wordsworth, and Gothic Autobiography', *Studies in Scottish Literature*, 27 (1992), 218–40.

Porte, Joel, 'In the Hands of an Angry God: Religious Terror in Gothic Fiction', G. R. Thompson, ed., *The Gothic Imagination: Essays in Dark Romanticism* (Washington: Washington State University Press, 1974), pp. 42–64.

Punter, David, *The Literature of Terror: A History of Gothic Fictions From 1765 to the Present Day* (London and New York: Longman, 1980).

Ridley, Jasper, *John Knox* (Oxford: Clarendon Press, 1968).

Sage, Victor, *Horror Fiction in the Protestant Tradition* (London: Macmillan, 1988).

Samuels, Shirley, *Romances of the Republic: Women, the Family, and Violence in the Literature of the Early American Nation* (New York and Oxford: Oxford University Press, 1996).

Scott, Sir Walter, *Guy Mannering; or The Astrologer* (1815; Harmondsworth: Penguin Books, 2003).

Stauffer, Vernon, 'New England and the Bavarian Illuminati'. Dissertation, Columbia University, 1918.

Stevenson, David, *The Covenanters: The National Covenant and Scotland* (Edinburgh: The Saltire Society, 1988).

Stevenson, Robert Louis, *The Strange Case of Dr. Jekyll and Mr. Hyde* (1886; Oxford: Oxford University Press, 1987).

Walzer, Michael, 'The Puritans as Revolutionaries', in Cushing Strout, ed., *Intellectual History in America: Contemporary Essays on Puritanism, the Enlightenment, & Romanticism* (New York: Harper & Row, 1968), pp. 1–20.

Wilson, James D., 'Incest and American Romantic Fiction', *Studies in the Literary Imagination*, 7 (1994), 31–50.

12
Colonial Ghosts: Mimicking Dickens in America

Andrew Smith

Dickens's account of his first travels in America, published in 1842 as *The American Notes for General Circulation*, includes a moment, in his account of solitary confinement at the State Penitentiary in Philadelphia, where he employs a ghost in order to critique the penal system. This represents a turning point in the narrative, one in which Dickens's attempt to understand the institutions of democratic America (its schools, hospitals and prisons) is replaced by an assertion of a supposedly superior British difference.[1]

In Dickens's account he uses the image of the ghost to illustrate the feelings of self-haunting which he believes characterize the experience of solitary confinement. Self-haunting provides Dickens with an image which represents a particular sense of psychological and cultural alienation. Why this indicates a colonial interjection on Dickens's part will be explored later, but before discussing the prison episode it is important to acknowledge that the roots of what becomes an argument about visibility and invisibility are to be found in earlier parts of the book, in encounters which go someway to explain why Dickens introduces a ghost into his travelogue. This chapter focuses on his 1842 journey to America rather than his happier return visit in 1867–8. Also, although much has been made of how Dickens's negative experience of America was incorporated into *Martin Chuzzlewit* (1843–4), that is not the subject of my argument.

Throughout *The American Notes* Dickens responds to what he perceives as a language of mimicry. Such moments represent feelings of uncanniness, but also correspond to Homi Bhabha's conceptualization of a colonial ambivalence. Mimicry for Bhabha indicates just how far the colonized 'Other' has internalized ideas that are foreign and that are intended as forms of regulation (political, educational, and bureaucratic). However, such moments of mimicry can also appear to the colonial gaze as unsettling parodies of colonization so that 'Mimicry is also the sign of the inappropriate' because it suggests the presence of 'a difference or recalcitrance' that subtly subverts colonial power (or at least is seen as such by the colonial gazer).[2] The uncanny also plays a role in this. Uncanniness, according to Freud, occurs when images of the past intrude into the present, so that such images are strangely familiar although repressed and this can be applied to a language of colonial gazing which in asserting the difference between self and other is, paradoxically, prone to integrating such terms (as they become doubled, or linked through mimicry).[3] Thus, as we shall see, Dickens's assertion of difference comes back to haunt his narrative as doubled, uncanny, versions of exclusion – of blind children that can read, incarcerated ghosts and regional obsessives. In other words, Dickens gets back an image of himself as an unconsciously inflected, but politically loaded, parody. The effect is that throughout there is a pervasive undertow of alienation and estrangement which inheres within images which reflect on Dickens as a national outsider, and as a writer who struggles to make sense of American idioms.

Dickens's sense of alienation can be seen in his early account of The Perkins Institution and Massachusetts Asylum for the Blind in Boston. Initially, Dickens extols the virtues of what he regards as a just regime in which forms of employment (making brushes and mattresses) create alliances between the children in the school, ones which, for Dickens, takes them out of their otherwise inner and psychologically locked worlds.

At first, he is impressed by the apparent candour of the pupils at the school because:

> It is strange to watch the faces of the blind, and see how free they are from all concealment of what is passing in their thoughts; observing which, a man with eyes may blush to contemplate the masks he wears. (p. 81)

However, this spirit of openness disappears when Dickens finds himself confronted by behaviour which he finds unfathomable. He encounters Laura Bridgman, a twelve-year-old who is deaf, blind and mute. He notes of her:

> Like other inmates of that house, she had a green ribbon bound round her eyelids. A doll she had dressed lay near by upon the

ground. I took it up, and saw that she had made a green fillet such as she wore herself, and fastened it about its mimic eyes. (p. 82)

The doll is a mimic representation of the pupil and this challenges the notion of immediacy and authenticity which had earlier characterized the seemingly open expressions of the children. The girl is in possession of an image of herself (the doll) which baffles Dickens and suggests that she is trapped in a self-referential world which is generated by her blindness (her inability to see out to others). For Dickens she has become entombed 'in a marble cell, impervious to any ray of light' (p. 81). Dickens discovers a written history of the girl and he quotes approvingly from it the claim that 'her mind dwells in darkness and stillness, as profound as that of a closed tomb at midnight' (p. 86), an image of mental solitary confinement that foreshadows the more literal solitary confinement in his later account of the prison. Dickens has been struck by the presence of Laura Bridgman's doll which is a mimic version of herself and he focuses on a passage in the history which emphasizes:

Her tendency to imitation is so strong, that it leads her to actions which must be entirely incomprehensible to her ... She has been known to sit for half an hour, holding a book before her sightless eyes, and moving her lips. (p. 89)

For Dickens this mimicry poses a problem for interpretation. She appears to represent a familiar world, a child playing with a doll or reading a book, but her blindness defamiliarizes this, and it becomes an unconscious conceit for Dickens's wider inability to account rationally for the perceived peculiarities of America. For Dickens, America is familiar, possessing similar institutions and a shared history, but it is also culturally unfamiliar and strange in how those institutions are organized. Also, the scene turns Dickens into an oddly liminal, or spectral, presence who is both there (observing) and not there (unobserved), and this is closely bound up with the ideas of colonial mimicry suggested by Bhabha. For Bhabha, mimicry becomes identifiable, or visible, when it appears as implied mockery, so that:

It is from this area between mimicry and mockery, where the reforming civilizing mission is threatened by the displacing gaze of its disciplinary double, that ... instances of colonial imitation come. What they all share is a discursive process by which the excess or

> slippage produced by the *ambivalence* of mimicry (almost the same, *but not quite*) does not merely 'rupture' the discourse, but becomes transformed into an uncertainty which fixes the colonial subject as a 'partial' presence. (*LC*, p. 86; emphasis in the original)

Crucially, it is an experience in which colonial regimes of power – and the instances which Dickens discusses (schools, hospitals, prisons) concern institutionalized power – marginalize, or spectralize, the colonial gazer because they no longer represent the older authority which once held such regimes together.

Dickens's sense of exclusion is further dramatized in his account of the 'State Hospital for the Insane' in South Boston, where he is full of admiration for a benign regime which develops self-restraint in the inmates. However, he also finds that it is an institution in which mimic forms of behaviour appear to be actively encouraged. One inmate, for example, is supported in her belief that she owns the institution, and it is at this point that images of European difference appear because the woman is described as having pretensions to European aristocratic lineage. Dickens notes that 'she was radiant with imaginary jewels' (p. 95) and that on introduction she puts down a newspaper 'in which I dare say she had been reading an account of her own presentation at some Foreign Court' (p. 95). He also discovers that the hospital holds a series of dances and marches which are much discussed by the inmates, who practise dance routines in preparation for them. In effect a version of polite European society is used to control behaviour.

Dickens is thus confronted by another type of acting, here a performance of polite European society, which is both familiar and unfamiliar. However, in Bhabha's terms we can see that the means of controlling 'insanity' appears to be a lampoon of European mores and Dickens cannot help but be struck by the mimicry (and mockery) of it all, and by the fact that it contains a covert national narrative. These issues of visibility and invisibility – of what is being shown and why – are given a particularly dramatic turn in his account of ghosts.

His discussion of the Blind School and the hospital suggests the presence of spectrality to the degree that they imply that there exist occulted, or hidden, realities concerning power, realities Dickens cannot quite see. This idea of a hidden presence is readdressed in his account of solitary confinement. He writes of the emotional anguish suffered by such prisoners: 'that there is a depth of terrible endurance ... which none but the sufferers themselves can fathom' (p. 147). Like Laura Bridgman, the inmates are there but not there, physically present but mentally entombed: 'He is a man buried alive; to be dug out in the slow round of years; and in the mean time dead to everything but torturing anxieties and horrible despair' (p. 48). He describes an inmate's bed which 'looked like a grave' (p. 150). Another is summoned from his cell and stood in the corridor 'looking as wan and unearthly as if he had been summoned from the grave' (p. 150). Dickens, who had been unable to comprehend the actions of Laura Bridgman or the inhabitants of the hospital, makes a supreme effort to understand the psychological effects of solitary confinement. He imagines that an inmate would be aware of others in adjacent cells and would create narratives about their lives and personalities. Such a line of thought leads him to employ an explicit language of ghosting. He imagines of his imaginary neighbour 'How was he dressed? Has he been here long? Is he much worn away? Is he very white and spectre-like?' (p. 154).

These disembodied figures represent Dickens's attempt to explain otherness – as a desire to account for the emotional life of the marginalized, the excluded and the culturally disempowered. To this degree it constitutes a moment of crisis in the narrative because they are also moments of projection and transference. Dickens is a national outsider who cannot make sense of what he sees, and his emotionally fraught account of solitary confinement reflects his sense of isolation and exclusion.[4] His attempt to imagine imaginary people illustrates the presence of this projection and importantly it is one in which haunting becomes self-haunting, as the self is unable to transcend its boundaries (national and cultural) in order to properly embrace otherness.

He argues that an inmate would see 'an ugly phantom face' (p. 154) peering in at them through the cell window, a phantom which is not externalized, but one which participates in the mental life of the prisoner and so is, in reality, an aspect of their own psychic life. What is horrifying is the 'feeling [that the phantom] gave birth in his brain to something of corresponding shape, which ought not to be there, and racked his head with pains' (p. 154). The phantom haunts the prisoner wherever he goes because he is his own ghost, created by his burial alive in solitary confinement so that:

When he is in his cell by day, he fears the little yard without. When he is in the yard, he dreads to re-enter the cell. When night comes, there stands the phantom in the corner. If he have the courage to stand in its place, and drive it out (he had once being desperate) it broods upon his bed. In the twilight, and always at the same hour, a voice calls to him by name. (p. 155)

Such a process of self-haunting could generate a range of speculative readings concerning Dickens's psychological state; however, this image of ghosting represents a political (rather than strictly private) drama.

Dickens uses the Gothic in this instance as a mode of interpretation that illustrates the depth of feeling of a prisoner held in solitary confinement. To that degree the Gothic is used as a means of reading this plight, rather than merely being employed to capture a sense of the experience. It becomes a moment in which Dickens asserts a peculiarly European mode of the Gothic (concerning the plight of the non-American othered, i.e. himself) which is an outsider's way of reading what otherwise appears to be unthinkable, beyond representation. It is also, as in the earlier encounters, an experience in which Dickens becomes the strange, othered, spectral presence. This doubling suggests the uncanny, although in Bhabha's terms it is the presence of an implied mimicry which also unsettles such encounters because it is this 'repetition of *partial presence* ... that reverses "in part" the colonial appropriation by ... producing a partial vision of the colonizer's presence; a gaze of otherness' (*LC*, pp. 88–9; emphasis in the original). The problem confronted by Dickens the writer is to find a trope that can adequately capture such an experience.

It is significant that any sense of horror is generated rather than simply observed, because in reality Dickens has to imagine the whole thing. That it represents an imaginative construction indicates this position of the outsider looking in, and it enables Dickens to articulate the first moment in which he explicitly condemns an American institution (the penal system). The Gothic therefore functions here as a political critique and this might appear to be overstating the case were it not that after Dickens's moment of unconscious textual insight (in which he reads Gothically), he increasingly deploys a more confident narrative concerning national and cultural difference, rather than attempts to pursue an analysis of America through comparisons and implied similarities.

We can see this in the change of tone in the *The American Notes*, which begins in a mood of jaunty optimism on his arrival in Boston, a mood tempered by his inability to 'read' the apparently inexplicable behaviour at the Blind School and the hospital, then darkened in his account of solitary confinement, after which the growing sense of disillusionment and pessimism culminates in his final major chapter on the Gothic horrors of slavery. In slavery he reads the mutilated and branded bodies of the slaves as signs of a culture which has generated horror from within and created the potential for national self-destruction.

Dickens's use of the ghost therefore functions as a colonial interjection into the narrative, one in which the sympathetic attempt at reading America is superseded by a more belligerent assertion of difference.

Allan Lloyd Smith has argued of American Gothic that although American fiction in general had its roots in a Gothic idiom because its emergence coincided with the heyday of the British and European Gothic, nevertheless American Gothic is different in kind because 'the circumstances of their own history and the stresses of their particular cultural and political institutions meant that a series of significant inflections determined a Gothicism that differs markedly from British or European versions'.[5] This is because American-authored images of the frontier, ideas about the past and critiques of democracy have a particular national resonance. To this degree Dickens's use of ghosting functions as a European intervention – a way of accounting for feelings of defamiliarization and exclusion rather than operating as an internally generated critique of power. It represents the view of the cultural 'Other', who sees things from the margins, but who then turns a position of marginality into one of strength. To not belong enables Dickens at last to stand back and 'read', in highly nationalistic terms, what is for him being staged within American institutions. Another example is found in his account of a visit to the American frontier in the chapter 'A Jaunt to the Looking-glass Prairie and Back', in which the idea of mimicry is reasserted.

In the Blind School and the hospital he had encountered forms of mimic behaviour which he found inscrutable; and in his closing account of the prison he refers to an instance when an alcoholic had asked to be imprisoned in order to cure his addiction (or at least to be put beyond temptation). After two years this mock-prisoner, whilst working in the prison gardens, sees that a door has been left open and effects a mock-escape. However, at the frontier the idea of mimicry is politically repositioned. It no longer troubles Dickens as he sees in it a means of lampooning what he regards as a peculiarly American form of gullibility.

At the frontier he encounters a Scotsman who is selling fake medicines in the guise of 'Dr Crocus'. The shantytown that Dickens visits is in a swamp in which disease was rife, so creating opportunities for quacks and conmen such as Crocus. Dickens is introduced to him and they have a highly stylized series of verbal exchanges in which Crocus extols the virtues of American freedom in a bid to attract more customers to his show. Dickens implies a subtext which is that Crocus's concern about a lack of freedom in Britain is because he is probably wanted there on criminal charges, something which is broadly implied by Crocus and understood by Dickens, but which the gathering crowd do not register. Dickens colludes with Crocus in an exchange of banter in which Dickens ask him whether he intends to return to 'the old country', to which Crocus replies, 'You won't catch me at that just yet, sir. I am a little too fond of freedom for *that*, sir. Ha ha!' (p. 225; emphasis in the original). The suggestion is that frauds like Crocus can flourish in America because gullibility has, for Dickens, become a political trait. The attempt to build a town, to construct a model of civilization, in a pestilential swamp represents for Dickens clear evidence that its inhabitants have been duped into believing that such things are both possible and desirable. There is therefore a difference between the ideal and the real, between lived experience and political fraud. As he noted in a letter to W. C. Macready written around this time, 'This is not the republic I came to see; this is not the republic of my imagination', because instead of democracy he perceives a political con trick.[6]

This idea of political duping underlines Dickens's investment in his European credentials, and it is a position which is emphasized in his account of the prairie in which national difference frames his evaluation of it:

> Great as the picture was, its very flatness and extent, which left nothing to the imagination, tamed it down and cramped its interest. I felt little of that sense of freedom and exhilaration which a Scottish heath inspires, or even our English downs awaken. (p. 226)

To get to this point he has to relocate ideas used in his account of the prison – there too was an experience which was about taming and cramping the imagination, an experience articulated through the use of the ghost, one which had enabled him to exorcize such anxieties and assert the alleged freedoms and exhilarations of Britain.

However, there is another issue which relates to language. Dickens uses the image of the ghost as a conceit for how he perceives, and senses that he is perceived by, America. The ghost is thus part of the rhetoric of the Gothic and indicates Dickens's attempt to find a language which enables him to represent his ambivalent feelings.[7]

The ghost should be seen as part of a performative Gothic argot and this idea of a performative language is developed at some length in the protracted banter between Dickens and Crocus in which false realities are created for the benefit of the credulous observers. As Steven Marcus has noted, exploring how Dickens uses language is central to understanding his concerns about American democracy. Marcus claims that Dickens, following Tocqueville, believed 'that a new language was being born in America; that Americans were losing the habit of speaking conversationally and spoke in private situations as if they were addressing a public meeting'.[8] This is not a superficial linguistic tic, but is generated because the private self becomes public property in American democracy and this is not only due to the pervasive influence of what Dickens regarded as a pernicious media, but to itself. For Marcus, Dickens 'noticed several essentially related things about this new kind of social authority; its strongest tendency was to convert the private self into public property and into something wholly externalized – an externalization accompanied by reckless, aggressive self-inflation' (p. 244). Such images of publicly rendered private selves are suggested in Laura Bridgman's performative reading and in the mocking performance of a European aristocracy in the hospital.

It is the unreal nature of America which disturbs Dickens and this is why he has recourse to the Gothic in order to account for this disturbance. Marcus argues that Dickens concurred with Tocqueville in arguing that American reality was governed by economic forces of mass production that also created mass-produced selves, characterized by 'a certain mechanical type of human being' (p. 246). This was combined with the absence of older, European social hierarchies so that for Dickens, according to Marcus, 'Having almost nothing finally but themselves to refer to, Americans tended to develop narrowly and unimaginatively, their characters and personalities to become thin and superficial' (p. 248). Thus America seems to be inherently unreal and hence Gothic, and it is these related issues about language and identity which Dickens addresses in an account of a canal boat journey to Pittsburg.

Dickens open his account by discussing the use of 'fix' as a common term used to describe a range of disparate activities, from fixing food, to getting fixed (dressed) and being fixed (seen to). Dickens uses the prevalence of the term in order to imply that its use 'unfixes' meaning. The term is ubiquitous and so lacks precision and indicates the presence of an alternative linguistic reality in which meaning is constituted merely by contextual usage. Linguistic realities and social realities are quickly elided as Dickens discusses the social arrangements of life on the boat. Of significance here is how a literary language is used to refer to the passengers. Dickens notes of the cramped sleeping arrangements that:

> when going below, I found suspended on either side of the cabin, three long tiers of hanging book-shelves, designed apparently for

volumes of the octavo size. Looking with greater attention at these contrivances (wondering to find such literary preparations in such a place), I descried on each shelf a sort of microscopic sheet and blanket; then I began dimly to comprehend that the passengers were the library, and that they were to be arranged, edge-wise, on these shelves, till morning. (p. 193)

The observation associates the inhabitants with language and narrative because Dickens is there to tell their stories. However, it also has the effect of contributing to a sense of unreality that Dickens regards as inherent to America and which is captured in his account of the noises made by the croaking frogs as they make their journey down the canal: 'the frogs ... sounded as though a million of fairy teams with bells were travelling through the air, and keeping pace with us' (p. 193). Although on the boat ghosts become replaced by characters, there remains an insistent focus on how narrating America depends upon accounting for identity and this appears in an account of a man from Mississippi, and a man whom Dickens regards as overly inquisitive.

The man from Mississippi makes an impassioned speech which is designed to rid the boat of overcrowding caused by taking on too many passengers. The speech concerns his origins and suggests that other passengers, most notably from the north-east, would find him disagreeable company on such an overcrowded vessel: 'I'm from the brown forests of the Mississippi, *I* am ... I'm the wrong sort of man for 'em, *I* am. They won't like me, *they* won't' (p. 97). Many of the passengers leave on this account and as a consequence he is accorded special privileges by the others. However, Dickens notes that on other encounters with him he still seems to be trapped within this speech about his regional origins. When they are about to disembark he overhears him talking to himself: 'I'm from the brown forests of the Mississippi, *I* am,' prompting Dickens to claim: 'I am inclined to argue from this, that he had never left off saying so' (p. 197). This sense of being trapped within language implicitly echoes Dickens's own inability to find a language for America, so that such images subtly, unconsciously, rebound back upon him as moments of the uncanny.

Dickens's account of a man who is unable to break free of his regionally inflected, nationally-specific language, for example, not only renders that man as 'Other' to Dickens but also, at a more complex level, it reflects his own position as a cultural outsider struggling with the language. The ghost captures this earlier in the narrative but this later figure is also Dickens's *doppelgänger*. This is also clear in the only other portrait of a passenger that he gives. Dickens describes a man 'who was the most inquisitive fellow that can possibly be imagined. He never spoke otherwise than interrogatively. He was embodied enquiry' (p. 195). Dickens soon finds his questioning wearisome and tries to avoid him. However he notes that part of the reason that the man becomes tiresome is that his questioning never ceases because it is never satisfied, 'He was always wide awake, like the enchanted bride who drove her husband frantic; always restless; always thirsting for answers; perpetually seeking and never finding. There never was such a curious man' (p. 195). Many different Gothic-inflected narratives have been suggested as the source for the reference to 'the enchanted bride', but what is noteworthy is the claim about 'perpetually seeking and never finding'.[9] It is an image of curiosity which again reflects Dickens's position as an investigator into the attitudes and mores of America. Here, such inquiry is represented as overly intrusive and strangely exhausted. However there is also, as in the earlier examples, a sense of doubling which through a covert language of mimicry suggests that such doubling reveals the split within the colonial gaze identified by Bhabha in which there is 'the *splitting* of colonial dis-course so that two attitudes towards external reality persist; one takes reality into consideration while the other disavows it and replaces it by a product of desire that repeats, rearticulates "reality" as mimicry' (*LC*, p. 91; emphasis in the original). In such a process the colonial gazer is confronted by two possible images, that which narcissistically reflects their power, or that which makes a mockery of it and generates paranoia.[10]

Dickens is, of course, in a unique position because he subjects what had once been a colonial nation to a now redundant colonial gaze. However, Dickens ultimately cannot either stand outside of his national context nor properly embrace, or understand, an American one. Also the more or less overt images of mimicry that he frustratingly encoun-ters in the early part of the book become disabling covert presences as the narrative progresses, which add to the growing mood of pessimism.

However, if Dickens has a sense of unease, it is also significant that his presence also generated unease in others. Dickens, towards the end of *The American Notes* and whilst on another boat trip, recalls that:

> There was a gentleman on board, to whom, as I unintentionally learned through the thin partition which divided our state-room from the cabin in which he and his wife conversed together, I was unwittingly the occasion of very great uneasiness. (p. 241)

He later overhears the man say, '"I suppose that Boz will be writing a book by-and-by, and putting all our names in it!", at which imaginary consequence of being on board with Boz, he groaned' (p. 242). The anonymous passenger's fears illustrate anxieties concerning the possible content of an outsider's commentary – an anxiety which many conservatively-minded Americans, disturbed by Dickens's condemnation of slavery and the media, felt strongly. However, the roots of this are also to be found within the subtle anxieties of Dickens, who cannot produce the celebration of democracy that he had hoped to write as America becomes constituted as an unreal space inhabited by unconsciously projected colonial ghosts.

Notes

1. Charles Dickens, *The American Notes for General Circulation*, ed. and intro. John S. Whitley and Arnold Goldman (1842; Harmondsworth: Penguin Books, 1985). All subsequent references are to this edition, and are given in the text.
2. Homi K. Bhabha, *The Location of Culture* (London and New York: Routledge, 1995), p. 86. All subsequent references are to this edition, and are given in the text, prefaced by *LC*.
3. Sigmund Freud, 'The "Uncanny"', in *Art and Literature: Jensen's* Gradiva, *Leonardo Da Vinci and other works*, in Penguin Freud Library, vol. 14, trans. James Strachey, ed. Albert Dickson (Harmondsworth: Penguin, 1985), pp. 339–76.
4. A point also made by John S. Whitley and Arnold Goldman in their introduction to *The American Notes*, p. 31, n. 59.
5. Allan Lloyd Smith, 'American Gothic', in *The Handbook to Gothic Literature*, ed. Marie Mulvey-Roberts (Basingstoke: Macmillan, 1998), pp. 2–10, p. 2.
6. Letter dated 22 March. Cited in *The American Notes for General Circulation*, p. 316.
7. This use of the ghost is quite different to how Dickens uses ghosts in, for example, *A Christmas Carol* (1843), where they become devices to scare Scrooge into living a better life. Dickens does not really believe that there is a ghost in the State Penitentiary or intends to imply that there might be one there; instead, it is used as an image designed to rhetorically capture the experience of isolation.
8. Steven Marcus, *Dickens from Pickwick to Dombey* (London: Chatto and Windus, 1965), p. 219.
9. *The American Notes for General Circulation*, see p. 350, n 3.
10. See Bhabha, *The Location of Culture*, p. 91.

References

Bhabha, Homi K., *The Location of Culture* (London and New York: Routledge, 1995).

Dickens, Charles, *The American Notes for General Circulation*, ed. and intro. John S. Whitley and Arnold Goldman (1842; Harmondsworth: Penguin Books, 1985).

Freud, Sigmund, 'The "Uncanny"', in *Art and Literature: Jensen's* Gradiva, *Leonardo Da Vinci and Other Works*, Penguin Freud Library, vol. 14, trans. James Strachey, ed. Albert Dickson (Harmondsworth: Penguin Books, 1985), pp. 339–76.

Lloyd Smith, Allan, 'American Gothic', in Marie Mulvey-Roberts, ed., *The Handbook to Gothic Literature* (Basingstoke: Macmillan, 1998), pp. 2–10.

Marcus, Steven, *Dickens From Pickwick to Dombey* (London: Chatto and Windus, 1965).

Part IV
Coda: Other Directions

13
Translating Technologies: Dickens, Kafka and the Gothic

Barry Murnane

Recalling his first attempts to write a novel in a diary entry from the year 1917, Franz Kafka describes *Der Verschollene/America* in terms of his 'intention as I now see it to write a Dickens novel, but enhanced by the brighter lights I would have taken from these times and the darker ones that I would have found within myself'.[1] The link between Dickens and Kafka may not seem obvious, but it has been suitably traced in German studies, not yet, however, in terms of the Gothic. Tracing these connections along the lines of several Gothic voyages, and several senses of translation, in and outside the works of both writers, a specific interest in technology emerges which can be seen as a Gothic response to 'the brighter lights ... from these times', that is to Gothic's ambivalent discursive relationship to the processes of modernization as a form of 'shadow of the modern'.[2] By focusing on Kafka's 'Dickensian' translation, one can suggest a Gothic reading of a text not previously observed in this tradition, Dickens's *David Copperfield*, a reading which also points towards Kafka's own place in a European Gothic tradition. Secondly, both writers' presentations of the very technologies involved in the spatial translation of voyages, the planes, trains and automobiles of the machine age, expand the links between Dickens and Kafka in their comparable Gothicization of technologies.

Kafka's translation of Dickens refers to a text not commonly read in the Gothic context, *David Copperfield*. Yet this is no direct translation of 'the story of the trunk, the boy who delights and charms everyone, the menial labour, his sweetheart in the country house, the dirty houses *et al.*';[3] it is much rather a translation in the sense advanced by Walter Benjamin in his essay 'The Task of the Translator'.[4] As Benjamin suggests, the traces of the original are still present in the translation, here Kafka's 'blatant imitation,' as a ghostly, defamiliarizing presence, a trace of foreignness. The translation is much rather a *Fortleben* of the original, a further development and unfolding of the text,[5] made relevant to, and adapted by, the contemporary translator, Kafka's 'sharper lights … taken from the times'. In an essay written under the direct influence of his early work on German Romanticism, the notion of translation as a constant rewriting and expanding of the original (an original which, for the early Benjamin can only be seen as itself a Schlegel-style translation from God-given nature) seems to match Kafka's modernist 'enhancement' of Dickens. Likewise for Lefevere, translation always implies a process of rewriting and manipulation of the text, a rewriting dominated by ideological motivation, 'Translation has to do with authority and legitimacy, and ultimately with power.'[6] As Terry Hale has shown, the Gothic itself is a result of a furious process of translation and cultural exchange dominated by ideological motivations, leading to a situation where Germany became synonymous with terror by the 1820s (in spite of the fact Goethe and Schiller had long since begun to produce a body of classicistic works known in Germany as *Weimarer Klassik* which was far removed from the popular British fantasies of a 'terrible' German School of Gothic writing).[7] Read against this background, Benjamin's model of translation can also be extended to describe the dialogic process of intertextuality (as observed by Kristeva and Genette) in literary works which accounts for both intentional, marked traces and the broader elements of architextual references to literary modes and social discourses. Following Hale, these intertextual and intercultural borrowings are a crucial part of any account of the Gothic. If every text is 'haunted' by the traces of another text, as Benjamin suggests with regard to translations and transformations, then an intercultural mode of Gothic transformations across the borders of national literatures can also be observed in this wider order of architextual fields of translation. Viewed thus, the connection between Dickens, Kafka and the Gothic – suggested by Kafka himself – becomes a point of departure for a wider reading of European formations of the Gothic.

That what emerges in Kafka's *Der Verschollene* is a *Gothic* translation of Dickens's text is anticipated by Kafka when he writes of a 'heartlessness behind his sentimental overflowing style' in the same diary entry. Kafka identifies a series of motifs running through the novel that belong in any good Gothic novel, from the devilish father-figure Murdstone, who beats and then banishes David,[8] the monstrous tinker on the road to Dover,[9] to the demonically ''umble' Uriah Heep, who fills David with an incomprehensible instant hatred that draws on discourses of monstrosity and physiognomy familiar from the original Gothic of Matthew Lewis and Ann Radcliffe.[10] These are characters out of the mould of Fagin, Miss Havisham or Krook, 'the Lord Chancellor', figures that embody features of social reality, but transcend any sense of realism insofar as they become representative of a sense of social evil for which Dickens's narrative ensures they are punished. Murdstone may disappear fom the narrative, but Heep's machinations are suitably punished by the close of the novel. The final element Kafka identifies as Dickensian is 'the method even more so'. *David Copperfield* is coloured by dream effects and grotesque tableaux, a method that is produced through the perspectival colouring produced by the single focus through David's eyes – a focus on children that seems to be a defining trait of Dickens's Gothic fiction. As David encounters the grown-up world of London so incomprehensible to him,[11] it emerges as a fantastic, threatening place coloured by fear and uncertainty, the fear and anxiety with which a Gothic heroine like Emily St. Aubert enters the adult sphere of Toulouse and Venice. Here, as in *Bleak House* and *Oliver Twist* – more commonly read as Gothic novels – it is this focus on children that leads to the grotesque portrayals of reality indicative of Dickens's Gothic style. It is this, I contend, that drew Kafka most to Dickens – the presentation of a world coloured by angst and presented as a distortion of reality rather than realistic verisimilitude.

David Copperfield is informed by conflicts and chronic fears of father figures and by sexual tensions that extend into portrayals of the social realm of schooling and the workplace. In his youth David is haunted by the image of his father's grave which he can see through the window, a haunting that emerges in several dream sequences, and his childhood home is split by him between a maternal and paternal parlour, a paternal parlour in which he is overcome by constant fear. His mother's second husband, Mr Murdstone, extends this fear of paternal authority, beating and banishing David to London. London still stands under the sign of parental punishment, however. Creakle, the headmaster at Salem House School, and Quinion, Murdstone's London manager, both continue to carry out the law of the father (Kafka's 'menial labour' element): Creakle hangs a sign around David's neck, 'Take care of him. He bites!' and Quinion rules with an iron rod over the boy in the warehouse.[12] The paternal conflict is linked with sexual tensions, however, with Murdstone taking on the role of the devilishly handsome and brutally careless villain in David's eyes. This trope re-emerges in several storylines in the novel, most notably in Steerforth, whose combination of power, charm and sexual magnetism, coupled with a moral deficiency, reduces David's childhood sweetheart Emily to ruin among the down-and-out fallen women of London,[13] Kafka's 'dirty houses *et al.*' story.

Kafka's reading of *David Copperfield* in *America* condenses and magnifies these standard Gothic tropes of sexual and paternal deviancy and injustice, the Gothic subtext of the novel, into a series of repetitions of the same scene: the seventeen-year-old Karl Roßmann's banishment from his Prague home to America, a banishment that is to be immediately compared to the paternal conflict that sets Dickens's story in motion. This then is a voyage under the flag of an unjust Gothic punishment of a young, helpless hero. This dismissal stands under the sign of sexual tension and patriarchal law: having been raped by a housemaid, who subsequently fell pregnant, Karl is coldly dispatched to America by his father. This initial over-exaggerated act of paternal abuse and sexual tension, the law of the father, is repeated throughout the novel – from Karl's equally unmotivated expulsion by an uncle he miraculously discovers in New York, sexual rejection by Clara Pollunder, Kafka's 'country sweetheart', to his violent dismissal from the Hotel Occidental, when he is beaten and dragged around by the head porter – fusing *David Copperfield*'s 'dirty houses' and 'menial labour' themes – a dismissal couched in sexual innuendo and masochistic violence designed as a specifically Gothic over-exaggeration of David's childhood. Karl is dismissed after a 'trial' which consists of lies, mistakes and uninformed judges from the hotel management for abandoning his post as a liftboy for five minutes in order to help an acquaintance.

From his arrival in America Karl stands under the sign of a violent system of law and order similar to the social injustice that Dickens had uncovered in the London episodes of *David Copperfield*. Entering New York he is overpowered by a morphed version of the Statue of Liberty with a sword in her hand, a harbinger of the sinister, unregulated power, violence and abuse that subverts the myth of free America and points towards a perverted system of discipline and punishment. Kafka's Roßmann suffers constant and repeated acts of abuse without any hope of salvation – his final journey towards the theatre in Oklahoma is, in fact, a journey towards a lynching. The origin of his adopted name, Negro, is a picture of a lynching in Oklahoma which Kafka had seen in his main source for the novel, Arthur Holitscher's *Amerika Heute und Morgen*. For Rudolf Vasata the difference in style and form, the 'brighter and duller' lights that Kafka mentions, are socially retraceable.[14] The Industrial Revolution that Dickens catalogues has reached its natural conclusion in the machinery and violent social order of the Hotel Occidental with its telephonists reified into writing machines, with their inhuman twitching fingers. Kafka's translation, his modernization, of Dickens's novel points therefore to a reading of modernization and technology and machinery as it is socially interpreted, within the framework of the Gothic. Dickens and Kafka suggest a form of Gothic positioned in an ambivalent relationship to modernity and modernization, by which the 'brighter' lights of modernity become fused with literary projections drawing on the 'shadows' between these lights.

The particular problem literature has evidenced with regard to technological change has been the intellectual separation of people and things, and subsequently an intellectual separation of knowledge structures, a cult of heightened specialization in which *literati* and scientists were equally responsible, and which resulted in writers and cultural analysts becoming separated from the scientific discipline responsible for social change. Left out of the processes which create and implement technological advancement, the writer and the reading public are left to deal with technical objects whose construction they do not understand, whose implementation they cannot influence. The situation smacks of an academic creation of two cultures, for which literature and science are mutually responsible, despite the obvious continuous borrowings and crossovers that occur. It is here that a second sense of translating becomes relevant – namely the translation of technology into literature. This is an adaptation of Walter Benjamin's concept of translation to relations between two cultural spheres within one society, rather than the normal linguistic contact. Justification for this comes from Benjamin himself: 'Every expression of human mental life can be understood as a kind of language, and this understanding, in a manner, new contexts everywhere. One can speak of a language of music and fine arts, from a language of justice and technology ...'[15] The gap that is opened between these two 'languages' must be bridged, but this can never be complete – as Homi Bhabha has observed, there remains a hybrid space of mimicry and mockery, of assimilation, fear and rejection, a space in which the translated material becomes strange, disturb*ed* and disturb*ing*.[16]

Each translation retains a trace of foreignness, an uncanny returning of that which is to be translated, each text is haunted by traces of the technology it attempts to incorporate. Helmut Lethen writes of First World War poetry involving tanks that:

A technical item like a tank is barely incorporated into a text when it is subjected to the strangest alterations in which it seems to become lost. Because this tank is spread throughout the text in a normative-moralistic context, in an aesthetic, expressive dimension and in a performative gesture.[17]

The performative gesture is necessarily one of fear and uncertainty, owing to being shut out of the intellectual processes involved. It can come as no surprise that this technology is presented as something demonic, arriving uncontrollably:

> The questions the writer asks are aimed towards how and why technology has been made, and in order to expand on this they engage in wish-images, hopes and fears, with which people take part in the development of technology. In this way, one can say that writers build wish and fear machinery that exist in our heads.[18]

And out of this fear machinery emerge the demonized images of technology, the Gothic modes of dealing with 'progress'.

Two brief snapshots that point towards what I mean by Gothic translations of technology:

1848. Approaching the end of *Dombey and Son*, the would-be adulterer and all round bad egg Carker is on the run from his ex-employer Mr Dombey, when he sees his pursuer from across a train track. Carker slips onto the track in a trance and:

> felt the earth tremble – knew in a moment that the rush was come – uttered a shriek – looked around – saw the red eyes, bleared and dim, in the daylight, close upon him – was beaten down, caught up, and whirled away upon a jagged mill, that spun him round and round, and struck him limb from limb and licked his stream of life up with its fiery heat, and cast his mutilated fragments in the air.[19]

1914. A traveller in a penal colony has been observing the death sentence by torture of a prisoner, when the Officer – dismayed at the traveller's lack of willingness to speak up for him when he meets the Commandant – releases the prisoner and straps himself into the torture machine, only for it to self-destruct:

> The harrow had already begun to rise to the side with the skewered body attached, as it only usually did after the twelfth hour. The blood flowed in a hundred streams, but not mixed with water, as

the water-pipes had broken down this time. And now the last mal-function; the body did not fall from the long spikes, the blood flowed out and hung over the pit without falling ... the lips were shut firmly, the eyes were open, had an life-like expression, with a look calm and convinced, the point of the large iron spike through the forehead.[20]

While any sense of direct translation seen in Kafka's modernization of *David Copperfield* cannot be considered in this case, one can indeed identify concomitant modes of presenting the industrial modernity of the machine age in both texts that point both towards a specific Gothic demonization of the 'brighter lights' of modernization itself, as well as towards the broader outlines of a Gothic discourse on technological modernity that connects Dickens and Kafka.

For Nick Daly in *Literature, Technology and Modernity 1860–2000*, there is a history of the Gothic novel yet to be written that focuses on the role of technology and a specifically Gothic approach to the Industrial Revolution throughout the nineteenth century.[21] Indeed, from Mary Shelley's modern Prometheus inventing his own, albeit biological, machine-man in *Frankenstein* to the 'up to date with a vengeance' *Dracula*, with its trains, phonographs and telegraphs (not quite the trains, planes and automobiles encountered in Kafka's works), there seems to be a constant awareness of technology running through the Gothic. Contrary to the traditional Two Cultures debate of the 1950s, literature has never been completely separated from technological development. Indeed Daly's book shows how the assimilation of technology into everyday life was crucially assisted aesthetically by literature, how the fears and hopes of the railway age found an important outlet in the Victorian railway melodramas, sensation novels and their just-in-time rescue on the tracks (nowadays probably better known from old black-and-white films). This is the second sense of Benjamin's translation, whereby 'every expression of human mental life can be understood as a kind of language' to be translated.[22] Literature had a physical as well as an aesthetic importance in the attempts to create what Daly, following Wolfgang Schivelbusch and Georg Simmel, presents as a protective layer against the *shock* of modernity that emerges in encounters with new technology – either the railway or the factory.[23] Sensation novels focusing on the railway fostered a new reading culture *in* the train designed to distract attention from the landscape as it flies by, thus eliminating the shock of perception changes – a second skin, or stimulus-armour.

I would argue a position for a Gothic portrayal of modern technology that does not offer such friendly assimilation, but rather holds
up the dangers of technology like a distorted mirror to the reading
public. What emerges in the gory death scenes I have mentioned seems
indicative for this Gothic response: the assimilation of technology
cannot have been complete as long as stimulus-shields were constructed, as the spike penetrating the brain in Kafka's text suggests.
Carker's horrific death is foreshadowed over ten pages with images and
word clusters that recall Dickens's descriptions of the shock of his own
railway crash at Staplehurst, Kent in June 1865. As the story moves
towards Carker's death the stimulus-shield becomes eroded: the shock
at experiencing the speed of the train returns, just in time for Carker to
be run down by the demonically coloured train, the moment at which
the shock of technology emerges:

> Some visionary horror, unintelligible and inexplicable, associated
> with a trembling of the ground, – a rush and a sweep of something
> through the air, like Death upon the wing. (*D*, p. 644)

> Again the nameless shock comes speeding up, and as it passes, the
> bells ring in his ears 'whither?' The wheels roar in his ears 'whither?'
> All the noise and rattle shapes itself into that cry. (*D*, p. 645)

Two examples from 1868 reveal this shock, and also point towards
the traditional Gothic linguistic register on which Dickens draws and
which highlights the importance of Gothic registers in the processes of
technological modernization: the *London News* reports on a crash in
Wales with the phrase, 'A new horror has been added to the number
of horrors to which railway travellers are exposed.'[24] The Marquis
of Hamilton reports of the same crash in language worthy of Ann
Radcliffe:

> Not a sound, not a scream, not a struggle to escape, or movement of
> any sort was apparent in the doomed carriages. It was as though an
> electric flash had at once paralysed and stricken every one of their
> occupants ...[25]

These are images that Dickens had already incorporated into his own
railway novel *Dombey and Son* written between 1846 and 1848, partly in
Paris, where he broke up his working day with visits to charnel houses
and mortuaries. Dickens transforms the train into a metaphorical

monster, 'roaring, rattling, tearing on, spurning everything with its dark breath ... as it comes tearing on resistless to the goal: and now its way, still like the way of Death is strewn with ashes thickly. Everything is blackened' (*D*, pp. 236–7). The train is metamorphosed into Lucifer, rewriting the entire city and countryside erasing towns and areas of London such as Staggs Gardens, which on the second visit no longer exists. It even begins to define identities – Mr Toodle 'belongs to the railway' (*D*, p. 185) and is now Stoker Toodle, no longer Mr Toodle. It brings with it images of excess to the rewritten city, 'palaces now reared their heads, and granite columns of gigantic girth opened a vista to the Railway world beyond' (*D*, p. 184). The railway has even erased the natural sense of time, as there 'was even railway time observed in clocks, as if the sun itself had given in.' (*D*, p. 185). Through Mr Dombey's train ride, this shock is extended to travelling inside the train. The change to perception and modes of experience noted by Daly re-emerge in the very language of the novel: the rhythm of the train is repeated in the rhythm of the sentences:

> Away with a shriek, and a roar, and a rattle, from the town, burrowing among the dwellings of men and making the streets hum, flashing out into the meadows for a moment, mining in through the damp earth, booming on in darkness and heavy air, bursting out again into the sunny day so bright and wide; away, with a shriek, and a roar, and a rattle, through the fields, through the woods, through the corn, through the hay, through the chalk, through the mould, through the clay, through the rock, among objects close at hand and almost in the grasp, ever flying from the traveller, and a deceitful distance ever moving slowly with him: like in the track of the remorseless monster Death. (*D*, p. 236)

The dehumanization of the gaze inside the train is taken to its Gothic apogee with Dombey practically becoming a ghost, occupied only by his own thoughts of death, not taking part in the world around him, until he is finally aroused back to life by his travelling companion Major Bagstock (*D*, p. 238).

Yet this monstrosity, this 'evil' nature of the train, is not to be accepted as a pure aversion to the train as technology. It is the social use of technology that is demonic, not the technology itself. The railway is referred to repeatedly as 'Progress' and it is this Victorian myth of Progress that has turned the railway into something demonic. On its own the train can be a force of good, but caught up in a discourse of commercialism and mercantilism – that very cold-hearted, uncaring attitude embodied in Dombey who rejects his daughter simply because she cannot carry on the family business, but more invidiously and disturbingly in the Manager Carker, the immoral would-be adulterer who siphons off money from the destitute Dombey – the train becomes demonic. This link is made more concrete in the reference to Carker as a 'serpent' (*D*, p. 643) just before his final mangling under the wheels of the 'fiery Devil' (*D*, p. 651) with 'the two red eyes' (*D*, p. 652). Carker seems to know that Death is upon him. He is fascinated by and attracted to the railway tracks; he seems to ask to be mangled before finally falling in front of the train.

Dickens seems to have recognized the importance of the railway for the burgeoning Victorian capitalism. The railway must be understood as more than a mode of transport, 'rather it stood as both agent and icon of the acceleration of the pace of everyday life. ... As Dickens's case suggests, this vehicle of modernization also brought with it a new potential for harm; the early encounters between the human body and the discipline of the railway were not always happy ones.'[26] It did not take long for Dickens to experience the real dangers of the railway, being involved in a railway crash at Staplehurst, and the helplessness in the face of blind progress and the mechanization of transport, taking power of agency out of man's hands resurfaces in his Christmas ghost story that year, 'The Signalman'. Dickens has placed the train within a Gothic discourse that promises the delivery of justice on the villain Carker. This moves the metamorphosed, translated technology into the realm of moral judgement and execution, a realm, I will suggest, into which the Traveller in Franz Kafka's 'In the Penal Colony' also journeys.

The translation of real-life technology is one under-examined aspect of Kafka's work, which is all the more surprising, bearing in mind his work-a-day life involved compiling reports and analysing the dangers of industrial accidents at the *Arbeiter-Unfall-Versicherungs-Anstalt* in Prague. Kafka had a curious relationship with technology. He was fascinated by the mundane typewriter, the phonograph, the telegram, but at the same time he was positively paranoid about using the telephone. As an important and highly successful employee at the Insurance Institute, his knowledge of new industrial technology was second to none; he had undertaken numerous visits into the industrial landscapes of northern Bohemia. These experiences – and even the very technical details of machines he encountered – resurface in Kafka's texts, from the visits to mines, descriptions of technical apparatuses like Odradek or the torture machine of the Penal Colony. One particular case sticks out in relation to *Der Verschollene/America*, with the lifts where Karl Roßmann worked in the Hotel Occidental. In the summer of 1912, during work on the novel, Kafka was sent to Marienbad to survey the premises of a hotel owned by Norbert Hochsieder. Two weeks after his survey an appeal arrived on Kafka's desk stating Hochsieder's unwillingness to pay an extra insurance premium for his lift owing to the fact that he 'used no motor. The power with which the lift is moved is provided by the local electricity plant, and in our house there is only a switch to which nobody but the electrician from the plant has access. ... I am sure I need not offer any further information.'[27] Indeed he did not. Kafka's office rejected the appeal while he was on holiday in Germany, while he turned the legal system that allowed such a complaint into the horrific bureaucracy of the lifts in the Hotel Occidental, and later *The Trial*. If the case hadn't really have happened, one could claim it as a typically Kafkaesque invention.

Kafka was also the author of one of the first newspaper articles on the modern aeroplane in German, 'The Aeroplane in Brescia', in The *Bohemia* newspaper on 29 September 1909.[28] The article engages in a demystification of the aeroplane and the legendary air-artists, as they were then called in German – in effect, he reverses the metamorphosis of the machine that Dickens had undertaken – by casting his eye over every single element of the aeroplane, and reducing the mythical start into a farce of breakdowns. The pilot is reduced to mediocrity, the engineers appear much more important than the great pioneers Bleriot (first to cross the Channel earlier in 1909), Curtiss and Rougier. Rougier is portrayed as a Chaplinesque little man, with a noticeably hooked nose:

> He is definitely carrying out some kind of unclear task, he throws around his arms with the manic hands, feels himself all over while walking back and forth, he sends his engineers behind the curtain of the hanger, calls them back, goes himself ... (*D*, p. 403)

And yet this demystification of the magnificent men in their flying machines occurs at the cost of the audience. For Kafka's text is highly ambivalent, leaving open a critical subtext of the mystification process itself. The main thrust of his text seems to be the audience as it becomes dehumanized in what it makes of the aeroplanes – despite, or perhaps because of, their massive numbers they fade into nothingness beside the 'artificial misery' of the aerodrome. Even the very journey there is marked by this dehumanization through the masses:

> Beggars, monstrously fat from sitting in their wheelchairs, stick their arms out in our way, but the people are in too much of a hurry and are tempted to jump over them. We overtake people, and many people overtake us … Order and accidents appear equally possible. (*D*, p. 401)

Enthralled in the action, the audience grow silent; in fact, they begin to die out: 'There wasn't a word from them, only the sound of the screws that seemed to command everything' (*D*, p. 407). Bleriot takes off, and Kafka's description of the events seems to hint towards an emptying of life from the crowd watching:

> What happens then? Here 20 m above the earth is a man trapped in a wooden chassis and defends himself against an invisible danger taken up on his own free will. We, however, stand all pressed together down here, *without substance, dead* and watch this man. (*D*, p. 409)[29]

This emptying of life becomes clearer in the last paragraph of the text following the departure from the aerodrome, 'and finally independent existences once more, we travel homeward' (*D*, p. 411).

Kafka's interest in technology extends from the aeroplane to the mechanization of everyday life. Modern communication, like modern transport fascinates him, yet the social uses and their consequences frighten him – he sees dehumanization and a loss of freedom, through technological advancement. In a letter to his lover Milena Jesenská, Kafka writes of the mechanization of correspondence between people only increasing the ghostly mediality that already existed during 'old' written correspondence, 'humanity feels this [ghostly medial nature of the written word] and fights it, in order to exorcize the ghostly between humans and to achieve the natural communication, the peace of the soul, man has invented the railway, the automobile, the aeroplane, but it is no use, these are obviously inventions doomed to the abyss … the ghosts won't go hungry, but we will die out'.[30] Kafka develops a discourse of modernity as a ghost-machine, with the people – as seen in the crowd scenes at Brescia – reduced to ghostly traces in the machine. Viewed thus, Kafka's presentation of the spectrality effects of modernity identified by Jacques Derrida as an integral part of the 'rhythms of information and communication' of the 'techno-tele-media-apparatuses',[31] align his modernist translation of technology with the Gothic structures visible in Dickens's works:

Contrary to what we might believe, the experience of ghosts is not tied to a bygone historical period, like the landscape of Scottish Moors etc. but on the contrary, is accentuated, accelerated by modern technologies like film, television, the telephone. These technologies inhabit, as it were, a phantom structure.[32]

This opens up a discourse of ghostly technology that leads me to my last translation and voyage, namely into the monstrous landscape of 'In the Penal Colony', an image that links back into Dickens's Gothicized discourse of the mangled bodies of the Industrial Age, a discourse that is couched in terms of justice and legalese. The machine, it will become clear, also falls into the context of modern communication technology.

A visitor to a Penal Colony is introduced to a machine that writes the convict's crime into his body, not just as a tattoo, but with needles piercing the skin. It is entirely automated, working at the push of a button, and after twelve hours' torture, the victim dies and is automatically thrown into the bloody pit below. The most disturbing aspect is that the victim only learns his crime through deciphering the sentence shortly before death by feeling the wounds in his body. In his work travelling the industrial landscape of Bohemia, Kafka would have been in an excellent position to witness the exact dangers of the new technology, and indeed several sources for the torture machine have been offered, from a wood-cutting machine, to a watch-making machine with sharp needles, to a phonograph – or more likely, a metaphorical admixture of them all. Some of the cases Kafka had to deal with reveal the source of these Gothic nightmares: there was a man who had fallen feet-first into a saw whilst cleaning it; there was the worker who lost his right hand in a Dresher; and finally, there was a woman who had not tied up her hair at work and was pulled into an uncovered transmission shaft at a horse-hair weavers, thus losing her entire scalp and the skin on her forehead.[33] For if one thing emerges from 'In the Penal Colony', it is that technology in Kafka's view has not been aimed at reducing suffering; if anything, it has increased it.

This is no machine for the quicker, more painless execution – its very existence is based on torture – just as Kafka knew from his job, so too does technology malfunction here – it is no longer justice that is carried out, it is murder. And with the word 'murder', the machine is metamorphosed by the narrator into a being capable of agency   it malfunctions and kills the Officer. A monstrous technology indeed. There is no existential hope here as commonly argued. This is pure torture – saliva, blood and vomit dominate the description of the machine. These are images of crass, naked, bodily nature, in conflict with the cold steel of a machine. Yet there is a belief system here. If the mangling at the hands of the machine was only subconsciously willed in *Dombey and Son*, the Officer here openly and willingly seeks out his own crash with the machine age. If there has been a second skin, or a stimulus-shield, built up around technology in order to assist in its assimilation as Daly and Schivelbusch suggest, the Officer seeks to pierce through this of his own free will. The machine pierces his skin and leaves its imprint there, no longer writing – as it has malfunctioned – now only torturing and reordering his body completely by mangling it, not offering the redemption in technology he had wished.

Distancing himself from the Officer's conviction in the machine, the narrator suggests, however, that this has been an attempt to tie the Traveller into the power of a social order through rhetorical technique: the Officer has been lying all along. The machine is what it is because of the manner in which the officer has presented it as the *propagandist* of the machine, and of the tortuous machinations of humanity under the grasp of this twisted society. The rhetorical nature of his power becomes visible at the very latest with the malfunction of his machine. This torture machine is a concrete metaphor that fuses the two themes of technology and bureaucracy that define Kafka's translation of machinery in a Gothic context. Just as Mary Shelley had taken the discursive metaphor of the Monster at its word, so too does Kafka take the turns of speech 'legal apparatus', 'bureaucratic apparatus' and the curiously violent German saying *am eigenen Leibe spüren*, at their word and turns them into the violent machine here. Kafka reads these sayings at face value, as an ever-present threat to humans through social order and technology. In short, this is a story that fuses actual machines with social discourses of power to create a nightmarish vision of an unjust judicial system. These are the images of a 'progress' cult and a belief in a bureaucratic apparatus in Austro-Hungary that had led to the First World War, already in progress four months before Kafka sat down to write his story, with the first victims returning claims to his office in the Institute.

That this social power is couched in legal discourse is an important link back to Dickens in both *David Copperfield* and *Dombey and Son*, two novels with which Kafka was definitely familiar – for after all this is a Penal Colony, and the torture machine is there to uphold the law. For Kafka, as a Doctor of Law, the use of machinery in the process of conviction is automatically linked with Hans Groß (his teacher at Prague

University) and his attempts to reform the legal system by the introduction of phonographs and other recording machines into the conviction process.[34] Groß was, as is well known, also a believer in the racist and degenerative theories of criminal culpability made famous by Cesare Lombroso, and one of his many half-baked, abhorrent theories was the automatic deportation of all 'criminal types', the physically and mentally handicapped, and possibly foreigners. For Groß criminality is therefore, as with Lombroso, an objective given from the outset – the conviction process merely involves the mechanic recording of statements of guilt, traces of guilt to be recorded in order to hammer the final nail in the criminal's coffin. What is at stake here, and what is taken to its final Gothic proportions by Kafka, is the mechanized, scientific method of causality and detection by which a human is considered guilty as charged, before being charged.

For Wolf Kittler,[35] the needles of the machine, in leaving their imprint on the Officer's body, are the needles of the parlograph and the gramophone, the symbols of everyday industrial society in which the Officer blindly believed. This entry into a pseudo-judicial, or moral, framework is suggestive of a Gothic method of translating technology as metaphors into a literary form, thereby opening up these technological pictures into an ambivalent, hybrid relation to their real-life counterparts. This translation into literature allows both Dickens and Kafka to repeat the actual features of technological progress in their fiction, retaining a strange trace, or link, back to their actual social function. It also allows an implicit critique of the social appropriation of technology however, and thus Carker and the Officer get their Gothic justice in the end.

Notes

1. F. Kafka, *Schriften, Tagebücher Kritische Ausgab. Tagebücher*, ed. Hans-Gerd Koch, Michael Müller and Malcolm Pasley (Frankfurt/Main: Fischer, 2002), p. 841. My translation. All further references are to this edition and appear as *Tagebücher*.
2. M. M. Anderson, 'The Shadow of the Modern: Gothic Ghosts in Stoker's *Dracula* and Kafka's *Amerika*', in G. Richter, ed., *Literary Paternity, Literary Friendship. Essays in Honour of Stanley Corngold* (Chapel Hill, NC and London: University of North Carolina Press, 2002), pp. 382–98, p. 384.
3. *Tagebücher*, p. 841.
4. W. Benjamin, 'Die Aufgabe des Übersetzers', in W. Benjamin, *Gesammelte Schriften*, Band IV.1, ed. R. Tiedemann and H. Schwepenhäuser (Frankfurt/Main: Fischer, 1991), pp. 9–21. The practical consequences of Benjamin's theory for translation are not the main point of interest here; translation is meant more in terms of its meaning as transferral and mutating.

5. W. Benjamin, 'Die Aufgabe des Übersetzers', p. 11.

6. A. Lefevere, *Translation/History/Culture* (London: Routledge, 1992), p. 2.

7. Terry Hale, 'Translation in Distress: Cultural Misappropriation and the Construction of the Gothic', in A. Horner, ed., *European Gothic: A Spirited Exchange 1760–1960* (Manchester: University Press, 2002), pp. 17–38.

8. C. Dickens, *David Copperfield*, ed. Nina Burgis (Oxford: Clarendon Press, 1981), pp. 50–5.

9. Dickens, *David Copperfield*, pp. 152–9.

10. Dickens, *David Copperfield*, p. 217.

11. See, for example, Dickens, *David Copperfield*, pp. 129–32 and 142–5.

12. Dickens, *David Copperfield*, pp. 67 and 142–5.

13. Dickens, *David Copperfield*, *Ibid.*, pp. 579–87 and 611–17.

14. R. Vasata, 'Amerika and Charles Dickens', in A. Flores, ed., *The Kafka Problem* (New York: Schocken, 1963), pp. 184–9.

15. W. Benjamin, 'Über Sprache überhaupt und über die Sprache der Menschen', in W.Benjamin, *Gesammelte Schriften*, Band II, 1, ed. R. Tiedemann and H. Schweppenhäuser (Frankfurt/Main: Fischer, 1977), pp. 140–57, p. 140. My translation.

16. H. K. Bhabha, The *Location of Culture* (London, New York: Routledge, 1999), pp. 162–4.

17. H. Lethen, 'Freiheit von Angst. Über einen entlastenden Aspekt der Technik-Moden in den Jahrzehnten der historischen Avantegarde 1910–1930', in G. Großklaus and E. Lämmert, eds, *Literatur in einer industriellen Kultur* (Stuttgart: Cotta, 1989), pp. 72–98, p. 77. My translation.

18. H. Segeburg, 'Technik und Literatur. Oder: Was ist und wozu taugt eine germanistische Technikgeschichte', in *Akademie Journal 1* (2001) 29–32, 29. My translation.

19. C. Dickens, *Dombey and Son* (Oxford: University Press, 1999), p. 653. Page numbers in the text hereafter, prefaced by *D*.

20. F. Kafka, 'In der Strafkolonie', in der *Kritischen Ausgabe. Schriften Tagebücher. Drucke zu Lebzeiten*, ed., W. Kittler, H.-G. Koch and G. Neumann (Frankfurt/Main: Fischer, 2002), p. 247. My translation.

21. N. Daly, *Literature, Technology and Modernity 1860–2000* (Cambridge: University Press, 2003), p. 58.

22. W. Benjamin, 'Über Sprache überhaupt und über die Sprache der Menschen', in W. Benjamin, *Gesammelte Schriften*, Band II, 1, ed. R. Tiedemann and H. Schweppenhäuser (Frankfurt/Main: Fischer, 1977), pp. 140–57, p. 140. My translation.

23. G. Simmel, 'The Metropolis and Mental Life', in Georg Simmel, *On Individuality and Social Forms* ed. D. N. Levine (Chicago and London: University of Chicago Press, 1971), pp. 324–39, esp. pp. 324–6; W. Schivelbusch, *The Railway Journey* (Leamington Spa, Hamburg and New York: Berg, 1986), pp. 134–48.

24. Daly, *Literature, Technology and Modernity 1860–2000*, p. 22.

25. Daly, *Literature, Technology and Modernity 1860–2000*, pp. 22–3.

26. Daly, *Literature, Technology and Modernity 1860–2000*, p. 37.

27. Cited in B. Wagner, 'Kafka und die Statistik', in H.-G. Koch and K. Wagenbach, eds, *Kafkas Fabriken. Zur Austellung im Schillernationalmuseum, Marbach. Marbacher Magazine 100* (2002), p. 129.

28. F. Kafka, 'Die Aeroplane in Brescia', in Franz Kafka, *Schriften Tagebücher, Kritische Ausgabe. Drucke zu Lebzeiten*, ed. W. Kittler, H.-G. Koch and G. Neumann (Frankfurt/Main: Fischer, 2002), pp. 401–12. Page numbers prefaced by *D* hereafter in the text.
29. The German word *wesenlos* which Kafka employs is deliberately ambiguous, implying 'without-being' and the ghostly lack of being (i.e. death) incurred through the communal act of gazing at the aeroplanes.
30. F. Kafka, *Briefe an Milena* [Jesenská], ed. J. Born and M. Müller (Frankfurt/Main: Fischer, 1983), p. 302.
31. J. Derrida, *Specters of Marx. The State of the Debt, the Work of Mourning, and the New International*, trans. Peggy Kamuff (New York and London: Routledge, 1994), p. 79.
32. J. Derrida, 'The Ghost Dance. Interview', in *Public* 2 (1989) np.
33. F. Kafka, *Schriften, Tagebücher Kritische Ausgabe. Amtliche Schriften*, ed. K. Hermsdorf and H. Wagner (Frankfurt/Main: Fischer, 2002), pp. 547–50.
34. See W. Müller-Seidl, *Die Deportation des Menschen: Kafkas Erzählung 'In der Strafkolonie' im europäischen Kontext* (Frankfurt/Main: Fischer, 1989), pp. 51–9.
35. W. Kittler, 'Schreibmaschinen, Sprechmaschinen. Effekte technischer Medien im Werke Franz Kafkas', in W. Kittler and G. Neumann, eds, *Franz Kafka: Schriftverkehr* (Freiburg: University Press, 1990), pp. 75–163.

References

Anderson, Mark M., 'The Shadow of the Modern: Gothic Ghosts in Stoker's *Dracula* and Kafka's *Amerika*', in Gerhard Richter, ed., *Literary Paternity, Literary Friendship. Essays in Honour of Stanley Corngold* (Chapel Hill, NC and London: University of North Carolina Press, 2002), pp. 382–98.
Bhabha, Homi K., The *Location of Culture* (London, New York: Routledge, 1999).
Benjamin, Walter, 'Über Sprache überhaupt und über die Sprache der Menschen', in Walter Benjamin, *Gesammelte Schriften*, Band II, 1, ed. R. Tiedemann, *Schweppenhäuser, H.* (Frankfurt/Main: Fischer, 1977), pp. 140–57.
—— 'Die Aufgabe des Übersetzers', in Walter Benjamin, *Gesammelte Schriften*, Band IV.1, ed. R. Tiedemann and H. Schwepenhäuser (Frankfurt/Main: Fischer, 1991), pp. 9–21.
Daly, Nicholas, *Literature, Technology and Modernity 1860–2000* (Cambridge: Cambridge University Press, 2003).
Derrida, Jacques, 'The Ghost Dance. Interview' in *Public* 2 (1989) np.
—— *Specters of Marx. The State of the Debt, the Work of Mourning, and the New International*, trans. Peggy Kamuff (New York, London: Routledge, 1994).
Dickens, Charles, *David Copperfield*, ed. Nina Burgis (Oxford: Clarendon Press, 1981).
—— *Dombey and Son* (Oxford: Oxford University Press, 1999).
Hale, Terry, 'Translation in Distress: Cultural Misappropriation and the Construction of the Gothic', in Avril Horner, ed., *European Gothic. A Spirited Exchange 1760–1960* (Manchester: Manchester University Press, 2002), pp. 17–38.

Kafka, Franz, *Briefe an Milena* [Jesenská], ed. Jürgen Born and Michael Müller (Frankfurt/Main: Fischer, 1983).

—— *Schriften, Tagebücher Kritische Ausgabe. Tagebücher*, ed. Hans-Gerd Koch, Michael Müller and Malcolm Pasley (Frankfurt/Main: Fischer Verlag, 2002).

—— *Schriften Tagebücher, Kritische Ausgabe. Drucke zu Lebzeiten*, ed. Wolf Kittler, Hans-Gerd Koch and Gerhard Neumann (Frankfurt/Main: Fischer, 2002), pp. 401–12.

—— *Schriften, Tagebücher Kritische Ausgabe. Amtliche Schriften*, ed. Klaus Hermsdorf and Hanno Wagner (Frankfurt/Main: Fischer, 2002).

Kittler, Wolf, 'Schreibmaschinen, Sprechmaschinen. Effekte technischer Medien im Werke Franz Kafkas', in Wolf Kittler and Gerhard Neumann, eds, *Franz Kafka: Schriftverkehr* (Freiburg: Freiburg University Press, 1990), pp. 75–163.

Koch, Hans-Gerd and Klaus Wagenbach, eds, *Kafkas Fabriken. Zur Austellung im Schillernationalmuseum, Marbach. Marbacher Magazine*, 100 (2002).

Lefevere, A., *Translation/History/Culture* (London: Routledge, 1992).

Lethen, Helmut, 'Freiheit von Angst. Über einen entlastenden Aspekt der Technik-Moden in den Jahrzehnten der historischen Avantegarde 1910–1930', in Götz Großklaus and Eberhard Lämmert, *Literatur in einer industriellen Kultur* (Stuttgart: Cotta, 1989), pp. 72–98.

Müller-Seidl, Walter, *Die Deportation des Menschen: Kafkas Erzählung 'In der Strafkolonie' im europäischen Kontext* (Frankfurt/Main: Fischer, 1989).

Schivelbusch, Wolfgang, *The Railway Journey* (Leamington Spa, Hamburg and New York: Berg, 1986).

Segeburg, Harro, 'Technik und Literatur. Oder: Was ist und wozu taugt eine germanistische Technikgeschichte', *Akademie Journal 1* (2001), 29–32.

Simmel, Georg, 'The Metropolis and Mental Life', in Georg Simmel, *On Individuality and Social Forms*, ed. D. N. Levine (Chicago and London: University of Chicago Press, 1971), pp. 324–39.

Vasata, Rudolf, 'Amerika and Charles Dickens', in Angel Flores, ed., *The Kafka Problem* (New York: Schocken, 1963), pp. 184–9.

14
A Voyage through the Phantom Museum

David Punter

The focus of this chapter is a specific museum, or perhaps one should say, since in a sense it no longer exists, the ghost of a museum. It is, or was, one of the most famous museums in the world: the enormous collection of 'things', as he called them, amassed by Henry Solomon Wellcome during the first three and a half decades of the twentieth century. Wellcome was the co-founder of Burroughs Wellcome & Co., an enormously successful pharmaceutical company. His motivation in becoming one of the world's most extraordinary collectors was, as he famously put it, to demonstrate 'by means of objects ... the actuality of every notable step in the evolution and progress from the first germ of life to the fully developed man of today'.[1] Wellcome was, one might suggest, to the world of objects what Hegel had been a century earlier to the world of spirit. His aim was, to put it in the terms used by one of the curators of a fairly recent exhibition of objects from the collection, 'no less than to trace the history of the human body, in sickness and in health, throughout the whole broad sweep of human history' (*The Phantom Museum*, p. 1).

In order to obtain these objects, he and his agents travelled through the whole of what was then the British Empire, and the objects range from the ancient (Neolithic jars and Greco-Roman votive offerings) through the magical and the religious (masks, charms, amulets) to the scientific (surgical instruments, microscopes, prostheses) – we are talking here about a collection that probably contained, at its zenith, well over a million things. We have to say 'at its zenith' because, with a fate utterly predictable with the benefit of hindsight, it became – quite rapidly, given Wellcome's enormous fortune – too big to handle. It was certainly far too big to catalogue, and many of the objects came with very little in the way of established provenance. A large number of the packing cases sent to Wellcome from all over the world have never even been unpacked and many still languish in a huge, decaying vault in West London. Many others have been sent – some would say 'returned' – to other museums, where again the colossal problem of how they fit into any reputable classification system has cropped up, and is now the collective headache of museum curators from Australia to Zimbabwe.

Many of the objects Wellcome collected are, again to quote from the exhibition curator – the exhibition to which I am referring was held at the British Museum in the summer of 2003, and contained only a tiny fraction of the available material:

> so mysterious as to be inscrutable. ... even the accretions of knowledge that accompany them sometimes awake suspicion. What should we make of the 'gall bladder, stuffed with rice' or the 'amulet for draining milk from cats'? Others are objects on the verge of annihilation: 'Human dust from vaults of St Martin in the Fields found by F. T. Buckland in 1859'. Some of the most mysterious objects now even lack the labels which might once have helped us to decipher them; their meanings have become impenetrable. (*The Phantom Museum*, p. ix)

It would undoubtedly be exciting to tour the vaults of what was once the National Savings Bank, Hammersmith, and indeed one such tour has taken place; but this is nevertheless not a pleasure open to the general public. Wellcome's ideal of using his collection of things as an educative resource, which was certainly uppermost in his mind, has long since faltered. What we are looking at here is the trace of a possibility, the relic of a relic, the residue of a mighty but doomed attempt at a collection, a vast, and now dispersed, Ozymandias phenomenon.

It cannot have passed unnoticed that the name of Wellcome's company was 'Burroughs Wellcome'; and the other partner in the company – though not in the acquisition of the collection – was an ancestor of William Burroughs, which might suggest an extraordinary looping of history. Wellcome the great collector, the tentacles of his operation encircling the globe, sucking evidence from five continents in the name of a vast, quasi-universal project; William Burroughs, the nihilist and the exterminator, as he refers to himself in *The Naked Lunch* (1959), but all the time presuming precisely the existence of a vast global conspiracy, which indeed pursues its objectives precisely through the pseudo-medical means of experiment and addiction, surgical intervention and the vulnerability and violability of the human body. 'In a white museum room full of sunlight pink nudes sixty feet high' – this is Burroughs in *The Naked Lunch* again, but one can still wonder whose dream we are seeing here:

> Followers of obsolete unthinkable trades, doodling in Etruscan, addicts of drugs not yet synthesised, black marketeers of World War III, excisors of telepathic sensitivity, osteopaths of the spirit, investigators of infractions denounced by bland paranoid chess players, servers of fragmentary warrants taken down in hebephrenic shorthand charging unspeakable mutilations of the spirit, officials of unconstituted police states, brokers of exquisite dreams and nostalgias tested on the sensitised cells of junk sickness and bartered for raw materials of the will, drinkers of the Heavy Fluid sealed in translucent amber of dreams.[2]

That, of course, is Burroughs in full narcotic flood. But we might be less certain about the provenance of this:

> Ivory anatomical model of a pregnant female with removable internal organs ... constructed tableaux ... from body parts including foetal skeletons, gallstones and kidney stones, veins and arteries. ... A shrunken head (tsantsa), Ecuador/Peru border, late nineteenth/ early twentieth century ... Memento mori brooch containing a graveyard scene made from [human] hair. ... Human skin tattooed with a male bust and flower stem. ... Bootlace threaded with corks, placed around the necks of female cats or bitches to drain away milk. ... Babies at a maternity hospital refusing to breast feed until the Houses (of Parliament) are dissolved ... Length of bamboo, apparently used as feeding tube for giving milk to snakes, probably from the Middle East ... (*The Phantom Museum*, pp. 193–202)

Perhaps one needs to focus on that last one: 'length of bamboo, apparently used as feeding tube for giving milk to snakes'. I particularly like the delicate use of the term 'apparently'. This, of course, is not Burroughs but Wellcome; or not Wellcome either, because Wellcome himself, as far as we know, never got round to writing anything about his collection. It is instead a description of some of his objects that features in one of two books published to accompany the 2003 exhibition. One of those books, called *Medicine Man*, is a relatively straightforward catalogue of the exhibits; the other, from which these descriptions are taken and on which I want to focus, is called *The Phantom Museum; and Henry Wellcome's Collection of Medical Curiosities*, and it is an unusual book. It emerged as a result of six writers being given the remarkable opportunity of a voyage to Hammersmith and being asked to write something relevant to their experience; it contains, therefore, six texts with pictorial accompaniment – some are recognisably stories, others are more in the line of photo-journalism. Some of them, I think – and that is why I have chosen to write on this topic – have a recognizably Gothic dimension, and at the same time serve as a further way into a field which is already, from some other aspects, well-trodden: namely, the complex relations between the phantom, the relic, the museum, the nature of collecting and that type of Gothic which we have come recently to know as 'imperial Gothic'. To wrap up, prematurely, this chapter into one proposition, it would be that the notion of imperial return, so aptly addressed in stories such as W. W. Jacobs' 'The Monkey's Paw' and many of Arthur Conan Doyle's stories – being written, of course, at much the same time as the relics of empire are flowing into Wellcome's coffers – has also what we might term a museological dimension, that what the fate of Wellcome's collection demonstrates is a Gothic turn in, at the very least, a series of dealings with the incomprehensible return of the dead.

The first of the images (Figure 1), and I have already alluded to its description, is a line engraving of a sculpture made entirely from body parts. It was done, we are told, by Cornelius Huyberts in 1709 as an illustrative plate for Frederick Ruysch's *Thesaurus anatomicus octavus*. Ruysch was apparently (and it is interesting how that term 'apparently' recurs; it is only the apparition of the phenomenon, perhaps, which is on offer as we try to reincarnate the multiple deaths which, seen from one angle, are the substance of Wellcome's collection) a Dutch anatomist and pioneer in techniques of preserving organs and tissue. 'The actual foetuses', we are also told, 'are now in the Academy of Sciences, St Petersburg' (*The Phantom Museum*, p. 194). I suppose we need to ask: Are they? *Why* are they? Or to be more precise, by what extraordinary route, through what remarkable impulse to collect, have these body parts found their way back to the site of a wholly different 'empire' – or, to put it yet another way, quite what empire of signs are we dealing with here?

I do not want to go into this picture in detail; in fact, I do not even want to *look* at this picture in detail. Indeed, fascinated though I am, I do not, I find, even really want to go into the Hammersmith vaults and examine Henry Wellcome's remains, and that is partly at least

Figure 1   Line engraving by Cornelius Huyberts, 1709

because I would not know what to make of them, I would not know
how to go about the superhuman task of recomposing them into a
unitary narrative. It would hardly be remarkable to suggest that Henry
Wellcome fell into the Frankensteinian heresy; into the trap of sup-
posing that if you collect enough fragments a body can be made to live
and breathe again. Yet that is not, perhaps, the whole of the message
of the palimpsest. For what we have here is a more extraordinary relation between the part and the whole, an impossible intermingling of
the charnel house and the domain of the aesthetic, a rearrangement
such that veins and arteries are made to stand in for miniature bones,
unspeakable anatomical tubing waves above the scene like forest fronds,
the whole beautifully and neatly mounted as though it could stand as
the centrepiece of any Edwardian mantelpiece, and it would only be
if you looked closely enough that you would see what is really there
to see.

But what would you see? From what perspective, and according to
what scale, would you be looking? Relics out of joint, relics superimposed

on relics – what does this tell us about human anatomy? Medical curiosities; one might suspect that behind Wellcome's impulse towards universalization, as ill-concealed in this collection as it is in that other, far smaller but far more available, monument to human – or perhaps largely imperial or anthropological – curiosity, the Pitt Rivers Museum in Oxford, lies another impulse entirely: not to assemble the 'typical', from which a continuous narrative might be woven, but rather to try to tie together the extreme instances, to provide what one might describe as a Gothic anthropology, a huge cabinet of curiosities which demonstrates not the progress of human science but rather the limit cases of a kind of perversion, such that even the apparently ordinary reveals itself as constructed from twisted and mutilated shapes.

Mutilation; the body, not in healed state but rather in visible anguish. One might be drawn to thinking of the well-known Lacanian trope of the body in fragments; or perhaps of its antithesis, Deleuze and Guattari's 'body without organs'.[3] For what we certainly have here is a set of organs without a body, and yet withal – is it? A certain kind of *jouissance*, a playing, the effect of what would happen if you cast the human, the physical into the air and saw what patterns would occur when the pieces came back down. But perhaps they do not always come back down.

In the case of the second image (Figure 2), the exhibition note to accompany this exhibit runs: 'Slip of paper, typed by William Witt, from a notebook of writing practice which accompanied Mr George Thomson's 'Mechanical Substitute for the Arms' (Scottish, 1919)'. The typescript reads (with many misspellings):

> Is it too much to hope that at least in British territory the night is finally gone. & that under enlightened & sympathetic rule the Negro will now have an opportunity of developing him self & his country? For a period of transition has arrived in earnest? The misionary the government and tyhe railway in very diverse ways are creating a new west africa making it difficult to write in the present tence of fashions that flourished ten yers ago.

And the hand-written note below reads:

> typed by William Witt (who has no arms) by means of the perfected model of the 'Mechanical Substitute for the arms' which is used for instruction at Roehampton Hospital. (*The Phantom Museum*, p. 51)

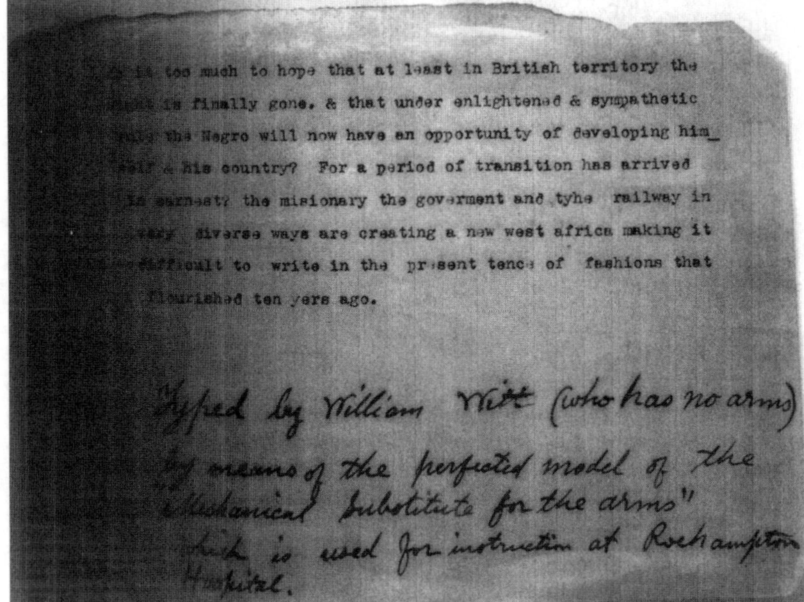

Figure 2   Slip of paper, typed by William Witt, 1919

Wheels within wheels; texts within texts. No more real provenance, of course. Is the typed text itself (as seems most likely) an exercise, a copy from some other, pre-existent text? Or could it be in another sense a plea from the armless Mr Witt, whose own skin colour we shall never (since, unlike many others, no piece of his skin is knowingly included in the Wellcome collection) know?

Hari Kunzru writes an account to match this surviving fragment, in which he invents, on the probability derived from the mention of Roehampton Hospital, a past for William Witt which hinges on imagining him as a wounded and mutilated soldier. Kunzru's account is in the first-person voice of William Witt:

> They were all brim-full of ambition. ... Thomson and his bloody contraption. All except me. They tried to gee me up, told me I had to make an effort. But I couldn't see the point. Not of writing. Not of anything in a world like this. A world in which things like the war could happen.
>
> There were forty-one thousand of us by the end. And even with all them armless and legless boys on the street people still couldn't

look me in the eye. Two little flaps just below my shoulders is what I had to work with.

Like a penguin. Couldn't have held my kids if I had any. Couldn't have held my girl if I still had her. But I sat there and they fitted me into Thomson's table and I knuckled down and did a bit out of the paper. A whole paragraph. The doctor leaned over and wrote his comment and said look on the bright side, now the generals can make you into a clerk and send you back. The he took the page of typing and put it in my file. Took me the best part of an hour. (*The Phantom Museum*, p. 50)

This, of course, is Kunzru's view, making up the evidence from the fragmentary manuscript as he goes along, as it were, finding a way to put the fragmented body, the fragmented text back together, trying to find some provenance for that which otherwise verges dangerously on the inexplicable. 'Knuckled down', 'look on the bright side'; how the bodily metaphors stare out at us from these relics, these inarticulate bits and pieces. Perhaps we should look again at those gleeful, dancing skeletons.

Or perhaps we need to move on. The third 'thing' (Figure 3) is another one that Kunzru's series of vignettes brings back to life. It is a shrunken head, of course, about the size (apparently) of an orange. We know that (though perhaps we do not really) from two sources. One is the exhibition catalogue itself; the other is Kunzru's imaginary provenance, told through the voice of the previous owner – indeed, one might say 'wearer' – of the head, Juan Ignacio Perez-Santos, out of Havana, but also Juan the Idiot, as he claims to have become known after his death and decapitation. Juan the Idiot because he fell prey to one of the oldest stories in the world, the story of treasure. Briefly: he meets a man in a cantina in Ecuador who shows him a map and assures him that the Indians of the interior, the Shuar, have much gold but no idea of its value. He agrees to accompany him on a voyage into the interior, where he learns that the man with the map cannot read it; indeed, he cannot read at all. They are lost; they are, as it were, at a loss, but they find the Shuar. Or, more accurately, the Shuar find them. To quote Kunzru, impersonating Juan:

It is a stupid story, really. There is nothing to it. We canoed upriver. We talked of gold. For food we shot sloths and roasted them over the fire. One evening as we tied up to the bank, the Shuar, who do not care much for gold but are fond of territory and manioc beer and heads, came for ours.

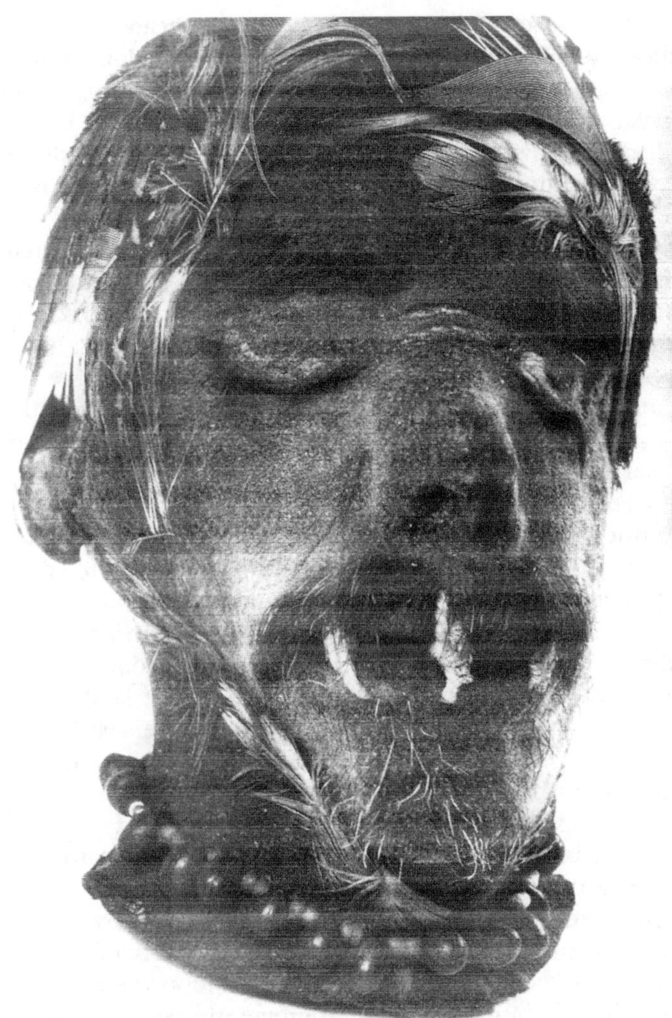

Figure 3   Shrunken head (*tsantsa*), late nineteenth/early twentieth century

He is shot by a dart and falls in the water.

It was not deep but the bottom was a sucking tangle of mud and creepers. I tried to stand but kept stumbling. As I flailed about on my hands and knees, trying to hold my breath, I felt someone in the water behind me. Then my head was jerked up by the hair and I cleared the surface and took a gulp of air which all at once became a gurgle of blood. (*The Phantom Museum*, p. 57)

A story told by a severed head; or by a talking head, a 'teraphim', according to the old Jewish mythology. A fount of wisdom which is at the same time a fount of blood; a warning uttered by a fool. As Juan – or, perhaps, as what has once been Juan – finally says, the Shuar 'believe humans have their origins with the sloths. We are closer kin than we like to admit. I wonder, was I just a fool? Or is this punishment for something more than stupidity?'

As far as we know (but of course we do not know the extent of Wellcome's collection, and never will, it has long since transcended the possible boundaries of containment) there are no sloths in Hammersmith. But there are other human heads – as well as arms, legs, feet, hands, penises, uteri, placentas, stomachs, all manner, as I have already said, of bits and pieces. It is, perhaps, the intimacy of their relation to writing, or to the places where writing – or, in this case, reading – cannot extend that constitutes the problem of Wellcome's collection. Can we understand anything unless it is written about? Or is the potential for our understanding, the potential of the long gaze, the movement around the cabinet of curiosities, simply further inhibited by the exigencies of writing, the phantomatization of the text?

The fourth image (Figure 4) is another head – or in this case, the reverse deconstruction and reconstruction of the head. In the case of the tsantsa, all the bone has been removed; here it is all the flesh that has been removed, to be replaced by – of course – writing, or at least inscription. This is an inscribed skull. What is inscribed on it (apparently – 'apparently' yet again, because the primary evidence is, of course, unavailable) is, on one side, the 'system of Gall', on the other, that of his colleague Spurzheim. One skull to demonstrate the contestation between two systems for assigning mental and emotional functions to the brain. You will see the catalogue above the head (perhaps it is a kind of substitute for the impossibility of the overall 'catalogue'), the catalogue that Wellcome's collection will never have – among its terms are 'Amativeness, Philoprogenitiveness, Adhesiveness, Combativeness, Destructiveness, Secretiveness, Acquisitiveness' – perhaps one should pause there, on 'acquisitiveness', the quality of wanting to group around the self as many artificial props as possible, to prevent ... to prevent what? To prevent loss, presumably; to prevent life from seeping away, to prevent the threat of mortality, by gathering around the self all these reminders, all these memento mori – mementoes to the loss and dissolution of the human form, of course, but also mementoes to the loss of universalist certainty, the loss of a master-narrative of human progress – after all, we are really simply at one with

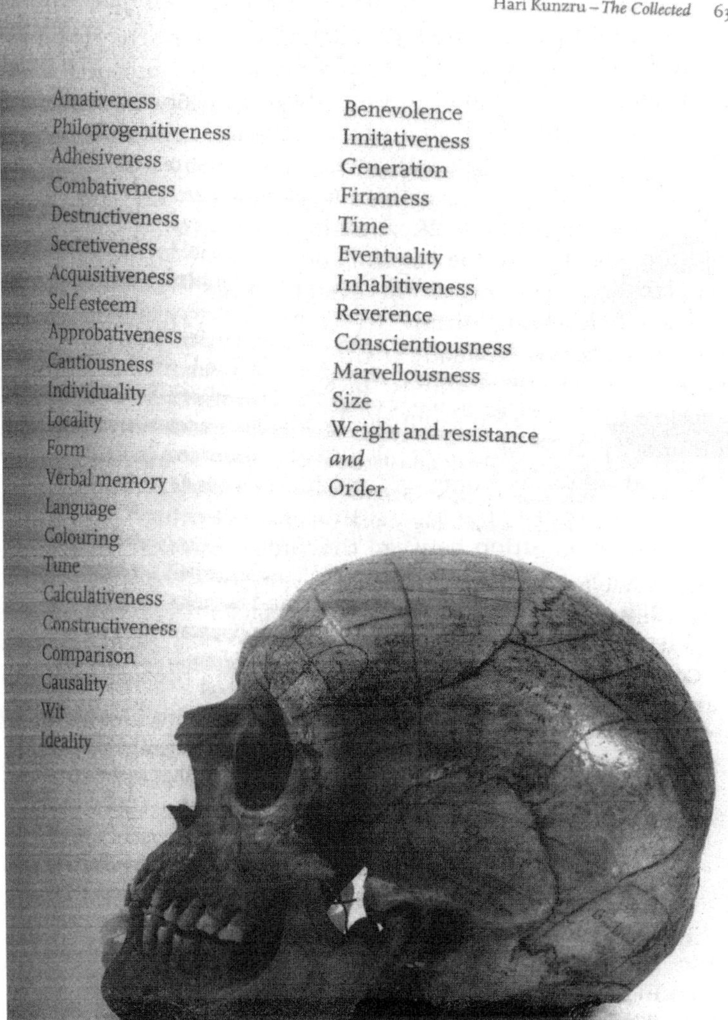

Figure 4 Skull inscribed in French with phrenological markings, nineteenth century

the sloths, until of course we start to kill and eat the sloths, an act which, we may suppose, Juan would live (were he to have remained alive, which he did not, and yet in a sense did) to regret.

'Benevolence, Imitativeness, Generation, Firmness, Time, Eventuality, Inhabitiveness, Reverence, Conscientiousness, Marvellousness', the list continues: those last two terms, 'conscientiousness' and 'marvellous-ness' sit marvellous well together, do they not? The conscientiousness that might impel one towards the total collection, the prospect of an overall explanation of human history and the human situation; and the sense of the marvellous that might leave one in a condition of permanent wonder at the extent of human difference, at the unreachability of interpretation. Perhaps if we inscribe it permanently on bone, hard-wire it into the brain, to use a different but parallel rhetoric, we might be able to construct at least the phantom of a perfectly organized body, might be able to sew together all this evidence from the past; but corruption sets in before that; already that collection in Hammersmith is rotting down, returning gradually to the earth. And that in a building previously occupied by, of all things, the National Savings Bank.

I would like to move away from Henry Wellcome's collection for a moment, and try to pursue a line of thought about museums, about the Gothic nature of museums. We might begin by thinking about what Foucault, of course, refers to as the 'order of things'; or rather, of the continual opposition between the 'order' and the 'things'.[4] A museum offers a narrative, it constructs a story or a series of stories; but the manner in which that narrative covers its objects is always an illusion, it is a cover-story for the haphazard. The things that are gathered into the world's great museums are not there because at some mythical point of origin the direction of museological development was decided; they are there, for the most part, by accident. They may be there because of the looting of armies; they may be there because of the grandiose aspirations of royal families and other tyrants; they may be there because of shady deals struck between shadowy Renaissance statesmen or churchmen, or between seedy antiquarians on the Charing Cross Road. The general voyage of such objects now, of course – of the most valuable of them, at any rate – is back into the shadows; out of the state-run museums which can no longer afford to protect them and into the heavily guarded vaults of newspaper barons, gambling tycoons, ever-changing corporate entities.

But the museum, as well as in some sense reflecting the shifting tides of power, also offers other peculiarities. The fantasy, of course, of so many ghost stories is of the museum at night, of what is left when the crowds have gone home, of what strange life might animate the relic, the talking head, the stuffed crocodile. Then the attempt to bring daylight into the world of lost objects would be strikingly reversed; we would be adrift in a world where the attempt to forge order, to assert a continuing memory of the past, would be revealed as the thinnest of veneers over the unattributable. The historian of paganism and witch-craft Ronald Hutton tells a whole series of stories culled from recent anthropologists and their attempts to verify, after the fact as it were, what had previously been taken for facts gleaned about tribal prac-tices and divine arrangements.[5] In many cases, there turned out to be nobody alive who had the faintest recollection of whole pantheons of gods solemnly written about in Western anthropology for decades. His conclusion is, in part, that these were tales made up specifically for Western anthropologists and collectors; in part that belief systems change, erase each other, supervene upon each other, far more rapidly than we have ever realized, and especially in societies and cultures where written literacy has been a relatively late imposition.

So far from the absence of provenance being a regrettable but minor state of affairs, a transient upset in the onward march of classification and progress, the labels and histories which make up the material evidence of origin are themselves always rotting down, becoming detached, under-going mysterious changes – perhaps especially in the night, when the museum is closed. This is when the things settle back into their custom-ary disorder, relax into their customary gaze of mutual incomprehension. But I must not become too mystical about this; I shall find myself drawn into the darkening museum, especially because the daylight museum, however spectacular, in the end always disappoints, always leaves us with a sense that these things are things of melancholy, things detached, often forcibly, from their origin and purpose. In the fifth of my images (Figure 5), we have a 'wooden hand with brass wrist plate and leather glove. The fingers and thumb are moveable. European, 1880–1920' (Hawkins and Olsen 2003: 196). Gaby Wood, in 'Phantom Limbs, or The Case of Captain Aubert and the Bengal Tiger', so reminiscent of Conan Doyle, describes it in greater detail as:

a delicate thing in a light-brown leather glove – perhaps a woman's. It was made in late nineteenth- or early twentieth-century Europe, and shows signs of wear – dark patches along the thumb muscle, heavy creases in the joints of each finger. There is something too intimate about it, perhaps because it looks so real, like any gloved hand; perhaps because of its polite gentility – the other hands on display are in a greater state of undress. This demure object seems to have more character than the rest: slain at the wrist, it offers itself up, palm towards the sky, pointing towards me two little clasps where, if it were living, an artery would be. In a moment of illicit curiosity I accept the apparent invitation, and undo the clasps.

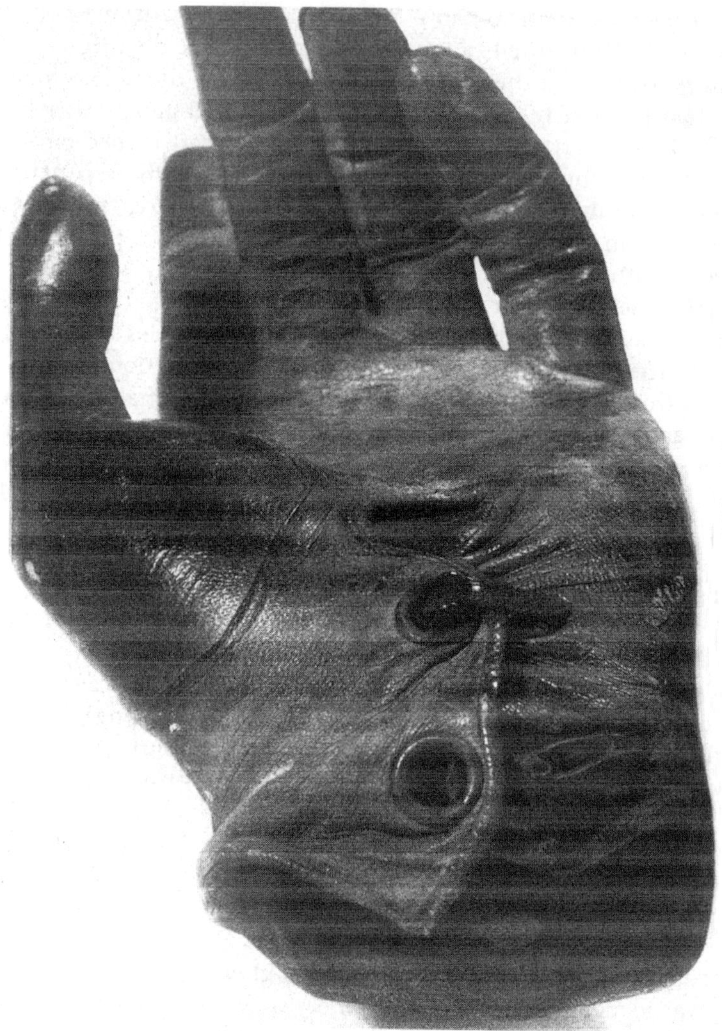

Figure 5   Wooden hand with brass wrist plate and leather glove, 1880–1920

As I slide the glove up over the smooth wooden wrist, the hand reveals more. Engraved into its surface, hidden beneath the leather, is a kind of message: two lines, like those read in palmistry. There is a head line, and a line for life, but there is no line for a heart. (*The Phantom Museum*, pp. 79–80)

'Apparent invitation': I wonder – apparent to whom? Only to the writer, presumably, only in the name of granting permission for an act of 'illicit curiosity' which seems uncommonly like an assault, the forcible revelation of a secret that its owner would have preferred to have held back in the darkness. When the writer says that there is something 'too intimate' about it, again one sense a curiously transferred epithet, or perhaps even an act of psychological transference: at any rate, something seems to be transferred between hand and writer, or between this dead hand and the living hand that peels away the leather in an act of – love? curiosity? rape? – removing, at any rate, its only protection and exposing it to the inevitable violence of interpretation.

But then again, wheels within wheels, further acts of transference. Is it really an accident that this writer, a woman whose name is Wood, is attracted to this hand of wood? Is she certain that its owner was female – there is no detailed provenance and it could surely have been a child – or is it rather that the hand offers an opportunity to revisit her own body, to imagine what it would have been like if ... Of course, all museums do that, invite us not merely to notice the synthetic narrative by means of which the things are arranged, nor simply to construct narratives about those things, but to enter into a series of interlocking fantasies in which we to an extent enter, or imagine, the reality of past lives, past deaths, past and continuing after-lives. Another object (which I have not reproduced here) is a 'woodcut illustration of an artificial arm from Ambroise Paré's *Instrumenta chyrurgiae et icons anathomicae*' (Paris, 1564), which takes the process of unpeeling, the stripping of the object, the attempt to uncover its inner secrets one stage further, by showing in a cut-away just how the machinery inside the hand worked, revealing the cog-wheels, the ratchets, the carefully balanced levers that would have contributed to a near-perfect simulation of life but which would at the same time have been the ancestor of that notion we tend to regard as so postmodern: the cyborg.

Nothing very Gothic there though, one might fairly say; if that hand, at least in Gaby Wood's textual reconstruction of it, reminds us of anything relevant to Gothic origins, it might more be through the notion of the 'demure'. Is it possible that, if the body of the innocent Gothic heroine in, say, Ann Radcliffe's works, had finally been exposed to the light of day through some monstrous act on the part of the villain, then it would have been discovered to be, not the perfect body of fantasy but a construct, a set of prostheses, wooden hands, arms, legs, or perhaps a construct of talismans, a magical body? Or indeed, to follow through the uncanny effects of the prosthesis, an automaton like

E. T. A. Hoffmann's Olympia, a 'living doll'? (One of Gaby Wood's published books is *Living Dolls: A Magical History of the Quest for Mechanical Life* [2002].)

The sixth image (Figure 6) is another version of 'mechanical life', although one with a slight problem of interpretation. This is the

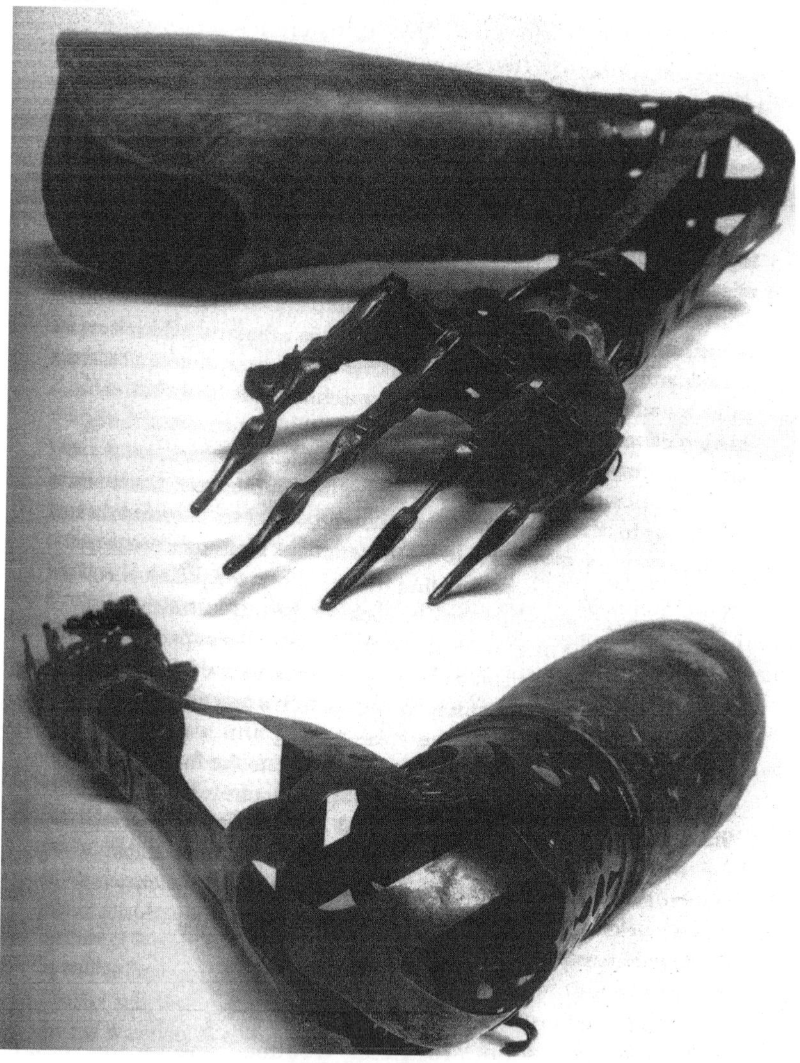

Figure 6   Steel hand and forearm with brass wrist mountings and leather upper arm socket, c. 1890

picture that occurs in the context of Wood's essay (which is mainly, and very interestingly, about phantom limbs); but the smaller version which is reproduced in what amounts to a photo-index at the end of the book shows only the upper object (I was going to write the upper arm, but that would not be appropriate), describing it as a 'steel hand and forearm with brass wrist mountings and leather upper arm socket. European, c. 1890' (*The Phantom Museum*, p. 197). I am not sure, and I have not been able to get enough detail on the main picture, whether what we have here is two views of the same arm; or two different arms, perhaps made by the same manufacturer; or indeed – a rather more alarming thought – a pair of arms. Not, of course, the arms of William Witt; that would set the sights of the uncanny far too high and the dates would be wrong – if we can trust the dates.

At all events, if we want Gothic arms, here they are, apparently life-less at the moment, but no doubt capable of reaching out from the museum showcase, or in this case the packing crate, after night has fallen. I am irresistibly reminded of the tabloid narrative around the figure of the British radical Muslim cleric Abu Hamza; I am sure you have seen pictures of him and of the prosthetic hook he wears because his hand was blown off by a bomb. Not for the tabloids any niceties or delicacies about disability; in their headlines he is referred to simply as 'Hook', and we all know what that means: Captain Hook, demon-ization, a ghoul with which to frighten the children.

But I am also reminded, of course, of the strange pieces of armour that have been lying around ever since the inception of the Gothic, since *The Castle of Otranto* (1765), the unaccountable things which erupt into the middle of everyday life and make a mockery of our real-istic assumptions. I have written elsewhere about the Gothic and the disabled body, but clearly the Gothic is a latecomer to this human scenario: blindness, lameness, deformity of one kind or another all have a long history, a complex mix of the taboo and the scapegoat. What would we like to know about this arm, or arms, if indeed they are two? We would like to know, I suggest, whether their owner wore them (is 'wearing' the right word?) discreetly covered up, or whe-ther he – or possibly she – felt some kind of strange power emanating from these phantom limbs. There is something uncanny which goes on for me too in this context, because I vividly remember a paper on phantom limbs I attended a while ago, and especially an example pro-vided by the speaker, which was of a man who suffered from a double misfortune on the same day. In the morning a sliver of metal got under his fingernail. In the afternoon, before he had time to get it out, his arm was severed at the shoulder by a machine. But that is not the bad bit. The bad bit is that for the rest of his life he suffered from pain under a fingernail he no longer had.

Still, we must not use these stories to frighten the children. I do not think Henry Wellcome especially wanted to frighten them, although he was by all accounts a melancholy and driven man, which might, I suppose, come as no surprise. On the other hand, one might suspect from one of his things that the children, for whatever reason, rather wanted to frighten him. And so to the next image (Figure 7), a coloured lithograph by J. E. Chaponniere of Paris, and the description is the one already mentioned: 'Babies at a maternity hospital refusing to breast feed until the Houses [of Parliament] are dissolved' (*The Phantom Museum*, p. 198).

Sometimes, as a critic it is possible – perhaps even advisable – to despair; perhaps it is in the nature of things to quail before this multitude of unattributable images. No date is suggested for this remarkable

Figure 7   Coloured lithograph of babies at a maternity hospital refusing to breast feed until the Houses [of Parliament] are dissolved, by J. E. Chaponniere, n.d.

work of art, although research into the life of M. Chaponniere might narrow the field. Nor is it obvious why somebody working in Paris should be interested in what was, presumably, a British event – if, indeed, it is the Houses of Parliament which is being referred to, because, in the passage concerned, the words 'of Parliament' are mysteriously bracketed. Which presumably means that the rest of the description is a quotation; but from whom or what, we are given no idea.

Peter Blegvad, who is mainly a cartoonist and who writes a spirited and, as far as I can see, completely mad essay on milk and his own milk obsession in the book, has other ideas. He rechristens the picture 'Zombie Tots', and pens a little poem about them:

> A sea of tots arrives in waves
> summoned from their tiny graves.
> Zombie babies in a trance
> are made to do a clumsy dance.
> Arms out like somnambulists,
> their chubby fingers forming fists,
> they slip, they trip, they catch their feet
> on mummy-cloth and winding-sheet.
> (*The Phantom Museum*, p. 113)

I have to say that I rather like that, although by now we might be beginning to sense that there are altogether too many arms about – arms attached to bodies, arms detached from bodies, organic arms and inorganic arms, a veritable arms race gone out of control. I also fear that perhaps I have been a little cavalier with Blegvad's milkiness. He is, indeed, very revealing about milk, and especially – obviously – about the unexpected places where milk crops up in connection with Wellcome. He has done a search of the Wellcome Library and 'churned up', as he engagingly puts it, 700 milk-related items, under such headings as 'Milk – chemistry'; 'Milk ejection'; 'Milk fever in animals'; 'Milk, human'; 'Milk hypersensitivity'; 'Milk plants'; 'Milk – radiation effects'; 'Milk – toxicity'; and so on. Milk, he says, represents all that we consider we have to get away from, to surpass in the process of maturation: the final temptation, the eventual solace, to abandon it all and relapse into a sea of milk. He does also point out that, because of the unfortunate fact that milk does not keep very well, there is something of a paradox about this dream – a wet dream, perhaps? – of milk as the eternal answer. He also, quite naturally, turns from milk to blood and to the case of the Sussex vampire, a Sherlock Holmes story, prefacing his comments on it with a rather nice quotation from Balthesar Gracian (1601–56): 'In order to see the things of this world correctly, you have got to look at them all upside down.'

The things of this world; Henry Wellcome's things; the case of the Sussex vampire – perhaps one should not go too far into that, but the brief passage Blegvad quotes occurs when Holmes's client sees his wife rising from their child's bedside having apparently drunk the baby's blood. But of course, to see the things of this world correctly, you have got to look at them upside down, and the woman was in fact merely going about a normal everyday task of sucking the poison out of a wound inflicted by a toxic dart. Not, of course, the same toxic dart that did for Juan the Idiot – like milk, toxic darts have a limited shelf-life. Apparently.

And now for the last image (Figure 8): the voyage round the museum is drawing to a close, and it is chucking-out time. But it might be fitting to end with a thing which is monumental in its mundanity; and yet has its own peculiarities, its own transgressions, its own uncertain boundaries. It is described in the photo-index as a 'cased induction coil made by E. Ducretet, 1870–1910' (*The Phantom Museum*, p. 205); and who am I to differ. My knowledge of induction coils has no doubt been restrained by gaps in my education. But the editors of the book place it in a slightly different context:

> Something that is apt to make any visit to the Wellcome objects in Blythe House a melancholy experience is the consciousness that everything here – including the building itself – is gradually falling into a state of decay. There is, however, a striking exception: a nineteenth-century inductor coil that oozes a hard, honey-coloured slime. In its setting – surrounded by some rather Heath-Robinsonish electrotherapeutic devices – it is so extraordinary as to seem mysteriously, unsettlingly alive. (*The Phantom Musuem*, p. xiii)

You must remember that I have not had the privilege of seeing this object, and in some ways I hope I never do. It is bad enough having somebody's second-hand account of a phantom pain stuck under the surface of my consciousness, and I have a suspicion that this object might not be easily forgotten. If, indeed, it is an object at all. Certainly the picture makes it look like an alien life-form, with one eye and a pair of nasty-looking feet. Apparently (it is that resonant word again) attempts to open the thing and discover why it is still continuing to operate – or perhaps 'to suppurate' would be a better term – have failed

Figure 8   Cased induction coil made by E. Ducretet, 1870–1910

because in order to do what you need to do you would need to break off the hardened secretion; and since nobody has yet found out what the secretion is, unsurprisingly nobody has yet been found who is willing to take the risk.

But I am in part making up my own story around this thing – this, perhaps, 'thing of things'. So does Tobias Hill in the last of the pieces in the book, titled 'Impossible Things'. This is a story involving one of Henry Wellcome's European buyers, the master-voyager, a man known as Captain Peter Johnston Johnston-Saint. Apparently. Well, according to Tobias Hill's imaginary reconstruction, this was the name and title on his passport, but bore no relation to either his birth name or his military history. At any rate, the story finds him in an antique shop in France, where he is introduced to the object by Rotgé, the proprietor. Understandably baffled, he initially refuses to buy it, but the vendor – and at this point we are being reminded, I think, of Robert Louis Stevenson's 'The Bottle Imp' (1893) and of the whole repertoire of folk tales where a dangerous object has to be got rid of – is determined to sell it at any price, and eventually a deal is concluded. Captain Johnston-Saint (or whoever he is) ends up saddled, like a phantom limb, or a phantom fingernail, with a dream:

> It always begins with the same thing: the nightmare of Wellcome's collection. He is there in the warehouse, with the smell of railways and factories. In the last of the long aisles, just out of sight, Rotgé's machine waits to be unpacked again. He has been looking for it forever, it seems, but no one can ever find it.
>
> The cargo crate creaks at the seams. In Peter's dream it never splits open. He never knows what lies inside, or whether it is dead or alive. There is only the sound of its pressure, the groan of rooms cracking at the keystones, the rooms of Wellcome's Museum filling as fast as they can be built. The past overtaking the present as the dead outweigh the living. (*The Phantom Museum*, p. 191)

This is such a compendium of Gothic themes that perhaps I need say no more: the insistent dream or nightmare; the impossibility of resolution or of release or relief from the pressure of the past; the question of what is dead and what is alive; the 'past overtaking the present as the dead outweigh the living'. Here is the blurring of boundaries between the organic and the inorganic, the fatal disturbance of the 'order of things', albeit in the form of a silent, slow, unresponsive object, which resists all our attempts at enlightenment. An 'induction coil' indeed; I may not know much about electromagnetism, but even I can speculate on what kind of induction might be at stake here, and what form of coil, mortal or otherwise, might entrap us if we were to get close to this different form of life, which carries on only in the darkened

Gothic spaces of a museum which is not even a museum but a decaying warehouse, where some of the last remnants of Henry Wellcome's collection are enjoying, or suffering, a secret afterlife of their own.

Notes

1. Hildi Hawkins and Danielle Oslen, eds, *The Phantom Museum; and Henry Wellcome's Collection of Medical Curiosities* (London: Profile Books, 2003), p. viii. Hereafter referenced in the text as *The Phantom Museum.*
2. William Burroughs, *The Naked Lunch* (London: John Calder, 1974), pp. 138 and 72–3.
3. See Gilles Deleuze and Félix Guattari, *A Thousand Plateaus: Capitalism and Schizophrenia*, trans. Brian Massumi (Minneapolis: University of Minnesota Press, 1987).
4. See Michel Foucault, *The Order of Things: An Archaeology of the Human Sciences* (London: Tavistock Publications, 1970).
5. See Ronald Hutton, e.g. *The Triumph of the Moon: A History of Modern Pagan Witchcraft* (Oxford: Oxford University Press, 1999) and *The Pagan Religions of the British Isles: Their Nature and Legacy* (Oxford: Blackwell, 1991).

References

Burroughs, William *The Naked Lunch* (London: John Calder, 1974), p. 138.

Deleuze, Gilles and Félix Guattari, *A Thousand Plateaus: Capitalism and Schizophrenia*, trans. Brian Massumi (Minneapolis: University of Minnesota Press, 1987).

Foucault, Michel *The Order of Things: An Archaeology of the Human Sciences* (London: Tavistock Publications, 1970).

Hawkins, Hildi and Danielle Olsen, eds, *The Phantom Museum; and Henry Wellcome's Collection of Medical Curiosities* (London: Profile Books, 2003).

Hutton, Ronald, *The Triumph of the Moon: A History of Modern Pagan Witchcraft* (Oxford: Oxford University Press, 1999).

—— *The Pagan Religions of the British Isles: Their Nature and Legacy* (Oxford: Blackwell, 1991).

Index